EX LIBRIS

VINTAGE CLASSICS

THE RICH HOUSE

Stella Gibbons was born in London in 1902. She went to the North London Collegiate School and studied journalism at University College, London. She then spent ten years working for various newspapers, including the *Evening Standard*. Stella Gibbons is the author of twenty-five novels, three volumes of short stories and four volumes of poetry. Her first publication was a book of poems, *The Mountain Beast* (1930), and her first novel *Cold Comfort Farm* (1932) won the Femina Vie Heureuse Prize in 1933. Amongst her works are *Christmas at Cold Comfort Farm* (1940), *Westwood* (1946), *Conference at Cold Comfort Farm* (1959) and *Starlight* (1967). She was elected a Fellow of the Royal Society of Literature in 1950. In 1933 she married the actor and singer Allan Webb. They had one daughter. Stella Gibbons died in 1989.

ALSO BY STELLA GIBBONS

STELLA GIBBONS

The Rich House

VINTAGE BOOKS
London

Published by Vintage 2011

8 10 9

First published in Great Britain by Longmans, Green & Co. Ltd in 1941

Vintage
Random House, 20 Vauxhall Bridge Road,
London SW1V 2SA

www.vintage-classics.info

Addresses for companies within The Random House Group
Limited can be found at: www.randomhouse.co.uk/offices.htm

The Random House Group Limited Reg. No. 954009

A CIP catalogue record for this book
is available from the British Library

ISBN 9780099560524

Penguin Random House is committed to a sustainable future for
our business, our readers and our planet. This book is made from
Forest Stewardship Council® certified paper.

MIX
Paper | Supporting
responsible forestry
FSC® C018179

Printed and bound in Great Britain by Clays Ltd, Elcograf S.p.A.

To Gerald Trice Martin

. . . . Everyday life—the practical life of each individual, with its home questions of health and sickness, of toil and rest, with its intellectual aspirations and tastes for science, poetry, music, what not, with its passions, loves and friendships—ran its regular course, without troubling itself to any serious extent about an alliance or breach with Napoleon. . . .

LEO TOLSTOY: *War and Peace*.

CHAPTER I

MRS. PASK was an elderly widow living in the town of
Seagate, where the meekness and simplicity of her nature
caused her to be somewhat despised by her acquaintances.
One cold winter night she was standing at her drawing-room
window. The curtains had been drawn by the parlourmaid two
hours ago, and she felt a little guilty as she gently pulled one of
them back to look into the street. But she did so enjoy looking
out of the window! and especially on a cold winter night when
there was not the smallest chance of her going out. Her favourite
view in all Seagate was the Hotel Bristol seen against the Pier head
and the Sunken Gardens, for she had watched them all being
built, in the course of the years that she had lived in "Avonlea";
and she thought that they never looked prettier and more mysterious than on a winter night when the red light of the Northstone Lighthouse was flashing over the black sea—flash—then a
pause, and suddenly the ruby spark growing in the darkness and
again—flash.

This evening a piercing wind swept along the clean empty
streets; the pavements and the lights in the shop windows and the
black sky itself looked as if they had all been polished by the cold.
The noise of the sea was loud. Mrs. Pask, bending her head a
little forward to listen, almost thought that she could hear it
through the glass of the drawing-room window. She could see
nothing beyond the lights on the promenade except a darkness.
That was the sea. The waves would be dashing forward into the
light of the promenade lamps and bursting on the shore, spreading
foam along the cold sands that had been smooth and untrodden
(except for Those Beach Dogs) since the tide went out that morning. The rowing boats would be drawn up high for safety on the
stone slope leading down from the pier.

Mrs. Pask sighed. A wild night by the sea had always excited
her, ever since her girlhood in this very town fifty years ago. But
nowadays she was Not Very Strong, and if she had said that she
wanted to walk along the sands beside the dashing sea at night,
everybody in "Avonlea" would have shrieked. Never mind,
I can look out of the window until Jean comes in, she thought,

smoothing down her dress, which had come from the Model Matron's Department at Boston and Lincoln's in Knightsbridge.

The drawing-room was in darkness except for the firelight. The little French clock on the mantelpiece ticked quickly, and everything was pleasant and peaceful. Mrs. Pask was enjoying herself: she turned to the window again.

Her house was on the Quiet Side of the High Street, but she had a good view of Cousin's the fishmonger's just opposite, and also of Just's Library.

The fish had been shoved away into the mighty refrigerator that was never cleaned at the back of the shop. The two fish boys, the hideous one who sang in the choir at St. Anne's and the very-good-looking one who was mad on football, were rinsing down the marble slabs. Reenie Voles, the cashier, was fumbling for change for a late customer and looking annoyed at being detained; she had her things on, and was all ready to go home.

It's a shame, thought Mrs. Pask, watching interestedly. She'll never get her shopping done. She's a good girl, though she is so fat and plain, poor thing. Not many girls would do all the shopping for their mother like that after a hard day's work. And *why* don't they wash those fish-scales off that little box she sits in? I do think Mr. Cousins might. I'm always meaning to speak to him. After all, I have dealt there for forty years. . . . Perhaps Reenie doesn't mind them. But I should. I should always be picking them off.

Suddenly there was a faint slam! and Mrs. Pask started. It was the distant sound of the front door closing. She just had time to see Pauline Williams, Mrs. Williams's eldest girl, going into Just's Library with that dog of theirs, before she glided rapidly away from the window and fell into, rather than sat down in, an arm-chair. At the same time she slowly reached out her hand for the *Radio Times*, looking with a smile towards the door.

It opened, and in came her companion, Jean Gaye.

"There you are, dear," said Mrs. Pask. "What a wild night! Is there a moon?"

"Yes, quite a gale getting up and bitterly cold. That means dead sparrows on the lawn to-morrow morning, I suppose. No, there's no moon. You would have seen it from the window just now if there had been. What a big fire! This new lot of coal burns very fiercely. Rather dangerous, I should think, and so uneconomical. But that's to Their advantage, of course."

Most people have a They. Some people, when they say They mean the Germans; others mean their relations or burglars or Communists. Miss Gaye meant the tradespeople.

"Come and get warm, dear, won't you? You must be frozen."

"No, thank you. I don't want to start my chilblains; they're late this year so I expect they'll be worse when they do come. Well, I saw Selby's and They'll call for the blankets on Monday."

"Not before then?"

"They can't. One of Their boys has run off, so They're short-handed."

"And it takes quite ten days to clean them!"

"A fortnight, They seemed to think. If I were you I should allow three weeks to be on the safe side."

"It's really very tiresome, the cold spell is going to last, it said on the wireless."

"You ought to have had them done before. It's leaving it very late, to send them in December."

"Yes."

"Yes. Well, I'll go and take my things off."

Miss Gaye then went upstairs to remove a miserable little hat of a suggestive shape, one of a family of such hats all in shades of beige that lived a dim communal existence in the drawer of her wardrobe. Some of them, as if maddened by the monotony of their days, had burst out into a nasty little coloured feather or a small hard loop of felt, but somehow these adornments made no difference to their general suggestiveness and misery. It was really a wonder, in this age of silly but pretty hats, where Miss Gaye had managed to acquire such depressives.

Mrs. Pask, left alone, stared into the fire and felt dashed. It was no use. Jean knew that she had been looking out of the window again. Now, if Mrs. Pask caught a cold, Jean would say as she always did on such an occasion: "It must have been that very cold night when you were looking out of the window."

Miss Gaye, who was Mrs. Pask's cousin, did not like Mrs. Pask to look out of the window. Miss Gaye liked scarcely anything except anticipating minor disasters and sombrely pointing them out when they arrived to those who had been trying to circumvent or ignore them. She also liked to pick holes; and she particularly disliked Mrs. Pask to indulge in pastimes which she called weird. "Do you *like* walking in the snow? How weird." Miss Gaye would observe to some young enthusiast. "I'm afraid I'm very conventional in my tastes. I enjoy a brisk walk in the winter as much as anyone, if there's no wind or frost, and it isn't muddy or that stuffy oppressive heat, but I can't say I like the idea of walking in the *snow*."

It says much for the better qualities in human nature that Miss Gaye had reached the age of forty-nine without anyone trying to kill her.

I wish Jean didn't mind me looking out of the window, thought Mrs. Pask, gazing into the fire. I'm nearly seventy and I haven't many friends left now. I pay a good salary to Jean and she has a comfortable home here, I'm sure. It doesn't *hurt* anyone when I look out of the window. I like to look at the people and see what everybody's doing, Reenie and Mr. Cousins and those two fish boys and Pauline Williams. It's something to do, when you can't go out at night or much in the day either because you're Not Very Strong.

And besides, why shouldn't I?

Pauline Williams pulled off her pixie-hood just before she passed the Hotel Bristol, and at once her brown curls blew out in the wind and the whole of her head felt cold. She endured it for a few minutes; then her ears began to ache, so she put the hood on again. She got neuralgia nowadays if she walked in a cold wind. It was annoying; when she was fifteen she used to walk for miles in a roaring gale along the shore and never get so much as a twinge. But now she was nearly twenty-two, and getting older made a difference, of course.

She had forced herself to walk past the Hotel Bristol.

When her mother had said at half-past five: "Pauli, change my book for me, will you? You might take Jumps, he'd like another run, wouldn't you, old man? And be as quick as you can, the Jamesons'll be here at seven," her heart had started to beat unpleasantly hard. For the quickest way to the library was past the Hotel Bristol, and for months, ever since the summer, she had been going the long way round in order to avoid passing the place.

But I can't go on like this for ever, she had thought, while she was tying the brown knitted hood in front of her mirror and putting on her new tweed coat (it was cold enough to-night to wear it, and besides it would cheer her up). I've got to go past the beastly place *some* time, and it's better to get it over by myself, at night, than when I'm with Mother or Marjie.

So she walked quickly past the long, cream-coloured, three-storied Victorian building with the fig-vine climbing along that veranda facing the sea.

On summer afternoons the large shadows of the leaves lay across the little tables, and it was so peaceful. Between the green tracery of the leaves the faraway sea showed faintly blue. The old waiter who did the teas on the veranda lounged against one of the iron columns supporting the vine, and read his *Daily Mirror*; and in the quiet it had seemed as if the music from the distant bandstand was made by some romantic gipsy orchestra and as if, in all the world, there were only two people.

But to-night, as Pauline glanced casually up at the hotel, she saw that the leaves were withered and the little iron tables were stacked at one end of the veranda. The blinds were not yet drawn over the lounge windows and she could see the two pictures, "Feeding the Swans" and "Two Strings to Her Bow" on the dark red walls and knew that on the other side were "Little Lady Bountiful" and "When Did You Last See Your Father?" There was the broad old table, with *The Field* and *The Lady* and the *North Essex Advertiser* spread on it. Two old ladies were sitting by the fire, with their knitting and one old gentleman. He looks fed up, thought Pauline, and I don't blame him. That lounge is frightfully old-fashioned; they ought to modernize it.

She walked quickly on.

Jumper rushed to the door of the library and turned on the very threshold to give her one of his dramatic looks. "Are we going in here? Am I right? Speak!"

"Go on, you flab," said Pauline, holding open the door for him, and he dashed into the shop.

"Good evening, Miss Williams," said Mavis Jevons, sitting at the library desk.

"Good evening," answered Pauline, to whom Mavis was only That Rather Pretty Fair Girl at Just's. "Isn't it cold!"

"Ever so cold. Still, it's seasonable, isn't it."

"Oh yes. I rather like it, really."

(*You have to walk straight into the wind and face it,* thought Pauline. *You can't moon about like you can in the summer. Cold weather certainly helps.*)

"I've brought this back for my mother," she went on.

"Oh yes, thank you. I'll just enter it. I've got her list." Mavis bent over the file. "Do you know what she particularly wants? I suppose she wouldn't like *I Was Hitler's Prisoner*? That's very good, they say."

"I'm quite sure she wouldn't, thanks. Have you read it?"

"Well, no, I can't say I have. The fact is, I like something— well, a bit more refined, really. And I like something to take you out of yourself, too. You want to forget what's in the papers when you open a book, don't you."

Mavis's voice was soft and shy and her small questions did not seem to require an answer.

"You do indeed. Well, don't bother, I'll just look round and find something."

Mavis returned to her work and Pauline went over to the fiction shelf, while Jumper lay down with his nose on his paws near the electric fire and watched her. The wind violently shook the door, making the gay clean jackets on the new novels, the bright lights, the tidy counters with red fountain-pens and Christmas cards and packets of blue or cream stationery, seem cosy.

Pauline's mother always said that she liked a nice story with plenty of descriptions and nothing disgusting and a happy ending only not too ridiculous; nevertheless, Pauline had almost insensibly observed that her mother seemed to read a good many books that were described by the *North Essex Advertiser* (if it ever got around to reviewing them) as Outspoken. This evening there did not seem to be many books about of the kind that Mrs. Williams officially desired, so her daughter chose one with an Outspoken bit on every other page and took it over to the desk.

"*Afternote to Experience*," said Mavis. "Oh yes, thank you. That's very good, they say."

"Have you read it?" asked Pauline, standing by the desk and smiling down at her without much interest or feeling in the smile. Suddenly she felt desolate, though she knew at the same time that she was better dressed and better looking and healthier than That Rather Pretty Fair Girl.

"No, I'm afraid l haven't. I don't get much time, really. I'm not always on the desk, you see, I'm just doing it this evening because Miss Gordon is away ill."

"Oh, I'm sorry."

"It's only a cold."

"Well . . ." said Pauline, and at the note in her voice Jumper quickly stood up, "I must get along. I expect this will do. I shan't read it myself, I don't get much time either. I'm crazy about Maurice Walsh's books but I haven't read any of his for ages. Come on, Jumps. Good-night."

"Good-night, Miss Williams." Mavis glanced at the clock while she was speaking and suddenly turned pink and bent over her work once more. Pauline turned up the collar of her coat and went out.

This time she did not go past the Hotel Bristol but went through the High Street (there was that fat cashier from Cousin's stepping through a little door in the shutters of Glory and Partners, the big grocers, with a basket crammed with parcels and tins, while one of the counter boys with a furious face dragged down the little door behind her). Pauline went down one of the quiet roads on either side of the High Street that ended on the sea front. Here there were the two kinds of hedge that are found in seaside towns; the kind with thick glossy leaves against which the wind pushes, and the kind with thin wispy shoots through which it hisses. When Pauline and her sister Marjorie were little girls they used to call the second kind "witches' hair."

Pauline held the book under one arm and put her hands in her pockets. The wind was so cold that she could not get her breath properly. The roads were deserted, except for one or two cars parked outside houses with a red or yellow glow in the windows, and through the black yet transparent air, rushing to land on the wind, came the loud noise of the invisible sea.

Well, I've been past the place, she thought, running a little way to please Jumper. Now I've done it once I can do it again. And to-morrow I'll buy that hat at Noreen's. I *will not* let this business get me down.

The road curved as it came near several fields not yet built on, which seemed like the sudden end of the town and the beginning of the country. Just before she came to the darkness that lay over them, there was a long row of iron railings through which bushes and branches had thrust themselves and beyond this could be seen some tall gates of wrought iron. On the opposite side of the road was a row of double-fronted houses that presented a cosy and prosperous face to the night and contrasted with the darkness of the grounds opposite, which were resounding with the melancholy and beautiful sighing of massive trees.

As Jumper rushed past the gates he suddenly stopped and began to bark furiously, staring in through the delicate bars of twisted iron.

"Shut up, you idiot! It's only a cat," and Pauline hurried up to the gates to see what was exciting him.

She could make out nothing but the wide path beyond the bushes, grey in the dimness, but suddenly she saw something moving towards her and the next instant a young man—a boy—was standing with his hands on the iron bars, laughing at the dog, which he teased with one foot stuck between them.

"Hullo!" he said, lifting his head to look at her. His hair was so long that it blew about in the wind.

"Oh, hullo Ted! (shut up, will you, Jumps!) I haven't seen you for ages."

"It's Pauli, isn't it? It's so dark I can't see your face, but I know your voice," and he laughed; a laugh that was plainly a habit and not because he was amused. He always had laughed for no reason, and cried too, and both displays of emotion used to annoy Pauline, sensible little girl that she was, when he and Marjorie and she had played together on the beach when they were children.

"Yes, it's me. How are you, Ted? We thought you must have gone to college or got a job in London or something."

"I only left school last week so I haven't had much time to look for one, have I?" and he laughed again.

"What are you going to do now you've left school?"

"Well, Grandfather wants me to go on the stage——"

He suddenly stiffened his body, and held out both hands to the dark rustling trees while he chanted dramatically:

"*Once more unto the breach, dear friends*——"

"You know, that sort of thing," he ended, looking sideways at her and laughing.

"That sort of thing's a bit out of date nowadays, isn't it?" she said spitefully.

She was a little embarrassed by him, as usual; he said and did the craziest things that weren't even funny, and his looks and manners were so different from the kind she most admired in a young man that the contrast made her feel miserable, and she shivered suddenly as she stood there in the cold wind. Yet she was sorry too, for Ted Early, who had always been so clumsy and queer looking, with such an odd habit of laughing out loud as he walked along the street that he was called "that barmy Early kid" by half Seagate.

"Do you want to?" she asked, more kindly. She knew that people of her age, and younger, often hated the careers described by their elders as "*Such* a wonderful chance for Rosemary!" Besides, it was impossible to imagine that great thump on the stage! Marjorie would shout at the very idea.

"Do I want to what?" He suddenly leant languishingly on the gate, gazing at her with his head on one side and an adoring expression.

"Go on the stage, of course." Pauline laughed for the first time that day. "You are an ass, Ted!" she added almost affectionately, for she remembered that even if he was always laughing himself he could make other people laugh, too.

"I shan't tell you," he answered after a pause. "It's a secret."

"All right. Be a mystery man if you want to. *Jumps! Will you shut up!* What on earth's the matter?"

The dog was staring at something in Ted's hand and whining with excitement.

"What's that you've got there, a torch?" she said, peering. He silently held it up; it was a cricket ball, but it glowed strangely. Jumper leapt at him, barking.

"Is that what you were doing just now, playing catch all by yourself? You'll get pneumonia." She bent to put on the dog's lead, looking up at the boy who was just visible in the darkness. One pale hand held the weirdly glowing ball, which cast a faint light upon his face, and the other clasped the slender bar of the gate, which was wreathed with iron leaves and grapes.

"I say, you do look extraordinary, like a prisoner in a film or something," she added. "Aren't you frozen without an overcoat?"

"I was bowling," he answered.

"Practising, do you mean?" Pauline was immediately interested. She delighted in games, at which she excelled.

"Yes." He held up the ball, gleaming with soft light. "Phosphorus. So I shan't lose it."

"What an absolutely brilliant idea!" she exclaimed, really impressed. "I say, do let me look."

He handed the ball over and watched while she curiously turned it about in her small sturdy hands.

"But why on earth do you practise at night?" she asked, giving it back to him. "I never heard of anything so weird."

"Grandfather," he said shortly in his other voice, the one he used when boys cheeked him in the streets or girls teased him.

"Oh Ted, don't be crazy! He lets you do just what you like, or he used to, anyway."

"Well, I don't want him to see me bowling, anyway."

"I think you're nuts."

"Thanks. I've got to go in now. Good-night."

"Good-night. I'm glad to have seen you again. Listen, do come over to tea one day soon, won't you? Mother and Marjorie'll be awfully pleased; we haven't seen you for such ages. Saturday about four is our best day. I'm at home that afternoon, of course, and Marjorie'll be in between the shows."

"Thanks awfully, Pauli, I'd like to. I'll come in the New Year. Well, good-night, lady fair!" and he made her a sweeping and awkward bow.

"Good-night. Come on, Jumps."

Ted walked off into the darkness, tossing the gleaming ball in the air, and she crossed her road to her home, which was opposite his.

When Pauline and Marjorie were little girls of six and seven, old Mr. Early, who used to be a famous actor years and years ago, had come to live at the big house opposite the Williams's home, with his little grandson and a dark thin woman named Louise Caller (who was supposed to be American or Spanish or something) to keep house for them. The two little girls had taken a half-fearful interest in the bony little grandson because he some-times had screaming fits at night. They used to stand at their bedroom window with their arms round one another, shivering and staring into the darkness and listening to the screams coming across the garden from the big house opposite.

But though the screams were frightening, there was no sinister mystery about their cause. Old Mr. Early neither thrashed his grandson nor stuck needles under his fingernails; he merely let him sit up as late as he pleased, eat salmon mayonnaise or veal and ham pie with coffee for his supper, and then march round the room to music from the gramophone until he fell exhausted on the carpet. When he did go to bed he not unnaturally suffered from night terrors. Louise was ready to explain this to anyone who chose to enquire. She would stand at the gate of the big house with her dark hand clasping the hand of little Ted, and drawl away in her sweet voice with her eyes fixed anywhere but upon the shocked and eager eyes of her questioner. "His grandfather loves him too much, that's all," she would always conclude.

Pauline and Marjorie used to peer through the railings on their way home from school on summer afternoons, trying to catch a glimpse of the yellow brocade curtains at the long dark windows, or the cream and pink and purple flowers pressing against the glass of the conservatory. In those days the house, which was made of that dark brick which preserves its appearance of good repair longer than other materials, looked luxurious and the well-kept lawns and large flowering bushes were beautiful. Sometimes if Pauline and Marjorie were lucky they would see the-poor-little-boy-who-screamed bouncing his ball on the lawn, while Louise sat near him in a garden chair, sewing something white and fine.

The little girls used to talk over all these wonders (that looked so different from the things they had at home) when they were in bed at night, and their name for the mansion was The Rich House.

Poor old Rich House, it doesn't look very rich nowadays, thought Pauline as she crossed the road. The windows get worse and worse (what *does* Louise hang up those bits of dyed rag for? They'd be much better with no curtains at all) and they never use the front door, and the dining-room must be fearfully draughty with all those broken panes in the conservatory. Whatever can it be like in the rooms they don't use? It simply *smells*; it's awful. Mr. Early ought to move into one of those new flats in Strathcona road; they'd be quite big enough for three. And fancy poor old Ted on the stage! I'm sure he simply loathes the idea.

She was just opening the gate of "Dorna" when she heard a

car coming down the road. It was a noisy sports engine, the only one of its kind in Seagate, and she knew it well. She let the gate swing back and quickly stepped into the shadow of the hedge.

The car stopped outside "Dorna." A door opened, and a slim and lovely leg came out, followed by another, and then came a fur coat, and at last a fair head. Two voices, a man's, and a girl's that was soprano and emphatic, laughed together and exchanged "good-nights." Then the car drove away, and Pauline came out of the shadows and opened the gate.

"Good god, Jumps, you nearly killed me—get away, you nasty old man!" cried Marjorie, coming up to the gate with her handbag, her hat, an attaché case, and a part which she was studying in a crumpled brown paper cover, and fending off the dog with her foot. "Hullo Pauli—my dear! *who* do you think that was? The Son of Frankenstein!"

"Good heavens!" said Pauline rather loudly, as they went up the path together. "Do tell me, I can't wait to hear."

"Well, I was charging out of the stage door and someone said 'Would you like a lift?' and I said 'What do you think?' so he brought me home. Lots of back-chat, we had. I'm not sure if he knew who I was."

"Don't be crazy, of course he knew!" Pauline was opening the front door. "You danced together most of the evening that time we went to the Bristol two years ago, anyway."

"Ah, but I've lost pounds since then. I say; he has got what it takes, hasn't he?"

"Definitely. Here's a postcard for you." She picked it up from the brass tray on the medieval chest and gave it to her sister, who read it.

The hall of "Dorna" did not smell. The little bits of sole, the skinny chickens, and unpretentious apple tarts that were cooked in the kitchen were not large enough to make smells. If they did make a faint one, it died in the kitchen in the company of Connie Letter, Mrs. Williams's maid, who had been taught to keep the door shut while she was cooking. In the summer, when the three ladies and the maid lived on modest salads and cut ham and dainty jellies in individual glasses, she was allowed to keep the door open. Mr. Williams had been dead for nearly four years.

"It's from that old so-and-so Cissie Curtis," said Marjorie. "Will I call on her to-morrow at eleven. No, I will not. Second leads twice nightly at Castleford for two-ten a week. I shall stay here, where at least I'm comfortable, until the New Year." She tore up the postcard and put the pieces in her pocket. "I should say Brian was definitely rather a swine though, wouldn't you?"

"Oh, definitely."

Jumper pattered along the passage and disappeared through a half-open door into the kitchen, where a female form was moving about preparing a meal. She said something to him; he responded eagerly, and then she shut the door.

"Pauli, is that you? What did you get me?" called a voice from the drawing-room.

"An outspoken one," called Pauline, beginning to go upstairs. "*Afternote to Experience*."

"Pardon me?" said Marjorie, looking at herself in the triangular mirror over the medieval chest and shaking her head over the untidiness of her hair-do (she tried never to frown, because frowns make wrinkles). "Mother, who *do* you think brought me home?"

"Who, dear? (Pauli, you know I can't bear that sort of book.) Do tell me, Marjorie!"

Pauline laughed; she was nearly at the top of the stairs, walking slowly, as if even she, twenty-two years old and accomplished at games, were tired.

"The Son of Frankenstein!" said Marjorie gaily, going into the drawing-room.

"That very good-looking boy whose father keeps the Hotel Bristol? Come and tell me all about it!"

Mrs. Williams was sitting over a rather resigned little fire. Marjorie put her possessions carefully down on a chair (she never threw her handbag or gloves about, no matter how casually she might seem to be treating them) and crouched over it and warmed her hands as she began to tell. Pauline heard the story beginning again as she shut her bedroom door.

CHAPTER II

THE shops in the back streets of a town sit up later than those in the prosperous ones. When Reenie Voles turned aside into Lavender Road there were still several shops open down its length, and she was able to dart into a little ham-and-beef one and get the pickled walnuts after all! While she was in there she saw Mavis Jevons walk quickly past, with her nose in the air, as usual. (In fact, Mavis usually looked at the ground while she hurried along, but when Reenie said that she had her nose in the air she meant that she, Mavis, did not see her, Reenie.) Mavis lived in Mrs. Voles's house, and Mrs. Voles and Reenie disapproved of Mavis because she was proud and a hypocrite and no better than anyone else. Only people who were hypocrites and wanted to suck up to the Vicar went to church; real Christians stayed at home. Thus argued Mrs. Voles and Reenie, whose choice it was to stay at home.

Mavis was hurrying. A wide road called Church Avenue led into Lavender Road and at one end of it was St. Anne's, her church. This evening, of course, she had not been able to go to Evensong because of Miss Gordon at the library being away ill; she had had to do part of Miss Gordon's work; but she knew exactly where she would meet someone else who had been. He always took a short cut through Lavender Road on the way to his home in Station Road on the other side of the town.

She could see the church and a little group of people just coming out, while Mr. Pent, the verger, was shutting up for the night. The figure in the black robe slowly drew the doors to; and suddenly the beam of light from the open doors had gone, and the church, dark against the dark sky, stood with its steeple among the stars. The wind rushed down the street and the group of people came with it, talking as they came. They were walking smartly and Mavis walked faster as she saw them.

It was all quite natural, really; she was on her way home from work and he was coming out of church, and after all, they did sing in the choir together. It wasn't as if they were strangers.

And now she was actually passing the little group of people. He was talking ever so interestedly with Mr. Reeves, but he noticed her and turned quickly, with a smile, and raised his hat:

"Good evening, Miss Jevons."

"Good evening, Mr. Somers." Her voice was a murmur carried away by the wind, but she smiled eagerly.

When she got to the gate of Mrs. Voles's house she lingered for a moment, watching him out of sight.

Pretty smile that girl has. The thought went through the head of young Mr. Somers (full, as usual, of Bach's music and Handel's music and Palestrina's music) as if it were itself a tune.

"Come in, if you're coming," said Reenie, not ill-naturedly, pushing open the gate while Mavis was still standing and gazing up the street. And she accidentally shoved her shopping basket past Mavis and out fell a tin of salmon. At the same instant Mrs. Voles, who had been hovering between the kitchen and the workroom in front of the house as she did every evening to see if her daughter were coming, charged slowly yet irresistibly out into the hall and flung open the front door.

"Come on, Reen, the chips'll be ruined!" exclaimed Mrs. Voles in a deep voice. "And we're nearly out of tea. Evening, Mavis. Did you get the salmon and the walnuts, Reen? Come on in, both of you, for goodness' sake, you're freezing me with that door open." As the two young women crowded into the narrow hall Mrs. Voles slammed the door, thereby securing victory for the smell of frying that had been wrestling with the fresh smell of the winter air.

"Oh Mum! Now I'll have to go out again!" said Reenie. "Isn't there enough tea for supper?"

"Oh, I daresay we can manage. Don't go out again now, it's perishing; you can pop round in the morning."

"O.K. I will. They open at eight."

Mrs. Voles and Reenie had good cause to know that they opened at eight, for there was seldom a morning that Reenie did not pop round to the shops for something, she and her mother having eaten—not more than they meant to, for they always ate as much as they humanly could—but all the food there was in the house.

The house was very small and Reenie and her mother were very large. As they went down the passage on their way to the kitchen they shut off the bright light and the cheerful red glow from the fire, and all that could be seen was their two massive forms moving along in the dim light to the sound of the chips sizzling. Neither of them took any more notice of Mavis, who went upstairs to the room which she rented from them at eight and sixpence a week.

She had chosen this room from many others five years ago, when she was looking for somewhere to live, because it had a pretty blue wallpaper and blue was her favourite colour. (Reenie had chosen it, for once overruling Mrs. Voles, who favoured a grey one with very large brown loops on it.) And from the three narrow windows that made an ungenerous little bay at one end Mavis had a glimpse, between the houses, of a dark blue line— the sea! That was enough for her; she took the room unfurnished, and moved into it, to the disgust of Mrs. Voles and Reenie, with only a divan bed and a suitcase, and here she had lived ever since.

Now it was her home, her pride, her refuge, the place where she could be peaceful and quiet.

The bed had a blue coverlet with apple blossom embroidered on it. There was a small fireside chair covered in blue, and a blue rug with roses on it; square, modern-sort-of-roses, but recognizable. The oilcloth was blue, like the sea. There was a chest of drawers and a dressing-table on which Mavis was still paying instalments to the Cosyhome Furnishing Company, Ltd., and about which she dreamed at nights, waking up crying "I can't pay it—I can't pay it!"

It was annoying that she could not dream about what she wanted to dream about. Surely, when a person was thinking about one subject most of the day, they ought to be able to dream about it at night? But no, she dreamt about falling behind with her payments on the furniture.

On the landing there was a small zinc safe on a table, where she kept her food. There was also a gas ring. She had to fetch water from the bathroom on the next floor.

But Mavis never did much cooking. Lumps of steak, muddy potatoes, tins with jagged edges stained with tomato sauce, would have spoiled the prettiness of her room; so she lived on eggs and bread and butter and the unmessier fruits, and milk, and those emasculate little cheeses wrapped in silver paper. And she always felt sick when the smell of the Voles's cooking floated up the stairs—until she had had her supper, that is, and then the smell did not make her feel sick any more.

She got out a little folding table and a clean tablecloth and some blue and white china and pulled the curtains across the dark windows, and lit the gas stove. She arranged a lettuce, a hard-boiled egg, a banana and two of the little cheeses. Then she made some tea and toast, and took down Rupert Brooke's Poems from her shelf, and propped them against the teapot.

But before she began to read, she leant back in her chair and looked dreamily, for nearly five minutes, towards the mantelpiece.

There was only one photograph on the mantelpiece, a snapshot of the St. Anne's Choir on their annual outing last year. They were sitting in a big circle in a sunlit hayfield, laughing and holding up their teacups, with their eyes screwed up against the strong summer light. Mavis was there, wearing the white linen suit that it had taken her nearly a year to save up for. She was laughing like everybody else, and she happened to be next to Mr. Somers— just while the photograph was being taken, of course; they had exchanged only twenty words and three smiles all that day. It was a good photo of Mr. Somers. He looked just like that when he smiled.

The photograph was unframed. The lightest head, resting upon a pillow, might damage a photograph in a frame if the photograph happened (as it usually did) to be underneath the pillow.

Mrs. Voles's kitchen was as small and hot as a stokehole, and this was not surprising because it really was a stokehole. It was here that Mrs. Voles and Reenie stoked themselves every morning and evening with unwholesome, indigestible and uneconomical food.

They ate and drank all the things the dieticians most disapprove of; golden chip potatoes, pink and silver salmon out of tins, slabs of rosy breakfast sausage, glistening black pickled walnuts, platefuls of spongy new bread, lumps of Best Fresh, blue mackerel drenched in vinegar, fat brown pickled onions, mounds of tinned beans, ropes of pork sausages bathed in tomato sauce, wedges of yellow Empire cheese, tinned loganberries swimming in coffee cream, pots and pots of tea the colour of burgundy with three pieces of sugar to every cup they drank, and bundles and bundles of spring onions.

Mrs. Voles seldom cooked a good nourishing joint or made a plain and sustaining pudding. Tins and the frying pan, like the Axis powers, ruled the kitchen. The more worthy vegetables such as carrots and spinach which are bursting with vitamins and pathetically eager to be properly cooked in order to do you good were ignored by Mrs. Voles and Reenie. "No taste to it" was the most awful verdict they could pass upon something to eat; and when once they had spoken the condemned article got no second chance. Fried onions held the field.

Dieticians would have pointed out that of course Mrs. Voles and Reenie had to eat so much, because what they did eat had no nourishment in it, and so they never felt satisfied, and had to eat more. But Mrs. Voles and Reenie would have answered that they ate such a lot because they liked it.

And were they martyrs to indigestion, like the people living in Midland towns who write to thank the makers of patent medicines? They were not. They were fat, of course, but they did not mind that; they never mentioned it, and as they had only a small acquaintance in Seagate and therefore but little social life, their friends did not mention it either—at least, not to their faces.

Every evening after her day's work, Reenie rushed off to Glory and Partner's to buy a tin of logans or a pound of Breakfast, and made her way home by a zig-zag route according to the shops she popped in and out of. At home, Mrs. Voles impatiently waited, with the stokehole door and window flung wide open to the little garden in the summer or heated to fury in the winter.

(The garden was not used, of course, for growing anything to eat. Why should it be, when the British Commonwealth of Nations spread a table in the sight of Reenie and Mrs. Voles? It had a cinder path bordered with fragments of white shell, and the flower beds were overgrown with red and yellow nasturtiums. At the far end was a small building which was, Mrs. Voles had decided, too far from the house to be of use. This was known as The Outside W., and in it Mrs. Voles kept such bulky objects as had, from age or incapacity, been discarded from their useful place in the household.)

As soon as Reenie had made the tea this evening, they sat down to supper. They always had Lyons Two Shilling, and they liked it frighteningly strong, the sort of tea that may be imagined brooding inside the teapot like a dictator in the sulks and positively leaping from the spout when it is released.

They stoked themselves in silence for ten minutes or so and then began to discuss the events of the day. Reenie usually began the conversation by asking what business had been like in the workroom.

A notice hung in the front room of the house, announcing that Madame Voles repaired all makes of corset, and also copied models; and in the front room itself Mrs. Voles carried on the business, the details of which she had learned as a young woman in the Corset Department of Godey's, the biggest drapers in Seagate. The late Mr. Voles had travelled in corsets, and he and Miss Manson, as she then was, had first met and had grown used to one another's looks and jokes in the large light upper storey of Godey's, where the windows looked out on the distant sea.

When Mr. Voles died, Mrs. Voles had carried out an ambition that she had impatiently suppressed for years, and started in business on her own. If Seagate had not been full of old ladies, the business would have failed in its first year; but the old ladies could not get on with the modern corselets and bras at all, and were relieved to have Mrs. Voles take charge of at least one side of their highly cautious and complicated existences.

"Been busy to-day, Mum?" asked Reenie.

"Nothing much. Pass the pickles, will you. That Miss Gaye came in."

"What she want?"

"Mrs. Pask's new corselet to be taken in round the waist."

"There! Didn't you say it would!"

"I'd have told her so, if she'd come to me last November like she has these fifteen years."

"You said she was going to get one in town when she didn't come in. Remember?"

"She didn't dare face me."

"That's about it."

"I knew a ready-made one would never fit her."

"Course not. Pass the pickles, will you."

Mrs. Voles did so, then picked up the tin of pineapple cubes that Reenie had just opened.

"Where'd you get these?"

"Glory's, same's I always do."

"It's that Golden Glow make. Got no taste. We had it before. Remember?"

Reenie stuck her fork into a cube and tasted it.

"No, it hasn't, has it." She leant forward and looked at the label on the tin, which showed some black men picking pineapples under a very blue sky.

"Hawaii," she read out stumblingly. "Would that belong to us, then?"

"How should I know? I expect so. We've got lots of places out East. You ought to know, you was at school last. Pass the cheese, will you."

"I don't fancy eating stuff picked by blacks, never mind who it belongs to," announced Reenie, sitting upright again.

"Well, don't get any more of it."

"All right, I won't."

When Mrs. Voles started on her cheese and spring onions she always picked up the *Daily Sketch*, which lay handily on the dresser, and Reenie unfolded the *Daily Mirror*, which she bought every morning on her way to work. They continued to stoke themselves while they read, but more slowly, and gradually as the evening wore on and the fire died down, they ceased to fish just one more walnut out of the jar or absently to reach out for just one more spring onion, and at last supper might fairly be said to be over. At nine o'clock they would clear away and wash up and leave the kitchen neat for the morning (they had discovered that a routine in the home left them more time for eating) and after an hour or so with the wireless in the little back parlour next to the kitchen, they would go to bed.

Once a week or so Reenie would go to the pictures—by herself, for she had no boy. She was plain, with a round pale face, frizzy brown hair, and gooseberry eyes; her only attractions were her excellent teeth and good-tempered expression. Mrs. Voles had been handsome; her small green eyes were set in her head at that enchanting slant that the eyes of Essex women sometimes have, but at sixty-three she was no longer handsome; her face was red and her mouth was thin and her hair was made up of little mousey curls and mysterious skinny plaits and sudden bald patches. She had two other daughters, who were married and seldom visited her, and one son who had a good job at Billingsgate. He also seldom visited his mother, but he was fond of Reenie and remembered her on her birthday and at Christmas.

Mrs. Voles was clever at her profession, which she exercised without talking as much as most elderly women do. All day she sat at the long table in the workroom, answering the door herself when customers came, but sometimes not using her deep harsh voice for hours at a time.

On this winter night the town went early to bed. One by one the lights went out in shops and houses, in the Theatre Royal where the Lenham Browne Repertory Company had been performing "The Wind and the Rain" with not one quiver to betray what a row there had been at the afternoon rehearsal, when someone had chucked a cup of tea all over the old character man without one *word* of warning, my dear, and at once everyone had rushed whooping into battle. The lights all along the Promenade went out and suddenly the winter stars showed cold and sparkling above the dark horizon of the sea. The tide came in, and as the noises on the shore died away, the voice of the sea grew louder, until at midnight that sound was the only one to be heard in the streets of the sleeping town.

CHAPTER III

ON the first Saturday after Christmas, Ted suddenly thought that he would go to tea with the Williamses.

The Rich House (its name was Parkfield) was still all over paper chains from Woolworths, branches of withering holly and sticky mistletoe, cigarette ash, and a very old actress named Myra whom Mr. Early had known for forty-five years. Myra was Going that afternoon, but she was still in the house, and Ted, who did not like Myra, was pretty sure that she would not Go after all.

After what would have been lunch in a conventional establishment, he went down to the kitchen to tell Louise that he was going out to tea and to hear what she thought about the proposed adventure.

Old Mr. Early and Myra were reclining side by side in the drawing-room, on a large sofa covered with grubby and gorgeous orange brocade, and talking; Ted heard their voices (they were both speaking at once) as he went past the shut door. They had not got out of their beds until twelve o'clock, and later still Louise had carried up to them kippers and coffee and two new packets of cigarettes and some chopped liver for Vinny, Myra's little dog.

Vinny was ten years old and one foot high by one and a half feet broad, and she had things the matter with her, poor darling. She always slept on Myra's bed, and her great age and infirmities entitled her, in Myra's eyes, to other privileges in the house which are not usually accorded to dogs.

Ted went noisily downstairs. The mahogany balustrade was dull and dusty and the stair-carpet, which had been an expensive Turkey one, was worn at the treads and all over bits of Louise's sewing cotton, and the brass rods were black. The walls were decorated with Mr. Early's collection of framed theatrical bills and nineteenth-century prints of once-famous actors, with real spangles on their turbans and sashes. They all hung crookedly and white patches showed on the wall behind them.

He went round a large wicker basket at the foot of the stairs which belonged to Myra and had her patchy fur coat and an empty milk bottle on it; she had asked Mr. Early to take care of the basket for her two years ago, and it had been in the hall ever since Carter Paterson's had left it there.

A door at the far end of the hall led into the servants' quarters, a maze of twilit stone passages and large dim rooms. Small caverns lined by cobwebbed wooden racks full of empty bottles, dark chambers where greenish taps dripped musically, black holes smelling of invisible coal, stretched away on all sides of Ted.

"Louise!" he shouted.

And her voice answered at once, as it had answered his calls ever since he was a baby·

"I'm in the kitchen."

He pushed open the door.

She was sitting at the table under the barred window with all the materials for stuffing a chicken around her, but a book was in front of her and she was reading. As he came in she slowly looked up.

"Is that for to-night?" he enquired, poking the chicken with a not very clean finger.

"Yes. Don't do that."

"Don't you put sage in the stuffing, then, you know I can't abide it."

"It isn't going to be stuffed with sage, it's going to be stuffed with prunes and chestnuts."

She put her chin into her hands and smiled at him. Her face always had the ghost of a smile on it, and this annoyed people in

Seagate. Her teeth were not her own and her lips were too full and she was forty-seven and not groomed, but she was beautiful. Ted was too inexperienced to know what was the force that made her face attractive. It was not intelligence, nor gentleness nor spirituality. Most women disliked her at sight.

He sat on the edge of the table and swung his legs.

"I'm going to tea with Pauline this afternoon."

"All right. Will you be back to supper?"

"I don't know. I shall stay if they ask me. I don't want to have to say good-bye to that ancient polecat upstairs."

Louise put her fingers into the frizzy black curls that hung on her shoulders, and yawned.

"She's not too bad," she said.

Her voice was pretty, and seemed to make love to each word it uttered, charming a listener like a warm breeze blowing music along. When he was a little boy Ted used to say earnestly to her: "Weez, I do like it when you *listen* to me," confusing the pleasure her voice gave him with his pleasure in his power of hearing, which he was just beginning to realize that he possessed.

"She stinks," he said.

Louise laughed.

"Pauline's getting awfully pretty," he added suddenly in a confidential tone.

"Is she?" murmured Louise, smiling so that a dimple came into one of her full sallow cheeks.

"Shut up! You're as bad as Grandfather. I get quite enough about Madame Costello and the Naughty Nineties belles without *you* starting! I thought I could talk to you."

"So you can, dear," she said anxiously. "I was only teasing."

"Oh well. . . ." His face had flushed and his full underlip had stuck out, but he went on more calmly:

"Well, perhaps she isn't strictly pretty but she's like a dear little pug dog with that nose and those big brown eyes and short upper lip. It's a charming face, I think."

"You ought to tell her so."

"She'd be furious!"

"Oh, I'm sure she wouldn't. But you wait till you see Marjorie. I saw her in Cousins' the other day, and everyone was staring at her. She's the beauty."

"P'r'aps she'll be there this afternoon. Hope so, anyway. It's passing strange, I never used to notice girls but lately I don't notice anything else."

Louise nodded, giving him a cautious glance, looked down at her book again, and began to whistle softly while she read, which was a trick she had. The kitchen was in a dim light except directly under the window, where the cold radiance of a sunny winter afternoon came in. Outside there was a small paved yard leading into a shrubbery of laurels and rhododendrons.

"Green sickness," said Ted suddenly, getting off the table.

"What?" she said, looking up startled.

"Nothing. I'm going to have a bath. Is the water hot?"

"Boiling."

She glanced across at a stove in a far corner. In another stood a refrigerator, for old Mr. Early liked his comforts and would have them. He did not mind from what dirt, debt, and disorder they sprang. He would suck up his coffee from a cracked mug without a handle, but it must be hot and strong and of good quality or he would return it to its maker with a long and awful oration. He was particularly impatient with what may be called the Dainty Mats school of domesticity, which does not care if the tea be cold so long as it stands on squares of delicately embroidered muslin; he took it for granted that food should be properly groomed and presented, but condemned women who sacrificed its quality to its appearance.

"Are you going to wear your new suit?" called Louise as Ted went out.

"I don't know. It's so tight."

"Ted, it *can't* be! You only had it in September!"

"Can't help that; it is," he said surlily.

She laughed, and pulled the book towards her and began to read again.

It was the life story of a French king's mistress, written in French and lavishly illustrated by pop-eyed eighteenth-century portraits with very low necks. She read the same paragraph three times, then realized that she was not really reading it, and pushed it away with a smile, and stared out of the window. He's just at the age when they're girl mad, she thought. Ted had always talked to her about everything since he was a baby and she had looked forward to the time when he would talk to her about his first love affair. The thought did not make her jealous, for jealousy never troubled Louise. She took a lazy yet lively interest in love affairs of all kinds and kept, without often mentioning it, a private dossier of Who was running after Who in every house in the road; the married postman and the pretty maid at Number Twenty-Four, that dark chap at Bellevue who always brought a redhead home in the car every Saturday, and so on. Ted had begun to notice this interest of hers, and sometimes to tease her about it; and she liked that.

Presently she took a letter from her overall pocket, written in an elaborate hand with large fancy capital letters, and looked mischievously at it but did not read it. Then she stood up, yawning and stretching her long arms, and began to move vigorously about the kitchen, drawing off water and washing up and singing to herself in a low warm voice that was as pretty as her speaking one.

"We're going to be quite a party!" said Mrs. Williams, handing Ted a cup of tea. "Marjorie said she'd bring Brian Kingsley in for sherry after the show and Pauline's asked Eric Somers!"

Ted could not express his appreciation of these promised delights, because his mouth was full, but he nodded approval.

"No more, Jumps; go away and lie down," said Pauline, pushing the dog with her foot.

She was sitting on a tuffet in front of the drawing-room fire, where tea was arranged round a handsome old silver teapot that dribbled. The bloom that is only bestowed by perfect health and maintained by exercise in the open air came from her presence like a perfume, and Ted could not keep his eyes off her.

He sat in a low chair which pushed his knees up to his chin, and wore his usual old pullover and grey bags instead of the new suit, but he was not in the least ill at ease.

"Who's Eric Somers?" he asked.

"He works in Pauli's bank."

"*My* bank, admission tuppence. Have some more to eat." Pauline took a plate off the cake-stand and held it out.

"Don't be absurd, Pauli; Ted knows perfectly well what I mean."

"No more, thanks." Ted gave the plate and the cake stand a rather hopeless once-over. He liked coming to the Williamses because their house was clean and quiet and peaceful and everything that the Rich House was not, but they certainly did have beastly food; never enough of it, and what there was was boring. Very thin dry bread scraped over with what he was pretty sure was margarine, sawdusty cakes with hard icing, too-sweet jam.

"Sure? Growing boys must eat, you know," urged Mrs. Williams, smiling at him.

He shook his head again. "Quite sure, thanks."

It's the margarine, thought Pauline. He always did hate it even when he was a kid. I told Mother not to mix it with the buttered slices, it serves her right. But heaven knows he doesn't *need* to eat any more. He's too fat now.

A young man of nineteen may have raw bones (whatever those

may be), untidy clothes, uncut hair, unkempt ands, grubby linen, scuffed shoes and no manners, and all these faults will be overlooked if he is thin. But let him be ever so slightly fat, and no one will allow him to be pathetic or interesting.

Ted's plumpness did not seem to belong to his tall body, and therefore looked doubly odd. His face was round and pale and his small head and sleepy grey eyes gave him an appearance that was almost Chinese. Poor boy, he *is* so plain, thought Mrs. Williams; but the smile faded from her eyes as he shook his head at the bread and butter.

"Do you know Brian Kingsley?" she asked. She was still an unusually pretty woman; slender and fair, with her hair dressed in a becoming knot and a beautiful complexion that suggested a pink roseleaf and matched her dress.

"Not to speak to. I've seen him hareing round the place in that repulsive little car of his," said Ted, gulping tea.

"Such a good looking lad!" said Mrs. Williams. "Pauli, more tea?"

"Thanks." Pauline put her cup into Ted's instantly outstretched hand and he passed it on.

Her mother's comment had affected her painfully, and for a moment she was only aware of the disagreeably heavy beating of her heart. Years of controlling her feelings on the hockey field and the tennis court had given her almost complete mastery over what had been in her childhood a lively face and voice, and she had even succeeded to some extent in managing her thoughts— no small conquest for a girl of twenty-one. But her feelings still gave her trouble. They were inherited from her father, the schoolmaster whose photograph looked at the room from its place on the piano. His face was masculine and tender, full of warmth and life. He had been a natural teacher who had loved his work and been loved by his pupils. Pauline had been his favourite daughter, and she still missed him and grieved for him.

For that moment, in the little silence while her mother daintily poured out the tea, Pauline felt as if she must get up and run out of the room. At any moment now she must use all the mastery of her face, voice and feelings that she possessed; she must laugh and fool about and not give even the fraction of a hint away to her mother or Marjorie—or to Ted, whose eyes at that moment she suddenly discovered to be steadily fixed upon her legs.

This discovery, in giving a turn to her thoughts, was almost welcome. She twitched her legs viciously to one side of the tuffet and gave the fire a smart poke. He *is* an ass, and so rude, too! she thought. He practically told Mother the bread and butter wasn't fit to eat. I'm only sorry for him because his nails are dirty and his shoes are so awful. I wish he wouldn't stare so, it's maddening.

"Well, Ted. What are you going to do with yourself now you've left school? Going on the stage, like all the young nowadays?" asked Mrs. Williams.

"Not if I can avoid such a fate, thank you," he answered, removing his stare from Pauline's legs.

"Don't you want to, you queer boy? Your grandfather's name would give you a marvellous start."

"You are weird, Ted," accused Pauline. "The last time I saw you you seemed quite keen." She was refusing to allow herself to listen for the sound of voices in the hall.

"No, I didn't. I said it was a secret how I felt. That was absolutely all I said."

"Oh well, I thought you were. Sorry."

"Granted, I'm sure. No. What I want to do is to join the ground staff at the cricket ground," and he gulped down the remainder of his tea.

"Whatever for?" exclaimed Mrs. Williams, but Pauline sat up crying:

"And be a professional! Marvellous!"

"Are you pleased?" He turned quickly to her. "I'm so glad. I hoped you would be."

"I think it's grand! I thought you must be pretty crazy about it when I caught you practising that night before Christmas."

"What was that?" demanded her mother, looking from one young excited face to the other.

Pauline rather impatiently told her; then turned to Ted again.

"But won't your grandfather mind? You said he wanted you to go on the stage."

"Haven't told him yet. I expect he won't let me."

"Well, I really can't blame him," said Mrs. Williams softly, smiling and lifting her necklace of small real pearls (a present from her husband) and letting it fall again; this was a trick of hers. Poor Ted, he looks so peculiar, one really dislikes having him to the house with nice people, she thought. And he'll be much worse when he's actually working with those common men who cut the grass on the cricket ground. It isn't as if he was going in for cricket as a *hobby*; lots of nice men do that. He's going to earn his living by it. But, of course, he might make a lot of money, you never know. They must make a lot, playing in all those Test matches and always being in the papers. And she smiled at Ted, somewhat comforted. But it was a cautious smile. He's crazy

about Pauline, she thought. About time somebody was; when
I was her age I was engaged. Of course, she hasn't any looks
compared to Marjorie but it isn't a bad little face.

Ted said nothing. At Mrs. Williams's remark he and Pauline
had exchanged one glance, in which the difference in their sex,
the important three years between their ages, her annoyance with
him for staring at her legs, were all forgotten in the mutual realization that they were both young and that older people, in small
ways and large, were everlastingly trying to stop them from doing
what they wanted to do.

"I suppose that really settles it, then; you'll have to go on the
stage after all," observed Mrs. Williams. "Is that Marjorie and
the Kingsley lad, Pauli?" she added, turning her head to listen.

"I don't think so, Mother; the show isn't over till five and she's
got to change. Perhaps he'll come round, Ted?"

"I don't care if he doesn't."

"But what will you do? You haven't any——"

She just stopped herself in time. She had learnt at an early age
that her mother disliked all references to money except joking
ones about being "stoney-broke," and having-to-go-to-my-nice-
bank-manager-again-poor-little-me.

"Haven't any money? Of course I haven't, but Louise would
always lend me some; Grandfather gave her a lot years ago, I
think."

There was an embarrassed pause. Mrs. Williams engineered it,
by infusing a careful lack of any embarrassment into her expression. When Ted and the Williams girls were children, it had been
months before Mrs. Williams would allow her daughters to play
with the little boy on the beach because of That Caller Woman,
and fifteen years had only made her take Louise more for granted;
they had not made her change her opinion.

She now said pleasantly:

"Pauli, get the sherry, will you, dear; I'm not sure if Connie is
back yet. And take Jumps and shut him in the kitchen, he worries
so."

"Come on, useless." Pauline went quickly out of the room and
Jumps followed her, leaving Mrs. Williams and Ted to sustain an
extraordinary conversation about film stars in which she praised
all the ones who caused him (he assured her) "to experience
actual bodily nausea."

While Pauline was setting the decanter and glasses on the tray,
she glanced up at the mirror hanging over the sideboard and
paused for a moment, staring moodily at her reflection.

She was proud and had a quick temper, as well as a warmth of heart that she was only beginning to realize, and at this moment she was deeply angry that she should have to endure so much secret pain and humiliation. None of it was her own fault; she could allow herself at least that comfort, but this conclusion made no difference to her feelings, which (she feared) might prove within the next few minutes to be as strong in January as they had been in July.

But as she gazed at herself her expression gradually became more cheerful. Her pretty, almost triangular, mouth looked soft yet firm; her neck was round above the round collar of her jersey, whose unusual shade of Indian red nearly matched the red of her nail polish and lipstick.

I don't look as if there's anything the matter with me, anyway, she thought.

Suddenly she heard the front door open, and then voices and laughter in the hall. Her face in the mirror assumed a listening look and her eyes opened a little wider. She stood there, with her head slightly bent, until she had heard Brian Kingsley and her sister go into the drawing-room and shut the door; then she rushed Jumps into the kitchen, where he settled himself into his fubsy basket with a bored sigh, and went back to the dining-room for the tray.

Now for it, she thought, going across the hall again with the tray. I can take it.

Outside the drawing-room door she called in a loud cheerful voice:

"Open the door, someone, will you?"

Until she spoke, she had not realized *who* might open the door; and she barely had time to compose herself for what she had most feared—an encounter face to face and virtually alone—before it was opened by Brian Kingsley.

CHAPTER IV

"HULLO, Brian! Thanks awfully."

"Hullo, Pauline, how are you? I say, do let me take that, won't you—welcome sight, isn't it?"

He had smiled at her; she had returned the smile; no trace of feeling (she afterwards congratulated herself) had showed in her voice or manner. But for the moment she was aware of nothing else but his presence, and as she followed him across the room into which he was cheerfully advancing with the tray, she was overcome by unhappiness. She had not seen him save at a distance for several months, and she now immediately discovered that his long brown eyes, and fair hair, and his smile, were even more charming than she had pictured them in those day-dreams which she had tried so hard not to have.

The discovery angered her so much that her unhappiness abated a little and was replaced by indignation and self-contempt. So many weeks in which she had carefully avoided the places where he might be, so many hours at the Bank in which she had steadily refused to let the thought of him interfere with her work, so many nights on which she had prevented herself from crying before she fell asleep! And now the work of all these careful days and nights was undone at the sight of a tall young man standing by an open door.

"I got your stockings, Pauli," said Marjorie, sitting in a chair near the window; she never sat close to an open fire, which might have harmed her complexion.

"Thanks very much. How much do I owe you?"

"Three and eleven."

"I say! Not very romantic, is it?" exclaimed Ted with his silly laugh.

Brian stared at him. "What isn't?"

"Knowing how much ladies'—girls'—stockings cost."

"You must try to bear up," said Brian, after a pause in which the two girls and their mother looked patiently at Ted. *Really*, said their look. "Sherry?"

Ted nodded and held up his hand for the glass. Pauline noticed how it contrasted, with its knobbly long fingers and black nails and very curved wrist, with Brian's square and more masculine hand, set off by a correct signet on the little finger. I'm sure Ted would wear an emerald ring, she thought, if somebody gave him one.

I do hate artily dressed men.

"Thanks," said Ted, and he cautiously sipped the sherry, smiling at Mrs. Williams, who happened to be looking at him. (Muck, he decided, utter muck. Never mind, I'll drink it, I adore looking at girls when my head's muzzy. And he turned himself round so that he could stare more comfortably at Marjorie.)

"Brian saw the show this afternoon," she said.

"Did you? Did you enjoy it?" asked Mrs. Williams.

"Well, I saw it in town in the summer. There was a big difference, of course. But I thought these people were very good really, on the whole."

Marjorie smiled but said nothing. Her nails were painted with a clear varnish that made them look like the little pale pink shells which she and Pauline and Ted used to collect on the beach when they were children; and her hair was slightly and touchingly untidy, as if the afternoon's performance had wearied it.

"And how is poor Mr. Taverner?" pursued Mrs. Williams, vivaciously. "Did Marjorie tell you, Mr. Kingsley, that some dreadful woman threw a cup of tea all over him?"

"It would be nice if you'd call me Brian," he said, smiling down at her. He had heard about and nearly forgotten the tea-throwing and was faintly bored by its resurrection; god, that was three weeks ago.

"Brian, then! Of course I will!"

"Thank you." He lifted his glass to her. He certainly has charming manners, she thought happily. Blasted flunkey, thought Ted, coolly staring. Flunkey. Flunkey. Good word, makes you think of funk and monkey.

"It didn't matter about Tav but it might have held up the show and that would have been serious," said Marjorie, holding out her glass for more. (How can she drink it? thought Ted. But she's so exquisite, it doesn't matter what she drinks. I can bathe in her eyes as if they were the sea.)

"That's the *end*, to you, holding up the show, isn't it, Marjie?" said Pauline, laughing. She was back again on her tuffet in front of the fire, and so stimulated by her unhappiness and by the need to hide it that her voice, her manner, seemed to sparkle like fiery garnets.

"Definitely. Ted, what's all this about your going on the stage? Tell us all about it."

Marjorie smiled at him and he eagerly leant towards her (just like Jumper when I say "Walkeys?" thought Pauline disgustedly. Really, he *has* grown into a flab; first he peeks at my legs until I could hit him and then he falls for Marjie so heavily you could hear it down on the beach. And just when I could have done with a bit of support, even from him! Shan't ask him here again for months).

"Grandfather wants me to," he answered, fixing his dim, slightly bloodshot grey eyes on Marjorie's face.

"But how marvellous!" she said; her voice was losing its tiredness and getting back its usual resonance under the influence of the sherry. "He'll be able to give you the most thrilling introductions."

"Well, I don't think he knows many people now; they're all dead," said Ted, going red and looking at her almost imploringly, as if asking her not to torment him. He added abruptly:
"You think he's ham, don't you?"

"My dear boy!" exclaimed Mrs. Williams, and Brian muttered "Good heavens, no!" and glanced at Marjorie, who was laughing.

"Of course not! What a suggestion, Mr. Early!" she said.

"But you do, don't you?" he persisted.

"My dear, how on earth can I tell? I've only seen him once, years ago when I was a kid, in that show the Copleys got up for the hospital. He stopped acting before I was even a gleam—before I was born."

"He was one of the greatest actors in Europe before the Great War," said Ted loudly. "He acted with Duse and Bernhardt and Mrs. Pat. He was as well known as Charles Laughton and Gielgud and Noel Coward."

"My dear, I'm *sure* he was!" she said soothingly, trying to look kind and to sound polite, and not even glancing at the others who were all openly smiling; Pauline had clasped her hands round her knees and thrown her head back and was laughing.

"Not that Noel Coward can act, really," added Ted in a quieter tone, pulling out a large dented silver case and taking out a cigarette; his hands were trembling.

Marjorie sat forward at this, and moved her feet just a little on the carpet, but all she said was:

"Well, after all that, you still haven't told us whether you want to go on the stage."

"No, I don't. I want to be a professional cricketer. I was just telling your mother and Pauli about it when you came in. I told them *all* about it," answered Ted in an exhausted voice, looking huntedly round the pale buff walls of the room where hung, at wide intervals, large birdscapes by Peter Scott. (Oh, he was thinking, if only I could get outside and go for a long walk by the sea, and think about her!)

The front door bell rang.

"That's Eric, I'll go," said Pauline, and got up and went quickly out of the room. (Oh, she was thinking, if only I could get outside and go for a long walk by the sea and not think about *anything*!)

"Hullo, Eric!"

"Hullo, Pauline. I'm a little late . . . *said he, nervously!* You did say six, didn't you?"

Pauline suddenly felt better at the sight of young Mr. Somers standing there against the darkness and apologizing for being late for sherry. He's a funny old stick but he's sweet, too, she thought, watching him while he hung up his damp mackintosh and his soft black hat like Anthony Eden's.

"Marjorie's here, and Brian Kingsley and Ted Early," she said, leaning against the wall with her arms folded. "We've been ragging Ted about going on the stage and he's thoroughly peeved."

He smiled, and as they approached the drawing-room door he said:

"Father has one of his colds."

"Oh dear, I am sorry!"

"That's why I'm late; I had to phone for Doctor Macqueen and then I waited to see what he had to say. . . ."

"Oh Eric! You said it!"

"What? . . . oh, 'phone.' So I did . . . hideous! I had to *telephone*, I should say (*said he, pedantically*) and then I waited to be quite sure that Mother wasn't worrying and then I came along."

"And what did he say?" Pauline's voice always took a teasing note when she talked to Eric; she had noticed that she was the only person who ever ventured to take this tone with him, for his own natural manner was serious and inclined to subdue any company that he might be in; but she suspected that he liked her to do it.

"Oh, it's nothing, just one of his usual colds. We shall just have to take care of him."

Pauline nodded, and opened the drawing-room door. Mr. Somers was over seventy and Mrs. Somers was not much younger; they had married late in life and Eric was their only child.

"Good evening, Mrs. Williams."

"Hullo, Mr. Somers . . . you don't know Ted Early, do you? . . . and Marjorie. . . ."

"I do, but it must be three or four years since we met," and he smiled across the room at Marjorie, sitting by the window with her fair hair close to some yellow tulips in a vase; flowers and hair were almost the same colour.

"How do you do," said Ted glumly.

Brian nodded to Eric, whom he knew slightly because they played at the same tennis club.

"Sherry?" asked Pauline.

"Thank you, I will."

"Beastly cold, isn't it," announced Brian, leaning his elbow on the mantelpiece; there were small electric candlesticks with rosy shades on either side of it and the light shone on his thick fair hair.

"I rather like it."

"Good heavens!" said Brian.

"But don't you *loathe* getting up in the morning?" asked Mrs. Williams, hissing through her teeth and drawing up her shoulders and screwing up her eyes and pattering with her feet on the floor.

"Not particularly. I always have a cold bath first thing, winter and summer, so weather doesn't make much difference to me."

"Don't tell us you're one of the people who make jokes at breakfast!" said Brian, and everybody laughed.

"I'm afraid I am. You see, my father and mother like it," said Eric.

The simplicity of his defence sobered everyone a little, and while they were seeking for the next thing to say, Pauline glanced at Brian and saw that an expression of sadness and reserve had come over his face. She knew why; he was thinking about his own father.

Mr. Kingsley had been badly injured many years ago in a boating accident which had crushed his body between the side of the vessel and the pillars of the pier, and he was a cripple. Few people had seen him in recent years, and he was said to have a very bad temper and to be generally Difficult. This reputation, and the fact that he had a suite of rooms in the Hotel Bristol into which no one except Brian and an old waiter named Dunfee and an occasional woman cleaner were allowed to penetrate, caused the youthful and heartless section of Seagate society, including Marjorie, to refer to him as Frankenstein, while Brian was naturally called The Son of Frankenstein.

Poor darling, thought Pauline suddenly. She could not bear to see that sadness upon his face, and turned her own quickly away. She had been angry with him for months, but now for the first time she realized how hard his life must be; dancing after Frankenstein and running the hotel and never having a minute to call his own. Perhaps the life he was forced to lead against his will accounted for the way he had behaved in the summer.

Perhaps he was not a swine; perhaps he was just unhappy. The sensation of relief and returning happiness that entered her heart at the thought was so delicious that she kept her head turned steadily away from Brian and towards the group that was talking about cars; she did not dare to look towards him lest her feelings should show in her face.

Eric was listening to the discussion about cars. His polite interested gaze moved past Mrs. Williams's face to Marjorie's; she was leaning forward and speaking with animation, twisting her empty glass about as she talked. His eyes rested upon her face for a moment, a shorter moment than they had given to Mrs.

Williams, then he glanced away to Pauline, with a slight movement of his mouth as though he had made an effort of some kind.
He shut his eyes for a second.

"Sleepy?" enquired Mrs. Williams, kneeling on the hearthrug
to attend to the fire and looking up at him.

"A little," he said pleasantly. "It's so nice and warm in here,
after the cold outside."

"Is it? Good. We always think this room is so difficult to warm
unless one has a fire halfway up the chimney," and Mrs. Williams
carefully put a small piece of coal upon a fire that was very far
from halfway up the chimney and went back to her chair. "I suppose you haven't seen Marjorie since she got back from her tour?
Oh no, of course you haven't, you said so, didn't you."

"I saw her once before Christmas when she came into the bank
one morning. I wasn't quite sure who she was, but someone told
me afterwards."

(*You mean you asked someone who she was*, thought Marjorie's
mother triumphantly.)

The gayer Seagateians said that Eric was dreary. That gesture,
as of one who wards off a wisecrack with uplifted arm, was never
made by him and he seldom talked about himself in a deprecating,
or in any other, manner. Most putting-off of all, he went to
church. Mrs. Williams had not been asked by him to call him
Eric, and she did not quite care to do so uninvited; he was generally called Mr. Somers, even by people at whose side he had sung
in the St. Anne's choir for years.

Now, he did not say that Marjorie was pretty or clever or
charming. He was silent.

Mrs. Williams went on:

"Of course, she's only got this job in this tatty little rep down
here until something better turns up in town, but there's an awful
slump in the theatre just now."

"All these crises, I suppose," he said.

Most young men would have said "crisises" and given a little
laugh and Eric knew it; but he had made up his mind some years
ago (he was just thirty years old) that, in small matters at least, he
would speak and think and behave as he chose. And if he preferred to say "telephone" and "cinema" and "photograph" and
"examination"; if he taught himself French and Italian from
gramophone records and from novels written by masters in those
tongues; if he believed in God—though not as most people who
went to St. Anne's believed—and was comforted by his belief,
these tastes and habits were his own business and no one else's.
But he did sometimes think "Good heavens, what a prig I am!"

2*

and then out came the little remarks in inverted commas, the gentle jokes at his own expense, just to show Pauline and his other friends that he knew all about himself and found himself funny.

"Yes. I always tell her she's got Hitler to thank for her being down here this winter."

"You must be rather grateful to him yourself, I imagine, aren't you?" he said, glancing across at Marjorie.

"Oh, I adore having her here, but of course this rep doesn't pay her much. Not that we care about that, Marjorie and I, we aren't gold-diggers. But every little helps, doesn't it! *You* ought to know that, being in a bank!"

He smiled but did not answer.

"I expect you know everybody's secrets, don't you? And how much everybody's overdrawn and what big cheques go out to all sorts of queer people they shouldn't go to! I've always thought it must be thrilling to work in a bank!"

"It is," he said. His eyes were fixed steadily on her face, with the gentle expression in their dark hazel depths that was always there when he looked at a woman.

"I'm sure you're laughing at me!"

"I'm not, really."

"You're a funny boy," said Mrs. Williams, suddenly, in a lowered voice. "I wonder——"

"Mr. Somers," said Ted loudly, getting up and blundering over to them, "you play cricket, don't you?"

"Occasionally, yes. For the bank."

"You played for Seagate last year against Chesterbourne, didn't you? In July?"

Eric nodded, and they began to talk about cricket, a subject which Mrs. Williams found so dull that she turned for entertainment to the group that was still talking about cars.

Pauline glanced at the clock; it said six-thirty, and Marjorie always had something on a tray at a quarter to seven before leaving for the theatre. In turning her head she saw, without looking, that Brian was leaning back on the couch, laughing, with his arms behind his head. That was how he had sat on that afternoon in the summer when he had come to fetch her in the car.

But now it was January, and whether he was a swine or whether he was only unhappy, he had fallen for Marjorie.

Her mother was making signs to her.

"Is Connie back yet?" she muttered, as Pauline crossed the room to her and bent to hear what she had to say.

"I don't know, I thought I heard the kitchen door shut just now."

"Go and hurry her up with Marjie's tray, will you?"

Pauline nodded and went out of the room.

Connie, a tall thin girl in her late twenties, was standing in the kitchen by Jumper's basket, talking to him in a quiet voice while he looked up at her with eyes full of love.

"I thought I heard you come in, Connie," said Pauline in that special firm yet gracious voice which she had unconsciously copied from her mother, who kept it for addressing maids. During Mrs. Williams's thirty years of housekeeping, that voice had addressed some forty-three maids, helps, dailies and chars, not to mention various obligers and outworkers.

"I just got in five minutes ago, Miss." Connie glanced at the clock. "I was just having a bit of a warm." She looked nervously down at the little stove which heated water for the house; she had been spreading out her hands towards its warmth, but now dropped them to her sides.

"Will you get Miss Marjorie's tray ready, please."

"Yes, Miss. I'll put it in the dining-room, shall I? as there's the party in the drawing-room." She looked towards the open door as she spoke; voices and laughter came from behind the closed door of the drawing-room across the hall, and the faintest possible expression of liveliness and pleasure came into Connie's dark-brown eyes behind her glasses as she heard them.

"Yes, please."

"And shall I just light the stove, miss? It's ever so raw to-night."

"No, you need not do that," said Pauline, shutting off the graciousness and emphasizing the firm note. These mean commands about not lighting stoves and keeping fires low had sounded through "Dorna" much more frequently since Mr. Williams had died, and now Pauline was as used to giving them as was her mother. But as she spoke, she suddenly remembered for no reason how her father had loved a big dancing fire; how he would come in from his work on a winter afternoon and kneel before the blaze and hold out his knotted yet delicate fingers to it, smiling at the size and beauty of the flames.

She turned away, saying "Walkies, Jumper?" and suddenly she remembered that Connie's father was out of work again; her mother had caught the girl crying as she made the beds that morning. But really, she felt so dreary herself that she could not ask firm and gracious questions about Connie's father; she knew that she ought to; it would be the kind, as well as the proper, thing to do, but it was no use; she felt too bad herself; and she simply could not. She went quickly out of the kitchen without saying another word.

"Someone's had a row with their boy-friend," said Connie softly, putting her roughened blue hands round the warm water-pipe for a moment. "Eh, Jumps? We know all about it, don't we? Uncle Herbert told us."

Jumper gave her an affectionate glance as his nails scratted on the tiles in the hall, but his before-supper walk was one of the most important rites of his day, and he would not forgo it even to gossip with Connie.

In the hall Pauline found them all getting ready to go. Brian had offered to wait for Marjorie and drive her down to the theatre, but no, she would not have that, so now he was pulling on his camelhair coat and teasing Mrs. Williams while he slowly knotted the belt, and Ted was turning up the collar of a large frieze coat of a gloomy shade that was neither green nor black. It was unusually long; so long that Brian remarked on it.

"I know; it belonged to a refugee we had staying with us," said Ted, glancing down at his skirts. "Grandfather swapped it for one of my old ones."

"Yes, why *are* their overcoats always so long?" demanded Pauline cheerfully, putting on her hood while Jumper danced round her.

"To keep out the snow. It's always snowing down there. And it stops the wolves snapping at their legs," said Ted. "Well, fare you well, Mrs. Williams, and thank you for all the baked meats and lucent sirops," and he bowed absurdly over her outstretched hand. She laughed without amusement.

"Won't you be cold without a hat?" suddenly asked Marjorie, leaning against the banisters with her arms crossed on the bosom of a black dress where a gold clip gleamed; and she smiled at him.

"Nobody wears hats nowadays," he said rudely, then swallowed and added: "Oh no, not a bit, a thousand thanks." He stared at her pale yellow hair, the only beautiful object in the subdued light and among the brownish tints of the little hall, where everyone was putting on gloves and coats and mufflers. She smiled again and turned away her head.

"Good-bye, Pauline," said Brian, pausing at the door. "Are you very busy these days? How about coming to see Marjorie's show some time?" and he gave her one of his special smiles, intimate and mocking and tender, the kind of smile she had not once seen him give to Marjorie.

"Thanks, I'd love to. Ring me up!" she called gaily, waving. Her response was immediate but quite without thought; she only wanted to look cheerful and to sound casual; the door closed on him before she realized what had happened, and she was left with a set of entirely new feelings and anxieties to deal with. Oh, I *can't* make him out! she thought wearily, buttoning her coat.

Eric Somers suddenly found that someone was helping him into his macintosh, and a waft of sweet scent told him who it was.

"Busman's holiday!" said Marjorie, as he twisted his head round. "That's what I've been doing every night this week." She laughed up into his face as he settled the coat round his neck; she was smaller and slighter than Pauline.

"In your show?"

"Yes, I've got a maid's part this week. Nothing much, but not a bad little part. More restful than last week, anyway; I was being murdered every night."

"Don't you get tired?" he asked, looking down at her while he arranged his scarf.

"Me? Heavens, no. I love it."

"Better than anything?"

She nodded, smiling. "Better than anything."

"That's the way I feel about music," he said.

She did not reply to this, but gazed seriously into his face with a listening look on her own.

"Good night." He held out his hand.

"Good night. Will you come and see me act some time?"

"Indeed I will. I—I love the theatre. I'll get Pauline to tell me when you're in something specially good—a really good part, I mean, and then I'll come."

"Grand. Good night."

"Good night, again."

He went slowly towards the door, putting on his hat and still smiling back at her as she slowly closed it.

Ted had observed this conversation; and had now huddled himself into the refugee overcoat in a state of misery so acute that after Eric Somers had gone on his way and Brian had driven off, Pauline noticed it.

"What on earth's the matter, Ted?" she said sharply, as they crossed the road towards Ted's home with Jumper bounding insanely ahead of them like somebody just let out on ticket of leave.

"Nothing."

"Well, do snap out of it! You're enough to give anyone the blues."

"I can't help it, I feel awful."

"So do a lot of people but they just have to get on with it," she snapped. "They don't make other people miserable too."

"More fools them. 'A grief bared is a grief shared.'"

"Tripe. It only makes it worse to talk about it. And who said so, anyway?"

"I did. I just made it up. '*A grief bared is a grief shared.*' I say, I think that's pretty good!"

"Do you? I don't."

"You're about as blue as you can be yourself, anyway."

"No, I'm not."

"Yes, you are. Come on!" He clumsily took her arm and pressed it to his side. "Tell Uncle Ted. What's the matter?"

"Nothing," said Pauline obstinately, shaking her head but letting her arm stay where it was, while tears came maddeningly into her eyes.

"Oh, yes, there is. Is it the ruddy bank?"

She shook her head again. They were walking quickly up the dark road towards the sea front, and for a few moments they paced in silence. No, thought Pauline, the bank was not too bad. She had not been enthusiastic about entering it, for she had wanted to get a job in the open air connected with dogs or horses; but her mother and sister had forcefully reminded her that all such jobs were messy, and she had therefore given up the idea. She detested getting dirty. Much as she enjoyed playing tennis and golf and riding when she could afford to and driving their old car, she enjoyed the getting clean afterwards almost better. Her brown skin and brown curls had a way of becoming oily, and it was only by keeping the strictest watch, a kind of grooming Gestapo, on them that she could prevent their doing so. To look their best her skin and hair must work in a clean, pleasant place. The bank was both, and her work left her plenty of leisure for games and dancing at the end of the day. It wasn't at all bad there, really: or it used not to be.

"Tell Teddy!" he coaxed in a sickly voice, squeezing her arm and putting a face down to her own that rather resembled, in shape and colour, the full moon dimly visible behind the un-moving clouds.

"Oh, Ted, don't be a *fool*!" she cried, laughing and angry and struggling to pull her arm away. "Do leave me alone, there's a lamb."

"All right. Let's run."

Suddenly he rushed her away down the deserted promenade, dragging her along with the ends of her scarf flying in the wind while Jumper raced and bounded beside them, wild with pleasure. There was nothing he enjoyed more than running, nothing; but usually people *would not* run. He was forced to implore, and crawl, and abase himself until he was *worn out* before they would feebly trot a mere six yards; and here were two people flying along as if they enjoyed it as much as he did!

At last they stopped short on the extreme edge of the cliff, and stood staring down on the enormous expanse of dim sea, that was no colour in the diffused light from the almost hidden moon.

"Better?" panted Ted, looking down at her.

She nodded. "There wasn't anything the matter, thanks, but I enjoyed that."

"Let's do it again."

"Oh no, I can't. I must get back. I want to listen in to something at half past eight and we've got to have supper first."

They walked slowly homewards; for a little while he kept a slack hold of her arm, but as he received no encouragement (now that they were no longer running she disliked the sensation of his hand clumsily grasping her elbow, and she was trying not to compare it with another's clasp, firm and charged with manly authority) he presently let it go.

"I say, won't you come in to supper?" she asked in a friendly tone; she felt better, and was grateful to him for shaking her out of her bad mood, but even as she spoke she thought, *Mother'll be livid if he does*.

"No, thanks. We've got chicken to-night," said old Ted firmly.

She really could not think of any reply to this; it was so long since they had seen one another that she did not feel quite enough at ease with him to say "Aren't you lucky!" which was what she felt.

At home there would be tinned asparagus on toast for supper with a trifle (no sherry) to follow, and her mother would sit opposite to her, eating small mouthquarterfuls off the extreme tip of her fork and wondering if the Kingsley lad were engaged? Pauline suddenly thought what fun it would be to go into supper at the Rich House.

Meals were always anything from half an hour to an hour late at the Rich House, and Ted played his gramophone while he made the toast (dishes cooked by Louise usually called for mounds of extremely thin toast, the crusts of which were flung out imperially onto the lawn where the birds as imperially disdained them because the garden was so rich in worms and insects): Mr. Early would sit in a deep chair in front of the fire reading old theatre programmes and smiling to himself; and a rich smell of frying floated up from the kitchen in the depths of the house and wandered among the old furniture covered with the threadbare orange brocade. All over the house, even in the lavatories, the lights would be on. Mr. Early liked the rooms to be as brightly lit as *Act I: Lord Mountmallion's Flat in Clarges Street*; he liked them to look as if, at any moment, the play might begin.

But Ted did not ask her in to supper, and as she was too proud to invite herself they walked in silence until they were nearly at the gates of Parkfield. Then Pauline said:

"I wanted some exercise. I feel better now. Do you?"

"Only temporarily. Oh god, I say, there's Grandfather."

A figure had emerged from the gates of Parkfield and was now bearing down upon them, saying questioningly:

"Is that you, Edward?"

"Hullo, Grandfather, yes, I'm just coming. I say, you remember Pauline, don't you?"

Pauline, who was gazing at old Mr. Early and thinking that he looked as eccentric as ever but was really strikingly handsome, was suddenly embarrassed to find that he was holding out to her a hand encased in a large mitten made of almost bald leopard skin.

"Indeed I remember Pauline," answered Mr. Early, making the words sound like the first line of a poem by Browning because he spoke them in his loud, deep and rich voice, which was beautifully produced in spite of its age and which carried to the very smallest earwig in the very farthest recess in the summer house, who corresponded to the last person in the back row of the gallery. "But you should have warned me, Edward. You should have prepared me."

"How do you mean, Grandfather?" enquired Ted, perhaps with more patience and less verve than a conscientious and experienced "feed" should display.

"For Pauline has grown into a woman," and the beautiful old voice grew soft and Mr. Early leant towards the girl and smiled at her. "The little girl who used to steal mulberries from my tree only two years ago has come into her kingdom, Edward."

He spoke slowly, and allowed his voice to die softly into silence. After he had ceased to speak, Pauline's embarrassment was acute; and at first she longed for the relief of laughter or some facetious comment from Ted; but as she stood gazing up at the old man in his old-fashioned coat with a wide fur collar and his broad-brimmed hat, her embarrassment slowly changed to a feeling that was completely unfamiliar to her. After her first impulse to reply smartly "It isn't two years, it's seven" had faltered and died, not a sentence would come into her head with which to answer him.

His face was in shadow, but behind it was the wide silver-grey sky closely covered by chilly clouds, and in that diffused light his pointed beard and full moustache could be seen as gleaming silver. His large eyes were no more than patches of shade in their deep ancient sockets, but because his face had been used and trained since his childhood to express every feeling within him, the fact that his eyes were in darkness did not matter; what was clear in his face was admiration of Pauline's charm and homage to her womanhood.

She was used to the appraisement in the eyes of one kind of young man, and she knew and disliked the confused, ashamed look of longing in the eyes of another kind; but no young man had ever looked at her as this old man was looking. As she stood gazing up at him, she remembered romantic scenes she had seen on the pictures: a gondola slowly moving between white palaces sleeping in the moonlight: a man and a woman standing silent and clasped in one another's arms under a group of waving palm trees beside the ocean. For a moment she experienced again the feeling that had come to her on the balcony of the Hotel Bristol, as if the far-off gipsy orchestra were playing. A memory of a poem once learnt at school returned to her:

> *And do accept my madness, and would die*
> *To save from some slight shame one simple girl.*

It must be wonderful to have someone feel like that about you and want to take care of you, she thought vaguely. I suppose that's how men used to feel about women in the old days.

The next moment the gipsy orchestra had ceased to play; and she was laughing up at Mr. Early and saying (but more cheerfully and less pertly than she had at first intended):

"But, Mr. Early, it isn't two years, you know, it's seven!"

"Is it indeed? Seven years?" repeated the old man softly, again making the words sound as if they were a quotation—from a story by Grimm or Andersen, this time. He was still holding her hand and gazing down at her, but there was a subtle change in his expression; some intensity had gone from it, and it was only polite and attentive. Pauline, despairing of regaining her hand and beginning to feel chilly, glanced at Ted.

"Well, I think we'd better be hastening away to the mountain brow, Grandfather," he said at once, taking a step towards the gates of the Rich House.

"Yes, indeed we must. Supper will be waiting for us. Go away, dog, go away. I dislike dogs. Shakespeare disliked them, too, if we may judge by the unflattering references to them in his Works," said Mr. Early, giving Pauline's hand a little shake and then dropping it, and at the same time moving away from Jumper, who was sniffing at his thin shapely ankles. "Good night, Pauline. Give my warm remembrances to your mother and sister."

"Thanks awfully, I will. Good night."

"Good night, Pauli. And a thousand thanks for the tea and cakes!"

"Oh, I'm afraid they were *awful*!" she called, with a burst of frankness—and of affection, too, for the two queer figures retreating towards the dark grounds of the Rich House like a couple of Robber Barons. "Come again soon!"

"Love to. Good night!"

She ran across the road, followed by Jumper, and Ted and his grandfather walked arm in arm along the pathway by the lawn towards the house.

It's awfully funny, thought Pauline; ever since I've known Mr. Early he's said things like that and sort-of admired me, but I don't ever feel he's a nasty old man. It *is* queer, because if old Mr. Foster or Mr. Gates said those things I should simply be sick. I suppose it's because he's an actor.

In the course of his seventy-eight years Mr. Early had many times been complimented by kings; but never had he been offered praise which he would have liked more than that.

CHAPTER V

ERIC walked quickly home, swinging his beautifully rolled umbrella and hoping, with a growing misery, that he was not about to fall in love again.

He was an easy prey to beauty, and had an affectionate nature which, if it received encouragement, became passionate and troubled him painfully. And he was one of those young men (fortunately they are rare but they exist) who cannot fall in love with the right girl; he was a predestined B.V. or Bitch's Victim. Some five years of his life had already been spoiled, if not completely wasted, by a most wretched affair with the daughter of a local doctor; she was an ugly but fascinating girl with a beautiful figure, skin and voice who made pretty girls seem insipid; and she enjoyed scenes and was unable to make up her mind. Eric was just beginning to crawl out from the shades of this affair and to feel that it was *truly* a relief that she had gone to live in London, when he saw Marjorie walk into the bank. Now he wondered if his sufferings were to begin all over again with somebody else.

While he was having a quarrel with the doctor's daughter (and that happened every few weeks) he would go about with girls whom he met at dances or at the tennis club or at sherry parties; but he always chose unkind ones who used him, and then let him down in small but humiliating ways. And when he returned to the one girl whose image was seared (this was how it felt to him) into his heart, he was less than ever able to manage her because of the way his makeshift, time-marking girls had treated him.

It will shock all those young men who can and do manage their young women to hear of a fellow man suffering such defeats in the field of love. Not natural, they will say. Chap can't have any technique or something. Nevertheless, this is the truth about the love-life of young Mr. Somers: despite those long warm evenings spent in making love with the doctor's daughter in a lonely hay-field, he was not one of your natural conquerors.

If a young man or woman is defeated again and again in love they lose confidence: this is one of the serious results of having a procession of unhappy love affairs. The hand, so to speak, is always lifted to ward off the blow; and the charming, gay, cool people whom such sufferers always desire can see it. They strike past the uplifted hand as if it were not there, and go on their way.

But why didn't he marry?

He had implored the doctor's daughter, again and again, to marry him; and she had refused because he had only his salary of three hundred a year and because she knew that she could not be true to him if they did marry. And he did not look about for a "really nice girl," even after the doctor's daughter had gone to live in London, because he knew that his marriage, in order to heal the wound she had given him, must be perfect. A second-best would not do. He continued to go baldheaded for beauty and charm, and to pick losers.

He is walking home through the streets faintly lit by the wintry moon, swinging his beautifully rolled umbrella, and the contents of his head are beautifully arranged, too. Here is a roll of silky Italian fitting exactly against a heap of glittering French; here is a shelf stacked with themes by Bach and there a row of airs from Palestrina; and in that corner stands a box of tunes by Handel. Everything is dusted and labelled, yet warm with love and use.

But look into his heart! The floor is strewn with forgotten appointments that he remembers too well; the walls (such a pretty paper, too!) are tangled with painful telephone conversations; the

shelves are overflowing with too-casual letters and misunder-
standings that no one has noticed but himself. And right across
the window, shutting out the light, is a great crack like a scar.

By this time the Gentle Reader is thinking that people who go to
church and sing in the choir should not make love in hayfields.

"There you are, darling," said Mrs. Somers, opening the dining-
room door and letting out a blast of totalitarian eloquence from
the wireless. "Did you have a nice time? Aren't you cold?
Supper's all ready; Father and I waited for you."

"You shouldn't have done that, Dumps." He turned to smile
at her as he hung up his hat. "Whoever's that carrying on?"

"Mussolini. Isn't it dreadful."

"Why on earth did you tune in to Rome? There's a very good
concert from Milan about now."

"I know, I've just been listening to it. But I did just want to
hear Mussolini's voice, then I can imagine it when I read the
Daily Telegraph tomorrow."

"Well do shut it off now, dear; it's quite drowning the smell of
the shepherd's pie."

"How *did* you know it was shepherd's pie?"

"Ah ha! My spies are everywhere!"

Mrs. Somers, who was a small pretty old woman of seventy in a
woolly coat over a Liberty dress, laughed delightedly and went off
to the kitchen to get the pie from the oven, with her hammered
silver earrings dancing.

Mussolini suddenly stopped.

The silence that at once filled the house was beautiful, and
broken only by small, ancient domestic sounds; the coals settling
in the grate, the clink of a spoon against a saucepan, the far-away
singing of a kettle.

" 'What I like about the wireless is you needn't listen to it,' "
said Mr. Somers as his son came into the room, quoting an obser-
vation by their charwoman that was a family classic.

"Did you have a good music-making to-night, son?" he went
on, looking at Eric over the top of his spectacles and *The Times
Literary Supplement*. His voice was hoarse and his eyes were
moist and a pile of paper handkerchiefs lay on the table beside
him.

"Father. Why aren't you in bed?" demanded Eric, putting his
shoulders back and drawing in a deep breath which he would not
let escape again as a sigh.

"Ah! I *knew* you'd expect to find me in bed!" cried Mr.
Somers triumphantly. "As a matter of fact," he went on, lowering

his voice to a confidential murmur, "about half an hour ago I nearly gave in and went, and then I thought Mother might be feeling lonely, and as we didn't quite know what time you'd be back from church——"

"I haven't been to church to-night, I've been to a sherry party at Pauline's."

"So you have, so you have! My memory! It gets worse every day, and I suppose this cold doesn't help it. I was only saying to Mother, it was funny you hadn't said what time you'd be back, you always do . . . that was why I asked you if you'd had a good music-making just now."

Here Mr. Somers interrupted himself to give a great sneeze, with the usual accompaniments. Eric had sat down in a deep chair in front of the fire and was silently staring into the flames.

"And now I think I can hold out till bed time," Mr. Somers said comfortingly, coming out from his handkerchief. "Yes, I really think I'll stay and have supper with Mother and you and hear all about this 'sherry-party' at Pauline's."

"Good," said Eric, sitting up with a smile and opening his eyes, which he had shut for a moment. His mother came in with the pie and a dish of leeks on a trolley, and he got out of the chair and helped her put the dishes on the table and even managed to observe: "Leeks . . . hooray!"

"Father, will you have yours by the fire?"

"Yes, I think perhaps I will, and pamper the flesh for once. I really do feel . . . but there! I can't abide people who talk about their ailments."

When Mr. Somers was comfortably accommodated before the fire with a tray, and Mrs. Somers and Eric had begun to eat, the old man said:

"Now, Eric. We want to hear all about the party . . . who was there, and what you drank, and what everybody wore and said. At least, I'm sure Mother does, don't you, dear?"

"How is Pauline, darling?"

"Oh, very fit. She sent you her love."

Eric filled his mouth, and hoped that no more questions would be asked. The pleasant room with the peacock blue wallpaper and Chinese and Japanese prints and black oak furniture was brightly lit and filled with peace: he did not want Marjorie's name to be the next spoken aloud in it. He could not endure that his father and mother should know about his anguish and defeat in his love affairs. He had managed to keep his five-year struggle with Madeleine Eames a secret from them, though he sometimes thought that his mother suspected something of it.

And now Mrs. Somers said, almost at once and giving him a bright interested glance:

"And was Marjorie there?"

"Oh, yes. Very much there," he went on, with an effort that was actually painful in some part of his mind or body. "A *very* sophisticated young woman."

"Oh, and is she as pretty off the stage as she is on?" pursued his mother.

"Well, not quite, perhaps. She was beautifully made up, of course. . . ."

(But she had not been made up at all. Her skin had looked like a child's; its innocence had matched her slightly untidy hair, such unexpectedly *gentle*-looking hair above her small, composed face.)

"They all are, nowadays," said Mr. Somers discontentedly, poking at his pie with his fork. "It's quite a pleasure to see a girl like Pauline who leaves her face as God made it."

Eric and his mother exchanged a little smile.

"Oh, come now, Father, I think it looks very pretty and it doesn't seem to do their skins any harm, either," said Mrs. Somers, soothingly. "More leeks, dear?"

"Thank you. And was she wearing trousers, pray?"

"Who, Pauline?"

"No, the actress girl, the other one."

"No. She . . . I think she had on a black dress, so far as I remember."

"Eric wouldn't notice what she was wearing, dear, men never notice anything but a girl's face."

"And figure!" Mr. Somers's cheerful laugh was drowned in another great sneeze.

"When I saw her in the summer she was wearing trousers," he went on, after blowing his nose. "Walking into the Fan Café with a crowd of young people, and half the girls were wearing trousers."

"Mother, shall I get the sweet?"

"Do, will you, dear. It's a chocolate mould. Your favourite."

She smiled lovingly at him. He was young, and the girls of whom his father spoke disapprovingly were his friends. One day, perhaps, he would marry one of them, but she hoped that this would not be for some time yet because she and Father and Eric were wonderfully happy together. They had the same love of music and the same sense of humour, and were in fact (everybody said) more like three friends living in the same house than father, mother and son. It was dense of Father not to notice that Eric was irritated at having his friends disapproved of, but then men were dense creatures. Even Eric was dense sometimes. He thought that she did not know that he had been rather sweet on Madeleine Eames two or three years ago. But she had known it. She had not spoken of it, nor shown in any way that she knew, but she had watched him struggling with the infatuation, and had been so relieved, and had thanked God so humbly from her heart when he had conquered it, and had become his usual serene self again.

A loose girl like Madeleine Eames—how dreadful if Eric had really fallen in love with her and asked her to marry him!

And now they were all happy together once more, with Mrs. Somers deftly managing the dense but beloved males.

In a moment or two Eric roused himself, and gave his father and mother a lively account of the sherry party in a slightly amused and superior tone that suggested he would rather have been at home with them listening to the very good concert from Milan. This put them both into excellent spirits; and when Mrs. Somers had cleared away and stacked the plates for the charwoman to wash up when she came in the morning, they drew the three small fireside chairs round the hearth and sat down cheerfully to chat for the rest of the evening.

Is it always like that?

As Eric was lighting his pipe with a spill from the fire, a lively memory of Madeleine's face came suddenly to him. She had turned to him as they shut the gate of his home, on the one occasion when she had spent an evening with his parents, and asked him the question in a mocking yet awed and disturbed voice.

Mrs. Somers knitted another woolly coat in gay cherry red, Mr. Somers sneezed and blew his nose and shook his head over the reviews of the modern verse in *The Times Literary Supplement*; and from time to time read bits aloud to the other two. Eric was trying to read Aldous Huxley's *Eyeless in Gaza*, but this was not easy with his father crying "Listen! You *must* just listen to this and then I *really* won't interrupt you again," and then interrupting himself with a sneeze and a long blow before he read.

"Do you know it's a whole week, darling, since you spent an evening at home?" said Mrs. Somers, about nine o'clock.

"Yes. Seven whole days since the gay young man condescended to grace the fireside of his ancient parents. At*ishoo*!"

"Is it?" said Eric, smiling.

"Now you're not to feel guilty about it, darling; you know Father and I love you to go out and be with your friends. But I couldn't help thinking how nice it is . . . just the three of us, cosy and warm and safe."

"I'm glad, Dumps." He leant over and patted her wrinkled little soft hand.

About half past nine, just as the distant knock of the postman could be heard approaching down Station Road, Mr. Somers got up clumsily from his chair and began to wander about the room, sniffing the white pheasant's eye narcissus in the glass barrel, fingering the *Daily Telegraph*, switching on the wireless and turning it off again.

Eric and his mother exchanged smiles. Mr. Somers shook his fist at them.

"Paderewski prowl," said Eric, and all three laughed.

"No, but Father, you ought not to go into the drawing-room with that cold, we haven't had a fire in there since Friday," said Mrs. Somers.

"Nonsense, nonsense. I'll be quite all right. I'll take the electric stove in with me," and Mr. Somers went out of the room.

"I don't think he's bad, do you?" said Eric in a low voice as soon as he had gone.

"Oh no, we must just take care of him, that's all. He's a naughty boy, though; he won't do a thing he's told."

Suddenly the first notes of a prelude by Chopin rang out, romantic and melancholy and splendid, and at the same instant, the postman knocked at the front door.

"I'll go," said Eric.

As he crossed the hall he glanced into the drawing-room through the open door. His father was sitting upright at the piano, frowning at the music with his lips puffed out and his shoulders swaying slightly as he played. His bulky body in the shabby tweed suit that he wore all the year round looked dignified and full of power and his bearded face was serene.

"Bless him, I hope he doesn't sneeze," thought Eric, as he picked up a letter from the mat. It was for his mother. The music was hurrying on, rippling and beautiful.

"It's for you, Mother."

"Thank you, darling."

Now the prelude was slow and powerful; a procession of big chords.

"How funny," said Mrs. Somers presently in a puzzled voice.

Eric did not look up; indeed, he did not consciously hear what she said, for he was reading his book for the first time that evening.

"Eric."

He looked up slowly.

"Sorry, Dumps. What did you say?"

"Do look at this. It's such a queer letter and I don't know who it's from. It isn't signed."

He took it from her and stared at it. The notepaper was pale blue and cheap, the writing was rounded and childish.

DEAR MADAM,

I have often thought how happy you must be with your dear son and husband, and your beautiful home. I should say a perfect life really wouldn't you. No worries. It isn't many that can say that nowadays. You are a very lucky woman.

That was all. The writing covered all one side of the single sheet and went over on to the other side.

Eric looked up, and he and his mother stared at one another. The music was hurrying again, racing on and then doubling back on itself.

"What an extraordinary thing," said Eric at last. "It must be someone playing a singularly pointless joke."

Mrs. Somers was staring at the letter.

"I can't make it out," she said. Her voice was quiet and thoughtful. "Of course I'm happy and I've got very few worries, thank God, and you and Father are as good as gold. Everybody knows that. Why should anyone want to write and tell me so?"

"Perhaps it's an appeal for charity . . . count your blessings and think of others. It'll probably be followed up by another in a day or two, appealing for the refugees or something. I shouldn't worry about it if I were you."

He returned to his book. He was tired, and thinking that it was about time for bed. Madeleine always used to mock at him about the early hours he kept.

The music had stopped and Mr. Somers could be heard shutting the piano and putting out the light.

Mrs. Somers continued to sit with the letter in her hand, turning it about and staring at it. At last she said decidedly:

"Well, I've no idea who it's from or what it means, but I don't like it. I don't like it one bit."

CHAPTER VI

MAVIS JEVONS was a very lucky girl. She earned thirty-five shillings a week.

The girls of her age and experience who worked in A. P. Beard's earned fifteen shillings a week and had to starve on that, or earn enough to live on as best they could. But there was not much spare time work to be had in Seagate nor many men with money to spend on girls. Beard's was a company with branches in many of the larger towns in Great Britain which combined the sale of ironmongery, groceries and whitewood furniture with a lending library. Seagate doctors, when a girl came to them in a run-down and nervous state from overwork and lack of food, would say at once: "Working for Beard's? I thought so," and prescribe an iron tonic.

Beard's treated their employees shamefully. The food in their canteens was ill-cooked and insufficient. Their cloakrooms were dirty and the manageresses were encouraged to harass the underlings. Rudeness, bullying and spying ruled their large, hot, brilliantly illuminated shops. The girls who worked in Just's spoke pityingly of Beard's, as angels moving about their cool heaven might speak of hell.

Just's was a family business, at present owned by old Mr. Just, that had been established in Seagate for half a century; and one or two of the assistants had been with (not "at" or "in") the firm for thirty years. Old Mr. Just took an interest in the lives and fortunes of those who worked for him; and five years ago, when Mavis had nervously presented to him a letter from the Vicar of St. Anne's recommending her for a possible job, he had decided that as she was an orphan without resources she must receive thirty-five shillings a week instead of the twenty-five on which he usually started his novices.

It cannot be said that there was no jealousy about this. The elder members of the staff reminded each other (and Mavis) that *they* had all had to start at twenty-five shillings a week, some of them on less. But as they were all now advanced in middle life and earned more than thirty-five shillings a week, and as they were sorry for Mavis and liked her, the grumbles soon died away and she was happy there.

This extra ten shillings made all the difference to Mavis's contentment and comfort; indeed, it *was* her contentment and comfort, for without it she could not have paid her rent. But with it—

twenty-five whole shillings were left to buy clothes and food and
medicine and entertainment and culture!

The salaries paid to the staff at Just's were adequate, but they
compared badly with those paid to the assistants at Jonathan
Brown's, the local branch of Brown's ("Brown's, the Household
Word"). Brown's sold drugs and beauty products. Their assistants held shares in the business. Their canteens were well managed and the food properly cooked and sufficient. The young
people had the run of staff playing fields and clubs outside the
towns; medical attention was provided by the firm and legal advice
as well, if anyone had a legal problem unconnected with their work
at Brown's. Assistants who had been there for twenty years
received a small pension on retirement at sixty. The assistants in
the large airy pleasant premises seemed cheerful and contented.
If none of them spoke of Brown's with devotion or even with
affection, that must be blamed on the peculiar waywardness of
human nature; perhaps Brown's, as an institution, was too large
and too efficient to inspire the warmer feelings.

Just's Library and Brown's The Household Word were pleasant
places to work in because they were controlled by good men.
Beard's was an unpleasant place to work in because it was controlled by bad men. These disappointingly simple facts will irri-
tate those who think in terms of economics and politics. They
would prefer to think of the Mr. Beards, old Mr. Just, and all the
Mr. Browns as cogs, symbols, social units, and symptoms. Nevertheless, the sun rises every morning and will continue to do so;
human beings have souls; and it is better to be good than to be
bad.

Mavis was the only child of a Seagate postman who had earned
three pounds a week, and his gentle, timid and religious wife.
They had been proud of her delicate prettiness and had "brought
her up to be refined". Her mother had washed and ironed every
day to keep her freshly dressed; and her father had made a habit of
sitting in their bit of garden on Sundays (he did not fancy walking
out into the country on the one day out of the seven on which he
did not have to walk) and talking to her in a muddled but tender
way about the flowers and birds.

He had had the touching respect of the uneducated for nature
and books, mingled perhaps with a little gentle snobbery that was
half reverence for the Good and the Beautiful, and innocent
enough. He had felt rather than thought that there was another
world than his own; a world where everyone spoke pretty and
admired flowers and knew about foreign places. The garden was
not a very successful one, because Mr. Jevons was too tired to do

more than potter about in it in his spare time and neither he nor Mavis's mother was clever with their hands, but they all enjoyed sitting out in it on sunny days, dreamily watching the sorrel and marguerites dancing in a field behind the house. It had been a happy little household, in a gentle, quiet, tired way.

Mr. Jevons died of pneumonia when Mavis was fifteen; and her mother, after two frightening and exhausting years of going out charing for a living, died too. Mavis had been working as a waitress at the Marygold, a teashop kept by two nice ladies in the High Street, but her mother had always wanted something better for her.

The neighbours who (in place of the relatives which Mavis did not possess) immediately interested themselves in her fortunes, decided that she Ought To Go To the Vicar. Mrs. Jevons had always been such a one for the church; now let the church do something for Mrs. Jevons's child (said the neighbours, not without hope that the church would do nothing at all and thereby justify them for never going to it).

But the Vicar had been ever so kind, and had given Mavis a letter to Mr. Just; and the next thing the neighbours knew was that she had a job, a regular job in the liberry; though she was that stuck-up she never would say How Much. As time went on she got more and more stuck-up; she moved out of the two rooms where she had lived with her mother and took a flat (all the neighbours swore that it was a flat) in the town nearer her work.

Occasionally one of the neighbours who had gone into town early to do some shopping saw her hurrying to work with a neat tatchy case, dressed in navy with those white washable gloves and her hair permed, looking quite a business girl. Never so much as smiled at me, though she must have seen me, goodness knows I'm large enough.

So gradually the neighbours came to disapprove of Mavis and her white gloves and her flat; and presently she was quite without friends, and there was no part of her old life remaining in her new one—except St. Anne's church.

When she was four years old she used to call St. Anne's "The Nice Place." She had been a good, unforthcoming little thing, who rather enjoyed than otherwise keeping quiet for an hour, except when she made earnest efforts to join in the hymns with a funny little droning noise. She would stare drowsily at the pretty colours in the windows, especially at a lady with long hair and a mauve dress, and she liked to watch the little boys in white walking about the church, and to see the kind old man, whom she knew was called Vicar, standing up in the little house on the wall and talking.

As she grew older, she enjoyed the putting on of clean clothes on Sunday morning, and the walk between Mum and Dad to church along the light, swept-looking streets where the sound of the church bells came echoing and there floated the wild fresh smell of the sea. She felt happy, with Mum's hand holding her own in its worn little kid glove and Dad marching along beside them; not too slow and not rushing ahead like, most girl's dads always seemed to, but just walking along nicely, with his umbrella under his arm.

Everything was just a bit different on a Sunday, and that made it a day to look forward to. Dad was at home all day, for one thing; and Mr. Robertson the baker always cooked the joint for the Jevonses because he had the ovens going: the joint was handed to Mum over the garden wall by Mrs. Robertson as soon as Mum had put on her overall again after they got back from church. And there was always a clean tablecloth of a Sunday, and the kind voices above her head saying, ".Well, and how's Mavis to-day?" in the porch after the service; and the walk home through the quiet streets now smelling of roast beef. Best of all, there was a kind of good feeling that came after she had been to church and seen the pretty colours and heard the music and the names of Jesus and Almighty God. She loved this good feeling, and longed to feel it more often. Sometimes it came on summer evenings when she was looking at the sea, but most often it came when she was in church.

As she grew older, she learned to love the words of the prayers and the hymns and the ritual of the Church's year; the palms and lilies at Easter, the crib and carols at Christmas, the days consecrated to the saints and the martyrs and the dead.

Church was always the same. Every Sunday morning the words were the same, and on Sunday evenings; sad yet comforting words, beautiful and kind. The sunlight always came in through the windows above the choir gallery in the same way, and the bells never changed their sound however often they changed their chime; she knew them from among all the other bells in Seagate and walked faster on Sunday mornings when she heard their warning summons, and glanced up from her work with a wistful look when they rang on weekdays for Evensong, and she could not be there.

When she was in church she could thank God for all His goodness to her; for her dear little room and her nice job and the kindness of the Vicar and Mr. Just and all the people at work, and for that extra ten shillings a week. She missed Mum and Dad ever so badly at first, but although she cried in church on the first Sunday that she went without Mum, she came away from the service feeling happier because she had been in the place where she and Mum and Dad had so often been together, and because she knew that they were looking down on her from Heaven and feeling glad that she, the one who was left, still went to church although she went alone.

She could not remember (and this puzzled and annoyed her) the first time she had seen Mr. Somers at church. It seemed to her that he had always been there, like the words of the blessing at the end of the Sunday evening service, which she loved.

She knew, from gossip among her fellow choir members, that he used to sing in the boys' choir when he was a little boy. So he must have been one of those figures in white that she used to watch as they moved about the altar, when she was a very little girl! She liked to think of that.

But in just the same way that the purple dress of Mary and the green water plants in the stained glass windows had crept into her childish imagination and charmed it, so the dark, good face of young Mr. Somers seemed always to have been in her thoughts.

She listened for his voice, a sweet high baritone, unforced and warm, when the choir was singing. When he and she sang together of the gates of pearl and the countless host, she felt as if they were sharing joy, and when they sang about the encircling gloom she felt as if they stood side by side amid the darkness and sorrow and terror of this world, and were brave together.

She knew all about him; where he worked and where he played tennis, and what a good son he was to his old parents, and how he was fond of country walks, and not engaged or Anything. But she knew nothing about his affair with Madeleine Eames, because he had been so careful to keep that a secret, and she never thought that he might be in love with anyone. He was so good, so clever! He must be above all that sort of thing. She had collected all this information about him without asking questions, simply gleaning it in the course of casual conversations with fellow church members and acquaintances, much as someone might collect the pollen of a favourite flower on their coat-sleeve while walking through a meadow.

Her feeling for him was so full of admiration, almost of reverence, that it could hardly be called love. The most she hoped for was that one day—oh! years and years ahead—they might get to know one another so well that he would take her for a country walk; a real country walk through the fields out beyond Happy

Sands, with the tall bronze corn standing on either side of the narrow path and rustling dryly yet richly against them as they walked by, and the silky poppies and the cool cornflowers crouching among the wheat stems like brilliantly dressed little people, as they used to seem to her when she was a child.

She had so often imagined that walk. It was her favourite waking dream at night, just before she fell asleep.

Next to God and St. Anne's church, Mavis looked up to young Mr. Somers (and there *were* times when the order was reversed) and her feeling for him made all her life richer and happier. She was (as it was pointed out at the beginning of this chapter) a very lucky girl.

One morning she got to the library at her usual time, which was exactly twenty minutes to nine.

It was a nice day. In any other town but one on the East Coast of England it would have been called springlike. But on the East Coast of England the March days never have that delicious softness; the air is too keen. They suggest the spring, because they are bright and the sea is a sharp fresh green and the waves run in roughly yet gracefully like young tigers with very white teeth; but they do not turn the heart to thoughts of love and primroses. They turn up the coat collar and they set athletic thumbs to the twanging of tennis rackets.

Mavis was not working on the library desk any more, as Miss Gordon was now well again; so, after she had taken off her outdoor clothes in the dim but clean and commodious underground cloakroom, she went upstairs into the shop and went behind the stationery counter, where she always presided.

The other assistants, Miss Gordon and Miss Rolls and Miss Fenwick and Mr. Forbes, were unhurriedly busy, preparing the shop for its opening at nine o'clock.

Books were being uncovered and pyramids of writing-tablets rapidly erected, trays of pencils were temptingly arranged and regiments of coloured-ink bottles alluringly disposed. The postcard stand was quickly stacked with views of the Sunken Gardens and the Roman Gate at Chesterbourne and Dovewood Abbey. Sunlight poured into the shop (the awning would have to come out presently if it went on like this!) and if anyone glanced up for a second across the road, there was the Sea, so big and green and near that it seemed about to pour into the shop at any moment.

In the midst of this orderly bustle and subdued cheerful conversation, the clock in the Town Hall tower struck nine. At once Mr. Forbes went forward and unlocked the door of the shop.

And the first customer to walk in that morning was Eric Somers!

Mavis's heart beat quickly but not painfully, and she did not blush or pat her curls, which were combed from her forehead and arranged high on her head like the curls of all right-minded young women that spring. She looked sweetly at him, as she did at everybody, and waited with her lips just parted to reply to his "Good morning, Miss Jevons."

But he seemed a little worried or absent-minded, and he did not glance in her direction until he had given Miss Gordon at the library desk the two books he carried under his arm (*Gentlemen, Old Bach is Here!* for his father, and *A London Girl of the 'Seventies* for his mother) and was on his way towards the door.

But while he was at the desk something happened.

The door of the shop opened again, and in came a short stout old gentleman with a pink face and silver moustache. He looked slowly but keenly round the shop; and at once Mr. Forbes started from behind his counter and came towards him.

It was Mr. Just.

Mr. Just did not want the assistants to leave their work and cluster about him like a harem ready and eager for orders whenever he entered the shop; he preferred them to stay where they were and attend to such customers as happened at that moment to require attention. They all knew his wishes in this matter, and therefore no one moved from her place or took any notice of him beyond assuming a pleasant and respectful expression. He entered into a low-toned conversation with Mr. Forbes, who listened with his head slightly inclined and nodded intelligently and helpfully at intervals.

But when he had been talking to Mr. Forbes for a moment, Mr. Just put his hand up to the back of his neck and a fretful look came over his face.

"Chilly in here, aren't you, Forbes?" he said, twisting his head round as if to see whence the chilliness came. "Shocking draught. Ah! the door's open!"

"Miss Jevons! Close the door, please!" ordered Mr. Forbes pleasantly but crisply. And Mavis, who had been in a dream, Mavis who had been staring at the back of young Mr. Somers's head and thinking how becoming was his new spring overcoat of a light grey sporting material, Mavis started forward and gently, ever so gently, shut the door. A deep blush of dismay and shame came up into her face.

"Thank you, Miss Jevons," said Mr. Just, giving her a kind smile before resuming his conversation with Mr. Forbes.

She began to arrange letter-cards, very slowly and carefully, with her eyes fixed steadily upon them.

Oh dear, she thought, that was my fault—leaving the door open when Mr. Forbes told me specially I was to keep an eye on it. How awful. I do hope no one noticed.

She did not admit, even to herself in thought, that she had forgotten the door because she had been staring at Mr. Somers.

The door of the shop had stood up well enough to the fierce blasts of an East Coast winter, but when the spring came it had taken the privilege of machines, window frames and human beings in the spring, and Gone Wrong. It refused to shut properly. This morning a man was coming to See about it, but until he came it was Mavis's charge to see that the door did not click open again after it was shut; she had been given this task because her counter was nearest to the door.

Mr. Just finished his murmured conversation with Mr. Forbes and went out of the shop to his waiting car with an absent-minded smile and a lift of his hat for the lady assistants. Mr. Forbes returned to his counter, refraining from giving Mavis a reproachful glance. He had seen her dismay and her blush, and knew that she had been punished.

It was such people that made Just's Library the pleasantest shop to work for in Seagate.

Mr. Somers turned quickly away from the library desk and came across the shop on his way out. Mavis had meant not to look up, for she felt that after her carelessness she did not deserve the joy of a smile from him. But it was useless; her eyelids lifted themselves, and her eyes were turned towards him before she knew what she was doing.

"Good morning, Miss Jevons."

"Good morning, Mr. Somers."

It was a smile, of course; but it was not as wholehearted as his smiles usually were, and as he went out of the door (pausing to shut it carefully after him—*oh dear, he must have seen me forget*) she was left with a sad little feeling that he was worried about something.

In fact Eric was only irritated because he was already a little late for work and because before he left the house he had been playing his annual part in the coquettish drama of Father's Tonic.

Every spring Mr. Somers was prescribed by his doctor a Tonic, to fortify him against the dangers of that treacherous season. He accepted it, but under protest, and he never could remember (so he said) to take the beastly stuff. The bottle stood about on mantelpieces all over the house, sticky and reproachful and making wet white rings on the paint. Before breakfast Eric had to go upstairs to fetch it, and at supper, and sometimes just before they all went to bed. Mr. Somers would sit back in his chair with a self-reproachful cry and Mrs. Somers would murmur apologetically to Eric and then a spoon would have to be wiped clear of tea or jam and at last, after a spirited tirade, Mr. Somers would swallow it. They would all three laugh and have jokes about it.

They had been having jokes about Father's Tonic for years.

The jokes were familiar to Eric; they were even dear to him. But on a spring morning when the sea was dazzlingly green and. brilliant with gold patches flung from the chilly new sun; when the waves were bouncing roughly in and rolling mussel shells over and over and flinging the glistening black green seaweed high up on the salty stones; when lilac buds were shaking in the furious gusts; when the pavements were parched by sun and breeze to the whiteness of marble; when girls at every corner were lowering their flowery new spring hats to escape the sudden leap of the wind and pressing down the blowing white frilled petticoats that were fashionable this spring——

How heavenly it would be to see Father's Tonic, stickiness and reproachfulness and all, sailing away, away, over the sea wall into the sea, and rolling over and over with the mussel shells and the seaweed until it sank fathoms, fathoms deep into the green ocean!

He went into the bank.

All that day people came into the library, and went away again with their choice: Miss Gaye with *Italy and the New Europe*; Colonel Bracebridge with *Europe—Whither?*; Mrs. Ullathorne with *Fallen Bastions*, and Mr. Cannondale with *Disgrace Abounding*; Miss Robinson with *Europe: Can it Survive?* and Miss Brown with *Can America Stay Out?*; Mr. Hapgood with *Insanity Fair*, and Major Morrison with *Africa: Unity or Collapse?*

The Island Race, indeed.

Towards evening the wind dropped. The colour of the sea changed to a beautiful and solemn blue that reflected the whole cloudless heaven, and the waves ran in with a majestic swaying motion below their ridges of foam. The sea looked cruel no longer, but as if it were the image, the reflection, of a sea in Heaven that was even more beautiful than itself. It seemed without guile, noble and good.

When Mavis came out of the shop at the end of her day's work she looked across at the expanse of two blues, the darker below and the paler above, filled with radiant dying light, and there came to her the good feeling that came to her sometimes in church.

She lingered a little while, gazing out to sea.

While she was standing there she saw a sports car go past in which there was plainly a Party of Pleasure: young Mr. Brian Kingsley from the Hotel Bristol and Miss Williams who came into the library sometimes and Miss Williams's sister Marjorie who was in the repertory company at the Theatre Royal—and Mr. Somers.

Mr. Somers looked ever so happy. The car stopped outside the Fan Café on the corner of the High Street and they all went in.

I expect they're going to have supper before they go to the pictures or to see Miss Williams's sister's show, thought Mavis, turning away to go home.

The good feeling had vanished. It was still a lovely evening and the sea looked as beautiful as ever and she had a nice book from the library to read when she got home; a life of the poet Cowper, it was, that the critics had spoken very highly of.

She was very glad to see him looking happy again. But she could not help wishing that she was sitting in the Fan (which was so expensive that she had never visited it) with the Williams girls and Mr. Kingsley and Mr. Somers. It would have been quite enough just to sit at the same table with them, and watch Mr. Somers. She did not want to butt in. But if only she could have sat there, in her navy suit and new spring hat with the snowdrops and primroses on it, and her white organdi blouse, and watched Mr. Somers!

She walked quickly home. Before she began to read the life of the poet Cowper she had stockings to wash for to-morrow and a pearl button to sew on to the organdi blouse, which had cost five shillings at Marks and Spencers. (You cannot expect buttons to stick like glue for five shillings.) And she would have to reset her curls and do her nails and clean her shoes and mend a shoulder strap.

There would be plenty to do. There always was.

When she got up to her room she found a letter lying on her dressing-table. She picked it up and looked at it curiously, as is the habit of people who do not often receive letters. It was in a cheap pale blue envelope and addressed to Miss M. Jevons in a round childish hand.

"I expect it's from Joan," she murmured, thinking of a girl who had been at school with her and who sometimes wrote to her from her home in the North.

But the postmark was "Seagate".

She began to open the letter.

Her little room was still filled with the fresh light of spring, lingering along the blue walls and on the daffodils on the window-sill. Through the bay window showed the grey roofs of nearby houses and the last glow of the sinking sun and the distant blue line of the sea. The chirruping of nesting sparrows came from Mrs. Voles's garden, and the beautiful voice of a thrush.

Suddenly Mavis sat down on the bed. She had gone pale and was staring at the letter with widely opened eyes. She began to tremble.

What a lucky girl you are. A nice cosy job and plenty of money to spend and nothing to worry about. My word you're luckier than some. No wonder they think so well of you up at Saint Anne's. You're a good girl too, not like some of them always running after the fellows. Saving yourself up for some-one. Lucky boy. You must love him very much.

It was the last words that had made her tremble and go pale. A dreadful feeling of shame and disgust overcame her. The words seemed to burn into her mind.

You must love him very much.

CHAPTER VII

THE young people now silently waiting for drinks in the Fan were there at the suggestion of Marjorie.

She had been on her way there with Brian, who was to buy her her evening meal, when she saw Eric and Pauline walking home together from the bank and said to Brian that they would stop and collect them.

Brian did not want to. They both looked exhausted and glum; he did not much like Eric, whom he deemed wet; and he wanted to avoid Pauline. However, as he never made fusses when he could evade them, he stopped the car and Marjorie leant out and called in the ringing full voice that came so strikingly from her small face:

"Hullo there!"

"Hullo yourself. We've been working late. Hullo, Brian," said Pauline.

Brian smiled and silently sketched the Nazi salute. A really bad go of influenza had left him looking interestingly pale, but Pauline angrily thought that she did not care how he looked. She had had 'flu, too, and everybody—old Mr. Somers and Mrs. Somers, Mrs. Williams, Marjorie, Eric, Ted, old Mr. Early—had had bronchitis and internal chills and colds, distributed among them according to their stamina and years.

That was why the young people had not seen much of each other for the past six weeks. But now it was a March evening, with the lights of the Regal Cinema shining brilliantly through the clear blue dusk, and people hurrying home with the afternoon editions of the London papers gleaming very white under their arms. (There was plenty of news from Europe; there always was in March.) Pauline suddenly felt a little stir of happiness and excitement beneath her boredom and after-'flu depression. The summer was coming, with swimming expeditions in her new brown swim-suit and dances at the Grand!

"Come and have a drink with us," said Marjorie. "I'm sure that's what Eric needs." And she smiled at him.

"Shall we, Pauline?" he asked, turning to his fellow sufferer.

"Swell!" she said—enthusiastically.

"Good," said Brian. "Get in, will you."

Eric opened the door for Pauline and they got in at the back.

Damn, thought Pauline. She sat back and put on a pleasantly interested expression and kept her eyes turned on the bright shop windows going past.

She had seen Brian once or twice in the last weeks, though never alone, when he had come to the house to see Marjorie or to bring her home after the show. She was getting used (she told herself) to their having a flaming affair. It would not last long, anyway, and when it was over she would not have to see him any more.

But meantime she did have to see him, and she felt no better.

She was still angry and puzzled and hurt. He got on her nerves. He made her remember that time when she was a kid and had a splinter under her finger nail and it drove her nearly crazy until Ted dug it out with his grandfather's razor. She told herself that she disliked Brian so much that she could hardly manage to be polite to him. But she made herself be polite, even friendly, whenever they met, because he must never find out how deeply he had hurt her last summer.

That was the one thing that she could not *bear* to happen. If he ever did find out she would . . . jump off the pier or something.

Oh, the unhappy, chilly English spring on the East Coast, with the cold sea tumbling in the gathering dusk, and the primroses and windflowers cowering in the wind-shaken woods!

As for Eric, he also was watching the shining shops go by, and thinking that he did not want to sit and consume, and pay for others to consume, expensive short drinks that upset his liver, while the girl he desired (for I don't *love* her, he thought bitterly) sat opposite to him with the man who could kiss her, and who of course did.

This was the third time that he had met Marjorie. Pauline had taken him to see her play the lead in "Love from a Stranger" before their colds had smitten them all down; and the picture of her in a dressing-gown stained with cold cream, her flowery blue eyes laden with violet paint, her lovely legs gleaming between the soiled edges of the old robe, had finished him. Her poise and beauty, her little air of knowing exactly what she wanted as if she were a single-minded child, enchanted and hurt him with a familiar spell. Mr. Somers was once more in an interesting condition.

Later on, when I can summon up the energy after this accursed influenza, I'll ask her to drive out to the Red Barn and have dinner, he thought. And on the way back I'll—I'll get what I can.

For once, he decided, he would treat a girl rough.

She was a small girl, and perhaps that composed manner was all bluff.

There was absolutely nothing in her calling him Eric; actresses called everybody Eric.

Probably later on she would call him darling.

This prospect was so exquisite and painful that he was obliged to speak in order to break the spell of his sufferings.

"How the evenings are drawing out, aren't they, *said he brightly*," he remarked in a voice faint from influenza and love.

"You're quite hoarse, you *do* need a drink, darling," Marjorie said absently. "Look, Brian, we'll go on upstairs and order while you park the car."

"O.K." They got out, and he began to back the car down the side street where the Fan's car park was. The other three went into the restaurant.

The Fan was the smartest café in Seagate for morning coffee and a one-and-sixpenny lunch or three-shilling dinner. It had a downstairs room where chocolates and cakes were sold to the common herd and (like another and more fashionable restaurant in London) an upper room where the top drawerites gathered. There they sat, in the bold curve of the great window that was the only piece of modernist architecture in Seagate (for the new block of flats out towards Happy Sands was not yet finished) and watched the sea or each other's eyes between sips of coffee and snatches of gossip. Huge fans were painted in brilliant colours on the dove grey walls and a small orchestra played a piano, a drum and a violin on a small platform at one end of the oval room.

Eric and Marjorie and Pauline found a table in the window and sat down.

"Pauline, Marjorie, what will you have?" enquired Eric a little stiffly as a waitress came up. The room was almost empty.

"Gin and lime, please," said Pauline.

"And me," said Marjorie. "Brian'll have a whisky, I guess."

"I'll keep you company," said Eric. He gave the order and had his hand in his pocket (drinks at the Fan had to be sent out for and paid for on ordering) when Marjorie said:

"No, this is on me. I asked you."

"Oh no, I can't have that," he said at once, more loudly and firmly than the occasion required. (Pay for his liquor she should not.) "Absurd," he added, smiling defiantly.

"How do you mean, absurd?" she murmured.

"Women paying for drinks," he said, putting his money back in his pocket after giving the waitress quite a lot of it.

"M'm, it does seem silly, doesn't it," she answered after a tiny pause. "I'm broke this week as a matter of fact, so I'm very glad to be a little woman for once." And she smiled at him.

What a beast I am, bullying her because I can't kiss her, he thought remorsefully, as he offered both girls his cigarette case. But I can't help it, I will not have women buying things for me, I will *not*.

That's a good thing, thought Marjorie, leaning comfortably back with a cigarette, at which she would not take more than a few puffs, fitted into her holder. How I do hate paying for drinks. She had trained herself to pay for a round as if she were a man when she was in mixed company and impoverished theatrical society, but she never saw her good money borne off on the waiter's tray without thinking *There goes a pair of stockings or some bath-salts*.

The three were silent, with their drinks before them. Eric and Pauline were dopey with the after-effects of 'flu and the disturbed state of their feelings, and Marjorie, who never talked much except when she was with other actresses or with actors, was quiet because she was content to sit and look beautiful in a place where she could be seen. She was fond of society and preferred to be with four people rather than with one; if she saw someone she knew, even if she was with a young man whom she did not mind kissing, she would invite the third party to join them.

But after the silence had lasted a noticeably long time and they were beginning to wonder sleepily why Brian did not come, Marjorie turned to Eric and said with her lovely child's look:

"You're awfully sad to-night, darling."

This was the truth, and as such it was hardly to be borne. It brought all his past miserable five years before him.

"Am I? I'm awfully dull, I'm afraid."

"Well, do drink up, then you'll feel better."

It's his boring old parents, I suppose, thought Pauline. Mother's bad enough but they must be ghastly. I mean they're awfully *nice*, of course, but quite ghastly.

"Here's Brian," said Marjorie.

Oh lord, why need he come back? I was just beginning to feel comfortably muzzy and not think about anything, thought Pauline, as Brian, the observed of all the waitresses, stalked across the room and sat down authoritatively at their table.

"Sorry I've kept you waiting," he said. "Is this mine? Thanks."

"Did you meet a friend?" enquired Marjorie innocently.

He nodded.

"Who was it?"

"Mrs. Cunningham."

"Oh."

"What do you mean, oh?"

"Just oh. Was she tight?"

"Not very."

"What did she want?"

"Nothing."

"Just passing the time of day, was that it?"

"That was it."

"Well, darling, could you order me a boiled egg now you are here? I can't sit carousing with you people all night, I have to be at the theatre and act, you know."

"Can you act on that?" asked Eric.

"Oh heavens, yes. I've worked out a scheme about my food. I eat hardly any breakfast and masses of lunch and no tea and hardly any supper and just orange juice when I get home after the theatre at night."

"It sounds Spartan. Don't you get hungry?"

"I did at first. I don't now. And anyway I'd rather be hungry than fat."

"Like Mrs. Cunningham," said Pauline.

A waitress came up, and Brian repeated the orders for their drinks and asked for Marjorie's egg.

"She'd be pretty if she weren't so fat," Pauline went on idly.

"She used to be lovely. Mother remembers her," said Marjorie. "But, of course, now she's a wreck."

"She's got masses of money, hasn't she, Eric?" said Pauline.

"So everybody says. She looks as if she had."

"And heavenly clothes. Her clothes are simply tops," said Marjorie. "Her furs are always real and she gets her suits from Creed."

"How on earth do you know?" enquired Pauline curiously. "You hardly know her."

"I don't know her properly at all; I've just been introduced to her once by Brian and then she was so tight she couldn't speak. But she was doing her face in the Ladies at the Bristol one day before Christmas when I was there and she'd chucked her coat on a chair and I saw the label."

"Quite the little sleuth, aren't you," said her sister. "Well, anyway, she's frightfully fat and rather repulsive, I think."

"Oh, yes, she's definitely an evil piece. Goody, here's my egg."

Brian, who had taken no part in this discussion, had been looking at Pauline for the last few moments and now said:

"Pauline, that's a very becoming hat."

She lifted her glass to him with a mocking, but not too mocking, smile.

"Thank you kindly, sir."

"No, but it is. Marjorie—Eric—don't you think that's a very becoming hat?"

Marjorie looked seriously at the hat. It was a little witch's one of scarlet straw, tilted over Pauline's eyes.

"Much better than those huntin' shootin' and fishin' things with brims she usually has," she pronounced at last.

"I do not!" protested Pauline. "I've only got one hat with a huntin' brim."

"I like women in brims," put in Eric, who might have left out the brims.

"Where did you get it?" went on Brian.

"Noreen's."

"Well, it's a dashed good hat, anyway. Here's to it," and he finished his drink.

It cost me twenty-seven and sixpence and I bought it to cheer me up when I was feeling so fed up after Christmas, thought Pauline, trying not to feel pleased. *If you want to know. And how absolutely extraordinary you are, going on the way you did in the summer and then dropping me cold and then saying things about my hats as if nothing had happened. I cannot make you out. I give up.*

3*

Nevertheless, the room now looked beautiful to her, and her heart seemed to be dancing lightly. She drank so little as a rule that the smallest quantity of alcohol affected her at once, but the sudden beauty of the room this evening was not due entirely to gin.

She pulled the witch's hat further over her eyes and leant forward with the big sleeves of her coat on the table. Suddenly they all began to talk and laugh, and everyone felt better. The room was beginning to fill up and the orchestra, after a last contemptuous glance round, had struck up "Black Eyes."

"Look here, I must go," said Marjorie, putting down her egg-spoon and glancing at her watch.

"Oh, don't go yet," said Eric. "I'm just beginning to enjoy myself."

"Must, I'm afraid."

"I'll be with you in a minute," said Brian, holding up his unfinished cigarette.

Marjorie pulled her cape round herself. It was a silver fox, one for which she was still paying a reputable firm in London, and like all her clothes it was both smart and of good quality.

"I think I'll walk," she said, glancing out through the window at the dark plain of the sea that was now almost indistinguishable from the sky. The Northstone Light had begun to flash and fade far out in the clear night.

"Oh god," said Brian.

"Why can't we all walk?" she went on. "It's a heavenly night and walking's good for your skin."

"My skin doesn't need doing good, thanks."

"I'll come," said Eric. (Damn, he thought. That sounded too eager and personal.)

"Goody," said Marjorie. "Pauli?"

"I think I'll stay here," said Pauline in what was for her a dreamy tone. The orchestra was playing a soft, sweet tune, and this was enough to remind her of the hidden gipsy orchestra whose music had haunted the veranda of the Hotel Bristol. The tune was not the same, and she was now sitting in a hot crowded room under bright lights instead of in the shade of the fig-vine on a summer day, but all the same she began to feel the same soft invasion of her mind and heart, as if something wonderful were about to happen.

So she received a distinct shock when Brian said:

"All right, Eric. You take some healthy exercise if you want to; Pauline and I are staying."

Look here ... good heavens ... I can't ... she thought wildly, slowly opening her handbag and taking out her flapjack. She had been looking at the other three and hearing the music and muzzily thinking how beautiful everybody was, and suddenly she heard that she was to be left alone with Brian.

She longed and yet feared to be left alone with him. Would he say anything?

Her face looked startlingly pretty in the little round mirror of the powder case and she could not help giving it a proud smile. I ought to go with them, she thought, putting on more lipstick. But she did not get up.

"So long, Pauli, that *is* a good hat," said Marjorie. Her voice was completely friendly; she was fond of old Pauli, who was so crazy about her games and who would never steal any of *her* young men, however good her hats were, because she had no oomph; and whose young men were not exciting but who had known her for ages, like that awful Wally Wade who used to be at Father's school.

And if Brian liked to stay there, Marjorie did not mind. He was marvellously good looking, of course, and he had what it took, and his car was useful and she quite liked kissing him; but already her mind had left them all—Brian and Pauli and poor Eric who was so clearly going to be a nuisance—and was in the dressing-room at the theatre. In fancy her white hands were deftly smearing grease-paint on to her face reflected in the spotted mirror with the prettily decorated Greetings telegrams stuck into its frame. Her mind was avidly speculating over the bits of news about Stuart and Lenny and Van that would have accumulated since the morning. Her sister and Brian and Eric were so dreary compared with the people in the company that she could hardly wait to get away from them.

She did not think all this out. Her contempt for the three at the table only showed itself by this running away of her mind towards the setting she loved best.

"Good-bye, darling," she said to Brian.

He lifted his glass. "I'll come and fetch you afterwards."

"Angel. Good-bye, you two."

Pauline smiled and Eric muttered: "See you to-morrow, *said he platitudinously*." He was wondering if the walk to the theatre would give him time to work up to the Red Barn invitation.

They went out. Pauline and Brian were alone.

CHAPTER VIII

THE orchestra had had a little rest, and was now giving petu-
lant preliminary pickings and tinklings before striking up
again; the waitresses were moving from table to table in the
crowded room taking orders; nevertheless, he and she were alone.

Brian leant back and surveyed the room.

He really is marvellous, thought Pauline, gazing at him. He's
Tyrone Power's type, more than anyone, but he's better looking.
Of course I'm still furious with him but he really is marvellous.
It's heavenly to be with him again. I've never felt like this with
anyone else.

Brian's eyes were half-shut and his fair head was tilted back as
he stared superciliously about him.

Heavens, I must look absolutely goofy, thought Pauline,
hastily looking away from his face; and at the same instant he
drawled:

"God, this place is badly run."

"Is it? How?" she asked, surprised, for the Fan was generally
supposed to be well managed and staffed, while its food, as
restaurant food goes, was good.

"Oh, everything. The orchestra's lousy, to begin with. They
ought to get a leader who can play the violin and croon, and fire
those dreary middle-aged hags. Women don't want to look at
other women when they come in for a sherry about six . . . or even
when they come in for coffee about eleven . . . in fact they don't
want to look at another woman at all unless it's to pick her clothes
to pieces. Our waitress had a dirty apron. There have been
crumbs and a dirty ash-tray on that table over there for the last
ten minutes. The piano's out of tune. A lamp on that table in the
corner isn't working. The pianist's shoes want mending. The
flowers aren't fresh. All small things, but they make the difference
between a badly run place and a properly managed one."

He leant forward and smiled at her.

"Like a girl who isn't groomed. No glamour," he said.

She was speechless. Did he mean . . . ?

"Now that hat," he went on softly, "has glamour."

"Has it?" she muttered foolishly.

It was thrilling that he liked her hat, of course, but why did she
always begin to feel angry whenever he talked to her? So long as
they were only playing tennis or dancing together it was divine,
but as soon as he began to talk to her she felt as if she were back

at school again; shy, and mad about games, and furious because
she was being lectured.

He always seemed to have some bit of advice.

There was that time in the summer when he didn't like her lipstick.

"Oh, definitely," he went on. "It gives you glamour, too, and
that's a very, very important thing for a woman to have."

You're telling me, she thought.

"It makes a big difference to a man whether a girl has it or not.
It may alter his whole way of thinking about her if he sees her one
day when she's looking unglamorous."

Pauline listened with her heart beating faster and the colour
slowly increasing in her brown cheeks, but her eyes were fixed
steadily upon his face and she was smiling a little.

Was that what happened last summer, she wondered.

He came that Saturday when Mother was out and I'd been
washing my hair at home because I was broke that week because
I'd had two rides. I had my head tied up in that old Paisley scarf
of Marjie's.

All the trouble started from that day.

But he was so sweet. He sat on the sofa and kept on staring at
me.

I suppose he was hating the scarf and thinking I had no
glamour.

He really is intolerable!

Frightfully rude!

"Some days, for example, you're quite glamorous," Brian went
on coolly, "and some days you haven't any glamour at all."

"Thanks," said Pauline.

She had to speak. Her temper was rushing up and she was
frantically catching at it, but it had nearly gone. And whatever
happens, she thought, I mustn't lose it. I *won't*.

"Mad?" he asked, smiling. He liked teasing girls.

"Well, no one likes being told they're glamorous one day and
not the next," she said, making herself speak in a quiet amused
voice.

"I'm speaking quite impersonally, you know," he said quickly.
"As a matter of fact your type is one that has great possibilities
for glamour. And I may say it is one that appeals to me very
much."

"Thanks most awfully," said Pauline in a low tone.

He glanced quickly at her. Such a steadily smiling but crimson
little face stared at him from under the witch's hat that he was
silent.

After a pause he said:

"That certainly is a swell'hat."

She did not answer.

He leant forward across the table.

"Pauline . . . about what happened in the summer . . . you know. . . ."

She nodded, unable to speak.

He hesitated, staring down at his hand with its correct signet. Then he tried again.

"I say . . . you must have thought it extraordinary that I didn't ring you up after I said I would that time at your place, didn't you?"

"No, I didn't," she said. "As a matter of fact I'd forgotten all about it."

"Oh . . . well, I did mean to, but just about that time things were very difficult."

Pauline, who had been staring at the handbag in her lap, looked up quickly.

"You see," he said, "I'm not my own master."

"Oh, I *know*!" she said earnestly, leaning towards him. "I do know that."

He smiled gratefully.

"It was only that I—it was so queer . . ." stammered Pauline, and came to a stop.

I really can't remind him that he kissed me like that in the car last summer out at Happy Sands and then didn't write or call me up for six months.

"I know," Brian said. "I knew you'd think it very peculiar. But you see, it was all so difficult."

She nodded eagerly, watching his face.

"It's always difficult."

She nodded sympathetically.

"It must be awful," she said.

"I—I did *want* to ring you up, all last autumn, Pauli. That made it much worse."

"I'm glad you did," she said, almost in a whisper.

Her anger was dying away. He had spoken about that time in the summer and hinted at why he had dropped her so abruptly. He need say no more. She understood. She was not a person who went in for long discussions with her friends over the morning coffee, for long walks through unnoticed country lanes, while pouring out her love troubles and listening to theirs. She kept her feelings to herself and tried to control them, and she expected other people to do the same. At school, she and Peggy and Eileen and Vera had always done that, and they tried to do it still, though it was true that lately Vera had gone a bit weak (they had always said someone was "a bit weak" when she went against their code) over a married man.

She felt proud that Brian had confided in her. It must be simply awful to be tied to old Frankenstein. Stopping his son going out with a girl! He must be nuts.

Brian said suddenly:

"Marjorie knows, of course."

"About last summer, do you mean?" she asked, dismayed.

"Good god, no. About how difficult things are, I meant."

"Oh, I see."

Brian went on quickly.

"He's met her. He likes her. She knows how to handle him. She's grand, of course. All the glamour in the world but she'd never high-hat you. I love her to run around with, but . . ."

He broke off and smiled, then shook his head. The last of Pauline's anger vanished and delicious happiness took its place. Were things going to be all right? Would he take her to dances in the summer? He wasn't in love with Marjorie! He had just said so; well, as good as said so. It was heaven, absolute heaven.

And fancy Marjorie having met Frankenstein, and not saying one word about it. I simply must ask her what he's like, she thought. She really is extraordinary the way she keeps things to herself; she always did, though, even when we were small kids. Well, so do I, of course. But I don't think I could have kept it to myself if I'd seen Frankenstein and talked to him.

Neither said anything for a little while. Brian gazed round the restaurant but his expression was no longer supercilious; it was gentle and sad. Pauline sat there in a happy dream, not wanting to talk.

At last Brian said:

"Are you doing anything this evening?"

She shook her head.

"How about a movie? If we go now we'll be in time for the second house at the Regal."

"I'd love to," she said, and just managed to stop herself from adding: "Thanks awfully."

While he was paying the bill she stood pulling on her gloves and gazing out through the great window at the brilliantly illuminated High Street, its purple and golden lights looking dramatic against the background of darkness that was the sea.

Gosh, I'm happy. Never mind if I am unglamorous sometimes; I'm quite glamorous enough for him to take to the pictures

Gosh! I feel as if I'd won three sets of tennis and had a glorious
gallop along the sands and swum miles in a rough sea on a sunny
day! Gosh, I feel *marvellous*!

Eric coughed, and took his hand from Marjorie's furry elbow.
He had been guiding, rather than steering, her across the road.

"Do you like these spring evenings?" he began. (Damn. What
a fool thing to say. Like the man in Compton Mackenzie's novel
who said they were like swords and the girl said: Do you mean
you're cold?).

"They smell heavenly. But I don't often see a spring evening.
I'm usually at the theatre by now. Do you mind if we walk a bit
faster."

"Of course not."

(Now we're alone she doesn't say darling.)

"Yes, I suppose you're pretty busy. Don't get much time for—
for reading or dancing or anything."

"Not much. When I'm not acting I'm studying a new part or
asleep. I need masses of sleep."

She was rushing along with the hairs on her cape sleeked back
by the wind and its foxtails flying and her own yellow curls blown
back from her face, which wore a serious and slightly worried look.

"Do you care for dancing?"

"When I can get it I do."

"I was wondering . . . you're awfully busy just now but I was
wondering if you'd come to the Red Barn with me some time.
We could drive out and dance and swim . . . if you'd care to."

"I'd *love* it, thanks *awfully*. It would be swell. I've never been
there," she said absently.

"Oh. That's . . . grand. Well, perhaps you could let me know
when you're not quite so busy." He spoke with meticulous politeness and did not look at all pleased. She glanced at him. Oh
lord, she thought, I wasn't overwhelmed with joy; I ought to have
been. Blast. Now he'll get a thing about it. She sighed, and set
to work.

"I certainly shan't ask you when I want to go," she said clearly
in her ringing voice, increasing her pace until the shops seemed to
sail past them like magic glittering caverns and the cold wind took
their breath. "I'd adore to go, but you *must* ring up and *ask* me.
I'm so busy that I never get time to arrange treats for myself. But
all my friends are absolute angels and arrange them for me because
they know what I'm like."

I know what you're like, too, thought Eric. You make me feel
like hell because I'm included in a crowd as one of "all my

friends" and at the same time you give me the hope of becoming a special friend by including me at all. You're a witch of the first water.

"It would be lovely to dance again," she said, in a softer voice and as if to herself. "I haven't danced for months."

It would be lovely to dance with you, he thought. Perhaps you only seem to be a witch; one of my usual witches. Perhaps if I had you to myself for a whole evening and you weren't thinking about your blasted acting you might be different. At this hope he suddenly felt better, and said cheerfully:

"Right you are, then. I shall telephone you one morning and say firmly 'You're coming to the Red Barn this evening, madam,' and you'll say 'Oh, am I, sir?' And I shall say (all domineering-like)——"

"I say, do you mind awfully if we run? I'm on at the opening and I'm late now."

"Of course. I'm afraid it was my fault talking. . . ."

The last words were jerked out of him as they began to run.

The theatre was only a hundred yards or so away, in a side street lined by old houses which had had shop fronts built on to them. Eric and Marjorie darted past people hurrying home from work and Eric stammered apologies as he just avoided bumping into people; snatches of conversation came to him:

". . . awful that one man should have all that power. . . ."

". . . they don't want it any more than we do. . . ."

". . . told her straight I didn't. . . ."

Marjorie darted up an alley that smelled strongly of frying fish at the side of the theatre, and stopped outside the stage door.

"Thanks awfully! I'm sorry I made you run!" she said, standing on the step and smiling brilliantly at him, with her small hand in a black glove held out. "Good-bye. And I shall look forward to our evening at the Red Barn."

He took the little hand and shook it and said "Good night. I'll telephone you soon," and turned away.

As he came out of the alley into Lavender Road he saw a girl coming across the road whom he knew. It was Mavis Jevons. He raised his hat and smiled but made no movement to stop and chat to her; he was going round to some friends for music later in the evening and wanted to get home and change his clothes.

"Good night, Miss Jevons!"

Miss Jevons murmured what was presumably "Good night, Mr. Somers," and went on down the road.

I suppose she lives somewhere down here, he thought. Sordid little road by daylight, but it looks romantic by lamplight with those pale old plaster house-fronts and the coloured fruit on that stall, and the stars. Pretty smile that girl has.

He went on his way to the pleasanter part of the town where he lived, and only had occasion to raise his hat once more that evening. This time it was to a face that was familiar to him but to which he could put neither setting nor name: a large pale fat face with a cheerful expression. He was too absorbed in his thoughts to wonder why he should connect this face with a smell of fish.

CHAPTER IX

REENIE was bouncing along on her way home, but first she had to buy some tomatoes. She had a new spring hat, like the rest of the Seagate girls; it was a black straw plate decorated with green flowers and anchored to her head by a green ribbon at the back, and it was very silly and she looked a sight in it, but owing to the softening influences of the Christian religion upon the vile cruelty of human nature, nobody had yet told her so and nobody was likely to.

She was always cheerful except when with her mother, who did not like cheerfulness; but this evening she felt extra cheerful because on her way to work that morning she had stopped a dog-fight. One of Those Beach Dogs, the big black one, had gone for Mrs. Pask's Jack who was out for a walk with Mrs. Pask's companion, Miss Gaye.

Jack was an old Airedale, sulky and stiff, who gave no trouble to any dog so long as he was left alone; but there were fearful stories told by Miss Gaye of what a fighter he had been in his youth; how he had once fixed his teeth in a collie's throat and hung on until the collie was dead and then it had taken two police-men half an hour to make him let go, etc., etc. There was a story about the Beach Dog, too; once he had rescued a child or helped to rescue a child or nearly rescued one or something; anyway, he was the handsomest and most outstanding of the Beach Dogs and the one in whom the people who said that Something Ought to be Done About Those Beach Dogs took the most melancholy interest: his rude yet noble qualities had been squandered, and replaced by a morbid craving for excitement that could only be quenched by a ceaseless throwing of sticks into the sea.

He was not a fighter by nature, but when he accidentally on purpose bumped against Mrs. Pask's Jack while on his joyous way down to the beach and his waiting band, and Jack flew at him, he flew at Jack.

Miss Gaye squeaked and flapped at them both with her gloves and people passing looked at the two hopefully, wondering if there was to be a brief snarling set-out or an epic battle to a finish which should find its place in the dog annals of the town. No one, however, tried to stop them; and Miss Gaye went on flapping and squeaking. They dashed round in a snarling yelping mass of black and brown, and suddenly Jack sank his teeth into the beach dog's neck and stayed still, growling horribly, while the beach dog struggled and shrieked.

"Jack! You *bad* dog! Let go at once!" said Miss Gaye, stamping her foot and dropping her handbag and gloves. A small crowd began to collect and give advice. Someone picked up Miss Gaye's things. One or two elderly men dabbed at the dogs and then skipped back, laughing knowingly.

Suddenly up came Reenie, with the black and green hat flapping in the wind.

"Here, stoppit, will you?" she cried, darting forward and unhesitatingly gripping Jack by his collar and the black dog by his worn leather strap. Her fat hands in her fabric gloves began to pull and strain, and her face got red, and all the elderly men surged forward uttering encouraging cries.

"Oh, Jack! You naughty-bad!" cried Miss Gaye.

Reenie was enjoying herself. She liked the feeling of her strong hands, clenched and unmoving, controlling the struggling dogs. She put her feet a little wider apart and set her teeth and hauled at the wriggling mass as hard as she could, with every bit of her strength.

She began to smile a little, taking no notice at all of the crowd, and suddenly the two dogs flew apart and she stood there with a dog in each hand, shaking them heartily while they stood on their hind legs and yelped and choked.

"I'll teach you!" cried Reenie, shaking away. "Ought to be ashamed of yourselves, you arabs!"

Miss Gaye now approached and tremblingly put Jack on his lead. The beach dog, as soon as Reenie let go of him, bolted away towards the sea.

"Really, how could you!" cried Miss Gaye to Reenie. "Really, I never saw. I was simply. Jack is quite uncontrollable when he's in a fight."

"That's all right," said Reenie. "Good old boy now, aren't you?" And she patted Jack, who growled.

"Really, I was simply," said Miss Gaye. "I did not know *what*."

"That's all right."

"Are your gloves torn?" enquired Miss Gaye, peering. "Yes, see, there, on the thumb. A hole."

"Oh, that's been there for days!" said Reenie quickly and bashfully. "Well, this won't buy the baby a new frock, I must be getting along to work."

"*Good*-morning, then, and *thenk* you. Really, I don't know how you *could*," said Miss Gaye, her tone implying that there was unwomanliness in stopping a dog-fight singlehanded. "I will tell Mrs. Pask. Shall we go home and tell Mother, Jack?"

Jack took no notice, and Miss Gaye, with a pitying nod to Reenie, went on her way. She always brought Jack out for a short walk before breakfast, as it was not convenient to take him later in the morning when there were many errands and duties to be performed.

Miss Gaye knew who Reenie was, for she had paid the bill at Cousin's as long as Reenie had worked there, but she disapproved of Reenie's hat and therefore pretended not to recognize her save by implication when she mentioned Mrs. Pask's name.

Reenie bounced on her way to the fish shop, looking forward to telling Mr. Cousins and the two boys about the fight. Mr. Cousins was a dramatic character with black hair and red cheeks who loved a thrill, and the boys were only too willing to leave off ministering to the haddocks and plaice, and listen. And Reenie herself liked a bit of gossip and fun, though she did not get it at home with her mother.

Well, that really was a bit of excitement, she thought, taking off her dear hat and hanging it against the wall of the fishy little den where she sat all day. Quite a wrestle, that was. I enjoyed that.

"What do you think I've been doing?" she cried to Mr. Cousins, the shop being at that moment empty.

"Gawd knows and he won't split, sorry, Joe," said Mr. Cousins, who was filleting plaice under the running tap. Joe was the ugly fishboy who sang in St. Anne's choir. He looked up and grinned embarrassedly.

"Stopped a dog-fight!" said Reenie.

"What did you do—look at 'em?" Mr. Cousins winked at the grinning boys.

"No—sat on 'em," and Reenie began to tell all about it.

The incident coloured the remainder of her day with a cheerful glow; and when she left the shop in the evening she was whistling as she began to think about her shopping.

She had been impressed by that picture of blacks on the tin of Golden Glow pineapple. She did not fancy (as she had remarked to her mother) eating stuff that had been picked by blacks. All her days were passed in a small dingy kiosk with fish scales on its counter, within sight of fish's discarded interiors, with the strong smell of fish in the air. This situation made her unusually particular about the cleanliness of the food she bought to eat at home; she could not bear the thought of eating food that was not quite clean. Blacks were not—could not—be quite clean. This evening, therefore, she was going to look out for a brand of pineapple that was not picked by blacks.

Or one that was picked by blacks who Belonged to Us. That wouldn't be quite so bad. Blacks who Belonged to Us would of course be cleaner than blacks who belonged to other countries.

If I just look at the labels on the tins I can always see where the things come from, thought Reenie as she went into Glory and Partner's, and that's what I'll do. Never does any harm to know where things come from.

"Got any tomatoes?" she asked the boy behind the counter.

"Best Worthing, one and three," said the boy.

Reenie shook her head.

"Too much."

"Got some tinned. Eightpence." The boy jerked his head towards a shelf on his right.

"Let me see, will you."

He took one down and handed it to her. Following up her recent decision, she studied the label.

It was a large tin with a picture of a tomato on one side. Well, that was only natural. But on the other side was a picture of a mountain with smoke coming out of it above a blue sea and some white houses on a hill. "Naples Brand. Produce of Italy," said the label.

Reenie considered. Italy. Would that Belong to Us, then?

No; the *Daily Mirror* made it plain that Italy was far from Belonging to Us.

Italy . . . why, that was Mussolini's lot!

She shook her head and put the tin down on the counter.

"Haven't you got anything—well, from somewhere that Belongs to Us?" she demanded. "British, I mean."

The boy stared, then shook *his* head.

"No tomatoes only these."

"Well, all right, I'll have half of the Worthing, but somebody's going to die rich and it won't be me."

After she had paid for them and put them into her basket, she strolled down the shop (there were few customers on this fine spring evening) examining the labels on the tins to see where the contents came from.

Peach jam from New Zealand (with a picture of a snowy mountain with steam kind-of bubbling out of the ground) apricots from California (rows of white fruit trees under a pink sky with blue mountains); salmon from Newfoundland (a silver fish jumping over a waterfall and a man in big boots fishing); pineapple from Singapore (a Chinaman in a funny hat bowing with his hands in his sleeves).

Perhaps this pineapple wasn't picked by blacks.

Singapore; did that Belong to Us, then?

She was not going to ask that boy; he had given her too much of a look when she asked him for something British; so she tried hard to remember something about Singapore. Singapore . . . funny name, rather a pretty name, really, when you said it over to yourself. Weren't We building something or making something there? The *Daily Mirror* had put in a piece about it.

Oh well, she couldn't remember. However, she bought the pineapple, and on the way home she tried to remember how many of the other places on the labels were British. Really, I am awful, I can't remember a thing they taught us at school, she decided, as she pushed open the gate of Number Seventy-Eight.

I'll have to buy myself a natlas or a geography book or something and find out which places Belong to Us. Don't fancy eating things from other places.

Mrs. Voles slowly opened the front door as Reenie came up the path with her parcels, and stood watching her with slightly lowered head. It was nearly dusk, and her expression could not be clearly discerned.

"Hullo, Mum," said Reenie, not too cheerfully; Mum had been known to ask if she had come into a fortune when her voice was too cheerful.

"Hullo. Did you get the tomatoes?"

"Yes. Sevenpence ha'penny the half."

"The robbers," observed Mrs. Voles in her deep voice, turning to go down the passage.

But her tone was not really indignant. She earned about one hundred pounds a year from her corset-repairing business, and with Reenie's two pounds fifteen a week the two women were more than comfortable. The house was Mrs. Voles's own, having been left to her by Mr. Voles. She and Reenie could afford tomatoes at one and threepence the pound.

Reenie said nothing to her mother about the idea of buying a natlas. She never really talked to Mum; she knew that Mum did not like her.

CHAPTER X

A FEW days later old Mr. Early was sitting in the drawing-room at Parkfield reading *Antony and Cleopatra*.

The morning sun came into the dusty room and shone on his feet, in Chinese slippers embroidered with bright little flowers, which he had put up on the sofa, and upon his dressing-gown of dirty and gorgeous brocade. His brow was now so large and wrinkled with age that it looked like some superb deformity conceived by Blake below his long white hair. His heavy eyelids, the eyelids of a lover, were lowered and his eyes behind the old-fashioned glasses moved slowly on from line to magnificent line.

No one pities an ageing cedar. It occurred to no one to pity Mr. Early.

Like most people who have had a number of romantic love affairs in beautiful foreign places, he diffused an atmosphere of satisfaction; neither complacent nor self-conscious, but as innocently self-pleasureful as that breathed out by the largest dahlia at the flower show.

The walls of the Rich House were adorned by photographs of plump women dressed in white chiffon with diamond crescents in their hair and one finger on their chin, looking sorrowfully yet proudly into one's eyes; these studies were signed "A toi—toujours. Carmen H." or (more reticently) "Ethel, '09." Bundles of letters written on blue or lilac notepaper in scrabbly foreign writing were stuffed into Mr. Early's desk and the dresser drawer in the kitchen; occasionally, when Louise was waiting for something on the stove to come to the boil, she would amuse herself by reading them and smile and shake her head. One or two of the bundles had a little lace handkerchief or a delicate fan with broken sticks thrust through the old ribbon that bound them.

And Mr. Early's memory, also, was adorned by pictures. Often he took Ted, or whoever happened to be there, for a walk along those ancient galleries; but the loveliest, the most thrilling, of the pictures were kept for his own pleasure. He often dozed over *The Master Builder* or *The Importance of Being Earnest*, and it was

then that the rarest of his memories returned. He would awake
from such slumbers with a faint smile and without answering
those who aroused him.

He had no friends in Seagate. More than twenty years ago,
when he first came to Parkfield to live on the fruits of half a century
of superb acting, local hostesses had been tempted by his pictur-
esqueness and reputation, and had invited him to their houses.
But they soon stopped doing that. He was not precisely a bore;
his appearance was too impressive, his stories too romantic, for
that. But he had no small talk and no other social weapons for
dealing with the pleasant ordinary people among whom he found
himself. He had been at home in the glittering yet solid stage-
world of the years before 1914, when the cleverest and liveliest
people in Late Victorian and Edwardian society had cultivated the
acquaintanceship of actors and actresses because they found them
unconventional, un-"stuffy", and good fun. He came from an
acting family of good lower-middle-class stock; but like most great
artists he belonged to no class, and he had moved naturally in this
marvellous world where elegance, wit, generosity, beauty and
lavishness were the commonplaces. For nearly thirty years he
moved in it; and then the Four Years War came and he began to
lose his memory.

He had acted before he could talk. His father, playing Aaron,
had carried him on to the stage as the Black Child in *Titus Androni-*
cus at the age of two; his mother was expecting another child and
had welcomed the chance of a little rest in her dressing-room while
the lively Archibald went on to play his part. His father had been
surprised to see him hide his face in his hands when the actor who
played the Second Goth shouted at him. When the hands came
away (but that was not until father and son were back in the
wings) a little face with a proud smile was revealed to the astounded
parent. His mother, sitting in the dressing-room with her tired
head sunk in her hands and the winged helmet she wore as
Tamora, Queen of the Goths, on the table before her, roused herself to kiss him and laugh and cry with pleasure.

From that time he began to act seriously. He was a beautiful
and word-perfect Puck; the loveliest Ariel that ever mocked
Caliban; a pathetic Little Willie who made huge provincial
audiences silently weep. For nearly sixty years his life was like a
splendid procession marching along to the sound of trumpets and
drums, with flags flying and people cheering and the air filled with
showers of flower petals.

When his memory began to fail his friends said that he had
overstrained it; he had been learning parts since he was four years

old, and he had always been an uncannily quick study. The failure came at a time when the great tradition of romantic acting was dying and when the young cinema was beginning to threaten the ancient theatre, and managers became more impatient and less sympathetic as his memory grew worse. When Ted was born, and Ted's mother died, Mr. Early decided, of his own will and without persuasion from his wife and his friends, to leave the stage.

His reason for his decision was: "I can still act, but I cannot study." And so he put the splendid procession, the drums and trumpets and cheers and flying flowers, behind him.

He was always pleased with what he did, like a happy child, and so he was pleased by his gesture in retiring while still at the height of his acting powers. He relished the long notices in the press of the whole literate world, recalling his triumphs and saying that of course he would act again from time to time, and show the youngsters how to do it.

But he never did. He began at once to grow old. For sixty years he had been so many people; Hamlet and Mercutio and Ernest, Macbeth and Peer Gynt and Torvald Helmer, John Tanner and Jacques and Mark Antony, that now it seemed as if he had no personality of his own. He sank peacefully into memories and lived there, untroubled by the passion to act. When Ted looked at other old actors of his grandfather's age, who were troubled by the passion to act, he felt awed.

But Mr. Early could still behave only in that large-scale manner that was natural to him. He would orate for twenty minutes, or he would sit silent: not pathetically trying to understand the young people's chatter and join in, oh dear no, but miles away in the Chicago of the 'nineties or the Milan of the 'eighties, and content to be there.

Not surprisingly, he cast a blight over the mild gatherings of Seagate. It was like having an abdicated king to tea. Gradually the social life of the place moved away from him and left him alone, a figure who grew every year more romantic and strange.

In London there were one or two splendid old women, glossed with the graces that were fashionable before 1914, who could have understood him and even now enjoyed his company, but they were busy in their old age with committees and family interests and the social round; if ever they thought of poor beautiful Archie Early, it was to sigh and suppose him dead.

When Ted came into the room a few minutes later, he found his grandfather asleep.

He peered at him; then sighed, and sat down cautiously at the far end of the sofa and picked up the *Daily Sketch*.

He supposed that he ought to tell his grandfather about what had been happening to him lately, but he did not want to. His feelings were so confused; he felt at once so lazy and so energetic; so able to do *anything* and yet so incapable of doing a thing, that the last way in which he wished to spend his time was in explaining to Grandfather, for hours on end, just how he felt. He could talk —God! how he could talk to Louise; but then, she was easy to talk to. She just sat at the other end of the kitchen table, cracking nuts and sometimes smiling to herself, and he could say anything to her, and she did not mind; neither did he.

He had already discovered that he could talk more easily to women than to men.

Soon Mr. Early woke up, with a little jerk of his head, and was not surprised to find Ted sitting there. He smiled at him, but said nothing. Presently Ted asked:

"Did that refugee creature—Stanni-something—ever write to you?"

His grandfather nodded. "Yes, indeed. A most grateful, an almost affectionate, letter."

"Did he get a job?"

"Yes, in London."

"Oh, goody. What's he doing?"

"I cannot recollect," said Mr. Early after a moment's reflection and in an absent tone.

"Grandfather, you are the extent! Haven't you got his letter?"

"I may have. Louise will know where it is, no doubt. I am seventy-eight," retorted Mr. Early; this statement was the nearest to a reproof ever conveyed by his rich unhurried voice. He meant that someone aged seventy-eight who had kept their hair, most of their teeth, and the blueness of their eyes must be excused if their memory occasionally failed them.

Stanni-something had managed to smuggle himself across to Harwich, and had tramped into Seagate on a dim freezing winter afternoon. He had caught sight of Mr. Early standing at the gates of The Rich House, majestically taking the air, and had implored him in broken English for help. Mr. Early looked too large and beautiful to be a typical modern Englishman, but Stanni-something's instincts had not betrayed him: he found himself escorted into the large, grubby, luxurious house and given his native dish (something with raw garlic) which Louise happened to know how to prepare. While he ate, his host read aloud to him from press cuttings about a gala performance in which Archibald Early and Duse had appeared, in the capital city of the refugee's native land, some forty years ago (but in those days both capital and land had had another name).

Stanni-something had stayed with them for a month, eating a good deal of garlic and marvelling at this glimpse of English home life, and Mr. Early had written one of his rare but statelily worded and emphatic letters to a Refugee Aid Society in London, who had managed to find Stanni-something a job.

Mr. Early slowly let his eyes close again. The sunlight was warm on his face.

"Grandfather."

"Eh?" The eyes opened.

"About my getting a job."

"Ah, yes." An intelligent note came into Mr. Early's voice, as if he had been thinking earnestly about the subject every day for weeks; but Ted knew better. After some slightly irritable words that they had exchanged at Christmas about his becoming a professional cricketer, his grandfather had said no more about the matter, and Ted was sure that he had not thought about it at all. He never thought about difficult or unpleasant subjects unless he was forced to, and then he flung himself into the suffering entailed with such gusto that he irritated other people, who were really worried, to bursting point.

"I'm getting extremely bored at home here," Ted went on boorishly; he felt resentful.

Mr. Early nodded.

"I get up in the morning and there's nothing to do but read the paper and then go down to the Fan for coffee or take that lousy little Vinny for a walk."

Here there was a loud sigh. Ted glanced down, and saw that Vinny's basket was just at the side of the sofa; she was gazing up at him with large adoring eyes. Ted made a face at her, and she at once turned her head away. Mr. Early did not even glance down at her; he let Myra leave her there while Myra was on tour, but he avoided looking at Vinny whenever possible.

"Or I go to a movie——"

"No, no," interrupted his grandfather, "what do you want to do that for?"

"One must do something."

There was a silence. Mr. Early continued to look at the young figure sprawling sulkily on the sofa. He was wondering if Louise would succeed in getting fresh shrimps for tea, and wishing that Ted would either go away and leave him to sleep, or go to a dramatic school in Paris and learn to act. Has he The Spark, wondered Mr. Early, not for the first time (he always thought of the power to act as The Spark and so referred to it in conversation).

He sighed, and opened his eyes very wide in order to keep them from shutting altogether.

"Do you not want to be a professional cricketer?" he enquired.

"Hang it, Grandfather, you said you didn't want me to!"

Mr. Early did not reply.

"You said you wanted me to go on the stage!"

Mr. Early nodded.

"You *always* wanted me to go on the stage!"

"Rather, I would say, become an actor. Any nincompoop can 'go on the stage'."

"Become an actor, then."

"Certainly, that is what I wanted for you."

"And now you don't want it any more, is that it?"

"I should be overjoyed," (Mr. Early managed to make the word sound full of joy brimming over) "were you to become an actor, Edward. I wanted your mother to become an actress, as you know. But there was little hope of it after she married your father. He was her cousin, but a poor thing; a poor thing."

He turned his gaze towards a photograph on the yellow marble mantelpiece marked with cigarette burns. A round woman with a placid humorous face sat with her arm about the shoulders of a round young girl with a placid humorous face; Ted's grandmother and mother. "She was exactly like your grandmother," concluded Mr. Early a little severely. "Neither had The Spark." And he actually shook his head at the picture of these two disappointing females.

"Well, I don't want to be a professional any more," said Ted sulkily. "I went up yesterday to see the groundsman at the Club about it. It was a most putting-off experience."

"How was that?" enquired Mr. Early, gathering Ted's meaning from his cold bored tone rather than from the phrase, which was not familiar to him.

"I can't tell you *how*, Grandfather; it simply was. The setting and the man's manner and—and everything just wasn't—congenial to me."

Mr. Early nodded and put on a beautiful expression of sympathy and interest. He said nothing; his silences had once been famous in scenes by Shaw and Pinero, Shakespeare and Ibsen, and although he had forgotten so much he had not forgotten how to create them.

"He was such a stupid lout!" burst out Ted. "I had to think every time I opened my mouth in case I put his back up by using a word of more than one syllable, and I think he found me funny. Blasted cheek."

"When the gallery is puzzled or moved it often laughs in order to relieve its feelings—or so they used to tell me," muttered Mr. Early. "I remember once in Chicago in 1913 when we were playing 'Ghosts' the gallery laughed all through the most moving scenes—even, strange to say, some of those in which I appeared."

"I can't go and work with people who are laughing at me. It would put me off," went on Ted.

Mr. Early nodded, this time emphatically; the beautiful expression had gone from his face and he looked really interested.

"It's too lousy, because I was so keen on being a professional."

"You cannot be very devoted to the idea if the fact that the man laughed at you has made you decide to abandon it."

Ted was silent for a moment; then he said in a low tone:

"It wasn't only that."

Mr. Early waited. He was not conscious of waiting; he was only using a sixth sense, his wonderful sense of timing. He neither understood people well, nor greatly needed human relationships in his life, yet most of his human relationships had been satisfactory.

"I'm sick of the whole business, that's the truth," said Ted at last, getting up and beginning to prowl about the sunny dusty room, in and out of the chairs covered with the worn orange satin brocade. "I suppose I don't know what I want. Anyway, there's no hurry for me to get a job, is there?"

"If you are to learn to be an actor you should begin *now*," said his grandfather, opening his eyes and speaking firmly. "You can go to Hervé's in Paris to-morrow, if you want to."

Ted was standing at the window playing with the cord of the old cream linen blind and staring down into the garden, where the cherry trees were covered with their frilled white bells and the magnolia was in lovely blossom.

"Isn't Hervé's very expensive?" he asked at last.

Mr. Early nodded.

"But I suppose old Hervé might take me for a bit less, as I'm your grandson?"

"Never!" cried Mr. Early, with such feeling that he sat upright and *Antony and Cleopatra* fell on the floor. "He is a monster of avarice and never makes his bills one sou less for old acquaintance's sake!"

Ted stared at him, fascinated. By using the words "sou" and "avarice" and slightly pushing forward his head and subtly altering his face, he had suddenly conveyed all the *Frenchness* of the unknown M. Hervé; it seemed for the moment to be, not Mr. Early who sat there, but another old man; an old man posed against the strange yet familiar Paris of the novels of Balzac. Ted knew that Paris well, for there was a shabby set of the novels downstairs in the drawing-room bookcase.

"Oh well—but could you afford it?" he asked at length, coming out of his French daydream.

"If I could not, I should not suggest that you should go there," retorted Mr. Early. Even nowadays, actors usually keep their salaries a secret; when Mr. Early had been on the stage they had used to be even more reserved about what they earned; and to this day he kept his distaste for talking about money. When money suddenly appeared, glorious and unexpected as a rainbow, it was as gloriously spent; when there was little or none, everybody in the house was expected to grin and bear the famine in dignified reticence.

"Paris is a—it's a lovely place, isn't it?" Ted asked next.

Mr. Early nodded.

"Were you happy there when you were young?"

"Happy and unhappy. I lived. That is all that matters."

And he glanced at a very large painting of a lady in purple draperies with a sort of jewelled fender round her head, which hung over the mantelpiece. She was bending passionately over a flower.

Girls are much prettier now, thank god, and they don't make scenes either, thought Ted. If only going to Paris didn't mean leaving Her, I'd love to go.

"Well, look here, Grandfather, thank you very much for giving me the chance of going," he said, putting his arm round his grandfather's shoulders. "I want to, but I'd like a little while to make up my mind."

"Don't delay too long in beginning your training," said Mr. Early. "You are nearly nineteen. By the time I was your age I had been an actor for seventeen years."

And then they both burst into delighted laughter; it was one of the rare and charming moments when Mr. Early seemed to emerge from his prison of memories and to take a full share in the life about him. In such moments, Ted could *see*, instead of having to imagine, what he had been in his prime, and a feeling that was almost awe mingled with his love. He stooped and kissed the clean ancient brow that smelled faintly of a toilet wash most Englishmen would have called effeminate.

"Dear Grandfather."

"Dear boy," responded Mr. Early at once, lifting his face to the young one. Both had strong and deep affections that they had never been taught to hide, and the love between them was expressed and happy.

Then Ted went out of the room, his fancy already beginning to expand exuberantly in visions of Paris in the spring and delicious girls in black silk stockings.

Mr. Early sighed, and at once settled himself to sleep. As he shut his eyes, slowly banishing the strong spring sunlight and retreating into his memories, he was smiling.

CHAPTER XI

IT was a Saturday afternoon. Ted thought that he would go and bathe; the beach huts would be crowded, but his temperament was half-dreamy and half-active and he did not mind sitting on the sands awaiting his turn and watching the people. As he was taking his holey old blue bathing suit from the Spanish chest in the hall where he had flung it down the last time he came in from a swim, Louise entered at the front door with a full shopping basket.

"Hullo," she said. "Going swimming?"

"Yes. I say, Louise, how much money have we got?"

Louise sat down on the lowest of the dusty stairs and took off her white straw hat and shook back her frizzy black hair.

"That's the first time you've ever asked me that," she said, looking at him interestedly.

"Grandfather's just told me I can go to Paris and learn to be an actor if I want to, and I was wondering if he could afford it."

"We've got about six hundred a year."

"But that's quite a lot!"

"Not nowadays," she said, shaking her head. "Food's expensive, and he likes the very best of everything, you know that."

"Is—is all that Grandfather's?"

"Two hundred of it's mine. The house is his, of course."

Ted was quiet for a minute. They were getting near ground where, until this moment he had never cared to tread. But to-day was different; he felt that he must go on, and ask questions. This day was so lovely, lit by strong sunlight and blown through by a warm steady wind, that nothing mattered so long as he was alive and that wind was pouring over his lifted face.

"Your grandfather gave me that money, you know," said Louise suddenly, stroking her knee under her brilliantly striped rayon dress with her dark hand and looking down as she spoke.

"You know I nursed your granny down in New Orleans, and you too, when you were little. I've told you lots of times."

He nodded. There was silence for a little while. The front door had been left half open, and through it could be seen the magnolia tree, glory of the Deep South of America, shimmering in the green of the wild English garden.

Louise took a banana out of her basket and began to peel it. "Have one?"

He caught the one she threw him.

"It's—it's queer I never asked you about the money before, isn't it, Louise?"

"Oh, you just took everything for granted; children and youngsters always do;" she said indulgently.

"But if I go to Paris won't you and Grandfather be very hard up?"

"We won't have so much, of course, but I guess we'll manage. Do you want to go?'

"Extremely. But I'll have to think it over."

He stood up (he had been sitting on Myra's basket) and put his bathing costume round his neck.

"My husband left me a bit, too," said Louise, looking up at him with her lovely dark eyes; she seemed anxious to explain all about the money now that they had started to talk about it and to send him off to his bathe without one doubt or suspicion left in his mind.

"Oh, do tell me what he was like!" he cried, out of deep curiosity. For nearly nineteen years he had taken Louise for granted, but now that he had found out a little about the money he felt that he must go on and find out something about her.

"Handsome!" she answered at once. "Handsomest man I've ever seen. I like them handsome."

"What happened to him?" Her cheerful tone and the fact that her mouth was full of banana encouraged him to ask the question, in spite of the plain inference that Mr. Caller might be no more.

"Went off."

"Oh, poor Louise! I'm so dreadfully sorry."

"Oh, he didn't go off with another woman!" she explained, beginning to laugh. "He was crazy about playing the trumpet in a band and he just ran off with the band. I never heard any more of him, but presently he sent me five thousand dollars. Five *thousand* dollars! Think of that. He must have made a lot of money out of his trumpet playing, mustn't he? So I gave it to your grandfather to take care of and it's there still, or most of it."

"Tell me about New Orleans," he said, sitting down once more on the basket.

"You always did like to hear about New Orleans when you were little. Oh well, it's a kind of a sleepy old place, you know, and there's a lot of rich folks down there and they give a lot of parties. The girls are fond of sheer white dresses and there's a whole heap of flowers everywhere. It's a lazy kind of a place, New Orleans. But I've told you a hundred times."

She got up, and balanced her hat on her head.

"Well, I must get along. Will you be in to tea?"

"No, I'll get an ice on the beach or something."

"All right. Have a good time."

She went away towards the kitchen, whistling, and Ted went out through the garden with his bathing suit round his neck.

He was suddenly happy. There was an innocent reason for that present of money which his grandfather had made to Louise! that present which had so often made him feel miserable and ashamed. It had been horrible to suspect that they had once been lovers and were now growing old together, living with him and with their memories in the squalid luxurious house.

His imagination had been fed from childhood on the great works of poetry and history, and he was therefore familiar with passions and situations which conventionally brought-up children —even nowadays—never encounter except in stealthy conversations and reading. He knew, as if he had seen it reflected in a gorgeous mirror, what the world is. He had not walked there, but he knew what it is like. And as he grew older he had not been able to help the suspicion about Louise and his grandfather creeping into his heart; that heart which still, like the heart of a child, longed for at least *one* situation, *one* dearly-loved group of persons, *to be what it seemed*. Now Louise, using a delicacy which was not natural to her but which her affection for him had momentarily bestowed on her, had given him the comfort he wanted.

And he was happy! The blue and crimson framework of the Giant Thrill Ride stood out against the fresh blue sky and looked bold and beautiful and so did the green waves rushing in under their spreading head-dresses of foam. The thought of Marjorie struck across his happiness but did not spoil it. To-day even his pain was dear to him; he held it close and would not have been without it for the world.

4

For weeks he had been wretched about her, but had done nothing sensible about his misery; he had neither avoided her nor tried to win some of her time and interest. He had only haunted the theatre night after night, sitting in the gallery in a seat bought with ninepence borrowed from Louise, watching Marjorie in a dream of unhappiness and longing. Apart from her beauty and her air of not being attainable, of being cool and unhurt by anything, there was another fact about her that made him suffer. He had tried to deny this fact to himself but it was useless: he had to face it, and it made him almost more unhappy than did her beauty.

He sighed quiveringly; one of those long sighs that come only in early youth and that seem actually to relieve the pain from which they arise; and glanced across the road in the slight hope that she might be coming out of her house. His heart jumped violently, for there she was!

He blundered across the road, calling "I say, hullo!" and she turned round, not looking particularly pleased, and answered:

"Oh, hullo."

"I say, where are you off to?"

"The theatre."

"Have you got a rehearsal?"

"No, and I'm not playing this week either, but there's something I want to run through with Lenny."

"Who's Lenny? I say, can I walk down with you?"

"Good heavens, yes, what's the matter with you? Only we must hurry."

"All right."

At once she started to walk quickly down the road with her black linen dress flying about her knees and her hair blowing back from her serious face, and Ted had to pound along beside her with the bathing dress flapping round his neck. He could not keep his eyes off her, and presently she said without looking at him:

"Have I a smut on my nose or something?"

"Good heavens, no—you look—good heavens, no, why?"

"You keep on staring so."

"Sorry," he muttered; but immediately his pride was aroused and he began to feel angry. She thought so little of him, did she, that it never even occurred to her that he might be in love with her! I'm less than the dust, I suppose, like that gutless halfwit in the Indian Love Lyrics.

So he announced, casually yet boastfully:

"I'm going to Paris soon."

"To Paris? *You?*" exclaimed Marjorie, turning right round and staring at him in amazement. "Whatever for?"

"To learn to act."

"To *act*? *You* are? You're going on the stage?"

"Such is my intention," said Ted haughtily.

He was getting angrier every minute, and she was simply rushing along with her skirts flying out like a parachute; it made him breathless to keep up with her.

"Have you any objection?" he added, awfully; and at that moment the bathing dress fell off his neck and by the time he had picked it up she was ten feet ahead of him.

"Why shouldn't I?" he demanded, running up to her.

"Oh, no reason at all, of course; anyone can go on the stage nowadays if they think they can act—worse luck."

"I don't 'think I can act'. I'm going to learn."

"But why on earth should you want to go on the stage?" Her expression was disturbed and resentful. "It's all frightfully sudden, isn't it? I thought you were all set to be a professional cricketer."

"So I was, but now I don't want to."

"I see. Well, good luck and all that."

"Thanks."

"It's a lousy life. I suppose you know that."

He did not answer.

"And I still don't see why you should *want*——"

"My dear Marjorie," interrupted Ted, with his heart beating fast and his mouth feeling dry and a tender emotion coming over him as he said "dear", though he spoke so steadily and cuttingly, "I'm the grandson of one of the greatest actors of the past hundred years. Doesn't it occur to you that there may be a chance— just a faint chance—that I may have inherited his genius?"

She did not answer. Half a minute passed, and still she did not answer. Appalled, he peered into her expressionless face, but was kept by some instinct (probably inherited from his grandfather) from apologizing. At last she said:

"Well there is a chance, of course. But surely any talent would have shown itself before now."

"Not necessarily."

"I just can't—*imagine* you in any kind of part, that's all!" she cried, suddenly bursting into laughter and turning to him a face frank and childish with amusement. "You're so . . . utterly *hopeless*, Ted!"

He stopped dead. He had gone white, and as he faced her he slowly lifted his head in a gesture that made him seem even taller than he was, and threatening. He did not move, but he said slowly:

"And so are you. You're a bad actress."

Marjorie had been walking rapidly on, but now she turned, and also stopped. Several people walking on the other side of the road glanced across at them interestedly.

"How dare you!" she said in a low controlled tone. "You clumsy conceited little beast, how dare you!"

"I've been trying to pretend to myself that it wasn't true, but it is. You can't act. I've seen Grandfather, and I know what acting is. Besides, I can *feel* here"—he thumped the bathing dress—"what it is. And you haven't got it."

"I'll never speak to you again!"

He nodded. "I thought you wouldn't."

"I suppose that's why you sit in the gallery every night rubber-necking at me, because I can't act."

"That's because I love you. I can't help that. But I only love you because you're so beautiful, not because you can act."

"Oh shut up," she said, turning away. The people on the other side of the road could hear every word and their eyes were popping; this was better than the pictures.

"I've been in hell," announced Ted loudly, staring at her yearningly. "I hope you'll feel like that some day about some-body——"

"Thanks," she said, over her shoulder.

"——but you won't. You haven't the power *here*," and again he thumped the bathing dress. "That's why you CAN'T ACT," he ended, raising his voice to a shout.

But she took no more notice; she only hurried on faster and faster with her round black skirt flying and her pale golden hair blowing, and he stood watching her until she turned a corner and disappeared from his sight.

Then he sighed quiveringly once more, and gazed about him. The people on the other side of the road had gone grinning on their way and the place was deserted. The wind blew sighingly in the long green hedges of witches' hair. The sound of the sea came loudly, because the sky was filling with massive clouds, tinged at their rims with purple, bringers of rain. Ted's heart was beating heavily and he could still hear, ringing in his ears like witches' voices, the words he had said to her. I'm glad I said them, he thought; it serves her right for being a bad actress and making me love her. But his state was no better. He loved her still.

I hate this hole, he thought, putting his hands in his pockets and beginning to slouch along towards the sea. I'll tell Grandfather I'd like to go to Paris at once.

"Ted!"

He turned, and saw Pauline coming smiling towards him, in white shorts and a crimson coat and carrying a racquet.

"Where are you off to? Swimming?" she went on. "I'm going down to the Club."

"Oh, are you?" he said glumly, and she stared.

"What's up?"

"Nothing. I may as well walk down with you, though god knows I've had enough walking down with people for one afternoon."

"Why? Have you been fighting with someone?"

"Never mind. You look deplorable in those things; I do wish you wouldn't wear them."

"Don't you like them? I think they're rather good, myself," she said, glancing down at her shorts; she spoke in an unusually gentle tone because she saw that the poor old thing was unhappy and she felt sorry for him, but she also felt that he must not be permitted to criticize her appearance without reproof, and she therefore went on:

"While we *are* on the subject, why do you wear that ghastly old bathing dress? Is that the one you've had about ten years?"

"What's the matter with it?" He glanced down at the garment lying on his chest.

"My dear Ted, *no one* wears bathing suits nowadays."

"What do they wear, then?"

"Trunks."

"Who said so? The Melancholy Double-Crossing Waterfly, alias Brian Kingsley?"

"Yes, he wears them."

"Sometimes he does," said Ted, in a peculiar tone.

Pauline stared.

"What on earth do you mean?"

"Just what I say. You said the Melancholy Double-Crossing Waterfly wears trunks and I said 'sometimes he does.' Well, he does wear them sometimes. When he's bathing."

"Yes, but why did you say it in such a peculiar way. What are you driving at?"

"Nothing. I was speaking from the weed-embowered crannies of a shattered heart." He took her arm in a brotherly way and went on: "Anyway, I'll soon be out of it all. I'm going to Paris to learn to act."

"Ted! Are you really? How marvellous!" Pauline's face was

full of the warmest interest and pleasure. "Do tell me all about it . . . I am so glad!"

"Are you? Well, you really are a darling girl, underneath all that tripe about having clean limbs and playing the game," and he gave her arm an affectionate squeeze.

"Do go on about it."

"Oh well, I'm going to Hervé's, the most famous school there, you know. Grandfather knows the old bloodsucker, apparently. That's all there is to tell, really. I suddenly thought I'd like to go when Grandfather said I could and I'm more than weary of Seagate . . . just now. Pauline," he went on, in another tone, dreamy and earnest, and bent his tall height over her, "do you know that exquisite poem—no, I don't suppose you do, you only know awful little rhymes on postcards about passing through this world but once and helping lame dogs over stiles—it's the bit about Helen in Marlowe's *Faustus*:

> O thou art fairer than the evening air
> Clad in the beauty of a thousand stars.

Isn't that lovely?"

She nodded, but did not answer. For two things had happened to her: Ted's bathing dress had flapped against her cheek, with a whiff of salt water and musty wool that brought back memories of bathes together when he and she were still at school; and for the first time in her life she had listened to his voice. Why, it's beautiful, she thought, startled; it's so deep and rich.

"Isn't it lovely?" he insisted, peering into her face.

"Marvellous," she replied in a quick, embarrassed voice. She had always disliked it when people spouted poetry at school; not because the poetry meant nothing to her but because it meant too much, and aroused those wild, sad, strange feelings that she told herself she hated.

"It makes me think of—someone I know," he said, sighing.

Pauline thought it best, despite her sympathy for him, not to encourage this mood; it also annoyed her a little to hear someone sighing and groaning over Marjorie. Pauline had shared a bedroom with Marjorie until they were both fifteen and she knew exactly what Marjorie was. Her knowledge did not prevent her from being fond of old Marjie, but it did make her impatient when people sighed and groaned over old Marjie. Why doesn't anyone sigh and groan over me? thought Pauline. I'm really much nicer than she is. But of course no one ever does sigh and groan over the nice ones.

She said cheerfully:

"Ted, do you know you've got an awfully nice voice?"

"Yes, of course I do, I'm not deaf."

"It ought to be very useful to you on the stage."

"Everybody'll say it's ham."

"They always say that when you can hear what an actor says. The only bits I enjoy in Marjorie's shows are the bit that old character-man does. You can hear every word he says and he always looks different in every part he plays. But Marjorie and the rest all say he's ham."

"Fools. They're suffering from Cowarditis—throw your lines away and put all your technique into answering the telephone. Wait until I get going; I'll soon change all that."

They were now opposite Just's Library, and Pauline stopped, holding up a novel called *Young Woman at Large*.

"I must just change this for Mother."

He nodded and said that he would wait for her.

All the assistants in Just's looked unusually serious, and Miss Gordon at the library desk told Pauline that old Mr. Just was gravely ill with pneumonia. Pauline expressed sympathy and asked how he had come to be ill; her mother knew him slightly and often remarked upon his perfect health for all his eighty years.

He had caught a chill one day last week, said Miss Gordon; stood in a draught near an open door or window, perhaps. You had to be so careful with old people.

They must all be really fond of the old weasel, thought Pauline as she went out with her mother's book. That Rather Pretty Fair Girl looks quite pale and worried. As she was going out of the library she stopped to hold the door open for Mrs. Pask, who was coming slowly in attended by Miss Gaye (wearing a po of beige straw to greet the brighter weather) and Jack, looking sourly about him.

"Thank you, my dear," said Mrs. Pask. She was so small that she passed right under Pauline's arm, and as she did so she glanced at the girl and smiled.

"Making a triumphal archway for you," said Pauline, rather louder than usual in case Mrs. Pask were deaf.

"A very pretty archway; such a lovely colour," said Mrs. Pask glancing up at her crimson sleeve. "Are you going to play tennis? You are Pauline Williams, I think, aren't you?"

"Yes." Pauline smiled prettily and thought, oh heavens, I hope she won't keep me talking.

"You mustn't mind my asking and I won't keep you for I'm

sure you want to be off to your tennis, but I think my late husband knew your father slightly. Lionel Pask—perhaps you have heard your father speak of him?" went on Mrs. Pask nervously.

"Oh yes, often," said Pauline, trying to remember. Pask? Pask? Oh yes—"one of Seagate's rich men."

"It would be very nice if you could come in one afternoon when you have nothing to do and—and have tea with me," continued Mrs. Pask, standing at the door with the strong rays of May sunlight pouring down on her beaver coat and hat with purple quills and her small pale face. "That is, I expect you are very busy . . .?"

Pauline was conscious that Miss Gaye was standing in the background, silent but disapproving, staring at her shorts. She also felt (why, she did not know) that Mrs. Pask was making an effort in issuing this invitation; a great effort, for which she would pay later. She felt sorry for the old lady, and therefore said warmly with her friendliest smile:

"Thanks most awfully, I'd love to. It's very kind of you. May I phone you some time?"

"This is my cousin, Miss Gaye. You have heard me speak of Miss Williams, haven't you, Jean?"

"How do you do?" Miss Gaye showed her teeth and concealed them again.

"Good-bye, we mustn't keep you." Mrs. Pask held out a very small hand in a doeskin glove. "I will write to you and suggest a day, shall I?"

"Do, that'll be marvellous." Pauline was aware that her tone was more enthusiastic than the occasion demanded but she felt that she had made a blunder in suggesting that she should telephone, and she wished to cover it. She also wished to impress upon Miss Gaye, who plainly did not want her to come to tea, that she *would* go to tea; she would go to tea through storms and in the teeth of European crises just as soon as Mrs. Pask chose to ask her, because she was sorry for the old lady and thought Miss Gaye looked a witch.

The three ladies smiled at one another and Pauline went out to join Ted.

"Did you notice?" whispered Miss Gaye hissingly as she and Mrs. Pask moved down the shop. "She was wearing shorts!"

"Very practical," retorted Mrs. Pask, but she retorted it in an exhausted voice. It had required courage to invite Pauline Williams to tea under the nose of Jean. Everyday Jean grew more difficult about everything; more resentful of the few visitors who came to the house, more eager to report failures on the part of the refrigerator, the electric iron, the wireless and the Hoover, and more anxious to keep entirely to herself and Mrs. Pask the benefits bestowed by those blessings of civilization.

"I don't expect she will come. Girls are very selfish," pursued Miss Gaye.

Mrs. Pask was silent.

"And if she does come she will talk the whole time and tire you out. You know you are Not Very Strong and nothing is more tiring——"

Mrs. Pask stopped to pat a dog which was staring alarmedly at Jack.

"——than people talking all the time. But I don't expect for a moment she will come," concluded Miss Gaye, giving a haul at Jack's lead which he ignored.

"Well, I hope she will," replied Mrs. Pask gently. Really, she did wish that dear Lionel were alive to deal with Jean. He had always been so good at managing her; he had teased her and kept her in a good temper.

But dear Lionel was not alive; he had been in Heaven for nearly twenty years, and there was no one now who could deal with Jean at all.

CHAPTER XII

IN his interesting and alarming book, *The Coming Struggle for Power*, Mr. John St. Loe Strachey tells us how Man has gradually bartered his liberty in exchange for his living. First he sold the tools he worked with to his boss; then he sold his time; and now (Mr. Strachey does not tell us this but it is a fact) he has begun to sell his most precious possession—his personality. That is what the high-powered salesmen, the pep-talkers and the power-and-glamour boys are doing: selling their personalities for a living. Some people suffer painfully in doing so, but most of them get used to it, and of course some of them enjoy it.

The next morning Brian Kingsley was sitting waiting for his breakfast in his small private room at the Bristol, opposite the reception desk, whence he could keep an eye on prospective visitors and pop out with a suave yet authoritative smile if there were any signs of trouble. The room overlooked a small retired lawn at the side of the hotel, shut in by a fine beech hedge and unfrequented save by thrushes and starlings; through the hedge, not yet covered with its full summer foliage, came the sparkle and dance of the sea.

Brian was smelling the delicious odour of coffee and bacon and watching old Dunfee, the waiter who attended upon himself and his father, shuffling towards him with the breakfast.

Dunfee was seventy, and neither in appearance or technique was he smart. His suit was not stained with tomato sauce and egg and soup, but only because he was everlastingly removing egg and tomato and soup stains with Cleano and Removo and Spottitoff. In the winter he used the two former, and in the summer when the hotel garage was full of cars he used petrol, begging a few drops from the garage hand. As a result of his exertions his suit throughout the warmest months of the year was so soaked in petrol that he was almost afraid to venture into the full sunlight, and he was fond of a nice sunny day, Dunfee was.

Brian never openly reproved him for the stains on his suit, but of course he had to let the poor old chap know that Mr. Brian noticed things of that sort, and he did it by staring hard at the latest drop of egg or tomato when Dunfee brought in his meals, and then raising his eyebrows. And the old chap was still quick on the uptake; Brian had to hand it to him for that. He always shuffled away quicker than usual on these occasions, and when he reappeared there was only a dark ring where the egg stain had been.

The harmony of their relations was not disturbed by these incidents, for Brian was sure that Dunfee was devoted to him because Dunfee used to take him for walks along the sands when he was a little boy; and as nobody asked Dunfee what he thought about it, the matter rested there to the general satisfaction.

This morning there were no marks on Dunfee's suit. He came up to the table with Brian's eggs and bacon and said:

"Good morning, Mr. Brian," momentarily creasing up his drooping, pale old face in response to the young man's absent-minded smile.

"Morning, Dunfee." Brian took the cover off his breakfast and poured out his coffee.

"Mr. Kingsley got his breakfast?" he went on.

"Yes, Mr. Brian. About half an hour ago. He's reading the paper." Dunfee paused at the door, towards which he was quickly shuffling. He was holding something behind his back and he looked towards Brian with a resigned, sullen expression.

"Good. Talking of papers, where's your *Daily Mirror*?" demanded Brian pleasantly.

Dunfee did not seem to have heard, for all he said was:

"Old Mr. Just's dead, Mr. Brian."

"Oh? I'm sorry to hear that."

"Yes. Last night, it was. Pewmonia."

"He'd been ill for some time, hadn't he?"

"Oh no, Mr. Brian." Dunfee sounded shocked. "Very healthy Mr. Just has always been. Wonderful, everybody said, for his time of life."

"Oh. Well, we've all got to go some time, I suppose. Let me have the *Mirror*, will you."

Dunfee silently let him have it, and turned away.

Disagreeable reflections were aroused in his mind by Brian's last remark, which Brian would not have made had he been seventy and Dunfee twenty-nine. Never mind, there's many a young one goes before the old ones, nowadays, with all this speed mania, thought Dunfee as he shuffled to the door.

"Who gets the business?" asked Brian, without looking up.

"Young Mr. Just, I expect, Mr. Brian. The one as lives in London. Changes, that'll mean. Some of them young ladies will be out of work, I expect."

Brian did not reply, for he was absorbed in the day's misadventure of Jane (who was as usual stuck up a tree in camiknickers) and Dunfee went out of the room and shut the door.

Drat, thought Dunfee, gowing slowly down the corridor.

Mr. Brian had got the *Daily Mirror* again.

Every morning, ever since Mr. Brian had left the Commercial College at Chesterbourne and taken over the management of the hotel, he had borrowed Dunfee's *Daily Mirror* to read at breakfast: Dunfee's *own Daily Mirror, paid* for out of his wages, *ordered* by him at Leach's in Lavender Road, *delivered* to him at the hotel with his *name* on it . . . and yet he could never get a really good read at it. Never read it all through from cover to cover, from the bathing girls on the front page to the bad business in Japan on the back. After the staff breakfast there was just half an hour when he could have read it all through—if only Mr. Brian hadn't always got it. In the afternoon there was no time because of Veranda Teas in the summer and Lounge Teas in the winter. If he did take it out of his pocket for five minutes while he was waiting for more hot water to come up, there was bound to be someone wanting another portion of cress or jam, and then he put it down in a hurry and one of Them Others picked it up and had a read at it and when he found it again the picture page was always missing. He had tried keeping it downstairs in his drawer, but it was no use; Mr. Brian always asked for it and Dunfee did not dare make excuses, much less refuse to hand it over.

It was a dratted shame, that was what it was.

He went on slowly down the corridor, which was covered by a good though worn crimson drugget and had a heavy cream paper, stamped with a raised design of water-lilies, on its walls. The pictures, like those in the lounge, were all Victorian favourites— "The First Quarrel," "Wedded"; indeed, all the decoration of the Hotel Bristol had an 1880 solidity that Brian detested and that he was replacing, as quickly as he could in face of some opposition from older guests who had been frequenting the place for thirty years and more, by fumed oak and reproductions of galleons in full sail.

If only the old chap wasn't so devoted to the hotel, and so fond of me, I'd get him into the alms houses at Nunby, thought Brian, while his eye devoured an article called "I Changed My Mind About Women." But I really believe it would kill him to leave us. He's been here—what is it—forty years? Something incredible. If he retired, he'd be dead in a week.

'Ole, thought Dunfee, still shuffling down the corridor and looking gloomily at the graceful staircase, now illuminated by the early morning sunlight, that led through a series of arches to the upper part of the building. 'Ow long is it I've been 'ere? Forty years? Forty years too long if you ask me. If only I could get into one of them little places at Nunby! Quiet. Peaceful. Bit of garden. Keep a rabbit if you want to (Artie does). Read the *Mirror* right through from cover to cover.

He thought irritably about Mr. Brian, sitting in the sun reading *his*, Dunfee's, paper. Always grinning at you and making faces at you about a bit of egg on your front. Never did like 'im. Never could stick 'im, when he was a nipper and the master used to make me take 'im on the sands. Used to pull off the crabs' legs, pore little things. What 'ad they done? Never could see what all the ladies see in 'im neither. That Miss Williams last summer—my great-niece Connie said she was upset for months after 'e'd done with 'er. Months. Got quite snappy, Connie said, and usually you couldn't wish for a nicer young lady. All 'is fault. Drat 'im. Drat this 'ole.

Nunby! That 'ud be the ticket.

The sound of voices and a woman's laughter outside in the corridor made Brian look up in surprise, and the next instant the door opened and round it, under a turban of leopardskin and velvet that matched the coat hanging from her shoulders, came the smiling face of Mrs. Cunningham.

"Good heavens, you're an early visitor," he said getting up. "Is anything the matter?"

"Only I'm gasping for a drink. I'm going up to town for some shopping and I thought I'd pop in and say good morning. Aren't you glad to see me?" And she pouted.

"You know I am. What'll you have? Do sit down." He put his hand on her arm and was guiding her to a chair and ringing the bell for Dunfee, as he spoke.

"A brandy. Don't you think it's naughty of me at this hour in the morning?"

"I'll be naughty too. Two brandies," he commanded of Dunfee, who had arrived, and was standing at the door with a resigned face.

"Is this your den where you work? Do let me wander round and peep," she said, getting up with difficulty from the arm-chair because she was so fat, and beginning to stroll round the room. She commented as she went, picking up account books and asking him about photographs. She had big soft eyes of the colour known as Bedroom Brown (as opposed to the brown that is sparkling and cool) and her large lovely face seemed to have no more bones than a petal. Furs and lace and satin and jewels had been piled upon her by herself because that was the only way she knew of looking attractive and she smelled of Nuit Noël.

Dunfee brought the drinks, and she gave him a look of interest as he shuffled away. She felt cheerful, for it was a grand morning and here was the first drink of the day. Perhaps everything was going to be divine to-day instead of lousy.

"Is that the family retainer?" she asked.

"Nearest thing to one we've got. Poor old devil, he's nearly past the work here but I haven't the heart to sack him. He's devoted to the place and he's known me since I was a kid and it would about kill him to leave."

"She nodded. "I know. You get fond of places. It's a scream, really, but I adore that old barrack of mine up on the West Cliff, I wouldn't leave it for anything you could give me."

"Wouldn't you, Eve?" he said, sitting on the arm of her chair and bending over her.

"No, I wouldn't," she laughed up at him. "That's the first time you've ever called me Eve. Do you know what it's short for?"

"Evelyn?"

She shook her head.

"Evadne." She finished her drink and put the glass down. "Weird, isn't it, but Dad and Mother wanted something distinctive for me. Distinctive!" She put her hand on her bosom, rolled up her eyes, and coughed. "I was an 'only', and they were fond of me—though you mightn't think it."

She struggled up out of the chair again and pulled her coat round her shoulders.

"Well, I must fly. Cheerio, and thanks for the little drinkie."

He went to the entrance with her and saw her out, standing smiling at the top of the steps while she went down to her handsome car and chauffeur. Miss Symonds who kept the accounts and helped at the reception desk, one or two waiters, the pageboy Dickson and a passing chambermaid were not much interested in the spectacle, being too used to others like it.

However, someone was interested. After Brian had returned to his room to finish his coffee and the *Daily Mirror*, a prolonged and angry ringing of a bell summoned Dunfee from his cleaning of the silver. Upstairs he hurried, along the corridor, through the hall where stood the well-kept palms, and up under the arches leading to the upper part of the building. Here, at the end of another long corridor carpeted in the usual red drugget and papered with the same water-lily design, he stopped outside a white door marked "Private," and knocked.

"Come in, you fool!" shouted Mr. Kingsley.

Dunfee opened the door, and was advancing into the room when his master went on with the same furious impatience:

"Wasn't that that woman? What was she doing here at this hour in the morning? Did she see Mr. Brian?"

"Oh yes, sir, I think that was what she come for."

Dunfee was standing with his hand on the open door, and over his shoulder could be seen part of a large pleasant room with white net curtains at the long windows, veiling a view of the splendid sea.

"Good! Good!" said Mr. Kingsley eagerly. "That's what I wanted to hear! More she comes here the better. Come in, can't you? Come in. These damned pillows are all over the place."

There was a sound as if the invalid were threshing about.

"Look at the weather. There's a morning for you! Wind perfect, not too much sea. God, what wouldn't I give to be out in a boat! Come in and fix these things for me, and then I want you to go round to Just's and get me my *Yachtsman*, the fools haven't sent it."

"Yes, Mr. Kingsley."

Dunfee went into the room and shut the door.

A week after the funeral, "young" Mr. Just came down from London to take over the business.

He was a solemn person of forty-odd with black hair and glasses with horn rims; he was not wealthy and had several children in their late teens whom he was most anxious to start in life. After he had appointed Mr. Forbes as manager and assured him that no changes would be made in the routine of the business, he proceeded to make just one small change: that Rather Pretty Fair Girl, what was her name, Jevons, must go. There did not seem to be much for her to do and she was probably living at home——

"Miss Jevons is an orphan," interrupted Mr. Forbes, trying not to look troubled, "and entirely dependent upon what she earns, Mr. Just."

"Oh well, she would get something else quite easily; it was always easy to get a job in a small town, it wasn't like London where the competition was fierce." And he, Mr. Just, would give her excellent references.

Mr. Forbes wanted to say that it did not matter how excellent the references were if there were no jobs to take them to; he wanted to say that he knew for a fact that there were no vacancies with Brown's, The Household Word; that it would disturb and worry him very much to see any young girl whom he liked and respected employed by A. P. Beard's; and that Miss Jevons was the last type of girl to find her feet and make her way in a place like Woolworth's or Marks and Spencer's.

But he said none of these things, because he was afraid. He had just been made manager with a slight rise in his salary that meant a great deal to him, and he was afraid Mr. Just might turn nasty and snatch these blessings away. So he protested no more; and that evening Mr. Just wrote (it happened to be a Friday) cheerfully to his eldest daughter and told her that she was going into Grandfather's business; and Mavis, watched by the sympathetic eyes of the entire staff, began to walk slowly homeward with her salary packet containing, as well as her precious thirty-five shillings, a week's notice.

She was terrified. She had never thought about the future because she had been so dreamily happy living in her little room and admiring Mr. Somers and thanking God for her blessings in St. Anne's Church. Her room, and Mr. Somers, and the church, had been like three big flowers; and nice books, walks on Sunday, her new hat in the spring and the autumn, an occasional tuppenny ice and other small pleasures, had been like little flowers set all round them; the whole making up the nosegay that was her life. Now the nosegay was scattered. She had no one to go to for advice, no kind older person to comfort her or lend her a little money until times were better. She was alone in the world, walking home through the bright streets of a little seaside town on an early summer evening, with the fresh blue sky getting darker and the red, green and yellow lights already glowing richly along the Marine Parade and round the cupola of the bandstand, while the lovely dark blue sea, already a little subdued by the laziness of summer, was rolling indolently forward among the scattered rocks, over the deserted sands. Young men and girls were hurrying to change into their best clothes and then come out again to dance or go to the pictures, and the air was charged with a delightful sensation of excitement and pleasure.

But Mavis was alone. And for the first time she knew that she was alone. Nothing stood between her and those dreadful things that happened to girls in the papers but her own power to work and five pounds five shillings in the Post Office. And she still owed twelve pounds on her furniture!

Slowly, gently, a dark cloud of unhappiness and worry seemed to settle on her heart and to stay there, making the brilliant streets seem strange and shutting her away from other people. She had always thought she was a lucky girl, and the anonymous letters assured her that she was. But she had been luckier than she knew, for she had preserved until her twenty-second year the confidence in life of a child. She had taken it for granted that if she were good, and worked hard, and said her prayers, she would be safe.

But no one is safe, and now she had suddenly found this out.

Reenie, also on her way home, was bouncing into the large stationers in the High Street to buy herself a natlas.

The young gentleman in charge of the atlases was none other than that awful Wally Wade whom the reader may possibly remember as an admirer of Pauline's. Of course he was not awful at all, but as he had a diffident manner towards pretty girls and did not smoke, he was despised by most females except his sister, who was a cripple, and with whom he shared a bungalow out at Happy Sands and who jealously loved him.

"Er—good evening," said Reenie.

"Good evening, madam. Can I help you?" enquired Wally pleasantly, pushing aside some price tickets he was marking and looking at Reenie over his horn-rims.

"Well, I want a natlas," she said rather defiantly.

"Certainly. What kind of an atlas, madam?"

"Well, a natlas showing all the bits that belong to Us, you know," said Reenie, looking at him very straight in case he was laughing because she wanted a natlas, and he could see she must have left school years ago.

Wally, himself a keen British Commonwealth man, was immediately interested. He was too experienced a salesman to look anything but cheerfully helpful, but there was a note of suppressed enthusiasm in his voice as he replied:

"Oh yes, madam." (He did some lightning guesswork on Reenie's social status and income.) "We have a very good one here—quite up to date, with all the mandated territories——" he checked himself, not wishing to scare off a possible convert to the New Imperialism by alarming her with long words—"quite the latest thing," he ended, as if the map were a hat.

For what he spread out on the counter before her curious eyes was not an atlas but a big comely map, slung on wooden rolls and fair with all the fine rulings, subdued yet gay colours, little figures, mysterious lines and shaded blues that make a map immediately attractive. And right across the top, in large bold print, ran the words:

"THE BRITISH EMPIRE"

Reenie stared at it. She could make but little of it and was too proud to ask Percy (as she had instantly christened poor Wally) for help. But soon she saw a little key at one side, and from this she gathered that all the parts of the map which were coloured red were Ours. (There was a lot of red.) Her large gooseberry eyes slowly followed the colour across the world; from little England up towards the top, down past Gibraltar and Malta to Africa—her gaze lingered on Africa—wasn't it big!—and then on to India, and Mandalay and Singapore (she looked hard at Singapore to see if she could find out what We were building down there, for she still could not remember) on to Sarawak and New Guinea and to many little crimson islands floating in the pale blue sea; and still on; on to Australia and New Zealand and Tasmania and more islands with peculiar names—Antipo-something, Auckland Islands—and then, taking a big jump right up to Canada (more islands; there seemed to be a lot of islands about) and so at last down to a bit of red all by itself at the tip of a big piece of land—more islands—The Falklands—oh, and one last little tiddy bit almost off the edge of the map with a funny name—The Sandwich Islands.

The shop was full of customers, for it was just on closing time and there was plenty of noise and bustle going on, but Reenie did not notice any of it while she was staring at the map. It had really taken her fancy and she could not take her eyes off of it. Imagine Us having all those places. She hadn't any idea We had so many.

"Is that the kind of thing you had in mind, madam?" asked Wally, who had been watching her interested face with sympathetic interest on his own.

"It's a bit large, isn't it? Where'd I keep it?" said Reenie, who always worked when she was shopping on the principle of running down anything she was offered. "How much is it?"

"This one is——" he turned the map over and glanced at the, ticket on the back—"seven and sixpence, madam."

Reenie shook her head. "Too much. Haven't you got a smaller one—in a book, like?"

Wally brought out a small school atlas and found the British Empire in it for her. The colours were not so pretty as those on the big map but she could see that the map was the same, and again she studied it, her eyes making the journey they had made before.

"That'll do," she said at last, opening her bag.

"How much is it?"

"Two shillings and sixpence, please, madam."

While he was wrapping it up she felt she must say something to pass off the awkwardness she felt in buying an atlas at her age, so she remarked casually: "Fancy all those places belonging to a little tiny island like Us and doing what our king tells them! Quite wonderful, isn't it?"

This was too much for the New Imperialist.

"But, madam," said Wally earnestly, laying down the parcel he was tying on the counter and leaning over it towards her, "they don't. That's quite the wrong idea of the Commonwealth—if you'll excuse my saying so."

"How do you mean—wrong idea?" she demanded, firing up. "All those blacks have to do what our king says, don't they?"

"*Indeed* they don't!" cried Wally, forgetting the parcel and forgetting to say "madam," forgetting everything except that here was someone else with the usual muddled ideas about the Commonwealth. "By the Statute of Westminster, passed in 1931, the Dominions became self-governing with their own ministers and laws."

"What, the blacks too? Do you mean to say all those blacks can do just as they like?" exclaimed Reenie, scandalized.

"Well, of course some parts of the Empire are more advanced in the art of self-government than others, madam. India, for example. India's going through a very troubled and thorny path just now. And the—er—the coloured tribes are responsible in most cases to their own Governor-Generals. But in many parts of Africa the native chiefs are encouraged to deal with their own problems. Indirect rule, the principle is called. You see——"

"But look here——" interrupted Reenie, "say we went to war (we shan't, so it doesn't matter supposing). Wouldn't all those other countries have to come in too, if the king said they was to?"

Wally shook his head, smiling in a superior way.

"Oh no. Nothing of the kind. They have absolute freedom of choice."

Reenie thought this over for a minute in silence. Then she said triumphantly: "Well, what's the use of Us having them at all if they won't do what we tell them?"

Wally shook his head again, patiently, this time. "It isn't a question of our 'having' those places, madam. They belong to themselves. But they are bound to the Mother Country by ties of tradition, and affection, and by the same language and religion. They—er—they like the *idea* of England, so to speak. The Commonwealth"—and here Wally stood up a little straighter and his eyes through the horn-rims shone as if they were taking light from a thought—"is as much an *idea*, really, as a reality. Yes, it's an idea. A great and glorious idea. The first voluntary and peaceful association of free peoples the world has ever seen. I tell you"—and here Wally leant confidentially over the counter— "I don't give that for your League of Nations. Not *that*. What is it compared with the British Commonwealth? It's ramshackle, that's what it is. Half-gone already. But the Commonwealth— that's still only at the beginning."

"Is it?" she murmured, her imagination struggling with these huge and unfamiliar facts. Slowly she put out her hand and Wally put the atlas into it.

"It is indeed, madam. I've talked a lot, I'm afraid, but it's a subject I feel very strongly about, the Commonwealth."

"That's all right. It's ever so interesting. Well, good evening, and thanks."

"Thank *you*, madam. Good night."

Reenie went homewards with her atlas, thinking about the British Empire and what a nerve Perce had to talk to her like that, as if she were still a school kid. But he had told her a good bit she hadn't known before and when she had said it was ever so interesting, she had meant it.

Some minds go hungry all their life without knowing it. They chew over the details of everyday—the strength or weakness of the breakfast cup of tea, the lateness of Miss Robbins at the office, that spiteful thing Mrs. Morgan said—and make them larger and more dramatic because of this hunger, and when such a mind is given a large, rich, nourishing, impersonal *Fact* to eat, it bolts it greedily, aware of a new and delightful pleasure.

Reenie only knew that she was glad she had bought a natlas

and that she liked thinking about all those places joining in with Us because they liked Our King and Our ways, not because they had to. Makes you feel sort of proud, thought Reenie, bouncing along. Have to be on your best behaviour, too. Course, We're better than anyone else, everybody knows that, but We ought to take care and stay better, so's all those places can go on looking up to Us.

"Hullo, Reenie," said someone, timidly, and she turned round and saw Mavis.

"Hullo. You're early, aren't you?" she said, more civilly than she usually spoke to the despised Mavis. She felt pleased with herself this evening and noticing at once that Mavis looked distressed, she immediately felt even more pleased with herself.

"What's up?" she went on bluntly. "You do look upset."

Mavis hesitated, for she was afraid that if she told Reenie her news Mrs. Voles might think she would not be able to pay her rent, and would turn her out of her room. But she felt so frightened and miserable! And after all she had known Reenie for some years, and her voice sounded quite kind and so, almost before she meant to, she muttered: "I've lost my job."

Reenie's eyes opened wide. The rent! she thought at once. Mum won't half be wild.

"Well, I *am* sorry," she said heartily, thinking how glad she was she hadn't lost hers. "After you being there all that time. It was Mr. Just dying, I s'pose?"

Mavis nodded.

"I s'pose they've given you a month's notice?" Reenie went on, as they began to walk onwards together, "just while you find something else?"

Again Mavis shook her head.

"There's meanness for you!" cried Reenie with consoling warmth. "You don't mean to say they've only given you a *fortnight*?"

"Only a week," answered Mavis in a low voice.

"Well!" Reenie said no more. She appeared to be speechless with sympathy but was in fact trying to decide whether she should make some excuse and hurry on to tell her mother. She was on the point of doing so when she suddenly changed her mind. Mum had been ever so disagreeable lately; downright nasty she had been, always forgetting to pass the pickles and going on at her, Reenie, about asking for a rise. It would do Mum good to get a bit of a shock.

"Look here," she said confidentially, "don't you tell Mum just yet. Wait till you got something else."

"Oh, don't you think it would matter?" said Mavis, eagerly yet doubtfully, for she had intended to tell Mrs. Voles that night. "I *would* rather wait."

"Never mind if it does matter," said Reenie stoutly. "You just keep it to yourself. And I won't say a word, neither."

"Well, thanks ever so much," said Mavis, as they came to the gate of Number Seventy-Eight.

"That's all right. Don't you worry. And good luck, I do hope you get something soon."

This was quite the friendliest remark Reenie had ever addressed to Mavis, and the latter was a little comforted by it as she went upstairs and opened the door of her little room; but as soon as she had shut it again and stood alone there in the beautiful but sad evening light, looking round at all the dear possessions that might soon be taken away from her, her fears and worries returned, and she began to move about and get her supper in a state of confused unhappiness. It did not make her movements less deft nor affect her memory, but already, while she set out the blue china and made the tea, her mind was beginning to run along a painful and well-recognized pathway, as it now did every evening.

It had been doing that since she had received the second anonymous letter a fortnight ago. The two letters now rested in a drawer beneath the case that held her clean handkerchiefs. The second one said:

That was a pretty new blouse you were wearing to-day. You must not mind me writing to you. I like to see a girl lucky and happy. You only want a nice young fellow to complete the picture. Don't you worry. Mr. Right will come along. Perhaps he has already. Perhaps he goes to St. Anne's Church.

The first letter had only disturbed Mavis and alarmed her lest someone had guessed her admiration for Mr. Somers, but this one had really terrified her. She felt an odious spirit coming forth from the words in pale ink on the blue paper; a close and gloating watch being kept upon her dear secret. All day, while she worked she was wondering, wondering, *who* this could be who had chosen her, out of all the people in Seagate, to spy on and write to.

The kindness of the words did not deceive her. At first she tried to persuade herself that the letters were written by some harmless busybody who was lonely and took an unusual interest in other people's doings, but she could not make herself believe it; and gradually the letters seemed to *invade her spirit*, until she was afraid to look at Mr. Somers in church lest the writer might be there, hidden among the quiet seated or kneeling figures, watching and mocking and planning another letter.

There was another thing, too, that she could not help worrying about (as these painful thoughts hurried through her mind she was moving lightly about, drawing the curtains, lighting the stove, and making toast)—I'm sure old Mr Just caught his cold that time when I left the shop door open. He shivered, and said that about the draught, two days later he was ill, and now he's dead, and perhaps—very likely—it's my fault. My fault that he's dead, because if I hadn't been looking at *him* (she did not mean Mr. Just) I'd never have forgotten to close the door.

So it really serves me right that I've lost my job.

And there's still that twelve pounds to pay on the furniture.

To-morrow I must go round to Brown's, The Household Word, and see if there's a vacancy there.

Mr. Just said he'd give me a good reference.

If only I don't have to go to Beard's!

They say it's terrible there.

I can't imagine how that person who wrote those letters knew about Mr. Somers.

Twelve pounds. If I have to go to Beard's I'll only get a pound a week and how can I pay for the furniture out of that?

I never talk to him, only look at him sometimes and say good morning. So I can't understand how they found out.

To-morrow I must go to Brown's.

She was sitting upright on the edge of her chair with her feet pressed closely together, swallowing toast and sipping tea without tasting either, and staring with widely opened blue eyes at the wall. The gas stove purred and the clock had a light cheerful tick. She sat there, staring at the wall, long after the toast was eaten and the tea cold.

Twelve pounds. . . I'm sure it was my fault . . . if only I don't have to go to Beard's . . . how *could* they have known? . . . twelve pounds. . . .

CHAPTER XIII

PAULINE dressed herself in her quietest suit to go to tea with Mrs. Pask, because she knew that old people can be divided into two classes about young people's clothes: those who are honestly frightened and dismayed by the bright, brief modern dress; and those who get no end of a kick out of cursing it and saying how disgraceful it is. She thought that Mrs. Pask was one of the first sort.

She put her head round the drawing-room door to tell her mother she was going, but Mrs. Williams, who had been sitting by the window with a novel when Pauline went upstairs to dress, was not there now; and her daughter heard her voice coming from the kitchen, so she went through to find her.

The back door was open, and just outside it, with his very blue eyes full of respect and his very red hands clasping his basket and his very black curls blowing in the May wind, stood the handsome fish-boy who was mad on football.

Connie was standing by the gas cooker, watching the scene with avid interest, and at the open door stood Mrs. Williams, looking charming in her first printed silk dress of the year (she always bought three, one in May, one in July, and one in September, and paid thirty shillings each for them from a big London store which sent her its catalogues) and scolding the fish-boy.

This fish-boy could never do right for Mrs. Williams. She said that he banged the back gate, loitered with the haddock, rang the bell too long, lost the bills, and kept Connie from her work by gossiping. The ugly one who sang in the choir at St. Anne's never offended in any way; he came, slapped his fish into Connie's hand, said it had turned out nice again, and was off. But so soon as the tall one with the blue eyes appeared at the back door, so would Mrs. Williams come out into the kitchen—sometimes she happened to be there making a cake or writing a list of groceries when he was expected—and lecture him. He always listened respectfully and said "Yes, madam," and "No, madam." Mrs. Williams could not complain that he was rude. But he always seemed to be doing something wrong, and of course he had to be spoken to about it.

"Well, you must try to respect other people's property," Mrs. Williams was saying, looking up severely into the fish-boy's sea-blue eyes.

"Yes, madam."

"I've already had to have that gate repaired once this year, thanks to you boys slamming it."

"I'm sorry, madam."

"I don't want to have to speak to Mr. Cousins about you——"

This time the fish-boy said nothing. He did not look at Connie; he continued to gaze seriously at Mrs. Williams. Yet the outraged look on Connie's face—*speak to his boss, the old cat, because he slammed her blasted gate*—was instantly reflected on his own, like the flung-back glow of sunset, though it showed itself only in an even more respectful look in his eyes.

"Mother, I'm going now," said Pauline, bored, standing at the kitchen door.

Mrs. Williams turned quickly round, colouring faintly.

"Oh, yes, dear. You look very nice. Give my kind regards to Mrs. Pask—though I don't expect she remembers me—it's years since we met."

"I will. Good-bye."

She went off, and Mrs. Williams brought her lecture of the fish-boy to an end—with a promise not to tell Mr. Cousins about him this time if he would, in his turn, promise not to slam the gate again.

"Yes, madam," said the fish-boy, and on receiving the gracious smile which he always got at the end of Mrs. Williams's lectures, he went whistling away with his handsome young face lifted critically to the sky (for the fish-boy had ambitions of becoming a pilot) and shut the gate with a tremendous and ear-shattering slam.

Connie did not dare to look at Mrs. Williams, who glided with dignity back to the drawing-room and her novel, deciding that she would have to speak to the tiresome boy *again*, and leaving Connie to her never-ending and self-imposed task of trying to make the kitchen look like a sitting-room.

To this end she always turned the FLOUR and BREAD bins to the wall so that their coarse revealing names might not be seen spread a cloth of clumsy lace bought by herself from Marks and Spencer's over the scrubbed wood of the table, arranged dusters and teacloths (ostensibly in order to dry them) across the top of the stove, and put the cookery books at the very back of the dresser so that they might easily be Tales or something else elegant and unkitchenish.

Pauline walked quickly through the air of May, that had not its complete summer richness in this East Coast town but was charged with a more than country vigour. A few of the better class of summer visitors had arrived, and were strolling towards the bandstand where the Royal Irish Fusiliers were playing selections from Gilbert and Sullivan and old and beloved military marches, much as their fathers had done when Mrs. Pask had been young. Concession was made to the taste of the August visitors in a sort of pit, shaped like a harp and painted electric blue with immensely elongated gold nymphs bounding all over the walls (so elongated that it did not matter if they did have nothing on because everything was so long drawn out) in the Parade at the other side of the Pier; here a series of hot bands with popular conductors looking like American college boys played throughout July, August and the first half of September, and girls with tinny voices sang expressionlessly into the microphone. The older visitors ignored the harp-pit and the younger ones ignored the bandstand, and thus harmony was preserved.

Pauline walked along in an impatient mood, bored at the prospect of tea with old Mrs. Pask and reluctantly forced, now that she was for twenty minutes alone, to think about Brian.

She usually managed to keep her leisure time either satisfactorily filled up or passed in his company. In either event she need not *think* about him. She could feel the delightful charm of his presence when she was with him, and let the consciousness of it run like a singing stream beneath her thoughts and actions when she was with other people. But when she was alone she had to face the fact that things weren't going too well.

Why doesn't he ever say anything, well, definite? He keeps on saying he's crazy about me and of course that's marvellous, but I do wish . . . I don't want to be like Madeleine Eames, running around with crowds of boy friends when I'm twenty-two and still not married by the time I'm twenty-nine. And it's no use him saying he doesn't run around with that ghastly Mrs. Cunningham because I know he *does*. I've seen him.

The worst of it is it doesn't matter how many lies he tells I go on being crazy about him.

It's sickening.

A nice state I've got myself into.

Thank heaven Peggy and Eileen and Vera don't know about it.

Of course, he still does make me furious. At least I haven't gone soft.

I suppose it's all his beastly old father's fault. I wish I could meet him! Marjorie was awfully close about what he was like, she'd hardly talk about him at all. This time six months ago if anyone had told me I'd be going about regularly with Brian I'd have been thrilled to death.

But now I'm actually doing it, it's marvellous of course, but there's always something to spoil things.

At this point her disagreeable reflections were interrupted by a loud shout which seemed to be almost in her ear:

"The Squire! God bless him!"

And turning round she was in time to see an extraordinary equipage going past, in which were seated Louise, old Mr. Early, and Ted. It was Ted who had shouted, and he was bending forward and smiling at her, flourishing his hat and looking even untidier than usual in his oldest suit, his hair blowing about.

Their carriage was one of the three victorias left in Seagate, lingering on in charge of their ancient drivers from the days of thirty years ago when they had done a flourishing business plying between the station and the boarding houses and hotels. It had been Ted's idea to hire one of these instead of a taxi; he never minded being conspicuous, in fact he enjoyed it, and he had a dislike (which increased as he grew older) to riding in cars. Mr. Early did not mind riding in a car. He was not nervous, for he had a feeling that no car would dare to go wrong or be in an accident while it was carrying *him*, but he gave way to Ted's wish, and Louise was always willing to do what her men wanted.

So there they were, bowling along in the graceful anachronism and obviously relishing the bright afternoon air while the pure sea wind blew over them as it never can over people who are crammed into a car with their knees in their mouths and the taste of hot petrol in their lungs.

The driver, a local character named old Maggs, and the well-nourished horse, old Nellie, and even the low, absurd, shapely carriage itself looked unusual and cheerful enough to have the appearance of a party of pleasure, and Pauline (though a little embarrassed by its novelty) smiled and waved with a sudden lifting of her spirits. Ted certainly did do the craziest things! *No one* rode in those awful old carriages nowadays. Still, it might be rather fun—Louise looked as if she were enjoying it, leaning lazily back and watching the shops go slowly past, and Mr. Early was sitting very upright, with no hat on and apparently asleep, with his long white hair lifting in the breeze.

Ted looked so full of high spirits that she could not help feeling a little envious as the victoria passed majestically on and out of sight. He was going to Paris, to an entirely new life full of change and excitement, while she was left in Seagate, grubbing away in the bank and bothered about Brian.

I'll miss him, too, she thought as she opened the gate of Mrs. Pask's house. He's a nice old thing. In the last week they had had a farewell walk along the shore together during which they had hinted darkly at the miseries that were preying upon them. Ted had hinted more than Pauline, but she had done her share, and his comments, though absurd, had been comforting and brotherly. Yes, she would certainly miss him.

"Is Mrs. Pask at home?" she asked rather subduedly of the severe elderly maid who stood regarding her.

"Will you come this way, please, miss?"

She stepped into a large, quiet hall, where a bunch of honesty leaves arranged in a Chinese vase seemed to draw into itself all the light from the clear day outside. The dark wood of the floor and staircase was highly polished.

The daughters of a widow of modest income in a small seaside town may have plenty of social life, but unless the widow be a county widow, the social life will not be formal. Pauline had a large and gay circle of acquaintance but she had never been to a dinner party where the only entertainment provided for the guests was conversation; she had never paid a call, or been out to tea with someone whom she hardly knew. Her manners were pretty, because her nature was sound and she had been conventionally brought up, but she had no social technique for dealing with an event like that of this afternoon, and in consequence she felt unexpectedly nervous.

At the door of the drawing-room the maid asked: "What name, please, miss?" and Pauline replied "Miss Williams."

She advanced towards Mrs. Pask across a large room in which the light was dimmed because of the velvet and net curtains at the windows and there seemed to be a good many tall cabinets. The air was so warm that some pink double tulips on the piano had opened right out and looked like orchids. Mrs. Pask was standing by a low table set with delicate cups and a tall silver urn, and beside this was a stand of sandwiches and sumptuous cakes.

"Miss. Williams," announced the severe maid, rather to Pauline's pleasure; she had never been announced before.

"How do you do. It is very kind of you to come," murmured Mrs. Pask, putting out a tiny yellow hand that Pauline gently held for a second, murmuring in her turn: "It's very kind of you to ask me."

"Do sit down," went on Mrs. Pask, looking distressedly round at all the chairs. "I think *that* little one is quite comfortable. We will have tea now, please, Ellen."

As soon as the severe maid had brought in a covered dish, and had gone out again and shut the door after her, Mrs. Pask's manner became less nervous.

She was dressed in an expensive jumper and cardigan of pale violet over a darker skirt and wore two or three heavy old-fashioned rings set with handsome rubies and sapphires. Old people so often have good jewellery, thought Pauline; I don't know anyone under thirty who's got any decent rings or bracelets, they have smashing wrist-watches now and then but otherwise it's all Woolworth stuff. Heaven knows when any of my boy friends'll earn enough to buy their wives modern rings like those! Eric and Wally will be about ninety before they can even think about it! Of course, everybody had more money in those days.

Mrs. Pask had been watching the door; and as soon as it had quite shut she got up briskly and said, looking down at Pauline with the kindest smile on her little face:

"Of course I don't expect you to drink *tea*! I know *just* what you young people like, and I've got some in specially for you— I do hope you'll like it, the man at the shop assured me it's very good——"

And to Pauline's utter amazement she made a dart at a dignified cabinet full of small ivory figures and glass, opened its lower cupboard, and turning round triumphantly, held up a large gaudy bottle of a ready-mixed cocktail labelled "Manhattan Marvel."

"Do excuse my hiding it away like this," she went on cheerfully, advancing towards the table and the dazed Pauline, "but my maids are rather old-fashioned in their ideas and—and so is my cousin, Miss Gaye. Perhaps you would be so kind as to open it— I've got a thing here that the man at the shop gave me"—waving it—"but I'm afraid my wrists aren't very strong nowadays. And here's a glass," she put the "Manhattan Marvel" down among the Crown Derby, and, going back to the cupboard, produced from it a rather large tumbler. "And now," looking round the room with a smile that enjoyed the fully open tulips, the bright sunlight veiled by the curtains, and the pretty girl sitting there in her suit the colour of a blackberry and staring at her with wide-open eyes, "I think we've got everything, don't you?"

You old pet, thought Pauline, trying hard not to laugh, and also to think of just the right words to say; words that should not hurt old feelings nor make an unsophisticated heart feel foolish. Offering me that poison at this hour in the afternoon because you've read in the papers that Modern Girls Drink Cocktails. You old duck.

"It's most awfully kind of you," she began quickly, putting all the warmth that was in her heart into her smile, "but I think perhaps I'd rather have tea, if you don't mind. You see, I play a lot of games and I have to keep pretty fit to do that, and as a matter of fact I drink very little. Sometimes weeks go by without my having a drink. But it really is most awfully kind of you to have thought of it."

Mrs. Pask's face wore a mixture of relief and disappointment.

"Really, my dear?" she said, sitting down at the tea table. "You are quite sure you prefer tea? You are not just being polite?"

"I'm quite sure, thank you. I adore tea. And those little cakes look heavenly."

"Well—that being so—if you are quite sure—I think perhaps I'd better put the bottle back. If Ellen came in and saw it—or Miss Gaye——" ·

"Let me," said Pauline, picking up the intimidating potion, which looked as if it might explode at any minute. But while she was stowing it away in the dark lacquered cupboard that smelled of pepper, she suddenly thought of something.

"Look here," she said, turning to look at Mrs. Pask, who sat at the tea table watching her with an expression that was now all alarm, "would you like me to take it along with me—if you're afraid of your maid or Miss Gaye seeing it? I could take it back to the shop and make them send you three bottles of soda water or lime juice or something."

"Oh, if you *would* be so kind!" breathed Mrs. Pask, at once restored to cheerfulness and beginning to pour out the tea. "I really was wondering what on earth to do with it. And if the maids or Jean saw it . . . so difficult to explain."

"All right, then." Pauline came back to the table, sat down, and took up her tea. "I'll wrap it in my scarf when I go—your maid will probably think I'm pinching the spoons but we can't help that—and no one'll be any the wiser."

And then they both laughed, looking at one another over their teacups.

I like you and I think you're an old squoo, decided Pauline, eating Mrs. Pask's delicious plain tomato sandwiches. (This was a childhood name she and Marjorie had kept for grown-ups they approved of.) What a lovely story to tell Brian!

No, she decided a moment later. He wouldn't—well, appreciate it, exactly. He'd just think it was a yell and wouldn't see that it's kind of sweet too.

I'll tell Ted if I write to him. He'd see what I mean.

The "Manhattan Marvel", of course, broke the ice as success-fully as only a guilty secret between two people can, and soon they were talking with mutual interest and pleasure, without awkwardness; and Pauline was no longer nervous and bored and Mrs. Pask was no longer frightened.

Mrs. Pask, too, looked with such open admiration and pleasure at her visitor that Pauline could not help feeling flattered: her own mother never looked at her like that! And Mrs. Pask's conversation was not disapproving or dull, like that of many old people, for her life had been so happy—until dear Lionel had died—in spite of their great grief that they had never had children, that there was no bitterness in her nature. She was now almost resigned to living without Lionel and to being Not Very Strong and being bullied by Jean. Almost; not quite. Her invitation to this pretty young person had been one of her occasional little flutters towards the beauty and quiet gaiety which she still yearned for.

(Where, asks the gentle reader, was Miss Gaye? Out; buying a horrid little scarf with part of a birthday cheque sent to her by her father, who was comfortably off and delighted to have his daughter living in someone else's house.)

So, as there was no hidden envy in the remarks and questions Mrs. Pask addressed to Pauline, there was no defiance or contempt in Pauline's replies; and by the time the wildly unexpected fact came to light that Mrs. Pask had at one time played hockey for her home county, Pauline was completely interested in their talk.

"Oh yes, I used to be mad about hockey. Quite mad," said Mrs. Pask meditatively. "For four years I thought about little else. I was always small, you know, but wiry. Very wiry. And fast."

"Weren't the clothes awfully uncomfortable? I've seen old photographs of teams and wondered how they ever managed to run."

"We thought them wonderfully comfortable and easy. Just as you do your shorts nowadays. And walking! How I did enjoy a good long walk! My husband and I used to walk along the shore every evening wet or fine, summer and winter, right up to the day before he died. I miss that very much. Often on a stormy evening," her voice became a little quieter and she glanced at the door, "I stand at this window and look out at the sea and I long—I really *long*—to go out and walk along the shore with the big waves breaking."

"Then why don't you?" (*That so-and-so of a companion, I suppose*) demanded Pauline.

"Well, I am Not Very Strong, nowadays," answered Mrs. Pask. "And of course I am seventy-two. It's my heart."

"I like rough weather, too," suddenly confessed Pauline, forgetting to say she was sorry about Mrs. Pask's heart: (an omission that did not offend Mrs. Pask, because she was pleased at her heart being treated with the casualness Pauline would have given to the heart of a contemporary). "Better than calm, I think."

They got on so well that, an hour and a half later when Pauline looked at her watch and said that she must go, Mrs. Pask decided to tell her something.

It was not much. It was a silly little thing, really. Probably it was just someone playing a joke. But all the same Mrs. Pask did not like it, and it had been worrying her ever since it had happened. She had not told Jean because Jean was always so unkind about the little things that worried one. But Miss Williams would not be unkind; she was a dear girl, and would be cheerful and comforting about this silly little worry.

So while Pauline was pulling on her gloves, Mrs. Pask said, no longer nervously but confidentially:

"There is something that is worrying me. It's only a silly little thing but I should like your opinion on it."

She had an unexpectedly clear and direct way of putting a point, for such a faded, ordinary-looking small being. Pauline had already noticed this and decided that it made her a little different from most old ladies, who always took ages to spit it out.

"Of course," she said at once, feeling competent and masterful as she stood there on the hearthrug, smiling down upon her hostess. "I'd love to."

"Thank you," said Mrs. Pask. "I won't keep you a moment."

She went across to a small desk made of yellow mahogany inlaid with circles of flowers in coloured woods, unlocked it, and took from a pigeonhole a letter. It was an ordinary letter in a pale blue envelope, addressed to Mrs. L. Pask, "Avonlea," High Street, Seagate, in an ordinary sort of writing. Mrs. Pask held it out to Pauline, who took it.

"Shall I read it?" she asked, looking curiously at her hostess's puckered little face.

"Please, if you will."

The letter began straight away:

There cannot be many women as lucky as yourself dear friend. Your dear husband's generosity has left you quite comfortable with this world's goods and a beautiful home. Kind friends and all the clothes you want. You must often thank God for all your benefits. How lucky you are.

That was all.

Pauline read it to the end, then she looked up. She was just going to laugh and say something about some silly thump playing a pointless joke, when she saw Mrs. Pask's face.

It was white with distress, and she was looking so eagerly at Pauline, with her hands clasped as if she were praying.

"What do you think of it?" she said at once, very anxiously.

Pauline hesitated. She thought—yes, she was quite sure that she thought it was some silly thump playing a pointless joke; but it was plain that Mrs. Pask did not see it like that at all. Mrs. Pask was frightened.

"Well," she began, "I don't know quite what to think of it, except that it's rather a neck—rude, I mean—to write to someone telling them they're lucky. It isn't any business of this person's," she waved the letter scornfully up and down, "if you *are* lucky. And anonymous too! I suppose," she went on, hesitatingly, because she felt that the question might prove a delicate one, "you haven't any idea who it is?"

Mrs. Pask shook her head. "No idea at all. I've thought and thought and puzzled, ever since it came, a month ago. But I can't imagine who it can be. I can't think of a single person I know who would do such a strange thing."

"I think it's silly," Pauline said contemptuously. She was angry with this unknown who had frightened her nice old squoo. "If I were you I'd simply ignore it. Burn it and forget about it."

Mrs. Pask shook her head again.

"I know it's foolish of me but I can't do that. I've tried to, but every time I put it near the fire I feel somehow that I *can't* burn it."

"You give it to me and I'll darn soon burn it!" cried Pauline. "Let me take it with the Manhattan Marvel when I go!"

"It's very kind of you, my dear, and I appreciate it very much. You are a dear girl to think of it. But I'm afraid even if you did burn it I should always remember what it said. It seems to haunt my mind, somehow." Her voice became lower and her anxious eyes were fixed mournfully upon Pauline's face.

"I don't really see why it should." (Pauline was using her kind-but-firm voice.) "After all, it's very nice to be lucky! You needn't mind someone telling you you are."

"But I do mind," said Mrs. Pask, at once, and decidedly, for her. "There seems something—something sinister, to me, in that letter. As if the person who wrote it knew my luck—if I *am* lucky —would soon be taken away from me."

"That really is nonsense, you know." Pauline saw that this obsession would have to be dealt with very firmly. "You mustn't give way to it. If you feel so bad about it why don't you go to the police?"

"But I should feel so silly! You can't complain to the police because someone writes you an anonymous letter—a *nice* letter, really, if you just read it on the surface—saying you're lucky."

"You could go to a private detective, though. It's just the sort of problem Lord Peter Wimsey or Poirot would love. 'The Case of the Nice Anonymous Letter'!"

"Yes, I suppose I could," said Mrs. Pask doubtfully. "But I should still feel very silly. And I suppose I am really; I must try to be more sensible. I can't make up my mind to burn it, but I'll lock it away in the spare room and try not to think about it. Yes, I really will."

"That's grand!" Pauline took her hand again and gave it the firm friendly little shake that was attractive.

"And thank you so much for letting me come, and please can I come again?"

She had not meant to say this. Her leisure time was precious and always pleasantly occupied. But she was chivalrous; her childhood had been full of attacks on little boys who were bullying other little boys or dismembering flies, and her chivalry had been aroused by Mrs. Pask's evident loneliness, fear of Miss Gaye, and worry about the letter.

"Will you? Oh, I should be pleased if you would! Would you come to lunch one day soon?—oh, of course, you will be at business. I suppose you couldn't manage to come in during your lunch time? I would have it all ready to pop into your mouth—but perhaps you go home?"

"No, I don't, it's too far. I go to the Fan or take sandwiches on to the front. But I'd love to come here one day, if it wouldn't be a trouble."

She was pretty sure that Miss Gaye and the severe Ellen would not want to have lunch all ready to pop into a strange young woman's mouth. So what?

Accordingly it was arranged. Mrs. Pask said good-bye to her affectionately with a much more cheerful face than she had had earlier in the afternoon, and Ellen showed her out, with a long stare that perfectly comprehended the "Manhattan Marvel" bulging in the pocket of her suit.

Pauline walked cheerfully home. She felt better. The Case of the Nice Anonymous Letter was amusing and interesting and she had quite enjoyed the old squoo's tomato sandwiches. Probably her lunches would be just as good. Save my hard-earned cash, too. (Not that I shall go there often enough to save much.)

5

CHAPTER XIV

SUDDENLY she remembered with annoyance that she had meant to buy some powder, and realized that she was well past the shop where she usually went. It was too late to go back; she was going to a dance that evening at the Grand Hotel with some friends and would only just have time now to get home and dress.

Bother! I'll have to go to Beard's.

Beard's was just across the road. It was blazing with light and crammed with shoppers and when Pauline pushed open the swing doors a blast of smelly warm air came out.

Beastly hole, she thought, pushing her way towards the Beauty Counter.

Next to the Beauty Counter was the Lending Library and Newest Fiction. Going by book jackets, only two events were occurring in the Newest Fiction; someone was lying dead on the floor in evening dress; and someone in evening dress was kissing someone else, also in evening dress, very hard.

Pauline was gazing, more absently than was her habit, at the books while waiting for her change when she suddenly saw among them a pale girl's face that she knew. Who *is* that, she thought, idly staring. The girl was serving a woman at the Library counter, and as she handed the book across Pauline remembered her as That Rather Pretty Fair Girl from Just's. What was she doing here?

"Your change." The grubby painted girl behind the counter thrust eightpence and a box of Coty's Apricot L'Aimant into Pauline's hand and turned to the next customer. Pauline took another look at the Books girl, and began pushing her way through the crowd towards her.

"Hullo!" she said cheerfully. "What are you doing here?"

The girl looked up, startled, from the entry she was making and the middle-aged women waiting to be served, who were all fat and bullyish, stared resentfully at Pauline.

"Oh—Miss Williams!" murmured Mavis, going red. "I didn't see you, I'm sorry. Oh, I'm working here now. I—I've left the—the other place."

"I haven't been to the library lately," Pauline went on, struck even in the midst of her own thoughts about Brian and Miss Pascoe and The Nice Anonymous Letter and the dance by the exhausted and miserable expression on the girl's face. "I'm so sorry you've left. Are you getting on all right here?"

"Oh yes, quite all right, thank you, Miss Williams." Mavis smiled but glanced quickly at a thick woman in a green smock with a badge on it, standing at a little distance away. "It's a bit— oh yes, I like it ever so, really."

"Grand. Well, I must dash. Good-bye. I'm glad to have seen you." She smiled and turned away, but something made her turn back. "Good luck!" she called, quite loudly. Mavis was staring at her, and when she heard that, she smiled faintly and just moved the fingers of one small hand in a little wave. Then she turned to a fat cross woman (whose life had been enough to make any woman fat and cross but no one cared) and Pauline, pushing her way out under the glaring lights and through the sickly bedroomy smell of powders and soaps, lost sight of her.

Poor little beast, she thought, it must be lousy working there after Just's.

She hurried home. Her dress was laid out on the bed with her new toeless gold slippers. She was going with Wally Wade and Phil Roberts and Peggy and it would be a good dance, for the Grand always employed the same excellent swing band and had a swell floor. But Brian would not be there, and so it was a case for saying "I'm darn well going to enjoy myself" instead of "It'll be heaven." He certainly does make a difference in my young life, she thought, standing in front of her long looking glass in an evening petticoat that she had made herself from rosy artificial satin and pale brown lace, and brushing her hair, and not looking at her reflection.

Damn him! I hate not being able to enjoy myself properly just because he isn't there. And when he is there I don't always enjoy myself. I'm always wondering if he's going to fall for somebody else, and getting furious and having to bottle it up when he does.

People always say it's such heaven being in love (not that I'm really in love with him; good heavens, I can get on without him; sometimes I forget about him for hours—well, half-hours, anyway). I don't think it's heaven at all. I used to be always trying not to roar last winter when things were all wrong, and even now, when they're all right, I'm always furious and wondering who he's with when he's not with me.

I wonder who he's with this evening?

The warm air came through the open window. Her room looked over long wide gardens and the nearest house was so far-away that she never troubled to draw the curtains. All the flower-

ing trees and shrubs were out and they glimmered, rich and heavy
and perfect, in the blue evening; the laburnum hanging down in
delicate yellow, the lilac top-heavy among its heart leaves, a bush
of early roses with every flower open and looking up at the twilight sky. The delicious smell of the motionless trees, and of
cooling grass, hung in the air. It was one of those evenings that
make people want to run away somewhere; to go on swiftly for
ever and ever under the darkening sky, among the flowers, escaping with perhaps one beloved person to the sound of music.

Heaven, thought Pauline, brushing back her hair and glancing
out at the still garden. Wish I were going for a drive. But he
hates the country.

What did Mrs. Williams do on such evenings?

The town was full of young men and women making love or
dancing or sitting at the pictures with their arms twined together,
writing or telephoning to one another, or having endless, murmuring, intense conversations across little tables in the Fan and all
the other cafés. The day might belong to the workers and the
nights to the properly married, but the evenings belonged to the
young; the romantic young, up to their necks in misery and
delight.

Mrs. Williams, like all the other thousands and thousands of
middle-aged people in Seagate about whom nobody much cared,
read a novel or did a bit of mending, telephoned a friend or went
to the pictures or listened-in or dozed. There *are* things for
middle-aged people to do, and they do them and manage to be
fairly contented; even though no one is imploring them over a
cooling cup of coffee to explain exactly what they meant when
they said that, or dancing very close with a hard young cheek
pressed against their own.

It is true that Mrs. Williams would have *liked* to be doing other
things, but she was an exception.

"Pauli, have you finished with the bathroom?" demanded
Marjorie, coming upstairs two at a time and going into her room
but leaving the door open.

"Ages ago. Are you going out?"

"M'm." Marjorie was carefully pulling her dress over her
head. Her bag and net gloves and a part had been laid tidily on
her bed.

"Who with?" (Not "Where to?" it will be observed.)

"Eric Whosit." Marjorie came out of the dress, and held it at
arm's length. "God, this thing is in rags." She placed it gently
down beside the gloves and bag.

"My old Eric, do you mean?"

"That's the man." She glanced across at her sister and made a face. "I say, that petticoat fits quite well."

"Don't you like him?"

"Not much. He's so wet he steams."

"I think he's rather a pet."

"You would. Be an angel and lend me some bath salts, I've run out."

"I've only got Verbena."

"Don't mind for once."

Pauline came into the bathroom, where Marjorie was running in the water, looking intent and calm, as usual.

Pauline went back into her room.

"Where's he taking you?"

"The Barn."

"I say, Marjie, that's frightfully expensive!" She came and stood at her bedroom door again, twisting short curls round her tail-comb and looking troubled.

Marjorie shrugged.

"He can't really afford it. I know what he gets a week," went on Pauline.

"What does he get?"

"Oh, the usual. About six."

"I shan't cost him that in one evening."

"All the same, you oughtn't to let him."

"Oh——" Marjorie, now in the bath with her hair done up in a net, said something coarse and fashionable. "He'll enjoy spending money on me. That hopeless sort always does."

"Well, I still think it's all wrong."

"You would. You know, Pauli" (she began quickly to wash her lovely arms), "you don't know a thing about handling men. That's why you've got in such a flap over the Son of Frankenstein."

"Thanks." Pauline, with a little white towel tied round her neck, was sitting in front of her dressing-table painting her face. She knew that red had come up under the foundation lotion that she had put on, but could see no change in her smooth pale brown cheeks.

"Don't be snooty. I'm only giving you a hint."

"I'm not snooty. You're like those know-all hags in the women's papers."

"All the same, Pauli, those hags are right. Men *do* need managing."

"It's such a bore."

"It's more boring to grovel about the place after someone. (I say, are you sure you can spare two cubes?)"

"(It's a bit late to ask, seeing they're in the water, but I'm quite sure.) I don't grovel."

"Not outwardly. But inwardly you grovel like fun."

"I do *not!*"

"My good soul you do. The more you seem to stand up to him the more you're inwardly grovelling."

"Well——" said Pauline suddenly, in a low tone, an almost helpless tone, and putting down her lipstick, "I suppose I—can't help it." And she stared gloomily at her delightful face in the mirror.

"Well, you should be able to." Marjorie was standing up drying herself and the bath water was running away. "One of the secrets of managing men is to like them, but to have something else you care about much more than you do them."

"Joan Oldham's crazy about her classic dancing and she's simply lovely, but no one's ever married her, and she's nearly thirty-two."

"She's arty. Men hate arty hags. Another secret is *never* to grovel to them. I don't mean be all independent. They hate that——"

"They seem a bit hard to please."

"They are, damn their eyes. Not that I need say damn them, because they seem always quite easily pleased by me."

"You're telling me." Pauline took off the little neck towel and looked earnestly at herself, from head to foot, in the glass.

"I'm not highly sexed," Marjorie went on, wrapping herself in a big bath-towel.

"My dear, *I'm* simply *seething* with it!" And Pauline half-shut her eyes and swayed out of the room, panting heavily.

"Ass!" said Marjorie, laughing; then, looking her over critically: "You look nice to-night, but why don't you have an up hair-do?"

"Doesn't suit me."

"That doesn't matter. You ought to look like everybody else. That hair-do is last year's."

"It keeps tidy when I'm playing tennis or riding, which is more than most people's do."

"You and your huntin', shootin', and fishin'! I give you up. Who are you stepping out with to-night? Brian?"

Pauline, pausing at the top of the stairs with her evening coat over her arm, shook her head. How easily the question had been asked and how surprised Marjorie would be if she knew the pain it gave! Marjorie was standing in front of her own long glass in the middle of her prim, rather sad little bedroom and slowly pulling in the wide black belt of a dress made of turquoise blue linen, which covered every bit of her except her back, and that was naked. Her hair was on the very top of her head with every large fair curl in perfect order. Pauline did not answer the question, but exclaimed:

"I say, *what* a frock! Where did you get it?"

"Bought it from Madeleine Eames, I ran into her when I went up to town on Friday. I remember now, your beloved—I would say, *our* beloved, but he's cooled off me lately—told me he was taking Ma Cunningham out to-night. Peculiar taste he has, I will say. If I were a chap I'd sooner have you, last year's hair-do and all. Well, good-bye, ducky. Enjoy yourself and tell Wally from me there's always hope."

Pauline went downstairs laughing over this ancient joke and trying to conquer the profound depression, mingled with anger, that had come upon her at hearing what Brian was doing that evening. If only her position with him were not so uncertain! If only they were engaged or even had an understanding! If only——!

And now he was cooling off Marjie, was he? Well, she had thought he might be; and at least it was one less hag to worry about. Dear old Marjie, it was a shame to call her a hag. She could be sweet when she liked.

Here a loud and festive hooting outside announced the arrival of the large draughty fifth-hand car in which Wally Wade took his friends to dances and parties. To-night it was open to the air, and there were Wally and Phil, with light coats and white silk mufflers over their dinner-jackets, and Peggy with her curls tied up in a refugee handkerchief, all looking eager and cheerful and ready to enjoy a delightful evening.

Pauline called out "Good-bye" to her mother, who was in the kitchen "speaking to" Connie, and was halfway down the garden, waving gaily to the party in the car, when Marjorie came flying down the stairs with her full blue skirts held up in both white hands.

"Pauli!" she called, pausing at the door.

"What?" Pauline turned; she was at the gate.

Marjorie seemed to want to tell her something without the others knowing what she meant. First she held up her skirts and shook them, then she called, subduing her ringing voice a little——

"You know my escort to-night—hullo Wally, hullo Peggy, hullo Phil!—you know—E. Whosit——"

Pauline nodded impatiently. She wanted to get away, to forget her anger and disgust—yes, it was disgust—to dance and laugh and not think about Brian.

"Wasn't he a friend of—you know——" shaking the skirts of the dress once more—"who I got this from?"

"Yes," called Pauline, "but that's all washed up now."

"Oh blast! Thanks." Marjorie turned away from the door, looking wonderful in the dimly lit, drab hall. "I can't help it if he *has* seen her in it," she muttered, going quickly upstairs again. "I'm certainly not going to take it off now."

CHAPTER XV

AT 45 Station Road, Eric was dressing to take Marjorie to The Red Barn.

His bedroom was small and austere, with a reproduction of Botticelli's "Nativity" over the mantelpiece, a long white bed that could not possibly have held two, and dark green window curtains that matched the rugs and linoleum. He had no long glass. He seldom saw himself at full length and so he did not know that he looked romantic in his dark trousers and fresh white shirt, like a scholarly aristocrat in the midst of a plot to restore the monarchy.

He never struggled with his evening ties. He tied one quickly and perfectly, looking at his fingers at work and not at his face. He was in the state of painful and pleasureful excitement that was so familiar to him, and wondering just how far he would get with Marjorie this evening. If only I don't fall in love with her! he thought, brushing his hair in front of the glass and staring unseeingly into his clear and unhappy eyes. I cannot and will not endure another five years of agony. Why should I?

Why, indeed? Some young men, seeing such rocks ahead, would never have asked the girl to go out with them at all. But Eric, as the gentle reader knows, was the original schooner *Hesperus* where rocks were concerned.

Two pleasant sounds were coming into his room: one made by his father, downstairs at the piano playing Josef Holbrooke's "Gulnare"; the other made by the bells of St. Anne's calling to evening service. Eric should have been there, singing in the choir. But since the end of the Madeleine Eames affair some months ago he had gone less and less to church. While he had been suffering so desperately in that girl's embrace, he had as desperately needed the comfort that the Church, with its beloved familiar music and its pardon for what it called the sins of the flesh, could give. But now that he was free of Madeleine and deliberately about to bark his emotional shins again, he felt ashamed and hypocritical to go frequently to church and participate in all the Church's rites.

He did not think of what he had done—and meant to go on doing—as a sin of the flesh. But the Church did, and the two points of view could not be reconciled. Something must be given up, and Eric was gradually giving up the Church.

He was in a muddle, and so steadily unhappy that a deep foundation of unhappiness, a coral-reef of frustration and pain, was growing in his nature. Sometimes he felt as if nothing could dissolve it but long years of delicate, tender, playful happiness; the kind of happiness that he had always dreamt of and never once experienced with any of the girls he had loved.

In this state of mind the young man was taking a girl to a roadhouse.

He sighed, and put on his white silk scarf with an elaborate "E" in one corner, and the dark evening coat which, as an elegant young bachelor, he had felt he owed to himself, picked up his gloves, and went downstairs.

His mother was standing in the hall, looking up at the stairs as he came down, and he suddenly thought how old and tired she had lately been looking. *Poor Mother*, he thought, and went up to her and dropped a kiss on her cheek. *But I ought to have a place of my own; it's high time*, his thought ended.

"How nice you look, darling," she said fondly, lifting her head to look at him so that her silver earrings tilted. Mrs. Somers, who had for many years taught drawing and painting at a large school for girls in Seagate, had been one of the arty hags that a man *had* liked; Mr. Somers, visiting music master at the same school, had loved and married her.

"Thank you, Dumps. But you look tired, darling. Are you?"

"A little, perhaps. I haven't been sleeping very well lately. Eric——" she suddenly took his arm and leaned her forehead against him—"something's worrying me. I know it's silly of me but I can't help it. I've had another of those letters."

"That anonymous advertisement-thing, do you mean, that came in the winter?"

She nodded, lifting her face from his arm to look up at him.

"I thought you would have forgotten all about it."

5*.

"Oh no—I've thought about it more than once. It was a queer business. But——"

"Well, I've had this this morning." She fumbled in her cardigan pocket. "Have you time to read it, darling? I don't want to keep you if you're in a hurry."

He shook his head, smiling tenderly and holding out his hand; and indeed he was in plenty of time for his appointment with Marjorie; he was the sort of young man who always gets there twenty minutes before the girl.

"I've got heaps of time. Let me see it."

She put the hateful blue envelope into his hand and watched his face with a grateful, worried, loving look on her own while he read.

Dear friend lately I have been thinking what a lucky lucky girl will be who gets that boy of yours. It is not many boys these days who are nice clean boys and never give their mothers a minutes worry. I am sure he tells you all his secrets. We all know who a boys best friend is.

Deep colour came into Eric's face. He tore the note across and across, screwed it up so tightly that he hurt his hand, and went into the kitchen without a word, and lifted up the lid of the stove and flung it in.

"Filthy thing. That's gone," he said violently, watching it burn.

"I was thinking of keeping it, to show to the police if I get any more of them," said his mother, timidly. She had followed him into the kitchen and was gazing, not at the burning letter, but at his flushed face.

"I don't think you can do that, Dumps. We should all feel such fools. Perhaps it's only some harmless lonely lunatic with a mania for writing letters. This is the second one, you say?"

"No, dear, the third. There was another but I burnt it."

"What did it say?" He was not looking at her.

"The same kind of thing—what a lot of friends you've got and how fond they all are of you and a lot more stuff like that. There wasn't anything in it that one could mind, really, only——"

"Dumpetta didn't like it! Never mind. It's burnt, and if you get any more just show them to me and I'll burn them too. It's only some lunatic trying to be funny. Don't worry about it. I really must go now or I'll be late. Good-bye, darling."

He gave her a hasty kiss and hurried away, turning to wave to her as he went out of the front door; an elegant young man amid the white and red geraniums and clipped grass of the little garden, all lit by the soft lingering light of the summer evening.

"Good-bye, dear! Enjoy yourself!"

His mother came slowly across the hall and shut the door after him. She did not watch him start up the car and drive away. Father was so tactless in that way! He never would realize that young people hated to be watched and asked where they were going and who with and what time would they be home. *She* realized it. That was why Eric and she were such chums.

Nevertheless, as she went back into the drawing-room, to work at her cross-stitch tea-cosy cover and listen to Father playing, she was more worried than ever. She had so longed to hear Eric laugh and make a joke of the whole business, and say, in his funny way that he was glad someone—even an anonymous someone—appreciated what a good boy he was!

He was a good boy, of course. He must be, or he would have married that dreadful Eames girl. But it wasn't true that he told his mother all his secrets. He never told her anything.

Of course, I don't expect him to. I understand him perfectly, and Father too. They're just two dear big schoolboys, the pair of them, and I'm sure neither of them ever have any secrets to tell me, bless them!

I won't worry any more about it.

Why did he go so red and tear it up like that?

I wonder if there is some girl he's serious about.

I suppose I shouldn't mind if she was a really nice girl.

He did seem upset.

She sat quietly in the deepening twilight, with her needle steadily moving in and out of her work. The music poured and rippled and Mr. Somers at the piano swayed slightly as he played. Whenever Mrs. Somers lifted her eyes she looked at a green pot in which a superb white double tulip was flowering. She worked mechanically on, with worry in her heart.

The car, which belonged to Eric's father, was a three-year-old Morris, comfortable and well-preserved. Eric got into it and looked at his watch; he was still too early, so he lit a cigarette, staring down the road but not seeing anything. Unless he pulled himself together the evening was going to be hell.

He had been quite worked up enough about Marjorie, without the added worry of the anonymous letter. He detested the thought of his parents knowing that he ran after witches who let him down; he had what Marjorie would have called a Thing about it; he had built up, to save his pride, a picture of the perfect son, and he did not want it spoiled. He did not want his father and mother to be miserable about him, either; but most of all he wanted to keep the family portrait of him untarnished and his unhappy affairs to himself. For he was ashamed of them.

And now this slimy letter-writer had put poison into his mother's mind.

He suddenly became aware that someone was standing by the car and saying "Good evening, Mr. Somers." For a second he did not know who it was; he only saw a rather pretty fair girl who looked very tired and was carrying her hat, and then he recognized her, and threw away his cigarette, saying:

"Oh, good evening, Miss Jevons! I'm so sorry—I didn't know you for the moment without your hat."

"It's such a lovely evening, I thought I'd take it off," said Miss Jevons, very softly. She was resting her hand on the door of the car, almost leaning on it, and Eric felt just a little surprised at the familiarity of the action, for as a rule she was so quiet and seemed so shy, flying past him with that pretty smile of hers.

"Are you going to church?" he asked next, as she did not speak. "I ought to be there, but I'm playing truant to-night."

She shook her head. "No. I've just come from business, but it was such a lovely evening I thought I'd walk along the front."

"But it's nearly eight!" he said, looking at her with more attention. There was no colour in her face; even her lips were pale and her eyes were darkly shadowed. "I thought Just's finished at six?"

"Oh, I'm not at Just's any more," she said, colouring faintly "I'm at Beard's now."

"*Beard's!*" exclaimed Eric; then checked himself and went on in a less shocked voice. "That explains why I haven't seen you in Just's lately. How long have you been there? Do you like it?"

"About a month. Oh yes, it isn't too bad. It's a bit tiring." And she faintly smiled.

Just behind her head was a climbing white rose that had been lured into an early flowering by the warm weather; Seagate was a great place for roses and all through the summer the porches of the double-fronted Victorian houses and the angles of the severe little modern ones were draped with them, while standard bushes of crimson, cream or white marched down the front gardens of each. The bush behind Mavis's head made a delicate frame for her delicate face, and just as she spoke the first puff of evening wind from the sea came down the road and struck from the flowers a scent so faint that Eric did not even recognize it as the smell of roses.

But he suddenly realized that Mavis was leaning on the door of the car because she was so tired she could hardly stand.

"I'm not always so late as this," she went on almost in a whisper, "but we're getting ready for the Holiday Sale"

"Are you on your way home now?"

She nodded.

"Well, may I give you a lift? Please let me, I'd love to."

"*Oh!*—thank you ever so much! But are you sure it isn't out of your way?"

"Of course not. In you get." And he got out of the car and opened the door for her on the other side and stood holding it while she climbed slowly in, for Eric had beautiful manners which he enjoyed exercising, but the girls he went about with were always in such a hurry that he seldom got the time.

Mavis leant back, and folded her hands slowly over a shabby little white handbag which she held in her lap, and turned to smile at him. He smiled back.

"That better?" he asked, going round to the driver's seat.

She nodded: "It's lovely to sit down."

"You oughtn't to go for a walk after a hard day like that," he said a little severely, starting up the car.

"It's such a lovely evening," she said almost pleadingly. "And I wanted to look at the sea. I love the sea," she went on, so softly that he hardly heard her. The car was going swiftly down Station Road, passing into the cooler air that came from the darkening sea.

"You have some hot milk before you go to bed," he prescribed, still in the severe tone that his usual girls called "Eric's fusspot voice." "Nothing like hot milk for making you sleep."

"I will," said Mavis dreamily, and then they said no more for a little while. Eric was thinking that this would just make him late for his appointment, and Mavis was not thinking about anything. The air blew past her face, smelling of flowers and the sea, and her tired back and aching feet were at rest at last. Every now and then she realized, with a faint shock as if she were coming out of a dream, that she was sitting beside Mr. Somers in his car. It's a pity I'm so tired, I can't sort-of take it in properly, she thought, as the car turned into Lavender Road. There's just half a cup of milk left from breakfast, so I'll be able to do what he told me to. I'm so glad.

"Which is your house?" he asked, turning to her.

"Oh—Number Seventy-Eight. It's down at the other end, close to the sea. But isn't that out of your way? If you put me down here, please, I can easily walk——"

"Please let me take you right to your own door. It isn't at all out of my way," he said, and drove on past the mean shops and the little grey and cream houses with the "Apartments" and "Board Residence" cards in the windows until they came to Number Seventy-Eight.

"There you are," he said, bringing the car smoothly to a stand-still, and turning to smile at her. And although he was by now quite five minutes late for his appointment, and she begged him not to, he got out again and opened the door for her while she slowly alighted.

The quiet little road was almost deserted. All the visitors were out at the pictures or the Band or the Lido Hall, and in the brightly lit parlours the landladies and their nieces and daughters could be seen lingering over the crumby tablecloth with their elbows on the evening paper. The sea was a dark line beyond the fiery coloured lamps on the Promenade, and distant music—from the band, the Lido and the wireless—filled the cool twilit air. And Mr. Somers was so beautiful in his dark coat and white scarf, looking down at her.

"Thank you ever so much," she said, looking up at him. "I do hope you won't be late."

"Oh no, I'm in plenty of time," he answered. And then—because (in spite of all his experiences and his unhappiness and his intention to rush ahead that very evening and let himself in for more unhappiness) he was a born lover of women and could no more help making love to them than he could help breathing—he went on in a tone of playful affection:

"Now you just go in and drink up that hot milk. Are you quite sure you aren't too tired to walk upstairs? Shall I come in and carry you?"

It was the sort of joke that his usual witches received with bored silence. Even as the sentence left his lips he was blaming himself: it was not only in bad taste, addressed to a girl whom he hardly knew, but it sounded most peculiar from a regular churchgoer and would perhaps get back, heavily embroidered, to all the other choir members and the rest of the congregation.

But, to his surprise and pleasure, Miss Jevons did just what he had always hoped a girl would do when he made a tender little joke of that sort. First she went pink, and then the tiredness seemed to lift from her face like a cloud, and instead there played over it a mingled shyness and mischief that made it a child's face as well as a young woman's. Then she looked down at the ground, murmuring something of which he only caught the words "Good night and thanks ever so much——" and then she turned away quickly and went up the path to the house.

But at the door she looked round and sent him one laughing

look—young, mischievous, sweetly friendly—that made him laugh in return as he waved to her and turned back to the car.

He felt better, as he drove away. I always start my affairs too heavily, he thought. I won't be heavy with Marjorie to-night, I'll handle the whole thing lightly. Take a sophisticated line.

"*Sophisticated line.*" What a repulsive expression! What am I coming to?

Mavis went straight up the stairs quickly, and lightly and proudly too, as if she were floating. The first time that the solemnity of a love that is half hero-worship is broken by laughter, the first time that the worshipper asserts herself, if ever so slightly and tastes the deliciousness of a feeling shared, *is* a proud one. For the moment Mavis's tiredness and worry about the payments on the furniture and hatred of Beard's and fear of the future were banished. It was not that she no longer remembered them: they were *not there*—gone like a headache or a thunderstorm.

She fell on her bed and lay there, staring up at the ceiling.

She was so pleased with herself! She had not been thinking quite so much about Mr. Somers lately, because all her other worries had left no room for much else in her mind, and this evening she had not—she truly had not—intended to walk past his house. But somehow she had just found herself walking down Station Road almost before she knew it, and then, when she saw him in the car, she had felt so really *dopey* with tiredness that everything had been like a dream, and when the impulse came— as it always did whenever she saw him—to go close to him, she had not resisted it. Why shouldn't I? Mavis had thought, so poisoned with overwork and tiredness and worry that even her nature (the nearest thing to the nature of a flower, as imagined by human beings, that a human being can have) had felt resentful and assertive. Why *shouldn't* I go up and talk to him?

So up to him she had gone. And here was the result! He had brought her home in his car and told her to drink hot milk and asked her if he should come in and carry her upstairs!

Oh, I'm so happy! I'm so happy! murmured Mavis, over and over again, lying on the bed. And then, because she had had nothing to eat since her breakfast, she began to laugh weakly and then found that she was crying. "Only with happiness," she assured the pillow earnestly, "only with happiness." But when she staggered up from the bed an hour later she was sobered to find that the half-cup of milk left from breakfast had gone sour; so she could not, after all, do what Mr. Somers had told her.

CHAPTER XVI

ERIC went quickly up the path of "Dorna," wondering if she would be furious because he was ten minutes late, and what sort of an act she would put on, and if the maid would open the door; or Marjorie herself, or——

The door opened almost as he rang, and then—he only just in time stopped himself from exclaiming violently: *My God, Madeleine*—for the girl who stood there was wearing the dress that he would remember until the day he died; the blue dress with the black belt that Madeleine Eames had worn on that last miserable evening of their five miserable years together; the evening that they had parted for ever.

"Hullo," said Marjorie, smiling; and observing his sudden start and pallor and perfectly comprehending the reason for both, and thinking in some dismay: *Oh god, he's recognized it. Now we shall have fun.*

"Hullo, Marjorie. I say, I'm afraid I'm late, *said he with illtimed obviousness*——" muttered Eric.

He hardly knew what he was saying. The sight of the girl he desired in the dress that had been worn by that other girl whom he had desired even more violently, and who had wounded him so deeply that he doubted if he could ever completely recover, had revived memories of such pain and anger that his one longing was to turn away and creep home—or drive the car miles out into the country—anywhere but to the Red Barn with Marjorie Williams.

"Are you? Never mind. I was running through my part for next week. Heavenly evening, isn't it?"

Marjorie's voice was cool but friendly. She felt, in fact, rather sorry for the poor sap. He must have fallen very hard for the Eames piece. Well, everybody in Seagate knew what the Eames piece was like, of course. No wonder he was struck all of a heap at seeing her frock on someone else, after she had been giving him the works for five years.

"Let's go," she went on, moving forward, as Eric still said nothing. "Shall we?"

"Of course."

As he followed her down the path he tried to pull himself together. The evening had to be got through somehow. Presumably Marjorie would expect to enjoy herself. As for him, he had come out on this little expedition with the object of asking her to sleep with him. But of course, now that he had seen her in that dress, nothing was further from his thoughts.

But was it?

Already, as he looked at the little jacket of black monkey-fur that covered Marjorie's shoulders, he was feeling the pull of her beauty. There was a terrible charm in seeing her in that dress. The smooth breast of it—or its double—had actually been marked on that night of parting by his anguished tears. And it *must* be the same. Madeleine had boasted that it was a model; there was not another like it in London. He gritted his teeth—an action he had long ago learnt is not performed only by "people in books" —as he shut the gate of "Dorna."

What sort of an evening would they—could they—have after this ghastly beginning?

In that old barrack of hers up on West Cliff Mrs. Cunningham was getting ready to go with Brian to the Red Barn. The old barrack was a large handsome house of red brick standing by itself among what only a few years ago had been a maze of wheat-fields and little country lanes. Now there were new houses being built all round Deepways and Mrs. Cunningham, who did not like neighbours, had had larches planted round her house to screen it.

She was walking round her bedroom in a satin petticoat with a glass of gin in her hand, trying to make up her mind which dress to wear. A white dress, a black, a blue, and an amber one were laid out on the quilted crimson bed coverlet. A doll with silver hair, dressed in a silver crinoline, sat on the pillow and another covered the telephone beside the bed. The luxurious room was rather dusty and untidy and smelled of Nuit Noël.

Mrs. Cunningham was talking to herself.

"Oh hell, I don't know which to put on and I'm getting into a state."

She drank up her gin.

"I've had quite enough, and I shan't enjoy myself if I'm canned."

She picked up the amber dress.

"Shan't enjoy myself anyway so what the hell does it matter? I'll wear this old rag, I'm comfortable in it, anyway."

She began to pull it over her head, but it got stuck, as her frocks always did, and she struggled with it for some moments, swearing and threatening to rip the bloody thing to ribbons. At last she flung it on the floor and put her thumb on the bell and kept it there, standing with her head thrust forward, breathing fast.

"Come in, for god's sake, and help me get into this blasted dress," she said to the tall, superior maid who at last knocked at the door. "Is Mr. Kingsley here yet?"

"Yes, madam, I was just coming up to tell you." The girl began deftly to get the dress on to her mistress, with an impassive face (Mrs. Cunningham always engaged good servants and one or two had been known to stay as long as six weeks).

When the dress was on, Mrs. Cunningham exclaimed loudly: "Oh Christ! Now where's that new lipstick?" and the two women began a hurried search, upsetting boxes of powder and flinging aside delicate undergarments and fine stockings.

"All right, here it is; thanks; I'm *sorry* I've left the room in such a filthy mess. Good night, Foster," and Mrs. Cunningham hurried away, putting the lipstick into her gold kid handbag and pulling about herself a long coat made of thick white tweed embroidered with gold thread.

Brian was standing by the brick fireplace, now filled with delicate ferns. He looked well in evening clothes and Mrs. Cunningham expressed her approval by saying:

"My god, you are ——" but her voice was lost as she put her fat arms round his neck and they exchanged a long, experienced and yet friendly kiss that would have sent the heart of any girl who was in love with Brian down into her shoes: such a blending of sensuality and good fellowship argued many tastes in common.

"You've got on the orange dress; I like it," he said, as they went out through the summer twilight to her waiting car.

"It's as old as the hills," she said, settling herself back against the cushions. "Pull down the blinds, will you, and tell him where to go, and turn on the thing."

Brian did as he was told; and as the chauffeur (also tall and superior, and leaving in a fortnight) sent the Rolls gliding down the new road with neat little houses on either side and all the neat little housewives glanced up from serving their husbands with macaroni cheese and exclaimed excitedly: "Look, Tom, there goes that dreadful woman—oh bother, she's got the blinds down!" the sweet sound of music slowly crept out upon the perfumed air of the small, darkened, moving box in which Brian and Mrs. Cunningham were sitting.

A modern poet should write a companion lyric to Browning's "In a Gondola" about wireless in a moving car. When the car is large and luxurious, and the set is a superb one, the gliding movement and the sweet sounds seem to be the same dreamy pleasure; and it is impossible to decide where movement ends and music begins. To complete the ecstasy the car should be chauffeur-driven, the time late at night, rain should be lightly falling, and the passenger a little drunk.

Mrs. Cunningham and Brian were not drunk yet, but they were making love so intently that they were only aware of the sensuous gliding of the car and the dulcet wandering of the music as a far-off added pleasure. They were not even aware that the music had stopped until, in the midst of a long silent kiss, Mrs. Cunningham heard a man's voice saying gravely:

"——*and open our hearts to receive the gift of Thy divine love, for the sake of Thine only Son, Our Lord and Saviour Jesus Christ*——"

She sat up, violently pushing Brian away, and her gold handbag fell on the floor.

"Turn that bloody thing off, will you?" she exclaimed angrily, pushing back her hair, and he leant over and turned the switch.

"——*life everlasting*——" said the voice, and stopped.

"I like my religion in church on Sundays," said Mrs. Cunningham, glancing at him and beginning to laugh. "That was funny, though, wasn't it? Give me a cigarette, darling."

He gave her one and lit it. The long closed car with drawn blinds was now going along a lane, which had no charms except two long, bright-green hedges on either side, from which the still closely folded heads of grasses looked out, and sprays of juicy climbing plants hung down among furry leaves.

"You won't ask me to marry you, will you?" she said suddenly, leaning across to pull up the blind and look out. "(God, how I hate the country in the evening!) Aren't we nearly there?"

"No."

"No, you won't ask me, d'you mean?"

"Yes."

"Why not, Brian?"

"Because you wouldn't have me."

"You're quite right, I'm not such a fool."

"As you're so candid about it you can't blame me for not asking you."

"No, I suppose not. Oh god, don't let's start on that, I want to enjoy myself to-night."

"All right. You began it."

"All right, all right, I'm sorry. Here is the bloody place."

CHAPTER XVII   .

SOME ten miles outside Seagate lay a realm of richer soil. There was a river called the Nunn flowing through this lonely tract, useless for sailing on, useless even for fishing except of the humblest kind, but it watered the flat meadows that gradually rose into gentle slopes and gave them the thick hedges and luxuriant grass and flowers and insects and animals that usually belong to an exuberant region. In this lush belt, lying across the sparse soil of northern Essex, the only two places of interest among the isolated farms were the almshouses at Nunby and the roadhouse called The Red Barn.

The Spring Developments Association, Ltd., had bought the group of dilapidated buildings standing about an immense and nobly proportioned barn with walls of black weather-boarding and roof of silvery thatch, and had turned the place into a roadhouse. All the directors thought and said that the place was simply made for a roadhouse. This was not true, as the place had been made for people who grew their own food to live in and store the food. That may have been why the barn, when floodlit, looked what can only be called "unnatural"; slightly sinister, definitely resentful and non-co-operative. It was this look that caused one of the directors to suggest calling it The Red Barn; you know, Maria Marten.

So they got a man to paint a terribly amusing signboard of a girl being murdered by a man, and hung it outside, built a swimming pool in the old farmyard, fitted up the buildings surrounding the yard as a restaurant and cloakrooms, put down a dance floor inside the barn and threw up a minstrel's gallery on its wall for the orchestra, and hoped for the best.

But, somehow, there was never a pleasant atmosphere at the Red Barn; not even the sense of space and relaxation that makes a roadhouse more agreeable than a crammed and stifling nightclub. The large areas of the Red Barn were empty rather than restful, the people who sat in silence or talking almost in whispers at the tables or round the swimming pool appeared to be listless rather than at leisure. The Barn itself seemed to suffer as it towered up in the floodlighting, with the terribly amusing sign swinging in the faint wind.

The fact was that Seagate, like many coast towns, had a section of society that was so dissipated as to be bordering on the vicious; comfortably-off people whose useless lives were so poisoned by silly quarrels, sensuality, and spite, that it might be truthfully said no one cared for them save God. It was these people who had adopted the Red Barn as their headquarters, and who frequented the field shut in by thick high hedges that lay behind the buildings. People of the same type came from Stanton and a few even from good-natured, winkly Bracing Bay and kept the Red Barn going; and although it had never had an open scandal, its reputation amongst respectable citizens was an unpleasant one.

Marjorie—a more determined young woman than Eric knew—set herself competently to squeeze as much pleasure as possible out of what promised to be a pretty dreary evening. She looked leisurely about her as they sat at a table waiting for dinner and observed:

"I rather like this place."

"Do you? I'm awfully glad," he answered, rousing himself from a long, miserable stare at the floodlit green water of the swimming pool.

"It's nice and quiet. I don't like noisy places full of smoke."

"Neither do I." (Neither did Madeleine, he remembered. The quieter the place, the more solitary the occasion, the better pleased was Madeleine and the more able to give all her energies to working up an agonizing scene. *Why, oh why, did you have to wear that dress?*)

"We might swim afterwards?" he went on suddenly realizing that here was a wonderful chance to get her out of the garment.

"Heaven," said Marjorie, lifting her cocktail glass to him with her lovely smile. Far away in the Barn, the orchestra began to play a sad and sexy tune. That, and the sudden splash as someone dived into the pool, were the only sounds breaking the languid silence.

The roof of the restaurant was supported by pillars painted to resemble old oak beams and these cast deep shadows which were not much lessened by the red lamps burning in little farm lanterns on each table. The tip of a cigarette glowed, or a woman's sequin jacket glittered, through the dusk and the ruby lights made every face look strong and tragic.

Eric ordered more cocktails (*I called for madder music and stronger wine*, he thought dismally as he did so, *But I was desolate and sick of an old passion*) and tried really hard to rouse himself and give all his attention to the calm and lovely little girl sitting opposite and amuse her with talk at once tender and witty; but it was no use. The anonymous letter, the shock of seeing the blue dress, the knowledge that he was going to lay up more trouble for himself, even the memory of poor little Miss Jevons worn out after a day in a job she hated—all these facts crowded in upon him and made him wretched; and the conversation consisted of short and dull remarks, with long silences between them.

At first Marjorie bore with him. Her dinner was good and she was enjoying it. She would rather have been at the theatre, of course, acting in *While Parents Sleep*, but since there was no part for her in it, she must make the best of her week out. And she was really sorry for him; the sight of the frock seemed to have turned him into a sort of gloomy imbecile. It was an awful tribute to the powers of the Eames piece and Marjorie thought of her with a new respect.

But as dinner went on she began to get cross.

She had only come with him because she never missed an opportunity of establishing herself in the opinion of a man as a gracious and desirable girl, and because he had been so eager to get her. She could have been at pleasanter places with half a dozen other young men. He ought to realize that he was very lucky. And in spite of her self-control her voice began to get offhand and her expression a little sulky.

Eric saw what was happening, and despaired. How lovely she looked in that frock! And every time he looked at her he saw— *Madeleine*; he was awfully reminded of torturing conversations in remote teashops, of scenes in hayfields and reconciliations on the tops of buses.

How could he possibly make love to her while she wore that dress?

Suddenly, while they were drinking their coffee, Marjorie said:

"Hullo, there's Brian!" and waved to a man and a woman who were settling themselves at a table among the shadows some distance away. The man waved back; the woman turned and stared, then looked away again.

"Who's that with him?—oh—the Cunningham hag," she went on. "Well, well. Wouldn't you think he'd rather take out my kid sister?"

"Pauline? Is he a friend of hers." asked Eric, and as he said her name he suddenly thought with relief of her likeableness; she was friendly and kind and not so beautiful as to hurt, like a sturdy yet delicate wallflower.

"I'm very fond of Pauline," he added.

"She's a pet and worth six of him," said Marjorie, pleased to observe signs of returning life in the corpse. "I hope she won't marry him."

"Why—is she thinking about it?" He sounded quite startled.

"I'm afraid so. But——" Marjorie put out her cigarette while she wondered whether to give her sister's secret away and decided that she would; he was beginning to look and sound almost human—"he isn't."

"How do you know? Is he a friend of yours, too?"

"We ran around together for a bit in the spring. I wouldn't quite say he was a *friend*," said Marjorie cautiously. "But I don't wish him any harm, you know. I only wish he'd stop keeping Pauli on a string."

"I've only spoken to him two or three times," said Eric, watching Brian as he instructed a waiter. "What's he like?"

"Oh well, he's a great glamour boy, and all us girls are mad about him, of course. And he has a good line in secret sorrows. Oh yes, and he's Public Nudist Number One."

"A nudist?"

Marjorie nodded, and gave one of her lovely childish smiles to the glamour boy, who happened at that moment to be looking their way.

"Oh yes. He comes out here almost every week-end," and she nodded in the direction of the field behind the Barn. "Didn't you know that this place is a club for nudists?"

"I may have heard so but I'd forgotten. I suppose there's no harm in it, but somehow one's conscious of a distinct sense of repulsion on hearing a person is a nudist. It's curious. I wonder why?"

"They're always bores," she said simply, thinking: *and so are you, but thank god we seem to have started the conversational ball rolling*.

"Is he a bore?"

"He'll do," she said pleasantly, too experienced to run another man down to an admirer.

"What kind of men do you like?" he suddenly asked, aware that he was no longer so painfully moved by the blue dress. If only I can get her to swim, I believe I'll manage to ask her on the way home after all! he thought.

"Actors," answered Marjorie at once, and colour came into her face. She looked away from him at the floodlit water. "I've often thought I could fall in love with a really great actor."

"Haven't you ever been in love?"

She shook her head.

"Only with acting."

"But you're so lovely! You're like a still moonlit night, so calm and cool. I should have thought——"

She gave him the first glance of true interest.

"What a charming thing to say. No, I've never fallen for any-one. I've got heaps of boy friends—and they really are friends, too ; I get on better with men than I do with women. But love——" and she shook her head.

This information did not cheer Eric as much as it might have. Firstly, he was not sure that he believed it ; secondly, if it were true, it was more than merely strange that so exquisite a creature had never loved : to a warm nature like his own it was definitely putting-off. And whereas five years ago he might have been fired by the thought that *his* was the opportunity to awaken the sleeping beauty, now he only thought that where doubtless better men had failed, why should he succeed?

So the conversation languished again. Brian and Mrs. Cun-ningham got up from their table and went away through the shadows, looking discontented and bored, towards the Barn where presumably they were going to dance, and Marjorie finished her cigarette and suggested that they should swim.

Eric's hopes revived and he agreed rather eagerly. Perhaps if he could see her without that dress he would again feel in the proper mood for making an improper proposal.

But whether it was the distance of the stars at which they glanced up while they were swimming, or the chill of the water, or her looking so much younger in a swim-suit, or the discovery that she swam rather better than he did—his mood when they came out of the water was still hopelessly depressed and hope-lessly friendly. It's like being out with one of the choir boys, only much more expensive, he thought, as he rejoined her at their table.

It's all that accursed dress.

For two pins I'd tell her about it, and why I've been so hopeless this evening.

Poor little thing, it's a shame she should have her evening spoiled because I'm a fool.

Not that she was looking forward to it much, I expect.

This will have finished me with her, anyway.

CHAPTER XVIII

IT was now after midnight, and the revels were at their height. People sat at the little tables, talking with their heads very close together, and in the Barn quite eight couples were slowly gliding up and down with their cheeks touching. Eric found that his cool fit persisted in spite of holding her in his arms as they danced; nor was his pleasure increased by the knowledge that this evening was going to cost him about three pounds ten.

Marjorie was no longer annoyed or even bored; she now felt a pitying interest in one who could be so abysmally, so unbelievably, wet. It's like visiting an asylum or a prison, she thought, going slowly in his nervous clasp across the shining floor, under the massive rafters and their splendid shadows. You feel you must *do* something about it.

Now what's he going to be like in the car on the way home? Thank god, he's driving, anyway. Suddenly she felt that she could bear no more.

"I'm sorry to break up the party," she said cheerfully, as they sat at a table having a drink between dances, "but I do really feel I ought to be getting some sleep. I've got to rehearse to-morrow. Would you mind awfully if we went?"

"Of course not," he said at once, going red. "May I—shall we have just one more dance, though?"

"Heaven," she said, getting up and giving him a really kind smile because she was so glad to be going home.

Round and round they went again. The snowy whitewashed walls towered above them and the huge rafters echoed with another sad sexy tune: a few grains of wheat were still hidden here and there in their crevices.

I wouldn't be surprised if a murder *had* been done here, thought Marjorie. Festive joint. *Mem:* Never come here again unless well canned,

Eric did not say one word. He was working himself up for the journey home. Never mind if he *didn't* want her any more; never mind if she *was* obviously a good girl who would probably hit him; never mind if he *did* feel she was a friendly human being to whom he could pour out all the evening's miseries and be understood; never mind all that. *He was sick and tired of being let down by women, and he was going to ask her.*

So ten minutes later they walked out of the Red Barn to the car, standing in the yard in the faint light of a moon in its last quarter, which even in early summer is not a soft or amorous radiance, suggesting rather gibbets, ruined castles, and witches' sabbaths. The sign painted with a girl being strangled by a man swung slowly to and fro in the wind. I wonder it doesn't creak, thought Marjorie, patiently waiting with a little white Neo-Victorian shawl round her head while he manœuvred with the car, and of course there *would* be a moon like that. It was all that was wanted.

Up came the car, and there was Eric with a face almost as white as his muffler. She got in while he held the door open and he carefully arranged a light rug over her. Still without a word! and it occurred to Marjorie that, in spite of the terribly amusing sign, girls had been murdered by young men before now.

The car moved off. A long grey lane, deserted in the faint moonlight, stretched before them with dark hedges on either hand. The air smelled of chilliness and dew.

Marjorie was perfectly cheerful again and quite in command of the situation. A glance at his face had showed her that he was more likely to burst into tears than murder her. Poor flab, she thought kindly, it'll be a grand chance to give him some advice. Unless someone does, he'll only go on getting into mess after mess. He's as bad as Pauli. *Why* can't people *manage* themselves?

He cleared his throat. He moved his hands nervously over the wheel.

Now for it, thought Marjorie.

Suddenly, without looking at her, he put his hand on the rug covering her knees.

"I—desire you," he said, in a hoarse and entirely unconvincing voice and through his teeth.

"No you don't, darling," she answered cheerfully. "It's sweet of you to say so, though, and I do appreciate it."

"How—what do you mean?" he stammered.

"You don't, you know," nodding friendlily at him. "But I can see you're terribly down and I do wish you'd tell me all about it? Come on, true confession," she went on coaxingly, peering round into his face.

The hand which had been snatched away from her knee as though it had touched a scorpion, was now clenched on the wheel and shaking. She noticed that with surprise; he must be in an awful state of nerves.

After a moment of silence he burst out.

"I know I've been hopeless all the evening. You must have been bored to tears. I'm exceedingly sorry. I—I—appreciate your—your patience very much. The fact is—you'll think me a fool, and

I am—that dress you're wearing is the exact double of one that belonged to—a friend of mine, a girl I knew some years ago. We were very unhappy together and when I saw you in it——"

"I know," she said calmly. "I bought it from her."

"Then it *is* the same one!" he exclaimed, and actually shrank a little away from her.

"Oh yes, but of course it's been cleaned since your day," she said, for she was nothing if not a realist, and probably the poor flab had howled all over it. Such fun for the Eames piece.

"How *could* you wear it when you were coming out with me?" he said violently. "You must have known——"

"My good soul, I didn't know one thing," retorted Marjorie warmly. "I had a vague idea you used to play ball with the Eames, but I never thought about that when I was buying the frock from her. And it looked such heaven when I put it on this evening I just couldn't take it off again, though I did ask Pauli——"

"Oh, you did ask Pauli? And she told you about—us?"

"I asked her if you'd been a friend of Madeleine's and she said yes but it was all washed up ages ago; that was all."

"And knowing that, you still came out with me, wearing that dress?"

"Looks like it, doesn't it?" She was beginning to get irritated. "How was I to know she'd blighted your life to that extent?"

"You must know——" He did not finish the sentence but Marjorie vigorously finished it for him.

"What she's like? Indeed I do. Who doesn't? She's bad medicine, that's what. Whatever made someone like you take up with her I can't think."

"I loved her," he answered proudly, staring unseeingly at the lonely road ahead. His reason might regret the waste of time and the barren ending, but his heart could never honestly regret an experience that had so enriched it: any truthful lover will make the same confession.

"Well, you shouldn't love people like that. They're meant to go to bed with, not love. Look at the waste of time! How long did it last?"

"Oh, about five years," he muttered. "Look here, I——"

"Five years! Think what you could have been doing all that time! Getting on in your job, or learning a language——"

"I learnt two languages," he interrupted her very angrily. "French and Italian. Not perfectly, of course, but——"

"Why, in five years you could have got to be a manager, I should think! Aren't you ambitious? Don't you want to get on?"

"I regard my work as a means, not as an end," he answered stiffly. "Man isn't put here to make money and 'get on'."

"What is he put here for, then?"

"To praise God," he answered at last, after a very long pause.

"Well, if you think you're praising God by loving the Eames witch you must have a mighty queer idea of God!"

"I sometimes think I have," he said wearily.

Marjorie went on loudly and clearly:

"Nothing gets me down more than waste of time and good energy. Almost everybody's the same. Hardly anyone organizes themselves properly. Now I will say that for Brian Kingsley. He knows just what he wants. Money and a good time. All right. So he goes straight where he can get both—Ma Cunningham."

"Merciful heaven!" he said, softly, turning the car round a corner.

"It's not one bit worse than you wasting yourself on the Eames witch!" she cried triumphantly. "Now perhaps you see what I mean!"

But he did not answer. He was remembering something. It was the quietness of the girl who had sat beside him earlier in the evening in the place where Marjorie sat now. He had hardly been aware of her presence except as a softness and a silence and the gentlest imaginable voice; a voice so quiet that it was not possible to think of it as raised in anger or exhortation or using strong ugly words. That's what a girl ought to be like, he thought, while Marjorie's vital soprano beat about his ears with excellent and truthful advice. Silent, and like a flower.

"Of course you're furious with me now," she was saying, "but you'll get over that and I hope we'll be friends. I like you, or I shouldn't have bothered to get on the blower at you about your taste in hags."

"I think it's very kind of you," he answered, observing with relief that they were nearly at her home.

"No, you don't, darling," she said with a return to her usual calm steam-roller manner. "But you'll come round. My males always do."

"Do they?" he said, thinking *I know one who won't.*

"Yes. And you will too. But one last piece of advice I *will* give you: beware of loving in types. And the next time you feel you're falling for a witch, run away! That'll begin to break the spell, and one day you'll find little Eric doesn't fancy witches any more."

The car stopped outside the gate of "Dorna."

"Here we are," he said.

There was a little pause; but Marjorie busily and naturally filled it by disentangling herself from the light rug and struggling with the car's door. He watched her for perhaps four seconds, thinking that for once in his life a woman should have from him the discourtesy she deserved; but it was no use; instinct and habit were too strong for him and he unwrapped her, and then got out of the car and went round and held the door open for her while she got out.

"Good night," she said, holding out her hand to him in the faint moonlight and looking up at him from the folds of the little Victorian shawl. The pavement was dark with dew and along the silent streets came the soft fall and wash of the sea.

"Good night," he said, taking her hand quickly and letting it go.

"Aren't you going to say something charming?" she teased, very confident in the power of her beauty, quite unmoved by their quarrel.

He did not reply for a moment. Then he said:

"I'm sorry it's been such a dreadful evening for you. I think you meant what you said kindly. Good night," and he turned away.

"Gosh!" breathed Marjorie, gazing after him, "you do hate my guts, don't you!"

He did not look back as he drove off.

CHAPTER XIX

" I RATHER wish you were sitting outside this café with Georges and Nina and me, dear Nut Brown Maid," said the postcard of the Eiffel Tower that Pauline was reading at breakfast on a Sunday morning some weeks later. "Last night I had bowlsful of heavenly lobster and hock, and God, did I feel sick afterwards, but it was worth it. Everything is, I find. How are all your clean limbs?

"A toi,
                "E."

"You've got one, too, haven't you?" she said, laughing and handing the card to Marjorie.

Marjorie nodded, looking a little cross. Her card was an extremely vulgar one, inscribed on its back with the single word:

SUCKS.

"What does he mean? What a very rude thing to do!" exclaimed Mrs. Williams, who had got possession of both cards and was now looking from one to the other through her pink-rimmed spectacles. "I must say I'm surprised at Ted. He's always been very queer and eccentric and clumsy, of course, really one sometimes wondered if he was quite right in the head, poor lad, but at least I thought he was *a gentleman*."

Marjorie said nothing but went on eating her grapefruit. She had a call for ten o'clock this morning or she would not have been down so early. The little cross look had gone. She was just realizing, in the calm, honest way that she had turned by practice into a habit, that in the last six months she had seriously angered two young men and had been cooled off by a third.

It won't do, she thought. My technique's slipping up or something.

Ted and Eric and Brian don't matter as men, of course. They're just good to practise on. But they're pointers, too. I don't want to be one of those women men don't really like.

When I've got through this big part this week I must think out what's gone wrong.

"Who are Georges and Nina?" pursued Mrs. Williams.

"People he's picked up there, I expect. His French will come in very useful," said Pauline. She was wearing her shabby riding clothes, having put by enough money this week for one of her rare and delightful Sunday rides.

"I didn't know he spoke any French." Mrs. Williams's tone was resentful; she liked to know every detail about her acquaintances.

"Oh yes, he speaks it fluently; Louise has always talked it with him ever since he was tiny."

Her mother said nothing.

"She is half French, of course," went on Pauline. "I wonder how they're getting on over there without him? I ought really to pop in and see Mr. Early some time. I think I'll go in on my way back this morning."

"It must be six years since I've set foot in that house," declared Mrs. Williams, making a shuddery face. "It was bad enough then; so dusty and untidy. Heaven only knows what it's like now."

"Oh, it's not so bad." Pauline got up, and pushed her chair back against the wall. "I like the old Rich House, don't you, Marjie?"

"I'd almost forgotten its existence." Marjorie did not look up from Mr. James Agate's column in the *Sunday Times*. "What's the point of going over there anyway? Now if the old man gave amusing parties it might be useful. As it is it doesn't get you anywhere."

"I don't want to get anywhere," said Pauline, and went out hatless into the sunny street; she suddenly thought that a little masculine society would make a pleasant change from the atmosphere of her home.

Women are always grizzling, she thought vaguely as she walked along in the Sunday morning hush. What's the matter with Mother and Marjie, anyway? They're always wanting things to be different. Either it's too hot or too cold or the food's not quite right or someone's behaving peculiarly. They really are a bit sickening. Why can't they just enjoy things?

Ted does sound as if he's having a heavenly time. Lucky blighter!

I rather like being called Nut Brown Maid. It's pretty.

That card he sent to Marjie must mean he's got over being crazy about her. And Eric looked awfully sour when I asked him how they'd enjoyed the Red Barn and didn't say a word, and when I asked her she just laughed and said he was all of a dither because of that Eames frock she wore. It looks as though old Marjie's man-managing has misfired for once! thought Pauline with a little sisterly malice. Serves her right; she ought to be sweet to my old Eric and my old Ted; they're both lambs, really.

"Hullo, beautiful," said a young man softly, and she turned quickly, with the thrill that always came to her at the sound of Brian's voice.

"Hullo!" she said, and her brown face, her eyes, her mouth, her very curls, seemed to dance with delight as she looked up at him.

"Where are you off to? Horse-riding?" he went on, looking at her with more approval than usual because of her riding clothes; if anyone he knew saw them together it might be supposed that she was rich and sporting. At a distance her worn breeches and coat looked elegant; her boots (he glanced critically down at them) were good even at a near view.

"Yachting," she corrected, and they both laughed. He was dressed for tennis and the white clothes became his good looks.

"Where are you going? The Club?" she went on.

He nodded. "You going to the stables? Let's go along together, shall we?"

She nodded, happily. *With all my heart*, as Ted would say, she thought. And then she thought how Ted would also say, if he could see them at this moment walking along in their riding and tennis clothes, that they looked like a snob-advertisement in *The Tatler*, and she nearly laughed, but not quite because she thought Brian might not like it.

He was looking down steadily at her, and presently she felt the pressure of his look and glanced up—to meet such an intent and desirous gaze that she at once looked away again, overcome by alarming yet delightful feelings.

"You look utterly charming in those things," he said in a low tone. "It's a pity we're both booked up this morning.; I'd like to take you away to a place I know out beyond Happy Sands and kiss you all ——"

She scarcely heard the last word but there was no mistaking what it was. She did not answer. The strength of her own emotion almost prevented her from seeing, let alone speaking. But mingled with her delight there was fear, and her strongest thought was *I mustn't go*.

"Would you like to come?" he went on.

She almost shut her eyes and lifted her head a little, half in an effort to regain control of her feelings and half in an unconscious longing to feel more fully the warmth and light of the sunshine pouring down from the deep blue sky, as if its heat and beauty were saying all the words she had never been able to say to Brian.

"You will come one day soon, won't you—darling?" He glanced quickly round the deserted street, then slipped his warm hand into hers and swung it gently. "There's a lovely quiet place out there——"

"Where we went before?" she murmured.

He shook his head.

"No. Another place, where we can be quite alone. I often go there. Just you and I, Pauline, alone, without any false shame or any of these horrible clothes that prevent me from seeing how beautiful you are. Just you and I, alone in the sunlight, naked."

Again he almost murmured the concluding words but she heard them as if he had shouted them.

"Darling, it doesn't shock your funny little mind to know I'm a nudist, does it?"

She shook her head. But in fact she was distinctly shocked; so shocked that her delight and fear had both vanished. It was not that she thought about the human body with shame; it was just that she hardly ever thought about it at all except as something to be kept exercised and which experienced strong delight when she was on the back of a horse or skilfully struggling at tennis or swimming in a lively sea. She was neither modest nor vain. Sometimes she looked at herself in the glass with nothing on and thought: the old bod isn't so bad as bods go, but her thoughts got no further than that.

No, the shock came from the fact that she had always regarded nudists as funny. And here was Brian, her troublesome and unsatisfactory but adored Brian, self-revealed as a *Daily Mirror* joke! Ted's enquiry on the postcard about all her clean limbs came back to her with doubled force, and this time she actually did the unforgivable thing: out of sheer nervousness and confusion she giggled.

Brian dropped her hand at once.

"I'm rather surprised that you should take my confidence like that," he said gravely, and as he spoke it seemed to her that a cloud went over the brilliant sun while the calling of the bells sounded mournful and full of warning. "I'm afraid you're rather inhibited, too; I thought you were broadminded and modern or else I should never have told you."

"I—I am," she stammered. "Only—I suppose it was silly—but I've always thought about nudists as a sort of joke."

"The human body is not a joke," he said austerely. "It's very beautiful. It's only all this false shame that makes some people laugh at nudism. False shame and envy. In their heart of hearts everybody would like to have our courage and fling off all their clothes. It's the natural thing to do."

But this was too much for Pauline.

"Well, I don't think it is," she said sturdily. "I'm quite sure I don't want to fling off all mine."

"Are you quite sure? Didn't you feel a longing to fling them all off—just now?" he asked, in a softer tone and bending a little towards her.

She shook her head. I felt a longing for you to kiss me, that's all, she thought, but then I always feel that. And I'm darned if I'm going to tell you so.

"Why do nudists always 'fling' off their clothes?" she said, smiling saucily up at him with her control of herself restored. "Why can't they just take them off like everyone else and put them quietly on a chair?"

He shook his head.

"You aren't in the mood to-day," he said quietly and sadly. "I wish I hadn't told you. But one day you'll—understand."

Oh go and fry! thought Pauline, for the first time since she had known him experiencing a violent wave of irritation unaccompanied by any softer feelings. Thank goodness here we are at the stables.

Something appeared to be going on in the stables. A very large pair of hindquarters the colour of a black plum was plunging about in an attempt to avoid being saddled.

"There, there, steady, Satan," said the groom absently, taking no notice of these goings-on.

6

"Oh good, am I going to have Satan?" asked Pauline, going forward into the yard with widely opened eyes and a smile of pleasure. "Good morning, Harris." ·

"Good morning, miss. Give over, Satan, will you."

"He's lively this morning, isn't he?"

"He's always lively. Gets livelier as he gets older," said Harris resignedly. "But a lot o' what he does is put on, mind you. Showing-orf, like, just to give the stable a name for lively horses."

Satan was now saddled, and standing quite still with his ears back and his beautiful eyes rolling.

Brian lingered for a moment at the gate of the little yard, watching. Pauline neatly mounted (to her relief and in spite of her nervousness because he was watching she did it in one spring) and settled herself in the saddle.

Looking at her, Brian thought he would really rather see her in riding kit than stripped. On the back of the big plum-coloured horse, with her brown hair shining in the sun and her pretty mouth smiling at him teasingly, she looked the very spirit of expensive sporting England, with a background of country houses, hunting, racing, bespoke shoes, and gloves at twenty-five shillings a pair. And Brian admired a rich girl on a horse more than anything, far more than he did a rich girl in a car or a rich girl in a theatre box. Advertisements of rich girls on horseback immediately commanded his respectful attention; he would linger over them for a long time. It was true that Pauline was not a rich girl but on horseback she looked like one.

If only Eve were twenty years younger and looked like that, he thought wistfully.

As for Pauline, as soon as she got on Satan's back she felt superior to everyone, as a rider always does. Him and his nudism! she thought, smiling down at him as he stood looking seriously up at her.

"Can I take him along the sands, Harris?"

"So long as you don't 'ave 'im down there after twelve o'clock miss. You know the rule."

"All right. It's only half past ten now. Good-bye, Brian. Have a nice tennis," and she very gently touched Satan with her heels and moved the reins so that he knew she wanted him to go out of the yard into the street.

Handsome horse and pretty rider went past Brian without another look, except that Satan (good for you, Satan! thought Pauline) went p-r-r-r-r! through his lips as though to blow the young man away.

"Got a good seat, Miss Williams 'as," said Harris, lounging to the gate with a straw in his mouth to watch them go down the road towards the sparkling sea. "Up to all 'is tricks, too. There isn't many ladies could manage 'im, but she can."

"Hope so, I'm sure," said Brian, feeling jealous of Pauline riding off so cool and free into the lovely summer morning. "I shouldn't care to tackle him myself."

"I daresay not, sir. Good morning," answered Harris indifferently, and unmistakably shut the gate. He was adequately paid for work that he liked, and there was no need for him to lick anyone's boots.

Brian went sulkily on his way; but presently began to console himself by thinking of the colour, the dreamy pleasure, that had rushed into Pauline's face. She'll come, he thought. I've only got to keep on at her, and she'll come.

Satan's hoofs sank into the sand, still marked by ripples from the early morning tide, and at once the hard noise that had been in Pauline's ears while she was riding on the road was replaced by a soft exciting muffled sound that made her think of desperate last-minute rescues and adventures.

There were not many people about. The good ones were at church and the bad ones were not up yet. A little old man was wandering by himself among some rocks, watching the crabs, and a fat woman was sitting with her back against the sea wall, reading; but no one else was in sight. Pauline sighed with happiness and put Satan into a canter.

It was delicious! The cool air poured against her face, already warmed by the sun; she felt the enormous strength of the horse beneath her putting itself forth in a wonderfully easy movement, so light! so effortless! There were his strange long purple neck, decorated with a frill of stiff dark hair like a spine, and his ears through which the sunlight shone, making them transparent and red; seen from the saddle, Satan looked as fantastic as a creature out of the deepest seas.

Horses are really queer-looking objects, thought Pauline dreamily, moving swiftly along through the fresh salt air. It's only because one's so used to them that they seem ordinary.

She was enjoying the ride so much that as yet she did not fully realize what Brian had said to her. She was still trying not to feel amused. That was what Ted meant, of course, that time when we were talking about bathing suits, she thought. Poor sweet, it's a shame to laugh at him, he takes it so seriously. How he *can!*

But suddenly, as if his voice were speaking in her ear, she remembered exactly the words he had said to her, and she was immediately so overcome by her former violent emotions that even there, in the pure air and the delight of rapid movement, her cheeks burned and she almost forgot where she was.

It was not that her modesty was offended, nor was she angry because he had assumed that she was a girl to whom such things could be said. Her present pain was because she felt, confusedly and miserably, that his feeling for her was so different, so very different, from hers for him!

And she was also extremely hurt because he had hinted that she was not broadminded and modern. It was awful to be inhibited and out of date; why, it was really an insult, to call a person inhibited.

Satan, encouraged by the increasing looseness of the reins and the absence of any pressure from his rider's heels, now turned his head and took a look at the sea. Presently he began to ease his way towards it. There it was, glistening with millions of silver sparkles from the sun, its waves spreading in thin sheets of delicate white foam over the smooth sands, its soft, regular, rushing sound coming enticingly through the almost breezeless air together with a pleasing smell of seaweed and fish. Satan did a sudden little dance, blew p-r-r-r-r! again, flung up his head, and suddenly did a sideways dash right up to the waves.

"Hey! Come up! Woa!" said Pauline, aroused and hastily shortening rein, and then saw to her alarm that she was almost riding down a hatless girl in a white coat who was walking stumblingly along with her back to horse and rider at the edge of the waves.

"Hi!" she shouted. "Look out!"

The girl started aside and one of her white shoes went into the foam. She turned quickly, staring up at Pauline as if but half awake, and Pauline saw that she was That Rather Pretty Fair Girl who used to be at Just's.

"Oh—oh——" she gasped, stepping backwards again so that her other shoe went into the foam. "I didn't see you!"

"I'm *frightfully* sorry," said Pauline, pulling Satan to a standstill. "I was half asleep and he thought he'd go off on his own; he does sometimes. I say, your shoes are wet! I *am* sorry."

"It doesn't matter," the other girl said.

She stood looking up at Pauline. Her fair hair glittered in the light as if it had a halo round it and her arms hung limply. Pauline thought she did not realize that she knew the person she was talking to; she looked so queer and exhausted and her face was as white as the foam spreading itself at her feet.

"Isn't it a heavenly day!" Pauline said, after the silence between them had lasted for long enough to make her sure that something was very wrong with the Rather Pretty Fair Girl.

Mavis shook her head as if she could not hear, but still stood there staring until Satan, bored, went p-r-r-r! tossing his head so that his bridle and bit jingled romantically.

"He wants to get on," laughed Pauline, feeling really uneasy about the poor little white-faced thing but not knowing quite what to do. "I say," she went on, leaning forward slightly and patting Satan's neck, "(Quiet, Satan) you mustn't mind my saying so but you *do* look tired."

Mavis made one or two movements with her lips before she answered and when the answer came it was so quiet that Pauline had to bend forward a little more to hear it at all.

"I'm all right, thank you," she said in a hoarse faint voice.

"Good. You didn't mind my asking, did you?"

Even two months ago she would have used to Mavis the kind-but-firm voice that she used for talking to her mother's maids, but in the last few weeks, since the fine weather came in and she had been increasingly troubled about Brian, she had stopped using it. She was sometimes so unhappy herself that she had taken to wondering if other people were unhappy too, and had decided that a good many of them were. And so her voice, from being the voice of a self-confident young middle-class woman used to dealing with inferiors, had gradually become the voice of a naturally kind girl who was really interested in other people.

But this new charm, unsuspected by Pauline herself, did not work on Mavis. She only shook her head and turned and began to walk uncertainly away; and Pauline, after watching her for a moment or two, decided that she could do nothing more, and turned Satan round and set him into a gallop on his way to the open country.

Old Dunfee looked up from his observations of the crabs as she dashed past, with her brown curls flying and her chin held up so gallantly. Pretty as a pitcher, thought old Dunfee approvingly, and better for 'er, too, than settin' about under that there fig tree with 'im, like she was this time last year. Do 'er a world o' good, that will. Pity Young Smartyface can't see 'er. Just as well, though. Only put Ideas into 'is 'ead. Oh well, time I was gettin' back to that 'Ole, I s'pose.

He went slowly back over the sands, past a much trodden patch where Those Beach Dogs were playing their primitive games. Their leader, the big black dog, left his rude companions for a moment to bump his sandy nose against the knees of the old man's baggy trousers. Dunfee never failed to stop and throw a stick into the sea for him, and he was the only person in all Seagate who troubled to give the black dog a name. It was not original; it was Blackie; but the black dog liked to hear it, and Dunfee was the only human being for whom he cared a hang.

"Pore old Blackie," said Dunfee, hurling a stick as far as his feeble arm could send, " 'ow'd you like to come and live along o' me at Nunby, eh? Nunby—that 'ud be the ticket! Just you and me in a cosy little room of our own—bit o' garden, read the *Mirror* all through, every mornin' at breakfast. 'Ow'd you like that, eh, Blackie?"

Blackie, however, was already down at the sea's edge dragging he stick out of the foam where the old man's cast had landed it.

Just as well 'e can't 'ear me, p'raps, reflected Dunfee, overtaken by a more sober mood. 'E'd be a bit large in one o' them rooms at Nunby. All over sand, too. Cost a good bit to feed. Better not say anything more about it, p'raps. Course, 'e can't under-, stand like a 'uman being can (no, no, Blackie, no more sticks to-day, got to go 'ome) but I don't like the idea o' disappointin' 'im. Goo'-bye, Blackie. See yer next Sunday.

He went slowly up the slope between the ornamental banks planted with flowering shrubs towards the hotel. A stone bridge crossed this slope, joining the West Parade to the East Parade.

Dunfee could remember The Slope forty years ago when it had been the natural approach from the growing little town that still lived by fishing to the sea. In those days little shops had lined The Slope on either side; treasure houses for the children who visited the place in the summer. There were big black lobsters for sale in the steamy windows, and boxes looking as if they came out of a merman's house, covered with dark blue shells and white fluted shells and little round rosy shells, with a border of tiny yellow shells around their lids. In those shops the children had been able to buy hoops, and white sand-shoes; spades and pails and sticks of bright pink rock with *A Present from Seagate* running magically all the way through them; and pints of rusty shrimps and villainous-looking winkles that could be taken home for the landlady to scald and serve up for tea. There were neck-laces too, of pointed pearly shells for little girls to buy. In those days Tom Gregson and his brother Joe, with Ben Bloomfield and Walt Attkins, had stood at the pierhead in their big blue jerseys in fine weather, when they were not fishing, waiting to take the children for a sail in the *Seagate Belle* or a row in the *Gipsy Girl*; and every dawn a fleet of fishing boats with wallflower sails had glided in as silently as sea ghosts, sunk low in the waves with their load of twitching blue and silver fish. Yes, it used to be a fine place, Seagate, forty years ago. Nowadays it's a fine place, too, of course; so clean and cheerful and all those dirty noisy little shops done away with; and Joe and Tom and Ben and Walt and the fishing fleet have gone, too. But perhaps the children still enjoy themselves there as much as their mothers and fathers did forty years ago: perhaps enchantment, like beauty, is only in the eye of the beholder.

CHAPTER XX

WHEN Mavis had been gone for some twenty minutes, Reenie (who was the fat one sitting against the sea wall) looked up from her book.

Yes, Mavis was still in sight, walking along by the waves in the direction of Happy Sands.

Must be walking very slowly, thought Reenie. Fair crawling. Feels bad, I reckon. Oh well, I done my best. Can't do more for a person than have a row with your own Mum about them and give them your breakfast. She'll come back when she feels like it.

After a contented survey of the sea she returned to her book.

It was a large *Social and Economic History of New Zealand*, full of facts and statistics and illustrated by double-page maps and photographs of cheerful Maoris with very little on. She had obtained it from the Public Library with the assistance of Mr. Cousins, who after some badinage had vouched for her general respectability and fitness to have it and any other books she might want.

After seeing all those places on the British Empire map she had felt a strong wish—kind of a longing it was really—to know more about them. Not tales, I don't want to read, she decided. Stuff you up with a lot of lies, tales do. Histories is what I want, I s'pose.

But my goodness, histories weren't half dry! The pictures were all right; she studied them carefully and was interested to see that the Maoris at the end of the book (after the white men had been at them) had a few more clothes on while looking as cheerful as ever; but it was all the maps and figures that got her down. Couldn't seem to make sense of them, somehow.

I daresay there's other books not so dry, she thought. There's enough books in that liberry, goodness knows, but I haven't got

anyone to tell me which ones to go for. Nuisance, that's what it
is. Make a nice way of passing the time for me (always did hate
knitting) learning about the British Empire, if only there was
someone to start me off right.

Goodness, Mum wasn't half wild with her this morning! Downright nasty to me, too. Fair gives me the sick, Mum does, when
she creates like that. Doesn't say much, but she makes you want
to run out of the place and never come back.

No. What I'd really like, best of all (and suddenly the *Social
and Economic History of New Zealand* fell forward on to Reenie's
lap and her round gooseberry eyes grew wider with excitement at
an entirely new thought as she stared out over the vast broken blue
surface of the sea), what I'd like best of all is to go there. See all
those places for myself.

They're all there. Only the sea (this sea, really, 'cos the sea is
all joined on) between me and those places. I wouldn't mind getting away from Mum, neither, when she goes on like she did this
morning.

The memory so disturbed her usual cheerfulness that she got
up and walked down to the edge of the waves and stood there for
quite a while, staring out across the rising and falling dark blue
water, feeling the wind on her face and neck and hearing the soft
rushing of the waves. Lovely day, thought Reenie.

Go there. See all those places with my own eyes.

Mavis walked slowly and stumblingly on. Her shoes were wet
at first but they began to dry quickly in the hot sun and presently
she did not notice any chill.

It was difficult to walk quickly while the sunlight poured on her
head and made it so muddled and hot. Presently, as she plodded
on, she slowly felt in her pocket and found a crumpled scarf that
she tied round her hair. She also took off her white blanket coat
and carried it over her arm; the one that was exposed to the sun
slowly became speckled with red and then began to sting but she
did not notice.

It was a fortnight since she had been sacked from Beard's.
They had told her she was slow and not the type for the job anyway and given her a week's salary and turned her off then and
there.

For a fortnight she had gone off in the mornings as usual with
her case and white net gloves in one hand; and for a fortnight she
had spent the day sitting on the beach or in the Sunken Gardens
until it was time to go home and pretend to Reenie and Mrs. Voles
that she had been at work all day.

Sometimes she had gone into St. Anne's and stayed up in the choir gallery for an hour or more, staring at the broad rays of green and purple and crimson light pouring through the St. Anne window; sometimes praying that she might find another job soon, sometimes confusedly remembering the sound of Mr. Somers's voice singing and how the sunlight falling through the high windows would light up his face.

At twelve o'clock, when there was less likely to be anyone in the shop who would recognize her, she went into a dirty little dairy in one of the back streets and drank a glass of milk and ate a ham roll. In the evening she had tea and bread and butter with the remains of a jar of meat paste. She was not conscious of being hungry because she felt strange all the time, like a person moving about behind a sheet of glass; and as the days went on she did not worry any more about looking for a job but only wanted to keep Mrs. Voles and Reenie from knowing she was out of work.

She went into Just's on the day after she was sacked, in the timid hope that they might take her on again, even at a much smaller salary; but Just's was in the miserable condition of all old-fashioned and contented firms when a new proprietor takes over, and although everybody was sympathetic, everybody was also worried, uncertain of their own jobs, and quite sure that there was no job for Mavis.

She had not liked to go to the Vicar of St. Anne's for help because she had the morbid fancy (nourished by her natural sensitiveness and by an unconscious longing to find some explanation for her seemingly causeless sufferings) that it was she who had caused Mr. Just's death.

It's all my own fault, she thought, lying awake night after night in the summer darkness because she could not sleep for hunger, and staring at the dim ceiling. I had a good job and I was so happy, and then I let the door blow open because I was staring at Mr. Somers and that was the start of it all.

I'd be ashamed to ask anyone for help because it's all my own fault.

The dreamlike, wretched days and nights went on, and became all alike, as they do to people who are very unhappy. She remembered words that she had heard in church:

In the morning thou shalt say, Would God it were even! and at even thou shalt say, Would God it were morning!

Her small savings in the Post Office had been used up weeks ago because she had been forced to supplement her salary from

6*

Beard's; and the payments due on her furniture, already some weeks in default, were a nightmare to her. Plans and ways and means revolved in her exhausted brain until they were no longer clear thoughts but a mass of painful hauntings, themselves a part of her helplessness and fear.

And then one Friday evening a man from the Cosyhome Furnishing Company had called to see her. He was an elderly man in a grey suit and very nice, really. He sat in her little blue fireside chair and listened in silence while she slowly told him, staring at the floor and trying to speak clearly, and not show how tired she was, exactly what had happened.

He quite understood. He said that kind of thing often happened these days to people when jobs were so hard to get and there was so much competition. He said it wasn't her fault and he was sorry. But he also pointed out that the Company had twice written to her reminding her that payment was in arrears, and that each time she had asked for more time to pay she had been given it. He said that the Company had to make certain rules to protect itself and those rules had to be kept and that to-morrow afternoon a plain van would have to come and take her furniture away.

She said in a whisper, would he please tell the Company how very sorry she was. But the whisper was so soft and her head was sunk so low that he never heard; he only looked back at her as he went out of the door and said "Good night"; and then he hesitated and then he came back and gave her two little pats on her shoulder, very quickly, as if he were afraid her shoulder would burn him; and then he went hurriedly down the stairs and slammed Mrs. Voles's front door.

Of course this visit did not pass unnoticed by Mrs. Voles and Reenie, though it was not referred to until the next day.

The next day—oh, the next day. In the late afternoon, just when the street was crowded with everyone out doing their Saturday shopping and the London trains had brought the week-end crowds of visitors to all the boarding houses in Lavender Road, a plain van stopped outside Number Seventy-Eight, and presently down the front garden came Mavis's little blue fireside chair and the rug with the modernist-but-recognizable roses, and the chest of drawers and finally the roll of linoleum that was the colour of the sea. One by one the plain van swallowed them up, and drove away. And Mavis was left alone with her divan bed, and two suitcases and the letter that had come by the afternoon post.

That was a wonderful bit of luck him giving you that ride home the other night wasn't it? I thought you both looked so happy. Lucky girl, happy boy, as the song says. When shall we hear wedding bells.

She read it through almost without feeling (she was past feeling except for this growing longing to get away somewhere and be by herself) and put it with the others in her suitcase. Then she lay down on her bed and put her face in the pillow.

By what can only have been a special Act of Intervention, Mrs. Voles and Reenie were out when the plain van arrived, having gone with a neighbour to the pictures to see Rosalind Russell in "His Girl Friday"; and they did not return until nearly ten o'clock. Mavis's door was shut and her room dark and silent. If they thought about her at all they supposed she was asleep.

But needless to say there was the usual Ain't-It-Awful-Annie ready to rush round first thing in the morning and break the bad news. In this case it was the old woman next door, who dramatically delivered her communiqué while Reenie was taking in the milk.

So Mavis, slowly lifting her dazed head from the pillow about nine o'clock the next morning as the door gently opened, was confronted by Mrs. Voles and Reenie, standing side by side and staring first at her and then slowly round the empty room. Reenie looked amazed and then shocked and sympathetic; Mrs. Voles's face was expressionless but redder than usual and her lips were sucked in.

Mavis said nothing. She had got thinner in the last weeks, and now she lay quietly on her side, looking like a child in her fresh shabby nightgown and staring at them with an exhausted expression in her blue eyes.

"Why, Mavis, what on earth's the matter? Have they taken your furniture?" exclaimed Reenie at last, as neither her mother nor Mavis said a word.

Mavis nodded.

"Nice disgrace, this is," said Mrs. Voles in her deep voice. She did not sound very angry. "That man who was here on Friday night"—actually it had been Friday evening but Mrs. Voles made it sound like the small hours—"did he come about the furniture? Or was he a friend of yours?"

Reenie glanced uneasily at her mother. That wasn't a nice way to talk to someone who was down on their luck, barmy though they might be.

Again Mavis nodded, and slowly pulled the coverlet up to her chin.

"What happened? Did you get the sack?" pursued Mrs. Voles. Her tone was no louder than usual but the natural hardness of her voice struck on the quietness in the room like something hitting at Mavis. Reenie began to feel worse and worse. Why couldn't Mum give over?

Mavis nodded.

"Is that why you haven't paid your rent this week?"

Mavis swallowed.

"I was going to tell you about it this morning——" she began.

"So I should bloody well hope," struck in Mrs. Voles. "There's been quite enough going on here I haven't been told about." Still her voice did not sound honestly angry. It was only hard; harder and harder, like a maddening hammer going. "Reen," she went on without turning her head, "go down and see to the bacon, will you, it'll be burning." (The delicious smell was now coming up from the kitchen.)

"It's all right, Mum, I put it on over ever such a low gas," said Reenie impatiently. "Look here, Mavis," she went on, feeling a desire to make up for the way Mum was going on and suddenly realizing from the look of her that Mavis was half-starved, "I'd better bring you up a rasher, hadn't I? You look as if you could do with it."

"She won't want to take charity and I'm not going to give it," said Mrs. Voles, never taking her eyes off Mavis.

Mavis was just going to refuse gratefully when suddenly the unexpected kindness and the effects of a fortnight's hunger and misery swept over her and she burst into violent tears.

"Snivelling now," said Mrs. Voles. "You shut your mouth, Reen. If you so much as set foot on the stairs with any bacon of mine, my lady, I'll smack your face."

"I'll give her mine," said Reenie, suddenly getting angry and not feeling a bit frightened of Mum. She went over to the bed and put her arm round Mavis. "Don't cry, you'll make yourself bad. I'll go down and get you a cup of tea and a rasher and then you'll feel better."

She turned, and advanced across the room upon her mother, who stood formidably in the doorway. Mavis was wiping her eyes and so did not see the impact of the irresistible force upon the immovable object; for a moment it looked as if Mrs. Voles would smack her daughter's face; she actually got as far as lifting her • hand, but Reenie bustled past her without taking the smallest notice, and it fell to her side again. After a last stare at Mavis, who was now blowing her nose, she turned and followed Reenie downstairs.

In the kitchen she sat down at the table and opened the *Sunday Pictorial*.

"She'll end up on the streets," she observed, pulling the teapot towards her without looking up from the paper.

"Mum, do give over!" burst out Reenie, stopping at the door with a plate laden with bacon in one hand and a large cup of tea in the other. "You're just like a—like—well, you're not like an English person at all, you're more like one of Hitler's lot. On a Sunday, too!"

"You shut your face. If your father was alive he'd belt the hide off you."

"Just as well he's dead, then," retorted his daughter. "What you'll be like when you're really old I don't know; you get worse every year. Regular old turn-the-milk, you'll be."

"Why don't you get married, then, and get out of it?" jeered Mrs. Voles.

This shaft fell harmlessly; Reenie was not one of those who are always pining and planning to be married, though she somehow (surprisingly, in view of her plain face) always took it for granted that she could if she wanted to.

"I'll get married when it suits me, not before," she pronounced, going upstairs with the plate and cup, "but I might go off and leave you, any day. So put that in your pipe and smoke it."

"Oh shut up!" shouted Mrs. Voles and kicked the kitchen door shut.

Mavis ate the bacon and drank the tea, but after breakfast, while she was dressing to go for a walk with Reenie (who said a blow by the sea would do her good and they could talk over her troubles) she was sick. All the way down to the beach she never said a word or even thanked Reenie for having given her her breakfast; and so by the time they reached the sands Reenie was feeling very hungry (she subsequently took the edge off this with three bananas, a Buzz bar, and a choc-ice) and rather cross with her.

It was Reenie who had finally suggested that Mavis should go for a little walk by herself to cool down like; she, Reenie, would sit here and have a bit of a read until she came back. Then Mavis had said:

"I shan't come back." But of course Reenie had taken no notice of that, because Mavis was all upset and enough to make anybody. And Reenie had settled herself with the *Social and Economic History of New Zealand*, and Mavis had walked slowly, stumblingly, away.

CHAPTER XXI

PRESENTLY she became aware that she was walking among people. Instead of smooth sands under her feet there were large smooth pebbles, grey, brown, dark blue, and white, that rolled as she walked on them, and the soft sound of the waves was mingled with the sharp noise of human voices.

She glanced up: facing the sea was a row of fantastic little cabins extending far into the distance, painted in pale pink or blue or yellow and adorned with wooden traceries over their open doors and verandas, that were crowded with deck-chairs and knitting women and drying bathing costumes. Unmade sandy roads scattered with empty ice-cream cartons and torn sheets of newspaper came down at intervals among the cabins, and along these roads could be seen more elaborately carved and painted chalets, with blue balconies and yellow eaves, named "Linga-Longa" or "Youanmee" or "Herzanmyne." These fantastic names, and the fragility of the little houses, their pale yet brilliant colours and the withered plants dying in the sand of their gardens, gave the pleasure-town a magical and temporary appearance, as if a genie had dropped it there in the night and to-morrow it would be gone. There were a number of shops to be seen, but they sold only food in brightly labelled tins, bread sealed in waxed paper, milk hidden in cardboard flasks. There were no signs of cooking or the solid and ancient rhythm of everyday life. The people who saved up their money to come here for two precious and longed-for weeks out of the year did not want to be reminded of the solid and ancient rhythm of everyday life: they wanted to live for four-teen days in one long, glorious, untidy, indigestible picnic, and that was what they did. The name of the place was Happy Sands.

All along the pebble slopes in deck-chairs sat the older people; enormous Mums in dark dresses printed with small white flowers, fat Dads with walrus moustaches, thin Dads with the *News of the World* spread over their faces, Aunties cackling with sudden laughter at young Derek or our Shirley, Mrs. Whosit from up the road with her little lot who'd joined up with us for the day, like; old Jim and old Perce and Ern and Wally and Stan and the beer; and hundreds of other fifty- and sixty- and seventy-year-old human bodies, lying comfortably back with the sun and the faint salt wind burning their faces; those knobbly English faces that have been affectionately and unflatteringly compared by an American visitor to potatoes. Here were the dear, the well-beloved people of England enjoying themselves and their holyday as they used to do when Chaucer walked among them; enjoying themselves in spite of there being few jobs and no safety nowadays and the fear of another war always hanging over them; enjoying themselves with roars of laughter and jokes about bottoms and babies and feet, and being at the same time so cheerful and kind and completely helpless that the heart almost broke with love as it contemplated them.

Down on the beach the old 'uns were having as good a time as young Derek and our Shirley, darting and screaming in and out of the waves; along the narrow concrete promenade in front of the bungalows the feeling was more elegant. Here the young beauties strolled in twos and threes, wearing thin frocks of artificial silk in brilliant colours and white toeless sandals, their thick shining hair swept up in ornate curls, their nails painted with Sudan or Coral or Copper Rose from Woolworth's; and only their Maker and the people in the Women's Pages of the daily Press who advised them how to get themselves up like this knew how they managed it.

And nearly everybody was eating; choc-ices, or Buzz bars, or bananas, oranges (what's the use of having an Empire if you can't have a banana whenever you fancy one?) or potato crisps, as well as Five-in-Ones, apples, Seagate Rock and Trays of Tea for the Beach. The sun burned down, white and grey gulls flashed and turned above, and dancing music from dozens of wirelesses sounded gaily through the soft monotonous poetry of the waves and the sharp roar of human voices.

Mavis found walking among all these people more and more difficult, and there were so many of them that she began to get confused and frightened. She felt she could not bear the noise for another second; through the steady roar of people talking and laughing and the dancing of the wireless music she was trying to hear the music of the sea, and it was so difficult! She frowned as she stumbled along with a listening look on her white face, One or two people glanced at her and thought, *she does look bad*, but no one said or did anything about her. It was a lovely Sunday and there were enough troubles all the year round without looking for any more.

Suddenly she turned away from the sea, unable to bear the noise and the people any more, and walked away up one of the unmade roads that led into the shallow heart of the town. Beyond the pink and blue bungalows with their doors open to the sunshine she could see green fields; empty, deserted, no one troubling to walk in them. Still listening for the sound of the sea, she plodded on towards them.

Happy Sands ended suddenly. Many years ago a dyke of flints and concrete had been built to keep out the sea that sometimes flooded over into the marshland in the winter, and this wall was the barrier shutting out Happy Sands from the meadows and deserted lanes beyond. The dyke was wide enough to walk on; it looked down into a marshy region immediately below on the other side, and Mavis mounted some steps that led to its summit.

Here there was strange contrast: the restless sea, the distant roar of voices and music, the dirty road and the pale flimsy houses on one side of the broad dyke; and on the other, marshland covered with old buckets, thousands of tins, broken basins, rusty bicycles and prams; and then an expanse of pure marsh covered with the greenest carpet the eye could dream of, and millions of Tom-Thumb white flowers. An old tower looked down over these unreclaimed meadows and fields of wheat. It had been built when Napoleon threatened to invade England, and was one of many that stood along this coast.

Mavis looked longingly at the fields of wheat. Suddenly a wind came rushing off them; first they all bowed together one way and became moving gold as the wind walked over them; then the wind smote her lifted face with honeysuckle and convolvulus.

She walked along the wall until she came to some broken steps; then she went down and crossed among the rubbish towards the distant fields.

The sound of the sea died away. Now the old tower stood out against the dyke and the blue sky. It was round, and coloured pale gold and patched with darker gold, as if the wheatfield wind was blowing on it, and the brilliant green marsh crept up to its lowest stones. Gulls were sitting along its ramparts. The strange smell of the marsh now came to Mavis; neither river nor forest nor stream. Another meadow near by was scattered over with pure brilliant little gold flowers, but she was walking on very dark green grass like wire, with dark purple thyme and trembling red sorrel in it; it was gratefully soft to her feet, and the sorrel made her think of the fields at the end of the garden that she and Mum and Dad used to like looking at when she was little.

Now she came to a stile set in a hedge, and climbed over it and found herself in a narrow lane looking on a field of wheat. It was a lonely place. The sea was out of sight and betrayed its presence only by a kind of liveliness and broadness and dazzle in the sky above it; something wonderful must be over there. The wheatfield was the first of many meadows threaded by tiny paths and little lanes with rather low hedges; nothing grew very tall or imposing here because of the strong winds from the sea, but there were the usual summer flowers and the delicious smell of warm grass blowing along in cool air.

She walked over to the wheat and stood looking at it for a little while; then she lay down on the grass, and put her head on her outstretched arm and stared in among the stalks. In a few places there were poppies, dazzlingly red yet delicate among the hot pale shine of the wheat; some of them were turned so that she could see the purple varnish and black trembling things in their hearts. There were a few cornflowers, too, going away in a scattered procession into the wheat stems and not so easy to see as the poppies; blue, cool and fringed, and coming out of a tiny green cushion. Poppy stalks, and heads of wheat, and stems of cornflowers were all covered with tiny hairs, and all the hairs were different. Wonderful things, flowers are, she thought, lying there in the blazing sunlight, quite still except for the slight restless movement of one hand playing with a grass stem; I always did think they were beautiful but I never looked at them properly before.

The hush, the warmth, the faint fragrance of the air, were soothing away her misery and shame and fear, and the relief was so delicious that it was not until she had lain there for a long time, and dozed and awakened more than once, that she began to feel how uncomfortable she was; faint with hunger yet slightly sick, and suffering from a headache and arms painfully burned by the sun.

I must get into the shade, she thought, but she did not move. And I *am* so thirsty. But she did not open her eyes.

Suddenly a cool pleasant sound fully aroused her; and she sat up, realizing that it had been going on for some time, and stared about her.

A Wall's ice-cream man was sitting on his tricycle, staring down at her and ringing his bell.

"Hullo, gorgeous," he said.

Mavis put up her hands and tidied her hair. This movement, and the sight of her face, slightly changed the look on his own. His voice was a little different as he went on:

"Having a bit of a doss, were you? Cor, it's hot to-day, isn't it?"

She nodded. The movement hurt her head and she winced.

"You ought to have a hat on," he said, watching her. He was a thick-set man of about forty. "Give yourself a headache. But you girls are all the same. Never think."

She was feeling in her coat pocket. She was almost sure——

"Feeling bad, are you?" he said suddenly. "What's up? Had a row with your boy friend?"

Yes! It was a sixpence. She brought it out and held it up to him.

"Please may I have a choc-ice and three water-ices?" she said in a hoarse faint voice.

At once he looked sulky, but got off his tricycle and took the ices out of their little cavern.

"S'pose I sit down and watch you eat 'em?" he said as he handed them to her.

She smiled slightly, like a polite child, without looking at him; and slowly peeled the deliciously cold silver paper from the choc-ice. There's a lovely lot of it, she thought, and after that there'll be the three water ices. Surely I couldn't still be thirsty after all that. And she carefully put the three triangular cartons into her pocket so that they should not melt, and bit into the choc-ice.

The man was leaning on his machine, watching her. He said nothing while she was eating the ices. They went down her dry throat in their refreshing yet solid coldness, glacial and tasting faintly of fruit. When she had finished the last one and wiped her fingers on her handkerchief, the man said in a quite new voice:

"You do look bad. If I was you I'd go home. Go home to your mum."

She did not answer nor look at him, but stared into the wheat wishing he would go away and leave her alone.

"What's the matter?" he coaxed, suddenly kneeling beside her and putting his warm dirty hand over hers. "In trouble, are you?"

She nodded, slowly pulling her hand away, and he stood up again.

"Well, if I was you I'd go home to your mum," he said, seeming to remember that he was out on a job, and looking sulky again at the recollection. "Go on, now. There's a good girl. Or I might send a policeman down here to keep an eye on you."

But still she did not answer or look up; so at last he mounted his machine and pedalled slowly away down the lane. Once or twice he looked back, but she did not move, and finally he turned a corner and was gone.

The afternoon moved on towards evening, and no policeman came. When it was about six o'clock and the shadows were beginning to lengthen, Mavis got slowly up and wandered on. She felt cooler now and the headache had gone and she was not worrying about anything any more. These were the fields where she had always dreamt of walking with Mr. Somers, but now she was not even thinking about him: she was only walking slowly down this little lane where the shadows were lengthening and the sound of the hidden sea was coming across the fields, mingled with the bells calling from a church further inland. In the evening light each tiny white yellow, or purple flower in the hedgerow stood up delicate and still, as if it were praising God. How beautiful everything is, she thought. If only I could trust God utterly and never be frightened again.

The lane continued beside wheat and barley and oatfields, and at last, when she had been wandering for nearly an hour, she came to the most beautiful of all: a wide expanse of unmoving gold in the fulness of the sinking sun, with a group of dark elms and oaks standing on its further shore. On the other side she could see sandhills scattered over with patches of coarse sombre grass towards the sea, and thought: I must have come a long way. While she was gazing at the white dunes two figures strolled slowly across them; a dark-haired woman in a dress with bright stripes and a man whose arm was about her waist; they stopped and took a long kiss, then moved on and out of sight.

Mavis was relieved when they had gone. She looked down at her feet: the hedge ended at this large wheatfield, and there was a little space of grass before the wheat began: it was thickly grown with white clover. She kneeled and smelt the clover, then lay down among it and stared up at the cloudless blue sky.

All was quiet! There was no wind. The shadows turned longer and longer and slowly the air cooled a little, but the light of the setting sun was fierce upon the motionless wheat. Mavis turned her head sideways and looked at the clover: the strange sweet little heads stood quite still, hundreds and hundreds of them, in colour neither green nor brown nor white, with little leaves like playing-card symbols, veined with white and as pretty as their flowers. It's queer, she thought, anything as beautiful as that growing so common everywhere and no one notices it except children. We used to pick it on the way home from school.

Presently she got up and moved to a place a little farther on. The grass was softer and thicker here and the clover had longer stems. She wrapped her coat round herself, pillowed her head on her folded scarf, and shut her eyes.

She awoke suddenly. Something had swooped out of the dusk very close to her face with the faintest possible sound of wings—yes—there! She sat up, and saw by the light of the rising moon an owl vanishing over the edge.

Moonlight was rolling up from the hidden sea out of a bank of heavy summer vapour, hot as its light. The air was warm and hushed; every now and then the wheat gave a prolonged faint rustle and then was still.

But there were bat squeaks in the silence, the swish of the owl's wings as he moused over the wheat, a cricket chirruping. She lay and listened to them, hungry and thirsty and frightened. I've never even sat up all night before, she thought, with her heart thumping, and here I am, sleeping out. Because I can't go home now, it's too late and I'm so tired and it 'ud be morning before I got there. I never thought I'd ever sleep out in the fields, I always thought it was an awful thing to do, like those poor girls that go on the lorries. I hope nobody ever finds out about it. Whatever would they say at church!

But gradually, as she lay there in the warm dusk breathing the scent of the clover, she became less frightened. Her heart beat more quietly and the surprising thought came into her head that she didn't care what they did say about it at church; there was no harm in it, she wasn't doing anything wrong. The moon got clear of the cloudbank and floated above the hidden sea, and its light slowly became thin and silvery. Ten o'clock struck from the church over the fields.

Presently she fell into an uneasy doze again, through which she was aware of the hardness of the ground and the crawling and tickling of grasses or tiny insects on her sunburnt arms.

It was long after midnight when she next awoke; there was a hush over everything and the moon was riding clear and high; the wheat stood white as snow in its light and the elms were black. And now (she heard it as she lay there half awake and knew that for a long time she had been hearing it through her dreams) there was another sound coming through the moonlit stillness: coming across the dunes; the soft faraway crash of the waves falling and spreading over the pebble banks; that sound beside which all music is coarse; that sound from which all music yet seems to come.

She lay and listened to it. Although the night was so silent except for this sound, there was no feeling of sleep in the silvered air. Intense and delicate excitement breathed through it, as if the elms, the wheat, the clover, were all awake and as alive as people. It's just as if something's going to happen, she thought.

But nothing happened. As she lay dozing and sometimes dreaming and always hearing the sound of the sea, she thought sleepily that ever since she was a little girl she had believed that something wonderful happened on moonlit nights. The moon would grow brighter and brighter, the silence deeper and deeper, and then—and then—— But nothing's going to happen, she thought. It's only going to be like a rainbow, that gets more and more beautiful while you watch and then suddenly you see it's fading.

And she did not see the moment at which the glory of the night began to fade, because she fell into a real sleep, and only awoke for a few moments in the dawn. She did not lift her head but gazed dreamily about her, and felt for the first time that the world was really sleeping. The bowed wheat had a heavy, exhausted look; as she moved her hand in the clover it was wet with dew, and the elms were no colour, mere blurs against the paling sky, and there was a cool fresh smell in the air.

But the sound of the sea was loud. It came clearly across the white dunes; first the fall of the wave and then the spreading of the foam and then that instant when the musical rushing almost dies into the silence. But always as the rush of the spreading wave thinned towards silence, it was broken into by the soft crash of the succeeding wave. Sometimes the sound so nearly died away that she believed it had, and in that instant, when the sound faded into softest rippling, wonderfully fresh and watery and musical and made up of hundreds of eddies and currents and tiny wayward whirlpools, it seemed to her that she was somewhere away from the world and completely happy.

It was such a lulling sound, that she became sleepy again as she listened; presently her eyes closed and she fell asleep again to the rush and ripple and pause of the waves. Clouds like grey shells lined with red suddenly appeared all over the sky and soon the sound of the sea was pierced by the sweet, wild little screams of birds flying up into the low sunrays.

CHAPTER XXII

MONDAY morning was so fine that Mrs. Somers decided she really would go out to St. Swythin's and finish that sketch of the church.

She made up her mind as soon as she opened her eyes at a quarter to seven, and broke the good news to Mr. Somers, who pretended to be still asleep.

However, by nine o'clock they were on their way to the village among the wheatfields beyond Happy Sands, Mrs. Somers nursing her sketching materials and gazing out of the car window and wondering a little unhappily why Eric had been so subdued lately and if the next anonymous letter would hint at the reason.

Mrs. Somers was a gentler and less self-confident woman than she had been six months ago. The letters had been quietly sapping her, and sometimes it seemed to her that she was always tired and worried and sleeping badly nowadays. Mr. Somers was driving and warning Mrs. Somers at intervals that they must be back in good time as he had to give a lesson at twelve o'clock, and occasionally expressing aloud his wonder at there still being churches open and people anxious to attend them.

For Mr. Somers was one of those atheists whose disbelief in God is livelier than the faith of most believers; he not only disbelieved in God, he actively disliked Him, spoke of Him rather as if He were a disagreeable old man living next door, and regarded all human progress as a series of, so to speak, smacks in the eye for the Almighty. He had what may be called the Booby Trap conception of the universe, in which God is always slyly setting snares and making apple-pie beds for Man, the magnificent hero-artist who sometimes manages to avoid them and get quite a good time in spite of them. Mr. Somers himself had had a very good time, what with his superb digestion, his passion for music and his practice of it, and his happiness with Mrs. Somers; and it is possible that his disbelief in God and his dislike of Him was due, not to thwarted hopes or bitterness, but to his secret belief that there was really no one in Heaven or out of it so sensible, kind, cheerful, wise and good as Mr. Somers.

It now need hardly be said that after much argument little Eric had been brought up as an atheist and had been serenely conscious of the existence and splendour of God almost from the instant he opened his eyes. This was a cause of wonder, rather than grief, to his father; he loved his son too much to protest even when he became a member of the Church.

The church of St. Swythin had some Saxon brickwork embedded in its Norman stones. Within, it was so small, dark and crude as to oppress the imagination and senses with its tremendous antiquity: here, the mind felt, men who were very close to the beasts had worshipped. Such *darkness* lay over all that landscape and time! But if the traveller thought for a moment, the small glimmering light of faith shone more beautiful by the contrast, and a fellowship was felt with those far-off, long-ago men in their squalor and darkness because they too had bowed at the name of Jesus; and the imagination was oppressed no more, but awed.

Mrs. Somers declined to enter the church on the grounds that she had been in there once and it depressed her. She sat on her little stool in the churchyard and finished a pleasing watercolour of the square tower, some deep brown yews with their red berries, and a limpid blue sky, while Mr Somers went in for a few moments and prowled about and then emerged again, observing that it smelt.

By the time he had shaken his head over one or two of the gravestones and given a short laugh or so over the hopes of heaven expressed on others, Mrs. Somers had finished her sketch and packed up her implements and was ready to go.

The fair morning had clouded over. Drops of rain fell on the windows of the car as it moved off.

They were approaching Happy Sands through a heavy downpour when Mrs. Somers exclaimed:

"Do look at that girl! Sitting on the grass in all this rain! She must be mad!"

Mr. Somers glanced up, and saw a little way ahead of the car a girl with fair hair in a white coat crouching rather than sitting in the long grass at the edge of a wheatfield. As they came nearer they saw that her face was buried in her hands.

"She's crying," went on Mrs. Somers, very interested, and turning to look back as the car went past. "Something's the matter. Poor thing! Oh dear, I do wonder—but perhaps——

The girl did not look up as the car went past; they could see that she was rocking herself backwards and forwards. They both stared at her curiously, finding it surprisingly disturbing to see a human being exposed to heavy rain and taking no notice of it.

When the car had gone a little further down the road Mrs. Somers suddenly exclaimed:

"Edwin! Do stop. We must go back. We simply can't leave her there, we must see if we can do anything."

"She's probably a bad lot," he said, feeling the distaste of a man who has been perfectly happy for thirty years at encountering violent grief, destitution and distress. "And I shall be late for Betty Matthews." But he began to back the car.

"Betty Matthews can wait," said his wife decidedly. She turned round in her seat and watched anxiously through the back window while they gradually came on a level with the girl.

She had not moved. Mrs. Somers let down the window, and was leaning out into the rain to call to her, when it suddenly struck her that such a manner of address was condescending and unlikely to comfort one plainly so wretched.

She opened the door, ignoring Mr. Somers's surprised and indignant exclamation, and got out into the rain and walked across the streaming road to the strip of grass. The long clover stems brushed wetly against her ankles.

"My dear," she said, putting her hand on the shoulder of the girl's soaked coat, "what's the matter? Can we help you?"

Mavis looked up, staring wildly. She saw through tears a kind face under a straw hat with raffia flowers on it, and her first, her strongest, feeling was one of deep shame that this kind, gentle, respectable lady should see her sitting out here like a lorry-girl in the streaming rain with no hat on. It seemed years since she had spoken to a human being; for nearly a day and night her only companions had been flowers and the sunlight and moonlight and the sound of the sea, and during that time she had almost forgotten her misfortunes and fears. They had all returned with a rush as the rain began to fall; hunger, exhaustion, bewilderment, had overwhelmed her, and for the first time she had realized what she had been doing and how she must look to her fellow beings. This kind old lady might think she was a bad girl.

"It's very kind of you," she answered, fumbling for her handkerchief and trying to speak as refinedly and prettily as she knew how, "I'm quite all right, really, thanks ever so."

Her fair curls had fallen from their arrangement and were lying limply on her shoulders and about her white drawn face. Her eyes were swimming in tears and as she spoke she suddenly gave a deep, terrible cough.

"But you can't be—here, in this rain—I wish——" said Mrs. Somers, who was not used to being a practical Christian. "I wish you'd come and sit in the car and tell me all about it. Just to get out of this awful rain."

"It's awfully kind of you. Thanks very much." Mavis managed to stagger to her feet but at once fell down, sprawling on the wet grass, and Mrs. Somers's cry of alarm brought Mr. Somers, cross and dismayed, hurrying up.

They were two sturdy old people, and together they got her across the road and into the back of the car. She had not fainted but was too weak to stand, and now lay back at once and shut her eyes without even troubling to smile at them, while they stood in the rain staring at her.

"We'll have to take her home," said Mrs. Somers at last. "We can't stay here all morning. Get in, do, dear, and let's make a move."

While he was slowly and grumblingly climbing into the car and Mrs. Somers was settling herself, Mavis opened her eyes.

"Be all right in a minute," she whispered. "Awful to give you all this trouble."

"That's all right," said Mrs. Somers briskly. The car began to move. "If you could just tell me where you live——?"

"Seventy-Eight Lavender Road. It's in Seagate. My name is Jevons," she went on, sitting up a little and looking at Mrs. Somers earnestly. "Miss Mavis Jevons."

"Oh," said Mrs. Somers, nodding. There did not seem anything else to say.

"I go to St. Anne's Church," said Mavis.

There was a sort of groan and jerk from Mr. Somers at this but Mrs. Somers took no notice.

"Oh yes, I know St. Anne's." She still spoke briskly, as if verbally protecting herself from some monster, but her expression became more natural. Bad girls were not anxious to tell you they went to church. So thought Mrs. Somers, an innocent woman.

"I lost my job," Mavis went on, speaking slowly and with difficulty, for she was not used to talking about herself. "I used to be at Just's Library."

"Thought I knew your face," suddenly shouted Mr. Somers triumphantly without looking round, and both women jumped.

"——and then I was dismissed when Mr. Just died."

"Back in the spring, I remember," nodded Mrs. Somers.

"And I went to Beard's."

"Beard's? Oh dear, that's a very bad place, they say."

"Yes, it is. Then I was sacked from there for no reason, really, except they said I was slow, and they came and took my furniture away because I got behind with the payments and my landlady was ever so unkind about it, and I came out for a walk and it was such a lovely day I didn't want to go home and I sort of walked on, not noticing, really, and it got so late, I slept out."

As she finished speaking she began to shiver violently and gave another deep cough.

"Well, you'll come home and have lunch with us, won't you, and get those wet clothes off. And then we'll see what we can do about you."

Mrs. Somers's tone was exactly as kind as she felt, and that was not overwhelmingly kind. It was plain the girl was telling the truth and she seemed a nice girl (though it was silly of her to go in for that hire purchase business) but the whole affair was a nuisance. She and Father and Eric never had mixed themselves up much in other people's troubles, their home life was too busy and happy to give them the time. But you couldn't leave a girl sitting out in a downpour. And those horrible letters had lately given Mrs. Somers the unfamiliar feeling that perhaps she had been *too* happy in her wonderful home life, and was Meant to share some of it with others. But it was not easy to make a start.

However, this tone of rather curt kindness suited Mavis. She had one of the rarest of human qualities: pride. It has always been a luxury that few people can afford, and in these times it is rarer than ever, but even nowadays it is to be found in poor people who have not yet discovered that they cannot afford it. The edifice of Mavis's whole life had been reared upon this foundation of gentle pride: her white gloves, her standoffishness, the temperateness of her thoughts about Mr. Somers, all sprang from the one delicate stem. She did not want to be fussed over or pitied; she was no piner for affection or kindness; and all she now said was:

"Thank you very much. It's very kind of you," and leant back again and shut her eyes, thinking that she had been silly to cry this morning and not trust God; He had provided for to-day and there was no doubt He would do the same for to-morrow.

As the car approached Station Road she slowly opened her eyes again, feeling cold and sick with hunger, and it was at this moment that Mrs. Somers chose to remark:

"I wonder if you know my son, Eric Somers? He sings in the choir at St. Anne's."

Five years of practice had given Mavis control of her manner when Mr. Somers's name was mentioned, but this sudden realization of *whose* mother she was talking to, and what car she was in, and which house she was going to, simply took away her power to talk. She just stared at Mrs. Somers with her lips parted. If she had blushed at that moment she would never have got into the house; Mrs. Somers's new charity would have stopped short at inviting to lunch a young woman who blushed at her son's name. But Mavis was feeling so exceedingly ill that there was not enough blood in her body to come up into her face, and as she did not answer but continued to stare at Mrs. Somers in silence, Mrs. Somers thought she had not heard, and repeated:

"My son? Eric Somers."

Then Mavis did manage to answer with an effort that left her trembling:

"Oh yes, I do, just to say 'Good morning' to."

And as she spoke the car stopped outside Forty-Five Station Road.

Like all the others in the road, it was a small solid house with a double front, built of red brick and adorned by a porch and panels of stained glass with birds and flowers in the front door. In every detail it was well kept; the standard roses were large and fine, the net curtains as white as the front step, the gravel path and the two small lawns well rolled. Mavis looked up at it as Mr. and Mrs. Somers helped her out of the car, and although she felt almost too ill to have any feelings except bodily ones, she thought how imposing and alarming it looked.

When she was at last sitting on the sofa in the drawing-room, Mrs. Somers took off the raffia hat and smoothed her white hair and said, looking at her doubtfully:

"You really do look ill, you know. I think you'd better come up and rest until lunch is ready."

Mavis could only shake her head. The smell of roasting meat was making her feel faint.

"I *really* think you'd better." And Mrs. Somers hurried out of the room murmuring something about a hot bottle.

Mavis at once shut her eyes. She had just seen that the room was cool and pretty, with lilac-patterned chintz hangings and a large photograph of Eric looking serenely down from the mantel-piece, but she did not want to see anything more; she could not bear it; she had come to the end of her endurance.

Mrs. Somers was by now seriously alarmed. The girl was very ill and was going to get worse. Now was the moment to put her kindly out of the house; in even half an hour it might be too late. She would be on the spare room bed in a state of collapse and only heaven knew what would happen.

But how can I turn the poor little thing out? thought Mrs. Somers, frowning as she pushed the potatoes back over the gas flame whence she had just removed the boiling kettle. They've taken her bed away and probably the landlady wouldn't have her back anyway, I expect she owed rent.

It's a dreadful nuisance and Father will be so cross and I expect Eric will, too; men do hate illness and fuss but—the fact is I simply haven't the heart to turn her away.

She'll just have to stay here for a bit.

After all, she does go to St. Anne's.

I can telephone the Vicar when she's asleep and ask him about her.

She explained to the daily woman who was preparing lunch that a friend had come back with them who was not well and would have some soup on a tray in the spare room; please open a tin; then she hurried with the bottle back to the drawing-room.

In half an hour Mavis was in bed. She had had a hot bath at Mrs. Somers's slightly embarrassed suggestion and was enveloped in an old locknit nightgown with long sleeves belonging to her hostess. The soup would be ready in a few minutes. She was now alone, waiting for it to be brought up.

She was not at all sleepy; indeed, she could not have slept if she had tried. She ached all over and thoughts raced exhaustingly round and round in her head and every now and again she gave the same deep harsh cough. Her cheeks burnt and her eyes were bright as she stared solemnly round the spare room at the little shelf of books—*The Roadmender, The Manxman, Sesame and Lilies, If Summer Don't*—on the tallboy, the faded yet gay pink chintz on the chairs and at the windows, the worn rosy carpet, and the enlargements of old family photographs on the walls. Her gaze found one of a dark-eyed little boy in a sailor hat, and lingered there.

Mrs. Somers had brought some Aspros, and after Mavis had slowly drunk the soup and eaten some bread she made her take two tablets.

"Now," she said in a low firm voice, bending a little over the bed and smiling down at her, "you're to go to sleep and not worry about anything. You can stay here for a day or two if you like until you're strong again. Does that make you feel any better?"

Mavis nodded slowly. The warmth and food had suddenly made her drowsy and she was so nearly asleep and so exhausted that she had forgotten whose mother this was, bending smilingly above her.

"Yes. Thanks ever so," she whispered, and turned her cheek into the pillow and shut her eyes. Mrs. Somers tiptoed to the window and drew the rose curtains; outside a day of summer rain had set in, and soft grey clouds moved slowly above the bright green grass and the lilacs where the browned blossom was falling. The room became dim with pink light. Mrs. Somers shut the door and came quietly away.

That evening Eric walked slowly home under his umbrella, dejectedly thinking. He had been disgusted with himself and angry with Marjorie ever since their evening at the Barn, but by now he felt only miserable. His love for her had gone and would never come back, and he missed the excitement and hope and pain that it had given to his life.

Intellectual pleasures were still, to him, only a substitute for love. He turned to them with real pleasure but only as second best. Now he would take up his music once more, take down T. S. Eliot's poems and Maurois's books from the shelf, and go regularly to church until the next bout of fever overtook him.

The prospect depressed him painfully. This evening he knew at last that he only found life bearable when he was in love, and he despised himself as a weak, useless creature.

Mr. Somers opened the door to let a youthful pupil out as his son came up the path. A ten-year-old slipped shyly past Eric, cheerful because her lesson had ended among the wholesome innocencies of C Major instead of in the perverse ingenuities of the Flat Minors, and ran down the road on her way home.

Mr. Somers looked irritable.

"Come in, come in, son." He shut the door after him. "Horrible evening, isn't it?"

"Why are you whispering? Isn't Mother well?"

Eric followed him into the drawing-room, but at once saw his mother sitting by a newly-lit fire.

"Mother's all right. But she's got a girl upstairs, ill in bed." Mr. Somers sat down at the piano and stared gloomily and longingly at the keys.

"A girl?" All kinds of wild thoughts at once ran through Eric's head. "What sort of a girl? Who on earth do you mean?"

"It's Miss Jevons, dear. She goes to St. Anne's, she says, and it's quite all right, I telephoned the Vicar this afternoon and he knows all about her and was so sorry to hear she was ill. She says she knows you, too."

"Oh, just to say 'Good morning' to, yes. And I gave her a lift in the car the other night. But what on earth's she doing being ill in bed here?"

Mrs. Somers explained, while Mr. Somers sat crossly twirling on the piano stool and Eric listened with much surprise and sympathy and some mixed feelings.

"I'm sorry she's been having a bad time," he said when his mother had finished, "but isn't it rather a bore her collapsing on us? Won't it make a lot of extra work for you, Dumps?"

"Just what I said. Wear her out," put in his father triumphantly.

Mrs. Somers glanced lovingly from one dear man to the other. The pets! After thirty years of family life neither of them realized that she was as strong—well, not quite as strong—as a horse, for there was always her leg, but much stronger than most women.

"Oh, she's better this evening, I took her up some tea and bread and butter and she was much cooler and had had a nice sleep," she said, taking out her embroidery. "I was afraid she was going to be really ill but she isn't. She can stay here for a few days, it won't be much trouble, and then we must try to find her another job. The Vicar said he would help."

Mr. Somers groaned. "Does that mean I can't play the piano for 'a few days'?"

"Don't be silly, Father, of course you can. If you play something soft and pretty it won't disturb her, I expect she'll enjoy it; she sings in the choir, remember."

So Mr. Somers opened a little grey book of German folksongs and began to play "Die Lorelei," and soon started to sway gently and look serene as he played; while Eric, for whom the old legend had painful contemporary associations, wished he had chosen another tune.

It was strange to think of that quiet little Miss Jevons upstairs in the spare room. Strange and depressing. For although she was a nice little thing and he wished her no harm, he did not want to see a girl or be polite to a girl just now; he never wanted (just now) to speak to a girl again.

> "*Sie kammt es mit goldenem Kamme und*
> *singt ein lied dabei——*"

hummed Mr. Somers, swaying contentedly.

Eric, who had been staring out of the window at the green garden hushed under the rain, got up suddenly and crossed the room to kiss his mother.

"You are a pet, Dumps," he said. "Poor little thing. It is bad luck. We must certainly try to put her on her feet again."

Some cautious instinct kept him from adding that he had always thought Miss Jevons had a pretty smile.

And although he never wanted to see or speak to a girl again, although he was depressed and irritated by the fact that she was in the house, he could not help glancing, as he passed it on his way to bed, at the shut door of the spare room. It was so strange, on this rainy summer night, to think of a girl lying asleep behind it.

CHAPTER XXIII

I'M getting to be a sort of walking Home for the Aged, thought Pauline cheerfully, on her way back from Mrs. Pask's one evening some days later. I like being with the old squoo, of course, but gosh! do I feel like running and shrieking at the top of my voice after I've been to tea there! And she sent a stone spinning along the path with a vigorous and satisfying kick.

I may as well charge in and see Mr. Early while I'm at it. And then there's tennis with Him, oh rapture!

Her visits to Mrs. Pask had begun in chivalry and were continuing from duty and real affection. She enjoyed watching the pleasure Mrs. Pask plainly got from hearing about her riding and tennis and dancing and the goings-on at the bank, as much as she enjoyed the delicious luncheons she got at "Avonlea"; and although her mother had annoyed and shamed her by suggesting that "Pauli might come in for something when the poor old thing passes on," she refused to limit her visits because she might one day benefit from them.

And she really did try not to daydream, after her mother's suggestion, about Mrs. Pask's handsome sapphire ring; she set herself little penances, such as not glancing at the Hotel Bristol as she passed it, every time she did daydream.

There had been another Nice Anonymous Letter. Pauline was walking home this evening with it in her handbag, having obtained Mrs. Pask's permission to show it to A Man. As the families of Mrs. Pask and Pauline were at present depressingly lacking in men, Pauline proposed to show it to Eric and Brian and Wally; she was looking forward to hearing what they had to say about it, and although not one of them was exactly what you might call a great rock in a desert land, surely they could rustle up some common sense and helpfulness between them.

The letter said how lucky Mrs. Pask was to have someone as devoted to her as Miss Gaye was and to have the friendship of a sweet girl like Pauline who left her boys and horse-riding to spare an hour to cheer up the old folks.

This annoyed Mrs. Pask more than any of the other letters; like most people over sixty she hated being called an old folk. And Pauline was quite as indignant at the adjective applied to herself.

Sweet! Gosh, I should hope not! she thought, walking quickly home with her pretty mouth pursed up in a soft cheerful whistle. But that's what Dad used to say I was—*Pauli's as sweet as a nut*.

She remembered Ted's postcard, and stopped whistling to sigh. She rather wished he would write to her again as his "dear Nut Brown Maid," it sounded so affectionate and brotherly and she was sadly in need of a brother's comfort these days.

It was still only half past five and the sunlight was very hot as she turned in at the wrought-iron gates of Parkfield, that stood slightly ajar, and walked up the short drive where the trees were already assuming the darkness of late summer.

Gleams of white appeared between the rhododendron leaves, and when she came out on the lawn in front of the house she saw that the large bushes of syringa and hydrangea were in flower, cream and snow rising from the lawn of long grass against the dark purplish brick of the house, with its two elongated towers, and slit windows and crenellated roofs.

Seated immediately in front of the bushes were Mr. Early and Louise, she in a white dress and shoes with no stockings, and he in a suit of yellowish-white silk and ancient cut. Letters and papers were scattered out of a large old wicker theatrical basket all about them on the grass, and both were busily reading. Vinny was lying on her back on a dirty old mat, with her legs in the air, panting.

Louise and Mr. Early looked up as she approached and Louise said in a low voice: "It's Pauline Williams. Hullo!" she added, louder, and waving her round brown arm. "We're having a mighty old turn-out."

Mr. Early removed his large white panama, slowly got up, and stood awaiting Pauline. He held her hand and bowed over it while she smiled up at him; then he slowly reseated himself and Pauline sat down on the grass by Louise and pulled down a branch of syringa to smell.

"How are you both? I just thought I'd come in and see how you were getting on."

"It was a charming thought," answered Mr. Early dreamily, folding his hands upon his knee and beginning a long stare at the hydrangeas, "we are both well, thank you. We both enjoy this very hot weather. And you? Are you well? But there is no need to ask. I can see for myself," and his eyelids began to droop as he gazed at the white papery flowers. "And your beautiful little sister, and your still-beautiful mother, are they both well? The Three Graces."

The last words were a murmur. He was almost asleep.

"They're both quite well, thanks awfully." Pauline was watching him with a smile of amused affection and thinking: I must tell Mum that; she won't be able to help getting a kick out of it.

"How's Ted? Have you heard from him lately?" she asked, turning to Louise—and was disconcerted to see Louise immediately turn away her beautiful brown eyes, which had been fixed with a curious sly look upon her face.

"We had a letter yesterday. He doesn't seem to be liking it much," she said.

Pauline laughed, thinking, *if she wants to stare, why doesn't she stare and get it over?*

"What's the matter with him?" she asked.

"He doesn't get on with M. Hervé," said Louise, and as she said the name her voice became a Frenchwoman's.

"I shouldn't have thought he had much to do with him in a place that size. It's fairly large, isn't it?"

"Yes, but M. Hervé teaches certain very promising pupils himself, and Ted's one of them, so he says."

"Is he? I *am* glad!" cried Pauline, drawing up her knees and hugging them.

"So's *he*." Louise inclined her head gracefully towards the now dozing Mr. Early, but her eyes had the same inquisitive and amused expression again as she watched Pauline's face.

"He thinks he'll maybe come back quite soon," she continued.

"But wasn't he going to be there for a year?"

"Yes, but he doesn't think he can stick it. He loves Paris (who wouldn't?) but he wants to hurry up and get a real job."

"But he isn't properly trained yet. It seems an awful pity to chuck it up halfway."

"Oh well, maybe he won't. We'll have to see," said Louise.

A little silence followed. Pauline stared into the grass and thought Ted must have changed a lot in three months if he was really eager to get a job, and Louise filled up the pause by a long, silent yawn. Then she began idly to turn over the papers on the grass.

"Do look at here!" she said suddenly, handing a yellowed postcard to Pauline. "Imagine wearing that!"

It was a cloak reaching to the knees of its wearer, Miss Evie Green, with rows and rows of white ruffles waterfalling down it. Her dress was white lace with a train that swirled about her hidden feet.

"Frightful," said Pauline, studying it curiously. "Do let me see some more," reaching out among the cards scattered on the grass. "I say, she's rather a pet."

The large eyes of Miss Dorothea Baird looked out tenderly from under the curls on her forehead, above a white blouse with capes on the shoulders and a high neck.

"And she's simply lovely! 'Miss Evelyn Millard,'" read out Pauline, below the photograph of a dark goddess in a black hat with a huge black ostrich feather caught by a star of cut-steel. "She's rather like you," she added, with a little surprise in her voice.

"Thank you for the flowers," drawled Louise, and they both laughed.

A look of pleasure lingered on Louise's face for a moment or two afterwards. She was studying another postcard, and after looking at it in silence for a while she held it out to Pauline.

"Gosh!" breathed Pauline, looking at it. "I say—*gosh!* Who on earth's that?"

It was the head and shoulders of a young man in the pride and bloom of youth. He wore a dark velvet cloak that left his throat bare. His hair was dark as the cloak, and worn long, parting naturally at the side and straying into thick loose locks in a way in which men's hair seems to have lost the power to grow. It was a face with a proudly carved mouth and large widely-spaced eyes and a round firm chin, yet it was something else that gave to it an astounding beauty. It did not belong to the modern world at all; it might have been seen in Ancient Greece or the Italy of the Borgias or the England of Elizabeth. It was like an old statue or painting come to life. Something in the face made Pauline think of a magnificent Sikh soldier she had seen in the tube in London at the time of the Coronation. *That's what the Almighty meant human beings to look like*, an old gentleman sitting next to her had suddenly snapped, to the embarrassment of the compartment as the Sikh got up and went out. *Yes, stare at him, all of you*, he went on rudely, *you don't often see a human being nowadays*.

"Can't wonder the women went crazy about him, can you?" said Louise.

"No indeed." Pauline was still staring, completely fascinated. "He certainly has got what it takes, and then some. But who *is* it?"

"Why—him," Louise whispered, opening her eyes very wide and turning to look at the sleeping old man. "Look on the back."

And Pauline turned the faded card over and read: "Mr. Archibald Early as Hamlet, Prince of Denmark."

Both women stared at the old bowed figure in silence for a moment, but found nothing to say. There was no breeze blowing through the hot evening sunlight but some syringa petals drifted down into the grass.

"Extraordinary the passion they had for stars and moons," said Pauline at last, picking up a postcard of Marie Studholme with a moon in her hair.

"They're pretty, though," said Louise. "It's all that hair that gets me down."

"And the hips! Forty-five if they're an inch!"

"And those clothes—all bits." Louise moved her long waist and high bosom comfortably inside her loose silk dress.

"Tatty," murmured Pauline, staring at Mrs. Patrick Campbell.

"Nevertheless," suddenly pronounced a judicial voice behind them which made them both jump, "they had the Right Idea. Man is enchanted by what is different from himself: a delicate complexion, draperies, long thick hair, large dancing expressive eyes."

After this there did not seem to be much else to say, so Pauline (controlling a desire to giggle that was obviously shared by Louise) got up to go.

But as she picked up her handbag from the grass she remembered the letter; and she suddenly decided to show it to Mr. Early. He might not say anything helpful (for his greatest admirer could not have called him a sensible old man) but it would be interesting to see if he, like Mrs. Pask, found in it something sinister.

So she went across to him and said:

"Mr. Early, please say if you'd rather not be bothered with it, but a friend of mine is very worried about some anonymous letters she's been getting. I wondered if you'd be very kind and read one of them and tell me what you make of it."

"I am honoured that you should ask me," he answered at once and held out his hand.

As she handed him the letter Pauline felt, not for the first time, that there was much to be said for the manners and traditions of the Oldest School. No cautious questions, no condescending protests; instead, a charming speech and an immediate, unquestioning response from his chivalry.

He put on his old-fashioned pair of glasses and read it twice, then handed it back, saying calmly:

"Very unpleasant. I am not surprised that your friend is worried."

"Oh, I *am* so glad you think it's unpleasant!" she exclaimed. "We thought perhaps we were just being silly about it, because, after all, there isn't a word in it that anyone could mind, is there?"

He was silent for a moment; then he answered:

"Happiness and comfort and contentment are very rare. When we have them we are like savages; we are afraid to bring them to the notice of the gods in case they become jealous and take them away. This letter brings your friend's good fortune to the notice of the gods, and therefore she fears that it may be taken away. I should say that it was written by a person who is envious and spiteful but not wicked; someone who has not the courage to write an abusive letter, and who may even hardly realize what pain they are inflicting."

"Do you think she ought to show it to the police?" asked Pauline.

He shook his head.

"It would be wiser to try and discover if anyone else has had similar letters. Then, if you could present the police with several cases, they might take a more serious view of it. At present, if they saw only one letter, they might say that it was a practical joke."

Pauline folded the letter and put it away.

"Thanks most awfully, you *are* kind," she said. "I'll tell my friend what you said."

He inclined his head. "I am honoured to have been of use."

She said "good night" to him again, stooped to pat the unappetizing Vinny, then turned to Louise.

"I'll walk with you to the gate," said Louise. "No, I'd like to, I'm tired of sitting still."

As they were entering the cooler shadows of the elms she suddenly asked in a teasing voice:

"You aren't engaged yet, are you?"

"Me? Gosh, no!" Pauline was a little startled; she had taken Louise for granted for many years, she had always been so passive and lazy and silent, that Pauline had hardly thought about her, and it seemed strange to hear her ask a personal question.

"I was just wondering. You and Ted and Marjorie are all growing up."

"Yes," said Pauline, embarrassed without knowing why.

"And I'm fond of love stories. I really do enjoy a good love story," Louise said, walking gracefully along with the shadows and sunrays gliding over her white dress. "If ever you get in a hole, and don't feel like telling your mother (I know girls never tell their mothers anything, I never did), you come to me. I might be able to help."

"Oh. Thanks awfully." Pauline was by now annoyed as well as embarrassed; what on earth did she mean? "But I'm not going to get in a hole. Why should I?"

"No reason at all." Louise shrugged her shoulders. "But girls sometimes do."

"Well, I shan't. I'm not that sort of girl." Pauline thought the only possible thing to do was to laugh, but her face was burning.

Louise looked at her amiably.

"You know, I've lived here twenty years now, but I still can't make English girls out," she said. "What's so funny? I didn't mean that sort of a hole, anyway—honey. I meant if you can't manage your boy I might be able to give you some hints."

"Oh—I see—I'm sorry——" stammered Pauline. "It's awfully kind of you, Louise, I won't forget."

"That's all right. Good night," said Louise, smiling and turning away down the shady avenue.

I'll boil myself in oil before I'll breathe a word to her about my affairs, thought Pauline, hurrying across the road with a hot face and beating heart. I expect she meant it kindly but she's so *nosey*.

Really does enjoy a good love story, does she? Yes, I expect she does. Well, she darned well isn't going to enjoy mine.

And why—why—*why* (she thought, running up the path to the front door of "Dorna") is everybody always hinting that I can't manage men? Even Mr. Early just now—telling me what men like women to be like!

I'm fed up with it.

Never mind, I'll have a heavenly game of tennis and forget all about it.

CHAPTER XXIV

BUT when she opened the door of her room the first thing she saw was her new dress, lying on her bed in the distinctive pale blue and scarlet box that showed it came from Noreen's, the smartest dress and hat shop in Seagate.

As she pounced on it her mother called up the stairs:

"Pauli, is that you? Your frock's come, dear. I put it on your bed."

"Yes, Mummy, I'm just opening it, thanks. It's an absolute lamb; you wait till you see it."

"Are you wearing it this evening?"

"No, I'm playing tennis. I'll bring it down when I come for you to see."

Mrs. Williams, who would have been a better mother if she had taken as much interest in the souls of her daughters as she did in their clothes, went back into the drawing-room; and Pauline opened the box, unfolded the dress, and laid it out on the bed.

It was even prettier than it had looked in Noreen's window.

It's simply ravishing, she thought, gloating. For two pins I'd wear it this evening and tell him I'm not playing.

Of course, he'd be furious.

But as she gazed at the frock, Mr. Early's words returned to her—"Man is enchanted by what is different to himself . . . a delicate complexion . . . draperies . . ." and for the first time in her life she wondered what would be the results if she deliberately made herself look as seductive, feminine and charming as she could?

She enjoyed her clothes and was always well groomed, but her "type" (she thought) was athletic, and so her clothes were tailored, with plain lines. This dress was different: it had called to some secret softness and longing in herself as it lay in Noreen's window, and so she had bought it and had thereby been set back four guineas.

It's *my* dress, she thought, staring at it. It makes me think of a gipsy orchestra playing, somehow.

I'll wear it.

Brian was sitting in his car outside the tennis courts, smoking and waiting for Pauline (he was a little early; he would not have waited had she been late) and thinking what a hole the pavilion was and how badly it needed doing up and how slack the Committee was about getting anything done to it, when he saw a lovely and exciting girl walking down the road towards him.

She was dressed in a frock of chiffon striped thinly in rose, brown, yellow, white and harsh bright green, cut low in a square to show her brown neck and bosom, with full sleeves that fell over her wrists, and a gold kid belt with a green jewel in it round her waist. She carried a crimson coat over one arm and had very high heels to her shoes and her hair was brushed so that it stood out from her head. She glowed and burned with colour; she looked like a gipsy princess.

Brian was enchanted but also rather shocked. That very low dress, those very high heels, that thick poppy pink (not red—a queer dull pink) paint on her mouth, that dancing, almost glittering, hair—it was all very ravishing but also very conspicuous, and who on earth could she be?

She was Pauline.

"Hullo!" she said, coming up to the car, and her usual fresh friendly voice came curiously out of the face of a gipsy princess. "I'm not late, am I?"

"Good heavens, I didn't know you for the minute," he said, staring. "What on earth—weren't we supposed to be playing tennis?"

"Oh yes, we were, but my new frock came home this afternoon and I was dying to wear it. Do you like it?"

"You look wonderful," he answered in a low voice, fixing his eyes upon the frock's neck. "Just as I always knew you could look if you cared to. But that dress—it's a bit—and your hair—and that lipstick—where on earth did you get it?"

"Pinched it off Marjie's dressing-table," she answered gaily, her spirits rushing up with excitement and pleasure as she saw the new look on his face. (*Wonderful!* Imagine him saying that to me!) "Don't let's bother with tennis to-night, let's go for a drive."

No "Shall we?" No apology for the lowness of her neck or the thickness of the paint on her mouth; just the cool assumption that he would do what she wanted! And so he would! He was immediately filled with strong desire for this unfamiliar, glowing, imperious creature, and was just opening the door of the car for her and saying:

"Of course, if you'd like that better, darling," when a large car drew up opposite; a window in it opened, and someone leant out and said in a confused voice:

"Brian, *darling!* Just person I wanted. Been trying to get you all afternoon, wher've you *been*? Get in at once, Collie said I was bring you *whatever* happened, so get in, darling, and make it snappy."

Mrs. Cunningham was already a little drunk and her large white shoulders were coming out of a beautiful black sequin dress. She took no notice of Pauline, whom in fact she did not see.

"I'm so sorry, Eve, I can't to-night," he answered cheerfully, wishing some lightning would strike her. "I'm just going to take Miss Williams for a run. I don't think you know each other, do you?"

He turned to Pauline, who was standing, completely at her ease in the consciousness of her new beauty and the Noreen frock, and looking composedly at Mrs. Cunningham.

For the first time Mrs. Cunningham turned her slightly blurred gaze towards the girl and stared at her.

At first her expression was haughty and angry, but as she continued to look at the brightly coloured dress, the young face flushed into beauty by excitement, the hauteur and anger in her own faded, and wistfulness came in their place. She said almost timidly:

"How do y' do. I don't suppose you care to come to party too, would you?"

Pauline shook her head. "No, thank you, but it's awfully kind of you to ask me."

Her voice was soft and polite. This half-drunk ageing woman disgusted her and she was very angry with Brian, but she could not be rude to her: she was something to be sorry for, with her fat body and diamond earrings and lovely ruin of a face; and the habits of chivalry and politeness to older people practised for twenty-two years do not desert a girl in a moment.

It is doubtful whether Mrs. Cunningham would have enjoyed the motives that prompted her courtesy.

"Thought you wouldn't wan'. Brian——" Her face puckered

and she fumbled for a handkerchief which she brought out but
made no attempt to put to her suddenly watering eyes: "Come
jus' please me, darling? So lonely."

"I'm sorry. Another time," he said, and caught the chauffeur's
eye and gave the slightest nod. "Run along now, Eve, there's a
dear girl, you'll be so late. I'll call you up to-morrow."

"Very good, madam," said the chauffeur suddenly, and the
car began to move.

"No fun without you," she said, turning to look at him as she
leant out of the window and apparently not realizing that the car
had started.

"Good-bye," he answered, smiling and waving and turning
away.

The car was now moving fast; Pauline saw Mrs. Cunningham
fall back on to the seat still turning round to get a last look at
Brian.

It passed quickly out of sight.

"Now, darling. How about it?" said Brian, holding open the
door for her and smiling. His gaze wandered over the soft yet
brilliant dress, her full brown throat.

I mustn't make a scene, thought Pauline.

But she was too angry to do what he wanted her to at once.
She longed to punish him, and for once she felt strong enough to
do it!

"We won't go just yet; I want to watch them playing," she said
coolly, and moved towards the entrance to the Club.

"Whatever for? There's nothing exciting on to-night," he said
in surprise; then he frowned. He had just seen the back of that
dress; it had four tiny green buttons and then a slit that showed
soft brown skin almost to the waist.

"Look here, Pauli," he said, slipping his hand through her arm
as she reached the gate, "I like that dress but it's hardly the sort
of thing to wear at a tennis club; it's almost fancy dress and it
makes you look awfully conspicuous—right out of your usual
line. I'd really rather not——"

"I like being conspicuous. It makes a nice change for me.
You go away if you don't like it," she said, and looked up with a
wicked, spiteful gipsy's smile on her poppy-pink mouth and in
her sparkling eyes. Her eyebrows were like the wings of soft
brown birds.

"Of course I'll come if you want me to," he said. His voice was
sulky and rebellious; the voice of a slave, and she was thrilled by
pleasure and triumph, for all her anger, as she heard it.

They went into the Club and round the courts (where several

people served double faults in trying to see who Pauline was, for the Kirriemuir Road Club had more rabbits who relished a good gossip than tigers who concentrated on a good game) and on to the veranda of the pavilion, where there were a few people sitting in the old deck- and Madras-chairs waiting for courts.

Brian and Pauline sat down in a far corner away from everybody, and he offered her a cigarette which she accepted.

"Reckless to-night, aren't you?" he said. (She seldom smoked, saying it was bad for her wind and hence for her games.)

"Utterly. Oh good, there's Wally, I always like to watch him, he plays an awfully good game."

And she waved to Wally, who peered to see who this gorgeous creature might be; then, recognizing her, went red and dropped his racquet.

Poor old Wal, now he won't be good for anything, thought his sister, the cripple, from her place on the veranda; and she darted at Pauline a look of admiration and jealousy and bitter envy.

Why should one girl have pretty, normal legs and feet and the devotion of one of the best boys in the world while another——? She felt the ugly iron frame and boot drag as she moved impatiently.

She was about twenty-five, sturdy and dark, with a pretty face a little marred by a downward curve of her mouth and a nervous frown. Her brother had coaxed her into coming this evening; she was morbidly sensitive and seldom went anywhere, but stayed at home, moving slowly about their bungalow that she kept as clean and pretty as a doll's palace. She was always elaborately and neatly dressed, with velvet bows in her curls, and old bracelets of thin Indian silver on her wrists that tinkled softly as she moved.

Now she was sorry she had come.

"Mad at me, Pauli?" asked Brian presently, in his famous girl-teasing voice.

"Yes. Oh, well *played*, Wally!" she retorted, not looking at Brian but following with apparent eagerness a desperate rally in which Wally was engaged.

He was silent. He did not know quite how to behave to her. For the first time since they had known one another he was the one who felt inclined to beg for kisses: he could tell when a girl was in the saddle with the bit between her teeth (so to speak); and he knew that Pauline was in that position now.

And he wanted exceedingly to kiss her.

He decided to be bold and injured.

"What am I supposed to have done? Ah!" as the rally ended with Wally's opponent missing the ball.

7*

"Good for you, Wally! I don't like you running round with Mrs. Cunningham."

"I didn't run round with her this evening."

"I should hope not. There are limits. Double fault; he's nervous or something."

"I don't see why you need mind. She's lonely and getting on— she likes running around with people a lot younger than herself, that's all."

"Brian, you must think I'm about thirteen and a half! I don't like being kissed by someone who's been kissing that face."

"I don't kiss her."

"Oh yeah?"

"I detest that expression."

Their heads, with flushed angry faces, moved quickly backwards and forwards as they watched the last struggle for game and set.

"In any case," he went on, "to put it pretty bluntly, it isn't any of your business who I kiss."

She went redder, her eyelids drooped for a second, but she retorted at once:

"It is my business if you kiss me, and I don't choose to go halves with Mrs. Cunningham."

Silence.

They continued to watch the game, but neither of them was thinking about it. Pauline had some softer feelings as well as her angry ones; she was fond of the tennis club, for her father had brought her here as a schoolgirl and taught her to hold a racquet and they had played her first games together; it was here that she had met Brian for the first time on a summer evening five years ago, when he was twenty-four and she seventeen, and she could never be in the place without remembering these events with mingled happiness and sadness.

The Club was openly situated with a view of the sea on one side, and on the others a prospect of the cream walls of distant boarding houses and a row of tall poplars with their rainy-whisper. Of course, the Club was not perfect, and the Pav. was very far from perfect. One of Pauline's recurring arguments with Brian was about the Pav., which he despised because its clock was either wildly fast or painfully slow, its deck-chairs had tops that collapsed on you because their screws were loose, and its washbasins had chains which frequently came away from that little thing meant to hold them to the rim of the basin. Pauline indulgently defended all these inefficiencies because she loved the place.

But although Brian despised it, he played there from time to time because one contacted (his expression) the few professional people in the town there and he might hear a scrap of news or gossip that would be of use to him.

Presently he said:

"This isn't particularly thrilling, is it? Shall we go?"

His voice was no longer angry, but she only said:

"Not yet; I want to see the finish of this," and at the same time slowly, without taking her eyes off the court, put up her hands to pin back a curl that had fallen over her eyes.

The graceful movement, and the grave look on her face as she watched the game with her chin slightly lowered, suddenly enchanted him. He leant towards her and said urgently:

"Pauli, don't let's fight. *Do* let's go. Haven't you seen enough? I've got to be back early and it's nearly eight now."

She dropped her arms and sighed. She did not want to fight any more, either. Half this lovely, lovely evening was already gone, and never again might she look so glamorous, never again might she feel that she had him at her mercy!

"All right." She stood up, and gave him a teasing little smile.

As they came along the veranda Estelle Wade smiled politely at Pauline. She was sure that they had been quarrelling and for Wally's sake she was glad.

Pauline smiled back and said: "Hullo, Estelle—heavenly evening, isn't it," then turned as Wally and his partner came triumphant off the court, and congratulated them. Wally said something cheerful and silly and everyone laughed; then Brian and Pauline went out of the gate.

"How pretty she looks to-night," said Estelle. She had learnt in long years of jealousy and bitterness not to grieve her brother and make him silently annoyed with her by saying unkind things about girls he admired.

"Smashing. Not at all her usual style. But certainly smashing," said Wally loyally.

And he did not sigh, but sat down beside his sister and kept her amused and content until it was time to drive her home.

Pauline got into the car and Brian drove away.

He made for the lanes and wheatfields out beyond Happy Sands, which was the nearest lonely place to the town. On the way they actually went past Mrs. Cunningham's house behind its larch trees; neither said a word but both were very conscious that it was there, and Pauline began to feel angry again.

At last he stopped the car in a deserted lane and silently took her in his arms. She struggled a little at first, but could not prevent herself from being kissed so fiercely that all the paint was bruised away from her mouth.

"Happy?" he muttered, defiantly, letting her go at last.

"I hope you enjoyed that. I didn't," she said, trembling; and got out the pink lipstick from her bag.

"No, I didn't," he answered gloomily, leaning back and staring down the lane.

There was silence for a while. Pauline painted her mouth. She was still trembling and her heart beat fast. Twilight had fallen, hushed and still.

"Darling," he began in a desperate whisper, (oh heavens, if he's going to sound like that I can't go on being angry, she thought) "it's all your fault. Ever since that day I asked you to come away with me, just you and I in the sunlight, I've been so wretched."

"What—that nudist business?" She sat up and made her voice sound brisk and cool. "You weren't serious, were you? I thought you were fooling."

"I'm perfectly serious. I want you to come out for the day with me, as I said——"

"And—and go all nudist together?" Pauline struggled, and succeeded this time in controlling an hysterical little giggle. "Is that all?" she went on, driven by the longing which she had felt for a year to know exactly what he *did* want of her.

"When we're alone—like that—we shall know just how we feel about one another," he answered solemnly.

"I can't see why we can't know it now. Other people do. Other people—get engaged or something," she went on quickly, "or they have an understanding. We haven't got anything. It's miserable."

"You know I'm not my own master," he said at once. "And I'm very hurt, Pauli—I can't help being—because you won't trust yourself with me."

"Well, good heavens!" she said, pushing back the hair from her hot forehead. "Doesn't it occur to you that it's—it's a most peculiar thing to ask someone to do—go sunbathing with them with nothing on? What do you suppose people would think if they knew about it?"

"People's minds are full of evil. It would be perfectly possible for you and I to lie side by side in the sun, naked, like two children."

Possible, but not very likely, thought Pauline, whose feelings were by now such a mixture of laughter and passion and unhappiness that her strongest wish was to go home.

"But I don't want to!" she suddenly cried, turning on him a flushed distressed face in the summer twilight. "That's the absolute truth, Brian."

"Think about it quietly," he said, taking both her hands and holding them. "Try to get used to the idea. Lots of people have false shame at first."

" 'Tisn't false shame. I just don't *want* to," she said tiredly, leaning against him. But no feeling of comfort came from her leaning, and in a minute or two she drew away again.

"Look here," she began again (and as she spoke she thought drearily how she had looked forward to showing him her new dress, and how well this evening, that was being so wretched, had started), "I'm a—a perfectly normal person, Brian. If we were— I mean—well, if we were married," (and poor Pauline stumbled over the word as though it were a shameful one), "I should be just like—well, anyone else about things. But honestly, I can't go and——"

Her voice died into silence. There, she thought wildly, that's absolutely a proposal. Now he'll *have* to say something definite. Oh well, it's out at last.

"I'd better tell you," he said after a pause in a voice without expression. "I didn't want to. I can't bear to talk about it or even think about it. You see . . . I can't ever marry anyone.' "

"Oh Brian, why not?" she whispered, and took his hand. "Is it your father?"

He nodded. "Partly. He doesn't want me to leave him, he depends utterly on me. But that's not the real reason. It's my mother. She died in an asylum."

There was a pause. Then she flung her arms round his neck, saying over and over again: "Oh darling, darling, my poor, poor darling!"

About eleven o'clock that night Marjorie had just come home from the theatre, and was doing her teeth in the bathroom after drinking her nightly orange juice when she heard someone coming slowly up the stairs.

"That you, Pauli?" she called.

"Yes," answered her sister's voice, sounding so strange and exhausted that she at once marched out on to the landing.

Pauline was leaning against the wall at the top of the stairs.

"My good soul, what is the matter?" Marjorie demanded, tying her dressing-gown round her waist. "Is that the new frock? It's heaven but you look exactly as though you'd been raped."

Pauline gave a weak giggle and began to cry.

"Here—here—shut up for heaven's sake, you'll have Mother on our tails," said Marjorie in an alarmed whisper, hustling her into her bedroom. "Do you want a hanky?"—giving her a clean one. "Now what on earth's up? *Have* you been raped?"

Pauline, still crying, shook her head and giggled.

"Well, then, what? Brian, I'll bet."

Pauline nodded.

"I mustn't tell anyone," she said wretchedly, blowing her nose.

"My foot," retorted Marjorie, beginning to brush her hair. "Did he ask you to sleep with him?"

"Nothing so straightforward," sighed Pauline.

"Well, do cough it up. Who do you think you are—someone in a Mrs. Henry Wood novel? No one has things they can't tell anyone these days. Come on, I'll guess!"

"Oh don't, Marjie!" cried Pauline, terrified. Marjorie had always had an uncanny talent for guessing the most unlikely secrets.

"Let me see." (She sat on the bed and nursed her foot in its violet slipper; this was her secret-guessing position.) "I'll bet it was some excuse for not getting engaged to you. M-m—he said his father would cut him off with a hapenny?"

Pauline shook her head.

"Mind you admit it if I'm right," said the sorceress sharply. "He said he'd got consumption?"

Pauline shook her head but looked conscious.

"Getting warm-er!" cried Marjorie. Then she dropped her foot and cried: "Got it! He told you his mother was nuts!"

"Oh, how did you guess!" breathed Pauline. "It's terrifying—honestly, Marjie, it's sheer black magic!"

"Just a gift," she replied, smiling to herself. "Well, now it's out, I don't believe a word of it."

"But it must be true! He *couldn't* make up a thing like that; it would be *too* mean."

"He darned well could if he wanted an excuse not to get tied up," said Marjorie, beginning to set her curls. "Hey, hey, who's had my Pink Poppy lipstick?"

Pauline guiltily brought it out of her handbag.

"I'm awfully sorry, Marjie, but I did so want to look different to-night."

"You've got your wish." Her sister ironically but affectionately surveyed her swollen face, ruffled hair, creased frock and smeared make up. "You look like somebody who's been arrested for telling fortunes. Now you go off to bed. I'll flit down and brew you a posset of milk while you're undressing."

"You are a lamb."

"Go hon. And I shan't rest until I've found out if Mrs. Kingsley was cuckoo. We might write and ask Mr. Kingsley, only maybe he wouldn't like it. Now, you get into bed, I won't be a minute."

She ran quietly downstairs.

When she came back with the milk Pauline was in bed, looking worn out and miserable.

Marjorie put the milk on the table and sat down.

"Those are my feet," said Pauline, grimacing and moving.

"Sorry. I'll bet he asked you to go to a nudist camp with him too, the saucy monkey."

Pauline went red.

"I hope you weren't dope enough to say 'yes' out of sympathy because his mamma was cuckoo?"

"I did say I'd think it over." Pauline spoke in a muffled voice with her face half-buried in the pillow.

Marjorie lit a cigarette.

"Honestly, Pauli, you are a dope. Are you really crazy about him?"

"I don't know, Marjie." Pauline raised herself on her elbow and reached for the milk. "I'm in such a muddle. I simply can't take this nudist business seriously. I mean, I *ask* you! And I only half-believe about his mother. At the same time I'm awfully sorry for him—if it's true. It's all so mixed-up and beastly," she ended gloomily, sipping the milk and staring at the floor. Her hair was brushed back into its usual style and her brown face washed clean from paint.

"You look about twelve," said Marjorie impersonally.

"I feel about forty. Do you think Mother remembers Mrs. Kingsley?"

"I'll ask her to-morrow."

Rap! Rap! Rap! on the wall.

"Look here, we must shut up or she'll come charging in. Drink up your milk, sweetie."

"It's marvellous; has it got sherry in?"

"It has."

Pauline lay down and Marjorie lightly tucked her in.

"Now you go to sleep. Everything's going to be fine (as they say on the movies)."

She dropped a cool kiss on her sister's cheek.

"Good night, bird-brain."

"Good night, Marjie. Thanks awfully."

"Pleasure."

She turned off the light and went out of the room.

CHAPTER XXV

"**M**UM, Mum, here's a letter from Mavis!" shouted Reenie, hurrying along to the kitchen on the following Wednesday morning.

Mrs. Voles was frying sausages and potatoes for breakfast, and just glanced up with one dart from her small green eyes as her daughter came in, then returned to her cooking. But Reenie knew that she was relieved.

"It's to me," she went on.

Mrs. Voles turned two sausages over and said nothing.

"She's at some people name of Somers in Station Road. Been rather bad but much better to-day (Tuesday, that would be). Will I go along and take her some things this evening after work. Looks as though I'll have to. Want to see?" holding out the letter.

Mrs. Voles shook her head and turned out the gas.

"Fancy, she slept out all night Sunday!" Reenie went on, sitting down with elbows on the table in the sunlight pouring through the open window and relishing the letter and her tea together. "Nothing to eat all day but a choc-ice and three water-ices! Well I never. No wonder she's been bad. Know anyone name of Somers, Mum?"

"Churchy lot. Father teaches the piano to the kids up that way. I did over a Berlei corselet for *her* last summer."

"Poor old Mavis!" Reenie put the letter in her bag and began on her sausages. "Well, I'm glad she's all right."

"P'raps you're 'glad' I didn't let you rush off to the police, too."

"Another day, and I would have," said Reenie in the sturdy way she had taken to standing up for herself lately. She was not afraid of Mum any more. All kinds of thrilling plans, Reenie had, and Mum did not come into any of them. "I'll go round there this evening. She's given me a list of what she wants. Oh, and she says can her big case stay here for a bit?"

There was a pause.

"I suppose so," said Mrs. Voles.

"Well, I must be off or I'll be late. Shan't have time to get her things now, I'll pop in at lunch time. Anything I can bring you in, Mum?"

"You won't have time if you're going traipsing off round there."

"Oh, I can get it on the way."

"You might bring a jar of Pan Yan, then. Large one. I fancy it."

"All right." Reenie was putting on her hat. "I'm quite looking forward to seeing poor old Mavis again."

"Silly little fool," said Mrs. Voles, reading the *Daily Sketch*.

"Who, me? Thanks."

"Her, not you. But you're nearly as bad."

"Now then, not so much of it, Mrs. Hitler!" said Reenie, and went giggling out of the back door.

The morning was lovely. The distant sea danced and dashed and sparkled, the nasturtiums in the garden glowed like red and yellow velvet and big balls of dew lay in their plate-leaves, the sky was a thick warm blue. Even the Outside W. looked less desolate than usual.

Nice in a salad, nasturtium leaves are. Used to drink the rain off of them when I was a kid, thought Reenie, shutting the back garden door. Funny I never got on with Mum, even then. Oh well, can't be helped. Shan't be here long.

She went bouncing cheerfully to work, thinking of all those other girls in those places on the other side of the world who were just coming home from work as she set out for it. In her tatchy case was a copy of *I Married Adventure*, from Just's Library. About Africa, it was, ever so interesting. The Public Library could not supply the newer books so she had joined Just's Twopenny (an innovation received at Just's with much excitement, not to say foreboding).

About half-past seven that evening she knocked at the door of Forty-Five Station Road.

It was opened by a young man with dark eyes and a newspaper in his hand. The wireless was going and there was a smell of distant supper; savoury, but fainter than it would have been in most of the houses Reenie knew.

The young man smiled enquiringly.

"Miss Jevons," explained Reenie. "I'm Miss Reenie Voles. I've brought her things."

"Good evening. Oh yes, do come in. Lovely evening, isn't it?"

"Lovely," said Reenie, beaming, and stepping into the hall and staring round her with interest.

Here, thought Eric, was that puzzling face to which he always raised his hat, that face associated in his mind with a smell of fish. She was Miss Jevons's landlady's daughter. But why the fish?

"How's she getting on?" asked Reenie.

"She's much better but she badly needs a rest, she's been underfed and overworked for months," he said gravely. It was shocking to him that one so quiet and gentle and good as little

Miss Jevons should have undergone all this, while none of his brilliant hard girls, who were so much better equipped to bear it, had ever endured a quarter as much.

"Always did say she didn't eat enough," nodded Reenie. She added: "It's ever so kind of your mum—Mrs. Somers, I should say—to take her in like this."

"My mother likes her very much," he said.

Reenie was rather surprised at anyone getting to like softy Mavis so quickly but of course you couldn't say a thing like that about anyone. So she said cheerfully:

"P'raps I'd better be getting upstairs, if you want to get on with your paper."

"Oh no, not at all, thank you, but I expect she'll be glad to see you. It's the first door at the top of the stairs."

Nice-looking boy but a bit washy, thought Reenie, marching up.

She banged robustly on the door, and a gentle voice answered. "Come in."

"Well, I *am* glad to see you!" cried Reenie, everything but pity swept out of her warm heart at the sight of Mavis. "I thought you'd fallen down a drain, honestly I did!" She sat on the bed and surveyed her kindly. "I've brought all your things (wish I'd of had time to press out your mauve frock; never mind, the creases'll soon come out if you hang it up). Well, how are you feeling?"

"Much better, thanks ever so. I'm awfully glad to see you, too," and Mavis shyly put out her hand, which was at once taken in a friendly squeeze.

Mavis was still pale and her natural curls were loose upon the shoulders of an old dressing-jacket belonging to Mrs. Somers instead of clinging elegantly to the top of her head, but she looked more serene and better fed than when Reenie had last seen her four days ago.

Food can work miracles. If everyone in the world had a little more than enough to eat we should perhaps see loving-kindness ruling the entire globe, and great new works of art created.

Reenie insisted upon hearing every single thing that had happened to Mavis, and Mavis was willing to tell; indeed, she had developed rather an appetite for a sympathetic listener (a thing she had never had in her life before) since the Vicar's visit on Tuesday. He had given Mrs. Somers a large bottle of Wincarnis for her, and made her laugh once or twice, and after he had gone she lay and wondered how she had ever got along without people: people to ask you how you slept, and to have little jokes with about the cat, and to discuss plans for the day with.

In the middle of her story there was a knock, and in came old Mr. Somers with a tray of roast lamb and mint sauce and vegetables and a dear little strawberry jelly and cream in a pretty glass.

"How do you find yourself this evening, eh?" asked Mr. Somers, absently, having bowed in silence to Reenie, who looked at him with much curiosity.

"*Ich hatt 'einen Kameraden*——" hummed Mr. Somers, putting down the tray beside the bed.

"Well enough to come down to breakfast to-morrow morning?" he continued, straightening himself and looking down at her over his glasses.

"Oh yes, quite, thank you," she breathed.

"Good. Good night. Eat it all up," and with another silent bow to Reenie, he sneezed and stalked out.

"Who's that, the father?" demanded Reenie.

"Yes. Oh, he does play beautifully. But we're afraid he's got one of his colds: he was out gardening yesterday evening quite late without his coat."

"They ought to send up the young one with your supper. Save the old one's legs."

"Oh—Mr. Somers." Mavis looked down at the coverlet. "I haven't seen him yet."

"All the better to-morrow, when you've got that mauve frock on! He opened the door to me. He says his mother's taken ever such a fancy to you."

Mavis looked up. Colour, and pleasure, came into her face.

"Mrs. Somers has? Oh, she *is* nice! I *am* glad."

"More than Mum has to me," said Reenie with a kind of cheerful gloom. "Regular old turn-the-milk she's been lately. I've half made up my mind to get out of it. Go on, eat your supper, it'll get cold."

"Where would you go, Reenie?" Mavis began to eat. "Try and get a job in London?"

"No. No more towns for me, thanks. I'm like Hitler, I want a bit more living-space or whatever he calls it. I'd emigrate. Go to New Zealand."

"Goodness, Reenie! All that way away?"

"Why not? It's a lovely place. I've been reading about it. It's got a bit of everything; mountains and lakes and towns if you feel like them, and farms and all that sort of thing. I've got sixty-nine pounds saved up and I expect my brother Ern up in London 'ud lend me a bit, him and me have always got on, and then off I'd go. Be a mother's help on a farm, that's what I'd like. Kids and animals to look after and no more fish, thank you very much *all* the same."

"But so far away from England!"

"Some things look nicer the further you are away from 'em," said Reenie darkly. "Mum would, for one. Besides, the fact is I'm simply crazy to see some of those lovely places, Mavis. Waterfalls, and those Maoris they have in New Zealand. Kind of blacks, well, browns really, they are, ever so good-natured and never worrying about anything and fond of a joke, too. I saw some pictures of them dancing with necklaces of flowers round their necks. Did you good to see them, they looked so happy. And wonderful talkers, they are, it said in the book. When they weren't fighting they were talking. Used to practise it, same as other people do tennis or the piano. Seems a funny idea, doesn't it, but I'd like to hear them all the same. And those geysers."

"Geysers?"

"Hot springs, they are. Coming up out of the ground. I'd give anything to see those."

She leant forward, the evening light falling on her round face, and said earnestly:

"There was a piece about New Zealand in one of the books I read. Poetry, it was. I've got it on the brain, you know how you do. It says:

"*Last, lone, loveliest——*"

"I can't remember how it goes on but it means New Zealand. 'Last' (it's the last country on the map, if you look, right down there at the bottom of the world), 'lone' (that's short for lonely but it doesn't mean sad), 'Loveliest' (most beautiful of them all). I had a good old think before I made up my mind where I'd go. I didn't want anywhere too big and cold or too little and hot, and I wanted somewhere where the blacks sounded all right—not nasty tempered, you know, or give you the miseries with grizzling. And after I'd read about all the places, I thought——

'*Last, lone, loveliest——*'

Well, that's the place for me."

She stood up.

"Now I must be getting back. Seeing you eating that nice supper's made me hungry. I'll pop in and see you again Thursday evening, shall I?"

"I may not be here," said Mavis, a little sadly.

"Don't you worry. You'll be here for a good long time yet," said Reenie confidently, and bent over and gave her a hearty kiss.

"Your landlady's daughter seems a good-natured girl," said Mrs. Somers, coming into Mavis's room after supper with her cross-stitch and sitting down by the open window. "I spoke to her as she was going out. Did you say she works in a fish-shop?"

"Yes, Cousins."

"We used to deal there. I go to Macfisheries now, but I thought I knew her face."

Mrs. Somers usually came in to sit with Mavis for half an hour in the evening. Mavis looked forward to these visits and also dreaded them in case she should give offence; but this evening she was newly fortified by Reenie's report that Mrs. Somers liked her.

Mrs. Somers sighed impatiently and moved her leg.

"Is your leg bad to-night?" asked Mavis, softly and anxiously.

"It is rather. Tiresome thing. It's all this rain. Miss Jevons," she said suddenly—and Mavis's heart jumped in alarm—"have you ever run a house and can you cook?"

"I—I always did my room myself. I never did much cooking since I was on my own. Mother did teach me a bit but she was always so busy and tired after Dad died, she didn't get much time."

"I see. Well, I've been thinking, and talking things over with Mr. Somers and my son, and they both think I ought to have more help in the house. Mrs. Gardiner is all right in the mornings, but she's gone by two o'clock and I always have to get a hot supper for Eric—my son. I can manage when this leg isn't bothering me but then there's the shopping (you can't do it all by telephone, or they rob you right and left) and I'm getting on, you know."

A pause, while she rethreaded her needle with her gaze fixed upon it. Mavis's heart beat quickly. Oh, what was coming?

"I wondered if you would like to stay here and help me instead of trying for another job? I would give you ten shillings a week pocket-money and your laundry and two evenings a week off and every third Sunday. We could try it for a month, anyway, and see how it works. How do you feel about it?"

For a moment Mavis could not speak. The prospect, with all its promises of peace and safety and daily encounter with the person she cared for most in the world—completely overcame her. At last she answered falteringly:

"I should like it better than anything. But do you think I could do it? I should be afraid of not being good enough. But I would try—truly I would."

"I'm sure you would," Mrs. Somers answered at once, "and I can always teach you to cook. I think we should get on together, too. I've quite enjoyed having you here, you know. It's been company for me."

"I'm glad. Oh, I am so glad."

"Well, is that settled, then?" She pushed her needle through the canvas and began to roll it up.

"Yes, please."

"And we'll get your things from your landlady some time this week. You can keep this room for the time being. If anyone comes to stay for a night or two we can always put you on the sofa in the drawing-room."

At the door she paused and looked across at Mavis, who was lying on her side staring at her with very bright eyes and flushed cheeks.

"I should think you might get up to-morrow, don't you?"

"Oh yes, please! To breakfast, may I?"

Mrs. Somers smiled, but she was pleased. "If you like."

"Please may I help you get it?"

"If you like. It's boiled eggs—nice and easy to begin on."

"I can do boiled eggs! I always had them at home—in my room, I mean."

"Well, they aren't as easy as people think. If you can boil an egg properly you know something. Very well, then. Breakfast's at eight o'clock. I'll see you in the kitchen at half-past seven, shall I?"

"Oh yes. I won't be a minute late, truly I won't."

Mrs. Somers laughed outright this time, but as she shut the door she said: "Good night, my dear. Sleep well."

Nice little thing, she thought, going downstairs slowly, because of her leg. And the Vicar spoke so well of her, too. He'll be pleased. I really am quite fond of her, I should miss her now if she went.

Oh dear, my leg. Well, we shall have to see how it works out.

Eric usually helped his mother carry the hot dishes from the kitchen into the breakfast-room, but on the following morning he stood in the sunlit window staring at the *Daily Telegraph* and feeling nervous and rather irritated. He had been told not to help because Miss Jevons was going to help, and his presence in the kitchen might make her nervous.

He disliked changes in his home. His parents had created a shell of habit and comfort that fitted him so well that he did not notice it except on the occasions when its very smoothness jarred

on him. He would be relieved when little Miss Jevons had become
a part of the daily routine.

But would she? At the back of his mind there lingered an uneasy memory of an unusually pretty smile.

Well at least, I shan't fall in love with *her*, he assured himself
morosely. She's much too nice.

And at that very moment the door opened and in she came;
slowly, importantly, bearing before her a little wicker basket
covered by a little padded cosy and containing four eggs.

Her eyes were fixed upon the little basket, but as soon as she
was inside the room she quickly looked up and saw him and
murmured: "Good morning, Mr. Somers," and gave him the
unusually pretty smile.

It was as pretty as ever. As Eric returned it, and answered
"Good morning, I'm so glad you're better," and put the *Daily
Telegraph* down and moved to the breakfast table, he suddenly
thought what a light room the dining-room was; it seemed to get
every ray of sunshine from the awakening brilliant garden outside;
and he noticed how the yellow bowl filled with crimson roses and
sky-blue larkspur on the table was reflected, as if by goblins, in the
fat silver stomach of the sugar-bowl; how white the tablecloth
was, and how the colours of his mother's embroidery glowed
upon it.

And Miss Jevons looked unusually pretty, too; that lilac dress
suited her, and surely her hair never used to be as fair as that? It
was pinned up like a little girl's who is going to be bathed.

"Milk and sugar, Miss Jevons?"

"Yes, please."

"You've got a lovely morning for your first day downstairs,
Miss Jevons," said Eric, beheading his egg.

"Yes, isn't it."

"Did you notice the little egg basket, Miss Jevons? It's
Japanese. Fancy, I bought it at Selfridges the last time I was in
London for sixpence. *Sixpence!* Just imagine plaiting that straw
and varnishing it that beautiful dark blue and making that little
padded cosy to go over it (with a *very* good design on it, too; those
little figures are charming) for sixpence."

"Their standard of living is so low," said Eric.

"Poor things. Wonderful artists but such nasty leaders."

"All leaders are nasty," said Eric.

"Father, what *is* the matter?" interrupted his mother, leaning
towards Mr. Somers. "Don't you like your egg?"

Mavis's egg-spoon was suddenly suspended in mid-air, while
she gazed, frozen, at Mr. Somers.

He was bending over his egg, scrutinizing it with his eyes half-shut, and shaking his head. "I can always tell," he said at last, nodding as if satisfied.

"What is it, Father? Now don't be naughty! Poor Miss Jevons——"

"Cooked by a strange hand," declared Mr. Somers, decapitating his egg masterfully, "I knew at once. There was something about the shape of it. Now, aren't I right, Miss Jevons?"

They were all three laughing. Mrs. Somers leant over and patted her arm, saying: "It's a shame to tease her. They're perfectly cooked, dear. Don't take any notice of Mr. Somers, he loves to tease people. You'll get used to it and you mustn't mind."

Mavis slowly smiled, looking with very bright eyes from one kind laughing face to another. After a moment of absolute despair she was suddenly as near perfect happiness as it is possible to be. While everybody was finishing their eggs she shut her eyes for a second and prayed: Oh dear God, I am so happy. Thank You dear God, and please, please, help me to be a success so that I can stay here, for ever.

On an evening towards the end of the week Eric came home earlier than usual, intending to change and play tennis at the Kirremuir Road Club.

He let himself in with his latchkey, and at once thought how quiet the house was. Windows were open and the smell of cut grass was floating in from the garden; evening sunlight filled the hall where the clock ticked loudly and slowly.

Suddenly a voice, small but rounded and sweet, began to sing loudly:

> "*The King of Love my Shepherd is,*
> *Whose goodness faileth never——*"

and then, getting ever louder and becoming filled with a kind of innocent triumph as if a lamb which could sing were dancing on its hind legs among the primroses under the catkins:

> "*I nothing lack if I am His*
> *And He is mine for ever.*"

The kitchen door opened. Mavis's voice called:

"Is that you, Mrs. Somers? I'm making the jelly," and she came out into the hall.

"Oh!" she said.

"It's me." Eric took off his hat.

"Oh. Good evening, Mr. Somers! I thought it was Mrs. Somers."

"No. It's—no."

He was staring at her. She wore a blue overall and the lilac dress and her sleeves were rolled up. A curl hung over one eye.

"I was just making the jelly." She put the curl back and rolled down her sleeves.

"Good. I hope it's an orange one."

"No, I'm afraid it's cherry."

"Oh. Well, cherry's very nice."

"Yes, I like—yes, cherry's ever so nice, too."

"Yes. I say, do you know what time supper is?"

"Seven o'clock, Mrs. Somers said."

"Oh. I shan't be in, I'm going to play tennis. Would you very much mind telling my mother?"

"Yes, Mr. Somers."

"Thank you very much."

He began to go slowly upstairs. When he came to the sunlight he turned back to tell her what a lovely day it had been; he had the absurd—he at once realized that it was absurd—feeling that she was still standing in the hall looking up at him. But of course she had gone back into the kitchen.

He stood at his window for a moment, before he began to change, staring down into the garden. "Hardly dare to breathe . . ." were the words repeating themselves over and over again; in his heart, rather than in his head. "Hardly dare to breathe. . . ."

CHAPTER XXVI

IT was three weeks later. Pauline was just going into the Fan to treat herself to a more expensive lunch than usual when she saw a tall and elegant young man sauntering down the High Street.

He wore an overcoat of camelhair with the belt untied so that a suit of thin cloth, not green nor grey, was revealed; a dark orange pullover, a square black hat, brown suede shoes, and a big rose in his buttonhole.

But it was the assurance, the unselfconsciousness, with which he was idling along in the sunshine that impressed her. He must be Somebody, she thought. A film star, p'raps. Do I know his face? She paused at the door of the Fan to look.

As he came nearer she perceived that she had known it for about sixteen years: it belonged to Ted.

Gosh! What a sight he looks! was her immediate and indignant thought.

She waited until he was nearly opposite to her and then stepped out upon him, intending to remark in an amused and superior tone: "Hullo, Ted!"

But when she was close to it the face under the black hat was so—different, somehow—that she suddenly felt shy, as if he were a stranger, and her amused and superior greeting emerged only as a quiet little "Hullo."

He stopped. He took off the hat. He made her a bow.

"Ah, Pauline!" he said.

Yes, he actually did say "Ah!" Afterwards she wondered if she had imagined it, but decided, in view of how he went on afterwards, that he did.

There was an awkward little pause. He stood and surveyed her coolly with his head on one side. His thick light brown hair was still worn long, but now it had been expertly cut and looked most becoming.

"Are you back for good or just for the vac. or something?" she asked at last.

"Oh, finally," he drawled. "That fellow Hervé was insufferable. I couldn't endure him. I told him so and came home by the next boat."

"Oh. I see. I say, won't your grandfather be awfully fed up?" He glanced at the restaurant.

"Have you lunched? No?" (as she shook her head, staring at him, fascinated, with her mouth slightly open). "Then will you lunch with me? Yes? Delightful."

He opened the door for her, stood aside while she went in, and shut the door after them with a competent click.

"*Up*stairs," he said, over her shoulder. "I seem to remember they do fish quite well here."

When they were seated at a table in the window and some of the local people in the room who knew Ted by sight were incredulously and gleefully trying to make out if it really were he, he glanced leisurely round the room and observed:

"Amusingly provincial atmosphere this place has."

Pauline could only nod. She decided to keep as quiet as possible. She felt shy and a little sad, for she had looked forward to her friend's homecoming, and he had come home a stranger.

And such a stranger! When he asked the waitress if the fish were done with mace, when he studied the modest wine list for some time and then pushed it aside with the contemptuous decision that they would drink water ("I wouldn't want to offer you an inferior wine, my dear, and I know you wouldn't want to drink it"), she did not know whether to be angry or laugh.

Fortunately he did not raise his voice, so people soon ceased to stare at them, but he had done something to it, of course; it was still beautiful but he sort of pushed it at you with a metallic, offensive ring. Charles-Laughton-and-water, thought Pauline, eating the fish they did quite well there and wishing it were the liver and bacon for which she had not liked to ask.

"And what have you been doing; have you had fun?" he enquired condescendingly, when he had done fussing about the details of the meal and they were both eating.

"Oh, the usual things. Not much. There've been one or two good dances at the Grand and I had a heavenly ride the other Sunday on Satan. I say," her curiosity overcoming her indignation at the way he had ignored her question the first time, "*do tell me what your grandfather says about your coming home. Isn't he livid?*"

"I haven't been home yet, so I really don't know," he said indifferently, looking about the room.

"But are you going on with the stage?"

"Oh definitely, I think. But I have no immediate plans. Is your sister still with the repertory here?"

"If you mean Marjie, yes." (*And she's still got the scar on her knee where you bit her when you were six, you affected thump.*)

"I might look in there sometime. Do you know what they're doing this week?"

"*Dear Octopus.* Marjie is doing the girl who goes wrong in Paris and gets all bitter."

"Really? Is she any good? I might go to see her."

"I haven't seen it yet. Mother and I are going to-night." (*She's not the only one who went wrong in Paris.*)

"Mother's quite well and so is Jumps," she went on, thinking that his manners also seemed to have gone with the wind.

"So glad. Jumps? Oh yes, your dog, of course. I'm afraid I've definitely inherited Grandfather's distaste for dogs."

Pauline glanced at her watch. She wanted to get away as quickly as possible and rage and laugh and blow off steam to someone, and then feel sad at her leisure.

"I ought to go, I'm afraid."

"My dear, what's the urge? Is the coffee drinkable here?"

"Try it and see," muttered Pauline, powdering her nose behind the shelter of her huge flapjack. "I should like some, thanks."

While they were drinking the coffee (blow me if I don't eat everything in sight and just gold-dig him, she thought) he said: "Are they doing anything interesting at the rep. in the next few weeks, do you know?"

"Oh, the great event is this play by Elizabeth Bayne."

"Bayne? Never heard of her."

"She wrote that frightfully funny book, I forget what it was called, a sort of skit. I didn't read it but Mother and Marjie adored it. This is her first play."

"Why are they putting it on in a backwater like this?"

"Can't imagine; I suppose no one in London would have it or something or p'raps they're just trying it out. Anyway, Marjie is very pleased, she's got an awfully good part."

He did not seem interested in Marjie's part, but asked her several more questions about the repertory which she did her best to answer. Perhaps he was going to be madly keen on work now? That ought to cheer me up, she thought; ambitious enthusiastic youth and all the rest of it; but she only felt that her friend was more lost to her than ever.

"Thanks awfully for my nice lunch," she said, as they parted at the entrance.

He raised his hat and gave her another of his bows.

"Thank you for your charming company. We must meet again, and soon." And he sauntered away.

And soon my foot, thought Pauline, hurrying back to the bank. Never would be soon enough. Oh dear, what with Brian, and now Ted gone all high-hat! Oh, and there's Eric—and *he* looks absolutely dopey. Probably got some horrible new girl.

"Hullo!" she said to him, and they walked along together the short distance to the bank.

"Hullo, Pauline. Was your lunch good?"

"The *lunch* wasn't so bad, I went to the Fan, but *who* do you think I had it with? Ted Early. He's just come back from a dramatic school in Paris and he—he—gosh, he has changed!"

"For the worse, I take it, by your tone?"

"Oh definitely, I'm afraid."

But she said no more. She suddenly found that she minded so much about the alteration in Ted that she did not want to talk about it.

"How's Miss Jevons?" she went on. (He had told her about the rescue of Mavis and she had been very interested, and related to him in her turn her Sunday morning encounter with Mavis on the beach.)

"Oh—er—she's much better, thank you."

"Has she got another job yet?"

"Well no. As a matter of fact I think she's going to stay with us for the present and help my mother."

"Oh good! I'm so glad. She ought to like that, poor little thing. I should think she's had a pretty thin time all her life."

"I expect she has. But I don't think that's the first thing that strikes one on looking at her. She's proud in a delicate kind of way, and brave too."

"She looks very pretty when she smiles," said Pauline, glancing at him rather curiously. "Oh well, here we are at the hell-hole. Good-bye for the present."

Gentle reader, are you a feminist? and are you impatiently wondering why Pauline did not find relief from her troubles in the interesting and manifold complexities of her job?

The answer is short: ordinary girls of twenty-two don't; and there are more ordinary girls of twenty-two in the world than there are highly educated ones. There have to be, to have the children and keep things going.

Feminists may not want things to keep going, or perhaps they want to keep them going in a different way. These desires do not alter the facts.

Pauline continued to get through her job conscientiously but without enthusiasm and to be most fully a girl when the doors of the hell-hole had closed upon her for the day.

She was still bubbling over about Ted when she got home that evening, and rushed straight into the drawing-room to tell the others all about it.

Mrs. Williams was sitting behind the wobbly silver teapot, surrounded by Jumps on the floor hoping for bits of cake and Marjorie on the sofa with her feet up and a huge cartwheel beach hat of black straw embroidered with Tyrolean flowers lying on her middle. She was drinking scalding hot tea, and staring solemnly over the top of the cup and looking white and tired.

"Hullo!" said Pauline, sitting down. "(Well, Jumpsie, you smelly old man!) How frightfully late you're having tea. I say, who do you think I had lunch with to-day?"

"It was this child wanted some; she's worn out," said her mother, with a proud anxious glance at the beauty.

"(Is it really hot?) Ted! He's come home! (I'll have a cup if it's really boiling.)"

"It's heaven," croaked Marjorie, cradling the transparent pink cup voluptuously. "Ted? Whatever for?"

"Oh, had a row with the head of the school in Paris or something. But my dear, you never saw such a sight as he's turned himself into! And his voice! And the most extraordinary manners——"

The telephone bell rang.

"Blast. You go for me, there's a lamb, Pauli," said Marjorie wearily.

"——and he said he 'seemed to remember' the Fan 'did' fish 'quite well'," continued Pauline, going into the hall.

A sweet derisive crow of laughter came from the drawing-room as she took off the receiver, followed by a faintly puzzled but dutiful "How absurd!" from her mother.

"Hullo?" she said.

"Pauli? Is that you? How did you like the chap you had lunch with?" asked Ted's voice—his old familiar charming voice.

"I think he was simply frightful! Oh, Ted, you are a wretch! You had me completely!"

"You don't mean to say you didn't like him?"

"Appalling isn't the word."

"Not the hat or the pullover or the vocabulary or anything?"

"Absolutely not one thing. Oh yes—the buttonhole wasn't bad."

"Well, this is extremely serious, because he's my new personality and I'm just trying him out. His name is Cudd Mott."

"*What?*"

"Cudd Mott." He spelt it at her. "All the charmers have these tough names nowadays; they're so convenient because you use them backwards. Mott Cudd would do equally well."

"Not with me it wouldn't. Oh Ted, have you seen your grandfather yet?"

"Yes. He didn't mind in the least. I think he was rather pleased to have me home again."

"What are you going to do now, about work, I mean?"

"That's where I want Marjorie to help me. Is she there? Can I speak to her?"

"She is here but she's awfully tired—I don't know——"

"I won't keep her a moment."

His tone was cool and decided and almost before she realized she was doing it, Pauline called:

"Marjie, Ted wants to speak to you."

"What about? I'm all in," Marjorie called after a pause.

"About a job or something. He says he won't keep you a minute."

After a minute Marjorie came out into the hall, looking irritable, and snatched up the receiver.

"Hullo?"

"Marjorie, will you give me an introduction to Lenham Browne?" asked Ted at once. "I want to get in as A.S.M."

There was a pause. Marjorie frowned, staring at the floor.

That was clever of him, she thought, not to apologize for saying that about me in the summer, or trying to woo me or anything. He knows I simply can't say no outright.

She said calmly:

"Yes, if you want it. There's a chance you might get in there just now, too."

"Good. Thank you very much; when shall I come down?"

"To-morrow morning, if you like, about eleven; I'll meet you at the stage door. 'Bye."

She hung up.

"Oh—I wanted to talk to him again," cried Pauline.

"Sorry." She went back into the drawing-room and lay down again. Their mother had gone out of the room. "Heavens, isn't it hot and how sick I am of this place. I'm going to town this autumn and stay there till I get something."

"Mother will fuss about giving you the money."

"Shan't ask her for it; I've saved enough to live on for a bit."

"Have you? You are a marvel, Marjie, I simply cannot save."

"You don't organize yourself," said Marjorie, shutting her eyes and putting the hat over them. Presently she opened them again to say:

"Ted may have been putting on an act but he has changed, all the same. He's grown up."

"How do you know?"

"I just do."

"He's a silly old thump," said Pauline happily.

Marjorie replaced the hat.

Most of us have a place where we feel it is natural for us to be. For someone it is the open air; she always feels her spirits droop just a little as she goes back into the house, even if she has only been hanging out the washing. For another it is a room lined with books; once, on the first occasion that he visited the British Museum Reading Room, such delight overcame him at the sight of those thousands upon thousands of books and the thought of all the knowledge and pleasure stored in them that for the moment he felt actually faint.

Perhaps we are not consciously happy in our natural place,

but we feel most fully ourselves there; body, mind and spirit are at ease, working in harmony and forgotten by ourselves while we revel in our native air.

This is the place for me, you know, thought Ted, following Marjorie along the greasy black stone corridors of the Theatre Royal, through the smells of make-up, and escaping gas, and lavatories. It's dirty and it's tatty and it stinks and I adore it.

She pushed open a narrow door, and there was the stage itself, the witch's cauldron for the moment off the boil. A rehearsal was in progress.

They stood in the doorway for a moment, looking down on the scene.

"Aren't you playing next week?" he asked. They had exchanged nothing but "Hullos" and some remarks on the weather since they met a few moments since. Marjorie's manner was her usual calm one and Ted could now match it by one as composed, and did.

"No; it's *White Cargo*. Joan Somerset's doing Tondelayo."

"Which is Browne?"

"Over there, sitting on the table."

"Come down, Marjie darling, and shut that bloody door if you're coming," called Miss Somerset fretfully, "it's bothering me."

They went on to the stage.

Nobody took any notice of them and they picked their way round the back between tall skeletral pieces of tropical scenery and across the dust on the boards; the sort of lively gritty dust that gets plenty of exercise in places where people are very much alive, not the sort that lies undisturbed and soft in places where people are half-dead.

"Lenny, I've brought Ted," said Marjorie, coming round at the back of the man sitting on the table.

"Oh, hullo, Marjie darling." He turned round smiling, but his gaze at once went past her to Ted, and while he went on in an easy friendly style, "she tells me you want to join this horrible profession?" his eyes, blue in his worn handsome face, were taking in every detail.

Ted nodded. "I wondered if there was a chance to get in as A.S.M., doing small parts."

His tone was quiet, unhumorous. His eyes steadily met the sad eyes of the actor.

"How old are you?"

"Twenty."

"My god!" said Lenham Browne feelingly. "I wish I were

twenty, don't you, Marjie darling? And you're Archie Early's grandson. My old man played with him in Shaw forty years ago. He must be as old as God now?"

"Seventy-eight."

"He was a grand actor. They just don't make 'em like that nowadays. Well, I can only offer you thirty," he added suddenly, getting off the table. "This is absolutely your first job, isn't it? I don't count anything you may have done in Paris."

"I'd be very grateful for thirty and the chance," said Ted; and suddenly Marjorie, watching him, realized that he was copying his grandfather's trick of making his voice convey every ounce of what he felt; now, those young tones simply brimmed with honest gratitude. You rat, she thought coldly, you can't like it all that.

"You'll have to learn, you know," warned Lenham Browne, looking rather ironically at his queer ugly-beautiful face. "Benny'll show you." He nodded towards someone in shirt-sleeves who was sprawling in a deck-chair and declaiming. "He's our stage manager. Are you a quick study?"

Ted nodded. "The head of the Paris school said I was unusually quick."

"Oh. We shall all enjoy hearing about Paris, shan't we, Marjie darling?"

"Sorry." Ted gave an apologetic (and natural) grin.

"Granted, I'm sure. (The old man's liver is often not so good of a morning.) All right, then. Can you start to-night? As a matter of fact," his manner became warmly confidential, charming, "the A.S.M. walked out on us on Monday. So you're really rather an act of God. There's my cue. Marjie, take him along to Benny, will you, darling? Au revoir."

He walked out to the middle of the stage, his face and body altering as he went.

"Let's go and have some coffee," said Marjorie, leading the way back through the tropical scenery. "Benny and the rest'll be along there in a few minutes, and I'll introduce you."

"He's a charmer," Ted pronounced, as they went down the corridors again.

"Lenny? He's an *angel*," she said bitterly, not looking over her shoulder. "He has a hell of a time."

"How come?"

"Oh, his wife's a cow and won't give him a divorce."

Ted said nothing.

"It's all right, I don't sleep with him."

"I didn't assume you did," he said mildly.

8

"Well, I thought you might have wondered. As a matter of fact I don't sleep with anyone."

"So I gathered."

"Why?"

"The signs of chastity are unmistakable."

"You really are the rudest rat I ever encountered," she said, pushing open the door of the café. "I don't know why I introduced you to Lenny."

"You thought I'd make a good A.S.M. and might even be able to act," he said. They sat down at a table near the window.

"Yes, I suppose I did," she said. "I certainly wouldn't have wished you on to my beautiful Lenny for any other reason."

He smiled without looking up, as he studied the menu, and did not reply.

I may as well face up to it, she thought, watching him; I fell for his voice on the phone. It's something new he's got into it. I had to see if his manner had it as well. Sometimes it has and sometimes it hasn't. Disappointing.

"You've lost about a stone in weight, haven't you?" she asked as their coffee came.

"Over a stone," he corrected. "It's a bore; I adore large rich meals, but if I eat all I want to I get bilious and fat."

"You've got a good figure now. Dieting's a bore, but there you are."

The door opened and in came six or seven people wearing refuhankies, slacks, and camelhair coats with the belts undone.

"God, Marjie darling, I'm *dead*! What a morning!"

"Sweetie, I adore your little hat."

"Is he the new A.S.M.? Lenny said——"

Marjorie introduced Ted to the company. He put on what she had already labelled his Manner Number One: Simple, Serious Modesty; and was soon chatting with them as if he had been with them for weeks.

She was rather silent, smoking and occasionally watching him.

He had something now, there was no doubt about it. His face changed as he spoke, his eyes were clear and full of light, and his mouth was beautiful, but of course the something was not in his features: it was personality, the fairy gift that everybody longs for nowadays.

She leant forward and put out her cigarette.

I shan't be surprised if he can act, after all, she thought.

She was surprised to find the thought not altogether disagreeable to her.

.   .   .   .   .

That afternoon a large and lavish tea party was in progress at the house of Mr. and Mrs. Letter, the parents of Connie Letter, Mrs. Williams's maid.

It was a queer little house called Railway Cottage, built into the actual structure of a railway bridge on the outskirts of the town in the days when the railways were still sufficiently new and romantic to give their name to a house, just as the telegraph did to the various Telegraph Houses up and down the country.

A steep bank with willow herb and marguerites growing all over it towered above the little house on one side, and on the other side of the road was its garden; a long triangular strip planted with cabbages and beetroots and runner beans. The back of the house went into the steep bank.

There were present at the tea-table: Mr. and Mrs. Letter, Connie (whose afternoon off it was), Mrs. Letter's eldest brother Herbert Dunfee, two small male grandchildren who had just popped round to see Gram as it was a Friday and there wasn't much for tea at home, and a married daughter with one offspring. As the offspring was taking its time about learning to walk, and continued to hang a contented bottom over its mother's arm long after less cunning infants were tottering perilously about on the floor, and as it was more or less permanently attached to its mother, they were known collectively as one entity, Edie-and-the-baby.

"But wot I want to know is," said Mr. Letter argumentatively, from his place by the hob where the black kettle simmered, "how did you come to know it was him put a spoke in your wheel?"

"It was the Committee, see," said Dunfee, who was sitting at one end of the kitchen table with a great-great-nephew on either hand. "The Nunby Almshouses Awards Committee meets every three months in our Banquet Hall, see (it's the old Dining-Room, really), and we always serves the tea to them afterwards. With watercrisses. (Paid for out o' the subscriptions, I s'pose.) And I was waiting, like I always do, that's how I come to overhear them talking. About me."

"Fancy, Uncle!" said Connie, sitting beside her mother with her plain pleasant face flushed by family interest, hot tea, and mussels.

Dunfee snapped his fingers playfully at Edie-and-the-baby, who acknowledged the gesture by a sudden wriggle.

"I sends up my name," Dunfee went on. "I'm seventy this year, born and lived all my life in the parish of Seagate, so it's all in order."

"But don't you have to get someone to sign the papers?" asked Mr. Letter from the fireside.

"The master did that for me. Said he was very pleased to. We never said anything to young Smartyface about it, neither. He don't want me to go, drat him."

"How do you know he don't?" demanded Edie-and-the-baby.

"Heard two of them talkin' about it while I was waiting when the Awards Committee was having tea. Two of the old bags—ladies, I beg their pardon—was eating their way through the sangwidges. '*Oh, I do so agree with you,*' says one, '*it's so important not to destroy their self-respec' by givin' them charity.*' '*Yes, and with so much done for them nowadays,*' squawks up the other, drinkin' half a cup o' tea and holding it out for more. '*Far better to let them die in harness if they have congenial work,*' says the first one. '*Now I understand from young Mr. Kingsley that this man Dunfee is perfectly happy here.*' (That was a bit of a shock to me, see, hearin' young Smartyface knew anything about it.) '*No doubt,*' says the tea-swallerin' one. '*I knows the type. Wrapped up in his work and it might kill him to leave it.*'"

There was a roar of laughter. Edie-and-the-baby bounced up and down appreciatively and even Dunfee himself gave a sour unwilling smile.

"So what I'll do I don't know," he concluded, picking up a mussel and peering discontentedly into it. If he don't want me to go and the Committee don't think I want to go because he says I don't, what's to be done?"

"Can't think why he wants to keep you on," said Mr. Letter. " 'Tisn't as if you was a youngster."

"Spite," said Dunfee briefly. "Like he used to be with the crabses legs."

"But seeing how you've sent your name in, they must know you want to stop work," argued Mrs. Letter. "No, Jimmy. No more mussels."

"*He's* told 'em something, I'll lay. Said I'm not right in the 'ead, p'raps."

"There's only one thing to do, Uncle!" cried Connie, "you'll have to do something downright horrible and get yourself sacked."

"That's about the ticket," said her great-uncle gloomily.

CHAPTER XXVII

AUTUMN had come. A note of wildness and melancholy, a rising wind, blew on cloudy evenings across the air and the sea. But the days were still warm enough to make bathing pleasureable; and a week or so later Pauline was sitting on the front, waiting for Brian to emerge (that was how one thought of his careful appearances) from the Hotel Bristol and bathe with her.

The military band was playing cheerfully; the mad-American-college-boy conductor was swinging hot tunes down in the blue pit; teas were being served on the veranda of the Bristol behind the fig-vine, and the sea lay dark blue and calm, swaying lazily under the late afternoon sunlight.

Pauline had her back to the sea, sheltered by a glass screen intended to protect old ladies. She was sitting in a deck-chair and absently gazing up at the windows of the Bristol.

This has been a rotten summer, she thought. Nothing but fights with Brian. And that evening in March I thought everything was going to be so marvellous!

Nothing's happened at all, really.

We're just where we were this time last year, except that then he hadn't asked me to go all nudist.

He's been so haughty ever since I wore that frock; I know perfectly well he's still sulking because I said no, but I'm darned if I mention it unless he does first.

She slowly opened her white straw handbag and took out a cigarette and lit it; a sign that she was going to have a serious think. She settled herself more comfortably, and lay back, smoking and staring up at the windows of the Bristol.

Here I am, she thought, nearly twenty-two and quite reasonably pretty, with heaps of friends and a good job and perfectly happy except for him.

Yes, except for him.

I'm not the sort of person who gets crushes on people. I suppose I'm not awfully highly sexed.

I like people I've known for years; and dogs and horses; and games; and shows; and dancing; and going for long tramps.

I'd like to get married and have some children, but certainly not unless it's going to last for ever.

I want my marriage to be the real thing, the sort of thing you read about in poems and see on the pictures. I want it to be beautiful and romantic.

Yes, I do, and darn being modern.

I want to marry someone who won't mind *how* much I love them and won't shy off like a scared seagull the minute I show I do.

I don't think I'm highly sexed, but I do feel pretty choked up and lonely sometimes. As if I needed petting.

But all *he* does is to pick at me and grizzle because I won't go nudist and try to bite lumps out of my neck.

I've got (and here she ground out the stump of her cigarette) a feeling something's got to be *done* about him, and pretty soon.

I'm just about fed up.

She was still gazing absently at the hotel as she came to this decision, and suddenly a curtain at one of the large upper windows was snatched aside, as if impatiently, and a figure was revealed, staring out across the sea.

With a little thrill of excitement she realized that it was a man seated in a chair, and knew that it must be Mr. Kingsley.

He did not stay there for more than a minute. After one long, intent gaze over to the horizon he dashed the curtain across again as impatiently as he had lifted it; and she could almost see the rough movement with which he trundled the chair back into the room.

She remembered Brian's story about his mother, and sighed. That was another complication. Was it true or wasn't it? Mrs. Williams had a vague recollection that Mrs. Kingsley had not been very strong and did not go out much, but that was all; and Pauline did not care, from delicate motives, to ask anyone else. Mrs. Pask, who had lived for forty years within sight of the Hotel Bristol, was obviously the person to ask, but so far Pauline had not had the courage.

Marjorie, who was handicapped neither by delicacy or cowardice, had been so busy lately that she had simply forgotten all about the matter.

Pauline glanced away from the hotel, and saw Ted coming slowly down the steps leading from the Upper Parade.

His hair was falling anyhow over his forehead, a crumpled part in a brown paper cover stuck out of one pocket, and he looked white and untidy and exhausted.

She gave the whistle they had always used on the sands when they were children, and he turned and saw her. Up went his hand in greeting (how much more graceful his movements were!) and a look of pleasure came into his face. He strolled towards her.

"Hullo," she said. "You'll probably be furious with me for saying so, but you look all in."

"No, I'm not; it sounds like heaven and you're a darling girl," he said and banged himself wearily into the chair next to her.

She did not smile but looked at him in affectionate concern. His odd ways and speech had ceased to embarrass her and she felt nothing in his company but content.

"We've been at it since ten this morning," he said. "And I've got to be back there in an hour for to-night's show. I'm on in the last act."

"Oh, *are* you, Ted? I did want to be there on your first night, you might have told me; I thought you weren't doing anything until the Elizabeth Bayne show."

"Oh, I'm only being a wicked Chinese; I haven't any lines," he said absently. "Me creepee about with armees in sleevee-sleevee and bang on a gong. It's a villainous poor play, about forty years old, called *The Idol's Eye*, but the groundlings love it."

"How's the Elizabeth Bayne show going?"

He opened his eyes and a livelier look came into them.

"Oh, just now it stinks, but it'll be all right on the night. There's a jewel of a part in it for me, right at the end of the third act (I got it because I'm doing props. up till then)—a cripple boy who gets the power to walk again. It's a honey."

She was watching him rather shyly as he talked, as if he were a stranger.

"Are you liking it?" she asked suddenly.

"That part? Enormously."

"Everything, I meant, really. The whole life."

"It's hell. Overwork and backbiting and indigestion and draughts and no sleep and smells and mad confusion and starvation wages and I adore it!"

They were still laughing over this, Ted leaning back and watching her pretty face crinkled up with amusement, when they became aware of a tall and elegant Presence slowly descending the steps, clad in grey Daks, sandals, and a striped sweater, with two huge and snowy towels festooned about its neck.

Ted turned his head and surveyed Brian but said nothing.

"Oh . . . hullo!" said Pauline, and her spirits sank even while her heart leapt to greet his beauty. "You do know each other, don't you?"

Brian distantly inclined his head and Ted nodded, looking lazy and nothing more.

"Ted's been rehearsing all day, he's simply worn out," she went on, getting up.

"Dreadful existence, I've always thought," drawled Brian, "but you people like it, I suppose, or you wouldn't do it."

Ted turned his head away so that they could not see his face, and answered in a low tone:

"It's not that, altogether. A good many of us are ill and some of us don't get enough to eat and we're all tired . . . so tired . . ." (his voice sank to an exhausted murmur and when he went on it was not quite steady). "But we keep on. Just—trying to give pleasure, that's all. Just faithful to our Public. It's—pretty hard sometimes——" He turned his head still further away and was silent.

After an embarrassed pause Brian said awkwardly:

"Yes, it must be. Sorry and all that, I didn't realize——"

"Ted!" cried Pauline, darting round and peering delightedly into his grinning face. "Just for the minute you had me, too!"

"That's my job," he said, standing up and giving Brian a cool look. "Well, I'm going to get some food. Good-bye. Have a nice little swim," and he hurried away, clutching at his part and a list of properties that was falling out of his pocket.

"Beastly little cub," said Brian furiously as they walked towards the tents. "I always did think there was something neurotic about him."

"Ted? Neurotic? You must be crazy!" she exclaimed: she was feeling a little remorseful and fonder of him because of that gruff apology. "He's about as neurotic as I am."

"You are neurotic in some ways. You're inhibited, anyway."

"I am not!"

"You must be, or else you'd do what I want you to."

Pauline stood still. Her hair blew in the wind above her frowning forehead and suddenly flushed face, and she clenched her hands.

"Brian," she said quietly. "I want to enjoy this bathe. Please don't say another word." He shrugged his shoulders.

"All right. But every word you say only shows I'm right."

"I saw your father looking out of the window just now," she said deliberately. "I should like to meet him."

He glanced at her.

"He never sees anyone. You know that."

"Why not?"

"Oh, well, he's so touchy and nervous and sensitive about his health."

"Marjie saw him once, you said so."

"Did I? Oh yes, I believe she did."

"Don't worry," bitterly, "she didn't tell me anything about him."

"What do you mean? I don't care if she did."

"Then why are you so peculiar and mysterious about him and —and everything?"

"I wasn't aware that I was 'peculiar and mysterious' about anything. I only know you're making me damned wretched." And he stood quite still, gazing out at the ocean with a suffering look on his face.

"I am?" Pauline began to tremble.

He nodded. "Because you won't do what I ask you."

She said nothing. He turned on her, roughly pulling down the towels from his neck.

"It's no use, I can't stand the sight of you while I feel like this. I might do something desperate."

She tried to laugh but only trembled more violently.

"What on earth do you mean?"

"You know what I told you that time in the car. I've got very violent blood in me, remember. If I'm driven too far I might— I don't know."

"Kill me, do you mean?" piped up Pauline; she was so horrified that her voice came out in a feeble squeak. Yet she also wanted to laugh.

"No. *Myself*," he said violently. There was a pause.

"Look here, we can't bathe now, it would be a farce," he said. "We'd better not see each other for a bit. I can't stand it. If you change your mind, ring me up."

And he sketched a gesture of farewell, as if he could not bear to look at her, as if he could not bear to touch her, and walked quickly away.

Pauline, not thinking at all of what she was doing, walked forward to the booth and took a bathing ticket and went into one of the tents and let the flap fall.

There was a dim green light coming through the canvas walls and the sand felt warm and loose under her bare feet: the tide never came up so far as this to wash away the sea's driftage, and in a corner there was one of those black seaweed pods looking like a beetle, with a fat stomach and two horns at each end.

There's a "beetle," thought Pauline, pulling up her bathing dress. Her mouth was dry and her heart beat fast. She could still see his face; that, and nothing else. Her outward eyes saw the beetle; but her inward eyes, the eyes of her heart, saw only his suffering face.

For heaven's sake let's go and swim, she muttered, and pulled the flap aside.

Suddenly she remembered how, when she was ten years old, she

8*

had been happy all day if she found a "beetle"; how she used to float them in a special pool among the rocks that she called Beetle Pool, and the fearful joy with which she used to "pop" their stomachs at last and throw them out to meet the incoming tide.

The tide was coming in now. The wind was getting up and the waves were beginning to roll. She waded out towards them; the water rushed round her knees and then over her waist and then she sprang forward into the heart of a blue wave sliding towards her and swam strongly out to sea.

She was alone. The roughening strength of the water held her up, under the sky now streaked with white whips of cloud. When she moved among the foam on the top of a wave she smelt the freshness of seaweeds and salt, and saw on a level with her eyes mile after mile of white crests coming on. The sea lifted her with its soft strong swaying; cold foam rushed over her nose and chin with a salt taste and made her gasp. The waves pressed buoyantly on her moving arms as she thrust the heavy water aside. Her body was warm and she was enjoying the struggle with the strong sea, but all the time she could still see his suffering face; and when at last she turned back towards the shore she suddenly realized that they had quarrelled; that unless she changed her mind and telephoned to tell him so, she would not be with him again.

CHAPTER XXVIII

DAHLIAS were out in the garden of Forty-Five Station Road; the eiderdowns had gone to the cleaners to be prepared for the winter; and Mavis had been living with the Somers for three months.

Gentle reader, perhaps you have sometimes imagined what it would be like to live in the same house with the person you love best in the world. (We address particularly our unmarried readers, for we hope that most of our married readers do live in the same house with the person they love best in the world.) What would it be like to hear that voice at breakfast, to take the afternoon letters from that hand, to receive that smile in "Good night" at half past ten every evening?

Mavis had never indulged in such fancies; her only daydream

had been that of the walk among the cornfields beyond Happy Sands. Yet a miracle, so unimaginable that it had never even crossed her mind, had overtaken her, and caught her up into itself. She was living in the same house with Mr. Somers.

It may disappoint realists (another name for those people who think everything is very disagreeable indeed) to hear that she found him even more wonderful at close quarters than she had found him at a distance.

Different, of course. Once or twice he had come down to breakfast just a little, but unmistakably, cross, and he went out far more often than she had imagined to sherry parties, and friends, and musical evenings. But in everyday life he was as gentle, kind and good as she had always believed him to be.

And lately he had taken to staying in in the evenings, listening to the wireless, and laughing. Before Mavis came, the Somers had never listened to the funny broadcasts, being impatient and selective in their listening-in; but one evening when they were boredly about to turn off "Band Waggon," Mr. Somers happened to glance up, and saw Mavis laughing silently away in her corner with her head bent low over her mending; and they were all so pleased to see her pleasure that they gave the funny men a trial and found them not so unfunny as they had always haughtily believed.

But they laughed as much from pleasure in Mavis's laughter as from amusement. Mr. Somers would watch her face as a joke unfolded, knowing the exact instant at which she would begin to smile that pretty smile, and Mrs. Somers would shake her head over her cross-stitch, murmuring: "Absurd creatures they are, really—such nonsense," and glance smilingly across at Mavis, whom Eric was watching too.

It was pleasant to see her laughing, when they remembered the white, thin, hungry creature she had been three months ago.

She had put on half a stone in weight; and although most of her weekly ten shillings went to pay back-rent to Mrs. Voles and to satisfy the reasonable claims of the Cosyhome Furnishing Co., she had managed to buy some pink rayon material with white cherries printed on it and to make herself a pretty dress. And the voice of the lamb singing under the catkins was now one of the familiar sounds of the house.

From seven o'clock in the morning until half past ten at night there was not a moment of the time that she was not busy and interested and enjoying what she was doing.

Every object in the house and all its domestic activities were important and slightly solemn to her. She made little jokes nowa-

days, but never about Mrs. Somers's hot-water bottle or Mr.
Mr. Somers's elevenses; and she was learning every day—with
that curious but definite satisfaction that comes from making
discoveries in a social sphere a little higher than one's own—how
gentle, cultured people spoke and lived.

Dad and Mother must be so glad I'm living here, she thought
over and over again. They always taught me to speak properly
and like things nice and told me there were people and houses
like this—gentlefolk, Dad always called them—and here I am,
living with them!

Her feeling for Eric had been part of herself for so many years
and was so quiet and deep that she was not aware how it showed
in her looks and ways. She waited on him without knowing it
and did not realize that she began to sing softly each evening as
soon as his key sounded in the lock.

And every Sunday morning they walked to church together.
They did not talk much on these occasions; sometimes Eric
observed that the chrysanthemums were early this year, or Mavis
murmured that she had enjoyed the visiting parson's sermon, but
usually they walked in pleasant silence. Their steps kept pace
comfortably together and he was a little taller than she was.

These Sunday morning walks were the high spot of her new
life. Walking to church with Mr. Somers! There could be no one
happier than she was in the whole world.

It was sad and puzzling that old Mr. Somers made those noises
about people who went to church; but she gradually realized that
he did not believe in God. However, he carried on so about God,
and seemed to think about Him so much, that she could not help
feeling that God knew all about old Mr. Somers and had His own
methods of dealing with him. And no one so kind as old Mr.
Somers could be really wicked, even if they did say they were an
atheist.

She at last decided that Mr. Somers only *thought* he did not
believe in God; and nothing ever shook her from this conclusion.

There had been no more anonymous letters since Mavis came,
and although Mrs. Somers was not a credulous woman she could
not help wondering if this was a Sign that she had done rightly in
taking Mavis in? And she had grown really fond of her. She was
so good, so affectionate and willing; so grateful for the home they
gave her.

When Mrs. Somers had been Miss Ethel Lindon, Art Mistress
at Seagate College for Girls, one of her favourite pictures had
been Rossetti's "King Cophetua and the Beggar Maid"; but it
was years since she had seen a copy of it and the legend never

entered her head nowadays. If it had, it might have rung a warning bell; as it was, she really had no more suspicions than the Dowager Queen Cophetua probably had.

Mr. Somers had suspicions. Mr. Somers, an old man who enjoyed teasing, had grown to love Mavis as if she were his own daughter; and he thought the whole affair as suitable as it was romantic and was rather maliciously looking forward to seeing the mine explode under his wife's feet.

I'm not worthy of her, I'm not worthy, mourned Eric's heart, by day and by night. *And yet I can't honestly say I wish I'd never loved Madeleine. If I told her that, would she understand?*

This was the only doubt he had. He did not doubt that she loved him. He had never seen that look, for him, in a girl's eyes before; but he knew what it was, and he found in it a wonderful soothing comfort; it was restful and sweet thus to be silently adored.

He had often thought how he would enjoy getting his own back for all his sufferings by cruelly dominating some horrid unkind girl, but lately this little daydream had faded, receding into the lustful unhappy past. And he felt close to God again, and could go to church and sing "O Praise Ye the Lord" with all his heart and soul and voice.

One October afternoon he came home early from the bank. Blue dusk was falling and leaves were spinning along the cool empty streets and the white-capped waves looked far off and lonely. The drawing-room was lit by a generous golden fire in the ample old-fashioned grate and a lamp with a rosy shade; by this illumination his father and mother were having tea, with Mavis seated in a fireside chair and tending the toasted buns.

The elders exclaimed with pleasure (rather like two well-trained dogs who do not see much of their master) at his early arrival, and Mavis looked up and silently smiled. Leaning back in his chair and holding the cup to his lips he indulged himself with a long tender look at her, quite reckless whether the parents saw it or not. She had on a skimpy black skirt and a poor little jumper, with a darn on one elbow; she's just like Cinderella, he thought, and now I'm going to be the Prince and the Fairy Godmother, in one go.

"It's the last dance at the Grand on Saturday," he began, setting down his cup. "Pauline wants to make up a party, and I think it might be good fun. Will you come?" he ended, turning to Mavis.

Mrs. Somers looked affectionately at him for a moment before looking at Mavis. Dear kind boy! so unselfish of him to think of the poor little thing's pleasure.

Mavis had gone deep pink, and was gazing at him with parted lips. Slowly an expression full of dreams came over her face: she continued to gaze at him, and he at her; and neither spoke, and it was a most fortunate fact that both the elders were no longer keen of sight, in spite of their glasses.

"Do come," Eric said at last. "I think we should enjoy it."

"Of course she must go!" cried Mr. Somers, plunging at the toasted buns, which were instantly thrust upon him by Mavis with something less than her usual care. ":Do her good, cheer her up, get away from us fogies, eh, Mother?"

"I should certainly go if I were you, dear," said Mrs. Somers. "There's a good floor at the Grand, I've heard, and they always have a very good band."

"Thank you, Mr. Somers. I should love to," Mavis answered, folding her hands together, and looking down at the toasted buns.

"Good, then I'll tell Pauline," he answered, and drank some more tea.

"By the way, what exactly *is* a fogey?" suddenly demanded Mr. Somers, "oughtn't to use a word one doesn't know the meaning of. Ought to look it up in the *Ox. Poc. Dic.*," and he began to struggle up out of his chair.

"Oh, Father, do sit still, you don't want to go rummaging in the dining-room, it's so cold in there!" said Mrs. Somers.

"Remind me to look it up at supper," he muttered, sinking back again.

"I've never been to a dance before," said Mavis unexpectedly. Her soft voice was completely charged with excitement; it was as if a little dynamo had suddenly begun to hum in the room. She sat forward a little in her chair, glancing from one face to another.

"Never been to a dance? Well——" murmured Mrs. Somers, peering at her cross-stitch, which was approaching one of its many crises.

"Don't tell me that means you don't possess a dance frock?" cried Mr. Somers, snatching up the last cold bun. "Behold a phenomenon! A young lady in the nineteen thirties who does not own a dance frock!"

"Oh yes—I—I—have got a dance frock," she said hastily. "I did go to a dance, once, and Dad bought it for me."

My little love, thought Eric, staring into the fire.

But for once Mavis was not thinking about Eric. The dance she had been to, once, had taken place at the school she attended when she was fourteen, and the limp white net frock that reached to her knees was still affectionately packed away in tissue paper in one of her suitcases.

But it would not do to wear to the Grand Hotel with Mr. Somers.

"Is that you, Reenie?"

"Yes. Whoever's that? It's not Mavis, is it?"

"Yes, it is. Reenie, I was wondering, could you have lunch with me to-day?"

"Half a minute. (Joe, has Eighteen The Approach's sole gone up yet? All right, see it goes with this lot, will you, she wants it for lunch.) What's up, Mavis? Anything wrong?"

"Oh no, nothing. It's only—I just wanted your advice about something."

"All right. Pleased to do anything I can," said Reenie, flattered. "Where shall I meet you?"

"Well, where do you usually go?"

("Thank you, madam, two and six, eightpence. Thank you; yes, quite a change, isn't it. Good morning.) The Geisha's quite a nice little place. On the corner of Marina Road, this end. I'll be there at about ten past one."

"All right. I'll see you there, then. Good-bye."

"And I was wondering," said Mavis, stirring her coffee and looking at Reenie, "what to do about it."

"Haven't got a summer one you could make do, I s'pose? Put something on the hem and lengthen it?"

"I've only got two cotton ones and my linen suit."

"Can't you ask Mrs. Somers if she's got anything she could let you have? I'd give you a hand altering it."

"Oh, I'd rather not do that. They've done such a lot for me already, I don't want to seem to be asking for anything more."

"Don't you worry, they like having you there, all right, and I'll bet she gets her money's worth out of you, too. Don't you know anyone else who'd lend you one. What about this Miss Williams?"

Mavis shook her head. "I hardly know her, really."

Not even for the hope of a dance frock would she approach that rather alarming girl who rode on horseback, Mr. Somers's friend, that lucky girl who worked with him in the bank.

"I was wondering," she said hesitatingly. "Reenie, you know that shop near the station, Smartway's. . . ."

"*Dress and Pay
The Smartway*,"

said Reenie at once, severely. "Now Mavis, you don't want to go getting into trouble with them. You still owe Mum a pound and there's all that owing for your furniture. You can't go paying something every week for a frock when you can hardly manage as it is."

"I know. I wasn't really thinking of doing it. It was just an idea."

"Forget it." Reenie vigorously stirred her coffee.

"I *do* want a frock so much!" said Mavis suddenly, staring across the crowded room. "I just want to look—very nice, for once. I want a *really lovely* frock like someone on the pictures."

"My Green!" cried Reenie, loudly, slapping her spoon down on the table and breaking into a beaming smile that showed her excellent teeth.

"What?" said Mavis, startled.

"My Green! My green dress my brother Syd gave me for me twenty-first before I got so stout. Never worn it since. It's as good as new. I was looking at it only the other day and thinking, I'll sell that, and put the money towards me emigration. But I wouldn't get more than ten shillings for it, the thieves and robbers never give you anything like what it's worth. You have it, Mavis. It may be a bit big for you but I expect I can alter it "

"Oh Reenie! You *are* kind, really you are. Wh—what's it like?"

"Go on with you, girl," and Reenie pushed at her with the coffee spoon. "It's chiffon. Kind of a pale bright sort of green, jade really it is, with wing sleeves and a round neck. Ever so pretty."

"Oh Reenie, I'd love it! But won't you let me pay you for it? Even a shilling a week?"

"It'll cost a hundred pounds if you do; take you a long time," said Reenie crushingly. "Now that's settled. I'll bring it round to-morrow night, shall I? And we'll see how it fits. It ought to suit you, being so fair."

CHAPTER XXIX

BEING so fair.

The ballroom of the Grand Hotel was crowded for the last dance of the season; and everybody was enjoying themselves the more, and finding the ballroom with its gleaming floor and cream walls and long faintly blue mirrors warmer and more brilliant than usual, because outside there were the dim stars and quiet misty sea of an autumn night.

But of course, as this was an English hotel, there were draughts in the corridors and people on their way to the bar shuddered as the icy breeze hit them, and Pauline had put on her velvet jacket to sit on the stairs and eat sausage rolls with Wally Wade.

"You're awfully full of beans to-night, have you come into a fortune or something?" she asked him. Wally was sitting on the stair above her, which he liked doing because he could look at her round brown head and brown eyelashes without seeming to stare.

She spoke a little enviously. She was thinner and her eyes no longer laughed when she looked at anyone.

"Oh help. I knew I should give it away." Wally, who was on the wagon for life, gulped some lemonade. "I'm on top of the world, as a matter of fact, but I was made to swear I'd ne-vah betray the fatal secret."

"Go on, you might tell. Pity Marjie isn't here, she'd soon guess."

They both laughed.

"Is she acting to-night?"

"Yes. She's awfully worked up about this show next week. It's been postponed twice, you know; the woman who wrote it had a baby and then it got ill—the baby, not the play. Marjie's got a good part and she seems to think Ted Early's pretty good, too."

"Are you going to the first night?"

"Oh yes," she said, watching the people going back in the ballroom. "Are you?"

"Well, we are, as a matter of fact."

"Both of you? Good." She knew how difficult it was to get his sister to go out anywhere.

"Yes. As a matter of fact, Pauline——"

He paused. The corridor and the little hall where they were sitting were now deserted except for themselves. They could see the dancers moving past the door of the ballroom to the sound of a sweet and slow waltz that echoed along the corridor and seemed to flow about their feet where they sat.

"We're celebrating," said Wally.

She turned and looked at him, questioningly.

He nodded.

"Estelle's engaged."

"Oh Wally, I am so glad! Who to?"

"Guy called Jack Caldicott. He's an estate agent-wallah in Happy Sands; that's how she met him; as a matter of fact, he sold us the house. He's an awfully good guy. About thirty. Very keen on gardening."

"I'm so glad. I do hope they'll be happy."

She spoke with feeling, and as she spoke the unhappiness of the past weeks overcame her, and she turned away her face that he might not see the sadness in it.

"I oughtn't to have told you, she wants it kept dark for a bit, you know what she's like," Wally went on, speaking more and more nervously, "but as a matter of fact—I had to tell you. You see, this makes such a thundering difference to me. Don't want to sound a low cad and all that, but it shifts my responsibility, if you take my meaning."

Pauline thought it best to keep her eyes fixed upon the dancers. Suddenly she felt a limp moist hand gently take her own. It was trembling.

"I expect you know about it, don't you?" he muttered. "How I feel, I mean. Lifelong devotion and all that. As a matter of fact," the hand tightened its clasp and trembled more violently, "I'm pretty sure, it's a case of no-can-do, isn't it? But I simply had to try my luck."

Pauline said quickly, so anxious to put him out of suffering:

"I'm frightfully sorry, Wally. Gosh, I'm so *sorry.*"

"I know. All right. Say no more." The hand slowly, gently released her own, and then gave it a timid and tender pat. "This discussion is now closed: editor. All you've got to do now is to say you'll be a sister to me."

"I will, if you like, but you don't want me to, I should think."

"Oh yes, I do, Pauline," declared Wally stoutly. "Always thought the guy was right who said half a loaf was better than no bread."

Pauline stood up. She suddenly wanted to say something that should match that "lifelong devotion."

"You've done me a great honour and I'd like to thank you very much," she said.

He stood up too, glancing at her, a little surprised but going pink with pleasure.

"That's what girls used to say in the days of the Good Queen, isn't it? Sounds pretty good coming from you, Pauline. There's a lot to be said for those old Spanish customs, I think myself."

"So do I," she said. She was thinking suddenly of old Mr. Early. He'd approve of Wally, she thought. Wally's got the Right Idea, even though he does put it into wisecracks.

They walked back towards the ballroom. It's nearly November, she thought, putting her hand on Wally's arm as they moved away into the dance. Suppose I rang up and said: You surely can't want me to go all nudist with you in this weather. . . .

He hates jokes.

"I suppose old Eric is getting it off his chest too," observed Wally, who had been glancing round the ballroom. "I don't see them anywhere."

"She's a sweet little thing."

Wally only looked down at her, and gave her a smile that made his face beautiful. Not to me, my only love, said the smile.

"What do you bet they'll come back fixed up?" he went on, the smile fading.

She shook her head.

"I'm *not* betting. I'm sure they will, too."

They moved quickly and lightly on, down the brilliant room.

How long have I got to be this sort of a slave? she thought. It's been going on for eighteen months. Shall I ever be free again?

At the top of the stairs where Wally and Pauline had been sitting there was a small sofa, covered in striped pink and cream brocade, with a palm nodding over it. On either side stretched away the shut doors, the dimly-lit corridors, of a hotel whose activities were temporarily concentrated downstairs.

On this sofa Eric and Mavis were sitting, with a space between them. It was dusk at the top of the stairs; and the music, the coming and going of the dancers, that had whirled like a stream about the feet of Wally and Pauline, seemed far below to Eric and Mavis, as though they were gazing down into a whirlpool.

They were silent. Mavis sat with her hands (they were not very white) clasped in her lap, but he could see the beating of her heart shaking the front of the green dress, and suddenly he longed that it should all be over; the proposal, and his confession; and that they should be married and at peace together. This moment was not completely like moments he had spent with other girls, but it was like enough to be painful to him.

All I want is to be at peace with her, he thought.

And then he thought: How selfish I am! I'm not thinking about her at all; and he was ashamed.

But they continued to sit there in silence while he struggled with the question: shall I tell her about Madeleine?

She thinks I'm a much better person than I am; I can see that when she looks at me, and it might hurt her so badly that she would say "No,"

But suddenly he knew he could not—he *could* not—endure years of keeping that secret to himself; of being afraid that she would find out; of perhaps having to answer her questions a year or two hence. It's no use, he decided; I'm too selfish, I *must* tell her, and then ask her with that load off my chest.

Without looking at her, he took her hand and held it. She made a quick little movement of her head towards him but at once looked away again, and continued to gaze down the stairs as he began to speak. But he saw that she breathed quickly.

"I want to tell you," he said, "for five years I was in love with a girl. I—I was her lover—we lived together as if we were married —you understand, don't you?" (for it occurred to him, so child-like was her personality, that she might be ignorant as well as innocent; but she nodded and her hand moved slightly). He went on:

"She made me very unhappy. She——" (he hesitated: poor Madeleine!) "she wasn't what most people call a good girl. But I loved her very much. She hurt me, and spoiled five years of my life, but I can't say I'm sorry I ever loved her."

He paused. Mavis said nothing. Her face had flushed deep pink and she breathed so quickly that he could hear the faint agitated sound.

"That's what I wanted to tell you. That I'm not sorry I loved her. I'm sorry we were so unhappy together and she spoiled five years of my life and made me into a hypocrite, but I can't say I wish I'd never met her."

Still she did not speak, but she turned her head very slightly towards him, with a listening look, while she continued to gaze down the stairs.

"I had to tell you. I just couldn't bear the thought of having that a secret from you. Dear—my dear little love"—he leaned towards her—"I love you. I want you for ever, darling. To—to marry me, I mean, if you will. Please."

Then she did turn quite towards him, but with such a dazed look that he realized she had not taken in what he had said.

He gave both her hands a little lift, and let them fall and lie in his. His spirits were suddenly light; unhappiness had rolled away. He was smiling.

"Darling, I don't love her any more, you know. That's all over and done with. I love you. I love you so much——" as he said it he was suddenly frightened: did he love her?—but he went quickly on, his ardour moved by her silence and her delicate waterflower prettiness so close to him: "Will you marry me? Darling little Mavis, do say yes!"

And then she said (looking full at him while on her face there slowly came her pretty smile, the smile of delight and shyness that she had once given him on the spring evening when he had driven her home in the car), then she said:

"Oh *yes!* Thank you *ever* so, Mr. Somers!"

"So I suppose it was a proposal, really," said Pauline, and put out her cigarette on the ashtray by Marjorie's bed, where she was sitting."

"I suppose it was; poor old Wally. Is that your first?" Marjorie was lying in the bed on her side. She had a cold and looked cross.

"First honourable one." Pauline took another cigarette.

"You smoke much more than you used to."

"So what?"

"That's the broken heart, I gather. Do you still have morbid cravings after the Son of Frankenstein?"

There was no reply.

"It's like a disease," said Marjorie. "You know he's poison but you can't shake him off."

"I haven't spoken to him for two months."

"I wonder you've survived."

"I nearly haven't," said Pauline, not lightly.

"What's eating you both, anyway?"

"It's him, not me. He's snooty because I won't go all nudist with him."

"In this weather? He must be nuts."

"Oh Marjie, I sometimes think he is! He goes on in the most extraordinary way—doesn't know what he wants, or his own mind. Talk about *women* being capricious and mysterious——!"

"Oh, I *know!*" Marjorie raised herself on her elbow in her earnestness. "We're as simple as bars of soap compared with males (young males, that is; they get simpler as they get older). I'm absolutely positive most of them go on in the extraordinary way they do because they don't know *what* they want. Now, we do."

Pauline nodded.

"Your friend Ted is another peculiar one," said Marjorie, blowing her nose and looking over the top of the handkerchief with one very blue eye.

"Ted? Oh, do you think so? I always think he's so comfortable and sort of brotherly."

"He's a rat of the purest ray," said Marjorie spitefully, putting the handkerchief under the pillow.

Pauline stood up.

"I must go to bed," she said. "Marjie——" suddenly leaning over her sister with both hands on the bed—"I saw him in the car to-day. He looks so ill. It's ghastly—I think about nothing else all day and half the night too—you don't think he'd do anything to himself, do you?"

She was pale, yet half-laughing, too, with a smiling, trembling mouth below her unhappy eyes.

"Good heavens, no!" said Marjorie in a sort of hoarse emphatic roar, bouncing in the bed. "Pauli, how can you be such an utter and complete fool? Can't you see he only said that—I suppose he did say something—to get you to give in to his nefarious scheme? And why he can't sleep with you and get it over I don't know."

Pauline stood upright.

"It takes two for that, and I'm not having any."

Marjorie looked at her, waiting.

"Besides, he's never actually asked me. And *I* can't see why he can't ask me to *marry* him. It has been done, you know."

"His sort is terrified of being tied up."

"He says he isn't his own master."

Marjorie said her favourite and fashionable plural word.

"What's Frankenstein like, anyway?" went on Pauline.

"Perfectly ordinary bad-tempered old man in a bathchair."

Pauline sighed and wandered to the door.

"I'd give anything to know if Mrs. Kingsley really was mad."

"When this show's over I'll get to work on the problem," promised Marjorie, burrowing comfortably into the bed.

"Oh god, yes, it's the first night on Monday, isn't it," said Pauline, yawning. "I wonder if he'll be there? Good night, ducky."

"Good night. Cheer up. Who cares if he is, anyway, I hope one of those gold cupids on the roof falls on him."

Pauline gave a forlorn giggle. As she shut the door Marjorie said, almost to herself:

"Your friend Ted may be a rat but he certainly can act."

CHAPTER XXX

THE Theatre Royal, Seagate, had been built in 1890, and it had gold cupids and red plush.

A theatre ought to be like a pretty little box. Then, when it is packed tightly enough, magic can be distilled there. Magic is not easily distilled, for some of us, in a dreary great drill-hall constructed of beige planes, with the roof looking as if it would fall on us for twopence; we pine for our red plush and gold cupids and do not feel we are properly in a theatre unless we have got them.

The Theatre Royal was small and dusty and cold and usually smelt of old orange peel and greasepaint; but it was a proper theatre, and this evening it was nearly full, and magic was already winding up through the chilly, brightly lit air.

It may be said that the audience consisted of nearly all the people in Seagate who were educated and lived on dividends. Mrs. Pask was there, with flushed old cheeks because she was looking forward to seeing dear Pauline's sister in this play, and Miss Gaye sat beside her, draped in a shawl all over storks whose long fringe kept catching in her heels, with an extraordinary bit of beige tulle swathed round her head such as they used to eclipse their profiles with in the Gay Twenties.

Mrs. Williams was in the stalls, too, wearing some white furs that would have looked tatty on any other woman but were showy and becoming on her. Pauline had put on an old velvet dress the colour of a wallflower; it was a favourite of hers and its familiar feel might comfort her.

Brian was not there, of course. It had been silly to suppose he might be. This was not his cup of tea at all.

She looked drearily round the theatre and discovered Wally gazing over the front row of the dress circle and waved to him and he waved back, with his faithful flush and smile.

He and Estelle and the fiancé were in the front row of the dress circle, partly because this was her favourite seat in a theatre and partly that she might not be reminded of her infirmity by often having to make way for people coming in and out. Her engagement was only a week old, but already she looked less resentful and there was a less aggressive tilt to all her little bows and a softer turn to her curls. Even the Indian bangles had a month-of-marriages-is-drawing-near tinkle: Estelle was learning to be happy.

What are we here for? wondered her fiancé, an admirer of the cinema, gazing about him. The air smelled of long-dead oranges and dust, most of the heads in the stalls were grey or bald, draughts whizzed and crept along the floor, and in the orchestra pit a mechanical musician thundered out a six months old tune. The programme was almost hidden in advertisements for the local tradesmen, most of whom were known to every member of the audience in their professional capacity and had been for many years: this made for stability rather than glamour.

Little girl's enjoying it, anyway, he thought, glancing at his betrothed.

"Oh, there's Elizabeth Bayne!" she said suddenly. "Look— in that lowest box on the left."

A large figure in a not very good black and white evening dress could now be discerned arranging itself, not without some confusion and dropping of things, in the dimness of the box. It finally sat down rather at the back, as if shrinking from the possibility of a frenzy of tumultuous welcoming applause, but need not have worried, since only about three people in the house knew who it was, and the rest only expressed wonder at anybody's choosing to sit in a box; everybody knows you can't see properly from a box.

"Looks quite ordinary," observed Estelle's fiancé at last, when the figure was settled with its hands folded in its lap.

"Yes, doesn't she. I was so disappointed when I saw her photo after I'd read the book, I thought she'd look very sophisticated and witty. Did you read it?"

He shook his head.

"Oh, you must, Jack. It's a yell. I'll lend it to you—don't let me forget."

Fancy such a nice sensible looking woman writing a book like that, thought Wally, also studying Miss Bayne. Quite dirty, parts of it were, too. Just shows you never can tell.

Some slight interest and confusion was now caused by the arrival in the stalls of Mr. and Mrs. Somers, Eric and Mavis, who were waylaid by Pauline and introduced to her mother. After general pleasantries had been exchanged, Mr. Somers drew Mavis's hand through his arm, threw a roguish glance at Eric, and roared out that they were celebrating the young people's engagement.

"Oh! How nice! Congratulations, Mr. Somers, congratulations," said Mrs. Williams, smiling and darting a needle glance at Mrs. Somers. The old man liked a pretty face, but what did the mother think of her precious son getting engaged to a girl who used to work in Just's and had got into debt with her furniture and slept out all night and been heaven knows what?

Mrs. Somers had cried a little and been angry with Mavis when she was alone with Mr. Somers in their bedroom after Eric had told them the news on the return from the dance on Saturday evening, but Mr. Somers had been stern and sensible as well as tender and pleading with her, and had convinced her that this was the best thing that could have happened to Eric.

And to prove his case he revealed that Eric had been serious about that dreadful Madeleine Eames! Doctor Eames had told him, Mr. Somers, as much with his own lips. Eric was definitely fond of the girls, Mr. Somers said. His father had suspected as much for some time. He was the type that needed marriage to settle him ("Oh dear!—to think of my Eric!" wept Mrs. Somers) and then he would make a good husband. And better, far better, surely, Mother, that he should marry this dear little girl whom we know all about and who obviously worships the ground his feet— his *unworthy* feet, repeated Mr. Somers severely—walk upon, than some girl we've never met and know nothing about?

"I can't get over your knowing all those things about Eric and I didn't, Father!" (Sniff, blow, sniff.)

"Women never really understand their sons," pronounced Mr. Somers. "They only love them. Use your reason about the affair, my dear."

Poor Mrs. Somers swallowed this; and spent most of the night lying awake trying to use her reason. And in the morning her reason had so far triumphed that she could see that she had no rational grounds for being either disagreeable or dejected about the marriage. Curiously enough this made her no fonder of Mavis.

However, every marriage is a social as well as an emotional contract, and therefore provides food for human interest as well as for human feeling. Mrs. Somers could not help being interested in the young people's plans, when the wedding would take place, where they would live and all the rest of it, and already, in the midst of an increasing excitement and busyness, she was beginning to feel better.

So she could return Mrs. Williams's needle calmly, and even direct a pleasant glance at Mavis, standing silently with her arm through her future father-in-law's as she answered.

"Congratulations, Miss Jevons! I'm so glad!" said Pauline in her friendliest voice, under cover of the jabbering of the elders. "I'm sure you're going to be marvellously happy."

Mavis looked up quickly.

"Thank you very much, Miss Williams."

Shyness and happiness were in her expression and, (so slight that it was barely noticeable) fear.

Eric did not say much. He stood smiling and listening to the kind voices and thinking: what have I let myself in for? If it's love I feel for her, I've never been in love before.

Still, I've hardly kissed her yet.

He knew from experience what an enormous, an unbelievable, difference kissing made.

And meanwhile the arrangements for getting married and setting up house were unexpectedly interesting and absorbing. And Mavis was unexpectedly sensible; suddenly making suggestions in her quiet little voice.

She's a pearl, he thought. And she's my last hope, my last chance to make myself into a normal useful happy person.

Mavis, sitting between Eric and his father, was not completely happy.

It was almost too wonderful to be engaged to be married to Mr. Somers; it had happened too quickly; she could still hardly realize it, and as she gazed down at the ring on her finger she remembered those evenings she used to spend in her little room long ago, before anything had happened, reading poetry and gazing at Mr. Somers's photo. I was ever so happy then, really, she thought.

The fact was, she could not help feeling rather upset and disappointed because of That Girl.

I used to think he was so good, she thought, and all the time he was—he was behaving like that.

She cautiously glanced at him. He was listening to Pauline's teasing with a smile on his thin dark face, and Mavis's heart lifted with love. "Mr. Somers," she thought, her mind repeating the beloved name as it had always done during the past five years, whenever she saw him in church or passed him in the street, "Mr. Somers," and up went her heart like a bird. But "Eric"— and she felt a little timid of being alone with him, and disappointed in him because he had behaved like that about That Girl. "Eric" and "Mr. Somers" were two different people.

But as she watched him she remembered he had been very unhappy about that girl, and suddenly she felt sorry for him, and wanted to comfort him. She looked down once more at her little ring (which had belonged to a great-aunt of Eric's and was made in the shape of a flower with a turquoise for heart and pearls for petals) and remembered the one kiss he had given her when they became engaged. Then, "Mr. Somers" and "Eric" had become one person; and her face flushed and her heart beat faster as she remembered.

She looked up again and smiled as she met the eyes of Mrs. Somers. She had noticed no coolness in Mrs. Somers's manner, because she so reverenced Eric's parents that she saw them always as two old angels who could never be anything but benign

"Enjoying yourself, dear?" asked Mrs. Somers,. leaning across to smile at her and moved by sudden affection for the really very good, harmless little thing.

"Oh yes, thank you *ever* so much, Mrs. Somers."

She gazed round the pretty little theatre, resounding with cheerful music, and full of kind people in their best clothes, and her spirits rose.

It's lovely being engaged, really, she thought.

Exactly in the middle of the fourth row of the stalls there sat a quiet stout dark young man in excellent evening clothes, who smelt slightly of snuff and had a small red rose in his buttonhole. He had been gazing about the house with an expression as if he were too intelligent to be completely bored in any situation, but had seldom been nearer to complete boredom in his life; examining the young women in their hopelessly undistinguished clothes and trying not to listen to the paneotrope.

Once he had smiled and slightly lifted his programme to Miss Bayne, who leaned eagerly forward to return the smile and half got up as if to come and talk to him, and then sat down again. A faint expression of relief came over his face, and he leant back with one arm along the back of his seat and surveyed the boxes. Upon one of them, immediately opposite to Miss Bayne's, his gaze gradually became fixed with some interest.

Two people were sitting in it; a woman and an old man. The interior of the box was dimly lit, and all that could be seen of the woman was a dark figure with something gold glittering about its neck; a shape that put forth grace and seductiveness with every slight movement. But the old man sat well forward with an arm resting upon the front of the box and his long white hair (it reached almost to his shoulders) gleaming picturesquely. His evening clothes were more than old-fashioned, they were exaggerated, antique, as full of personality and life as if they had been themselves alive upon his body. He surveyed the house with an absent dreamy air, and the young man noticed that two of the women in the stalls waved to him but that apparently he did not see.

Mr. Godfrey Hepplestall, deputy dramatic critic for a famous morning journal, studied the romantic pair lengthily, particularly the old man. Must have been Somebody, he decided. A man never loses the look he acquires from being a celebrity. That old buck has been used to big crowds. He opened his programme and studied it, idly wondering if the names in the caste might give a clue to the old buck's identity, and just as he came to the name at the very end that did give him a clue, and just as he realized with a sinking heart that the play was all about doctors, and even while his spirits rose at the prospect of a slightly more interesting evening, because of that name in the caste, than he had anticipated —the lights began to dim.

For a moment he savoured the enchantment of which he never wearied : the glow of footlights upon the yet-lowered crimson velvet curtain, and he was aware of the old man in the box suddenly leaning forward, as though to bathe in that glow—and then the curtain went up.

Oh god, he isn't going to have frustrated passages with the nurse—I can't bear it, thought Mr. Hepplestall ten minutes later. Poor dear woman, why couldn't she stick to comedy. And he sighed and glanced about him, but stealthily, because he did not want to set anyone else to coughing and fidgeting.

But they were enjoying it. They were not rapt, they were only entertained, but the laughs (especially at references to alcohol or common ailments) came readily and louder each time.

Nice audience to play to, thought Mr. Hepplestall. That's an extremely pretty little girl. He peered closely at his programme. Marjorie Williams. But *not* an actress, I think.

Oh god, he isn't going to tell us all about his duty to humanity —I can't bear it, he thought a little later. And all the speeches are exactly twice too long. Why will novelists try to write plays?

The curtain came down on the end of the first act with the surgeon standing alone and transmogrified among the blood-pressure gauges.

I suppose this kind of play is a nobler contribution to the Drama (thought Mr. Hepplestall, mooching along to the bar) than the Oh-who-will-sleep-with-who type. But how much less entertaining! And it hasn't the pluck to be as simple as "The Sign of the Cross" or the brains behind it to tackle a real Idea. Poor woman, it's dead on her already.

I think they're quite enjoying it, thought Miss Bayne absently, sitting in her box and furtively eating chocolate peppermint creams because she had come away from London in such a hurry that she had had no dinner. I wonder how Baby is? Only four more hours and I'll be home!

There was a tap at the door of the box.

"Come in," said Miss Bayne pleasantly, half turning in her seat. She was a rosy, rather handsome person with a straightforward manner that completely belied her nature.

The attendant from the Ladies' Cloakroom stood there, smiling as if she had a present to give.

"The Assistant Stage Manager's compliments, madam, and he's taken the liberty of 'phoning through to your house and the little darling—the baby's—had her bottle and she's sleeping beautifully, miss. He thought you'd just like to know."

Miss Bayne's eyes filled.

"Oh! Oh, how *very* kind of him! Oh please do thank him very, very much for me, will you, and say I'm so *very* grateful to him!"

"I will, miss. It's young Mr. Early, miss." And she went on to tell the writer who Ted was, and to point out his grandfather in the box opposite. Then she said: "I'm so glad the little darling's better, miss, if you don't mind my saying so."

"Oh—thank you very much. That's very kind of you. Everybody seems to know all about her!"

"Oh yes, we do, madam. The play being postponed twice, you see. We got ever so interested in her, bless her."

And all those actors calling the little angel the Blasted Baby! she thought indignantly. *Ought to be ashamed of themselves.*

"Would you like to see what she looks like?" Miss Bayne was fumbling with a large Victorian locket.

Two heads bent together over a snapshot of a bald and exceedingly imperious infant.

"There's a little love! What's her name, madam, if you don't mind me asking?"

"Carol."

"That's ever so pretty. American, isn't it?"

"Yes. Have you any of your own?"

"Four, madam. Two boys and two girls. But mine are all grown up now."

"It's so funny to think of Carol grown up."

"You'll have to give her a little brother one of these days, miss."

"Yes, I'd love to. Later on, perhaps."

A bell rang, and people began to come back into the stalls.

"I must be getting back, miss, I've left my niece on duty."

"Good-bye and thank you *very* much."

"Good night, madam."

Miss Bayne took another peppermint cream and turned smilingly to the stage once more. She was refreshed by the first incident that evening which had received her full attention. What a *very* nice young man Mr. Early must be, she thought.

"Enjoying it, sweetie-pie?" asked Estelle's fiancé, at the end of the second act.

"So-so. I wish there'd be some marvellous frocks, I'm bored with these nurses' uniforms. It isn't a bit the kind of play you'd think she'd have written. I thought it would be a yell. But I'm enjoying it all right, Jack," and she smiled and touched his hand.

Mrs. Williams was not greatly entertained, either. The love passages were of a lofty nature and everybody seemed to care more about serums and research than they did about kissing; which—you could say what you liked—was not natural.

It's lovely, thought Mavis, who had been watching with fascinated eyes. He's so good and Miss Williams is so pretty, oh, I *am* enjoying it. I like the scientist, too. He's a bit like old Mr. Somers.

I wonder where Brian is? thought Pauline.

"The play is strangely lacking in dramatic fire, is it not?" observed Mr. Early in his beautiful and carrying voice, to the great entertainment of the first six rows of the stalls including the by now almost comatose Mr. Hepplestall. "It lacks both emotional and intellectual force. The acting, too, is mediocre, with the exception of the leading man. He has The Spark."

"And what it takes, too," murmured Louise, pulling over her shoulders a little triangular shawl of black silk closely embroidered with flowers and leaves in dark red, dark green and dark blue.

She had been interestedly surveying the frocks and faces in the stalls. It's a good thing I always enjoy myself, she thought, or coming out, even to a one-horse place like this, would make me feel how little fun I get all the year round. Remember Paris and me thinking I was going to be a second Galli-Curci? Oh well, it's gone, and it's no use saying I'm miserable, because I'm not. A comfortable bed and good food and a hot book and a man now and then and the old boy and Ted to look after and I'm all right.

If it were not for this man coming on at the end of the third act, I'd walk right out now, so help me, thought Godfrey Hepplestall, glancing pleasantly towards Miss Bayne. And how am I going to be rude enough about her play to discourage her from writing another (for discouraged she must be) when she's a friend of the Old Man's and half the people I know in London?

Social life certainly does complicate dramatic criticism.

He got up and wandered out to the bar.

If this Edward Early really is related to Archibald Early (he thought, leaning against it and swallowing half his drink) and if that's the old legend himself in the box, the story'll be worth a quarter of a column even if Edward stinks as an actor.

The Bayne's given him a grand build-up, anyway; even I (who am not easily made agog) am all agog to see this touchy cripple who doesn't believe he can be cured. It does come off, and thank god there's *something* I can say does in my notice.

Now when was the old boy's last appearance? (He used his excellent memory, stocked with theatrical names and facts belonging to years before he was born.) Oh, yes; Command Performance in 1920, the Quarrel Scene from Julius Caesar with Arthur Keate as Cassius. And then he retired. Hove? No, Seagate, of course! It must be him!

Edward can't be his son; the old man must be rising eighty and if he'd had a son of forty-odd we'd have heard about him by now if we were going to. Grandson or great-nephew, perhaps.

He got some information from the barmaid; then wandered back to his seat again.

Glancing at the box, he saw that the old man and the graceful dark woman were both leaning forward and looking anxiously towards the hidden stage, and some of their obvious excitement got across to him. He looked round at the stalls and saw that other people were excited too; programmes were being lifted to short-sighted eyes and grey heads were close together, murmuring, while some of the younger people were whispering and smiling.

Well, here's to Edward, and let's hope he's got what it takes, he thought. Why, I'm beginning to enjoy myself, and that's a great big surprise.

Pauline sat upright with her hands tightly clasped and her heart beating quickly. Oh, dear old thump, if only he doesn't make too hopeless a mess of it! she thought. She had forgotten Brian.

Her mother was a little contemptuous and looking forward to a good laugh over poor old Ted after the show.

"Enjoying it, beautiful?" whispered Estelle's fiancé, leaning towards her and taking her small stiff hand. She had been rather quiet since the references to the crippled boy, and Wally was cursing his own luck for bringing her here and Miss Bayne for writing a play with a cripple in it. Weren't there plenty of happy things to write about? Same with books.

"Of course; why shouldn't I be?" she answered sharply, but after a moment smiled at him and squeezed his hand.

"How are you liking it, dear?" Eric asked, inclining his dark head to Mavis's fair one. He himself was a little bored; he did not care for the theatre, but he was enjoying, with a new tenderness, the sight of Mavis enjoying herself.

"Oh, I think it's lovely. I like the doctor ever so much, he's so good, isn't he. But I don't like his wife, she's so hard. Do—do you like it?"

"Very much." But he let his gaze move, as he answered her, over her hair and face until she turned blushing away.

The lights began to fade.

Then a little murmur and movement went over the house, made up of programmes dropping on to laps and shoulders settling more comfortably against the backs of seats, and there was a pause; and then the curtains parted. The audience looked at the doctor's consulting-room.

One lamp burned at the desk where he was sitting and shone on books and medical instruments, otherwise the room was in shadow; in the dimness the nurse moved quietly about, getting ready to go home.

The house was very quiet, watching. Some chord had been struck with the first glimpse of that silent room and the man sitting at his desk; a chord of interest and sympathy. It was late at night; the day's toil was over; he was tired after hours of hard work, and ready for bed. Everyone in the audience had felt like that. In a hush that slowly grew rapt as the simple scene progressed, the audience watched and listened.

(Now has she written that rarity, a good third act? began to wonder Mr. Hepplestall in dreamy amazement.)

NURSE MORGAN: "*Is there anything else, Dr. Frobisher?*"

DR. FROBISHER (without turning round): "*Nothing, thank you. Nothing more to-night. You must be tired. You'd better go home and go straight to bed.*"

NURSE MORGAN (coming down and standing by the desk): "*I'm not tired, doctor. But you must be. It's been such a long hard day. And I—I know I oughtn't to say anything, it isn't my business, but it's so disappointing——*"

DR. FROBISHER (turning round): "*Ransome, you mean?*"

NURSE MORGAN: "*Yes. After all that work! A year's treatment! And then to say he's no better!*"

DR. FROBISHER (turning back to his work): "*He ought to know, he says. And if he won't let himself be examined——*"

NURSE MORGAN: "*You ought to have insisted on his going into hospital for treatment, Doctor, instead of giving way to him and letting him be treated at home.*"

DR. FROBISHER: "*He was frightened.*"

NURSE MORGAN: "*Ransome? Frightened? Oh, no, Doctor!*"

That's only your—your kind heart. Ransome's never been frightened in his life."

While this dialogue was being carried on in low earnest voices that deepened rather than disturbed the trance now holding the audience, a door among the shadows had been slowly opening, and now a figure stood there, motionless except for a slight movement of its hands which continually crushed and released a cloth cap. It wore dark clothes and had a white face surmounted by a head of stiff light ginger hair, and the chin (though this was not visible until he came awkwardly forward into the light) was bristly with the same growth.

But what at once leapt straight into the entranced heart of the intently watching and listening audience was the fact that this figure, in merely standing there, *was performing an unfamiliar action.* He was balancing himself upon feet that had only just learned how to stand, and when the nurse and the doctor suddenly turned at his first loud hoarse words:

"Oh yes, I was frightened——"

and both exclaimed:

"Ransome!"

and the doctor sprang to his feet and·pointed at him and cried:

"He's standing! Do you see? He's standing! He can walk!"

the audience felt the same shock and amazement as the doctor and nurse conveyed by their tone, because the unfamiliarity and the wonder of his new accomplishment were so perfectly conveyed by the actor's movements.

He came forward into the light, walking as if his feet were made of wood and yet breakable, and stood by the doctor's desk, facing him.

"Yes, I was frightened all right," he said. His voice was full and carrying, and of a rough texture and uneducated pronunciation that matched his looks and belonged to him, and everyone in the audience heard every word, every inflection, that he uttered without receiving the impression that he was shouting. *"Who wouldn't have been? I thought you couldn't do it. Too good to*

be true, I thought. Twelve months of lying in bed and being mauled about and then being no better at the end of it—no, thank you, I thought. And when you'd got me to be treated at home I was still frightened. Got the wind up proper, I had, specially when I began to get a bit better. God, I hated you, Doc! I was afraid you'd never pull it off. You people"—he took a step forward, cautiously, and staggered a little and recovered himself—*"you people don't know anything about it. You don't know what it's like—lying still, day after day, week after week, month after month, year after year——"* (his voice began to rise) *"hearing the other chaps. That was what used to get me down, hearing the motor bikes go past of a Saturday afternoon, with a girl on the back. But this afternoon I heard them and I didn't care. Good luck to you, brother, I thought. Because I'm just like anybody else, now. In a month or two I'll be going out to Epping with a girl on the back. I can walk!"* (His voice had been rising steadily all the time he was speaking, and it was now filling the theatre, thrilling the audience with its fierce triumph. *"I can walk, I tell you!"* He lurched forward. *"I'm twenty-four years old and I've been a cripple since I was three, and now—and now—I can walk—I can—walk—— I can walk!"*

And at the last word, frenzied yet clear, he fell forward laughing and crying into the doctor's outstretched arms, and the curtain came down.

It gave Mr. Hepplestall genuine pleasure to join in the long and excited applause that followed, but he did not do so for long. He slipped out of the theatre while they were still clapping, went to the nearest telephone box, and put a call through to London. He did not usually dictate his copy but he was most anxious that this story should be in the first edition of his paper the next morning.

While he was waiting for the operator to ring him, he stared at the floor and decided exactly what line he should take. He was too experienced a critic, despite his youth, to be enthusiastic without qualification; he had seen so many first-night swans turn into geese. But this same experience of his strongly suspected that here (and even in his thoughts he fought shy of the abused word) was, well, oh dammit, genius.

There were faults, of course, he thought, staring at the floor. The make-up was Dickensian, grotesque (though expertly applied) and the playing of the character so strong that it threw the other characters into shade. But the beautiful voice, the control of the graceful body, the fire and power and *looseness* of emotion!

qualities so rare in English actors. They were all there, as they had been in the boy's grandfather.

The bell rang.

In a second or two, staring at the ceiling, he began to dictate:

"It is just possible that Miss Elizabeth Bayne's 'White Glory' will one day be remembered as the play in which Edward Early, grandson of the famous Edwardian actor, Archibald Early, made his first appearance. Much as I should like to, I cannot prophesy that it will live of its own merits.

"This young man (he is not yet twenty) . . ." and so on, half a column of stinging comment and praise that was the more impressive because it appeared reluctant.

There, my lad. Mr. Hepplestall sighed and hung up the receiver with aching fingers: he had gripped it in his concentration. That ought to do you a bit of good. And now I think I'll go behind and meet you, and see if you're the usual little——

"Ted?" said Marjorie, coming out of the shadows as he hurried into his dressing-room. Her painted blue eyes shone under her white nurse's cap.

He looked at her vaguely. The corridors were echoing with voices and hurrying feet and the slamming of doors. His own face looked grotesque in its white make-up below the coarse red wig.

"You were marvellous," she said in a low voice, following him into the untidy, bright, empty dressing-room.

He sat down in front of the mirror and pulled off his coat, staring at his reflection in the glass, as if he had not heard what she said.

"I mean it," she added.

"Is Pauli here?" he said suddenly, turning and picking up his grandfather's dirty old robe of Chinese silk. "I want her to come round afterwards."

He was tying the robe round his waist, not looking at her.

Marjorie went to the door.

"I *said*, you were marvellous," she repeated, turning at the door to look at him. "Didn't you hear?"

He sat down again.

"All my life I shall hear that," he said, as if to himself. "And it doesn't mean much. I seem to have been hearing it ever since I can remember."

"You do hate yourself, don't you," she said feebly after a pause.

He was cleaning off his make-up and did not answer.

"Oh, go to hell!" said Marjorie, turning away.

"You shouldn't say 'Go to hell!' when you mean 'Come to bed,' Marjie darling. Be an angel and run along and get Pauli for me, will you?" he said, smiling at her reflection in the mirror.

There was a conviction growing at the back of her mind that he was shortly going to be a person whom it would be very useful to know. So, controlling her mixed feelings, she went off on the errand just as a dark, square young man came nosing along the corridor.

"But I simply *forgot* it was Ted!" said Mrs. Williams, all the way home in the car. "That was what was so extraordinary. I was expecting to see Ted come on, and when he came I simply forgot it was Ted. I can't get over it. And that London critic coming round specially to see him! He was always so clumsy and plain and sort of half-dotty and just the boy-over-the-way, you know, and then not to remember it was him! Well! I *cannot* get over it!"

CHAPTER XXXI

PAULINE stood by her window and looked out at the wind. Large yellow leaves from the chestnut tree flew past, and low grey clouds raced across the sky, and the grass seethed. Gosh, I'm so miserable, she thought, and turned away and stood undecidedly in the middle of the room, wondering what she could do to relieve her pain a little. It was Saturday afternoon and the house was quiet. Mrs. Williams had gone to the pictures, Connie was out, and Marjorie still at the theatre.

The sea was hidden beyond houses and trees, but to-day the town seemed to belong to it, and its huge sad voice came sighing through the streets and over the roofs, making her heart more wretched than ever. She wanted someone to talk to. She did not often get into this mood, but to-day she felt almost at the end of her endurance.

I'll go and see Ted, she thought. He always cheers me up and if I can get my tongue round it I might ask his advice too.

The Rich House was so large and solid that outwardly it seemed to repel the furious wind, but when she pulled the patent string that opened the front door, all the frail old curtains and ramshackle pictures and worn carpets that furnished the hall trembled terrifiedly in the gust that pounced in, and a tattered book blew off a table and scattered loose pages as far down as the kitchen door.

She shut the front door after a struggle, and looked round.

Lowering wintry light made the hall more dim than usual, but a large banked fire smouldered in the handsome grate and the spangles on Mr. Early's collection of theatrical prints sparkled romantically in the gloom. Dear old Rich House, you smell but I love you, she thought, and wandered upstairs.

All the furnishings of the Rich House—the clocks and sofas and sideboards, the occasional tables and vases and fenders, the cushions and beds and books—were trembling upon the edge of becoming rubbish. When they were new, they had been solid and handsome and the best of their kind to be bought, but that was long ago; and for years now they had not been cleaned or repaired, the clocks had stopped and never been rewound, stuffing was coming out of the cushions and leaves out of the books, the springs of the beds were broken, the vases were chipped, the fenders scratched and dented. Living under this one roof, held firmly into a home by the power of the old man's memories, all these battered and old-fashioned objects had a life of their own, even dignity and beauty. But let them once be separated from one another, and the strength they drew from each other's presence be dissipated; let them once be exposed to the cool light of an ordinary day and the eyes of a crowd at an auction—and they would be junk; the sort of stuff seen on market day in a country town when the casual traveller, with an eye for the beautiful, hesitates over a pair of faded tapestry curtains lined with ragged scarlet silk, and finally decides they are not worth the seven shillings asked for them and turns away.

But they were not rubbish yet. The long sofa covered with orange brocade still had its honoured position in front of the fire in the drawing-room overlooking the garden; the naked marble Hermes on the landing, with his broken cap still looked unearthly white and beautiful as she approached him from the shadows of the staircase: she could remember him looking just the same when she was a little girl.

There was no one in the drawing-room, where the cold light of the winter afternoon fell upon a group of giant yellow chrysanthemums in a Chinese vase between the wide windows, and she went downstairs again.

I do hope they aren't all out, she thought.

Peering into the shadowy dining-room at the back of the house, which had formerly been the drawing-room, she suddenly noticed that the conservatory door was open, and saw that someone was moving about there. She went down the long room towards the glass doors, and saw that it was Louise.

A little anteroom, half conservatory and half lounge, led from the dining-room into the conservatory proper, and as Pauline entered this Louise glanced up and saw her.

"Hullo!" she said, looking pleased and standing upright from a delicate pink flowering plant she was tending. "I am glad to see you!"

"It's such a beastly afternoon, I felt I'd go crazy if I didn't have someone to talk to," said Pauline, stepping into the fragrant warm air of the conservatory. It was the frankest and friendliest speech she had ever made to Louise. Her usual reserve had gone this afternoon; she felt so desolate, so at her wit's end, that she must have comfort from somebody.

"Oh. Too bad." Louise's dark eyes shone as she pointed to an old Madras chair. "That's comfortable and fairly safe."

Pauline sat down in it and Louise went on with her cautious removing of withered leaves from the pink plant. The wind dashed against the clear glass walls and roof in sudden gusts.

"I say, you've had it all done up, haven't you?" exclaimed Pauline, glancing round. "I didn't notice at first."

Louise nodded. "That's Ted. He used to love the conservatory when he was little, you know, and now he says he wants it kept up again, like we used to have it. So he's paying for part of the repairs out of his salary and we've had a man in"—she nodded round at some pots of the same curled chrysanthemums that were upstairs—"and the heating's been put right and everything."

"It's lovely and warm," said Pauline, leaning back. Usually ten minutes in the languorous air of a conservatory were quite enough for her; she preferred freshness in what she breathed. But this afternoon the warmth and hush and fragrance were exactly what she needed.

"I didn't know you were keen on gardening," she said presently, smiling.

"I'm just as lazy as a terrapin about gardening and you know it," answered Louise, smiling too, "but anyone can pick dead leaves off a plant," and she took one and dropped it into a basket.

There was another silence. Louise moved about from one flowering exotic to another and Pauline watched her, not really thinking about her, but observing her with that mixture of irritation and pleasure felt by most people when they looked at Louise.

She was at her best in the summer, when her beautiful body was set off by thin clothes; but even on this winter day, in an old dark dress with a velvet jacket over it, she was attractive; attractive as a flower is, without culture, wit, kindness, real beauty or any apparent effort.

Warmth came from her, and that was what fascinated people against their will. But it was not a familiar or domestic warmth, for her housekeeping was slovenly, if comfortable; she ran Parkfield with the help of one or two impertinent and garrulous elderly charwomen who had been coming there for years and were used to the family's unconventional ways, and not so respectable as to be frightened away by the stories going round the town about the house's mistress.

In and out of some four rooms in the mansion moved Louise, cleaning and altering as little as possible; and with every year that passed the furniture that was moved and cleaned and used grew less and less; and all about it, in the untidy unused rooms full of broken furniture and clocks that would not go, there slowly and steadily collected a wall of dusty motionless objects surrounding the still-glowing life in the centre of the house where the three people lived.

Presently Pauline moved restlessly and said:

"Is Ted out?"

"He's gone to London again to see his agent."

"He's a busy man these days."

"He surely is."

"Has he heard any more about the Gielgud show?"

"He's almost certain to get the part; his agent 'phoned last night, that's why he went up. And he's having lunch with Elizabeth Bayne. She adores him after that business of phoning about her brat."

"How marvellous. I'm so glad." But she experienced a little unfamiliar pain that she was too unhappy to notice.

"He's thinking of changing his name to Edmund for the stage," went on Louise.

"Because of that mistake in the *Morning Herald*? He is an ass!"

"He says Edward makes people think of shirt-sleeves and bicycles."

"I like Edward best."

"Oh, I don't know, Edmund's kind of elegant."

"Is Mr. Early asleep?" Pauline was making conversation to ward off the unhappiness that kept attacking her like toothache.

"He's gone out for his walk."

"In this weather? He is amazing!"

"Oh, he's only gone down to the post-box at the edge of the

fields and back. That's his usual winter walk. He can see the sea from there and he likes that. He never did take any notice of the weather· or his health, you know, and he's got a wonderful constitution."

"You can see the sea from the drawing-room window now the trees are bare, I noticed it to-day when I went up to look for you."

"I know. I never look at it in the winter, it makes me feel so cold." Louise's voice came softly from the far end of the conservatory where she was bending over an ancient grape-vine.

Pauline said no more, but turned to stare at the wild copper light that was beginning to pour into the western sky as the clouds broke towards evening. Sheets of liquid blue were revealed from time to time as the monstrous masses of grey mist rolled on before the wind.

Louise came down the conservatory towards her.

"How about some tea——" she was beginning, when Pauline suddenly said:

"I'm fed up to the teeth."

"Why, I'm sorry to hear that," answered Louise easily, gliding into a chair and leaning back. "What's the matter?"

Pauline was silent, fighting with tears, her head turned away. After a minute Louise said:

"Back in the summer I guess I kind of annoyed you by saying I'd like to help, didn't I?"

Pauline shook her head, for she could not yet speak, and leant back and shut her eyes, from which the tears welled.

"Sorry," she said at last, using her handkerchief.

"It's all right, honey. Cry all you want." Louise was watching with her lips slightly parted.

This permission naturally made Pauline stop, but although the tears ceased to come she did not open her eyes, but sat still, with her head turned to the window, trying to control the trembling of her lips.

"What's the matter?" coaxed Louise after a long silence.

The lulling warmth of the air and the invitation in the pretty voice were too much for Pauline in her longing for advice and comfort, and she answered at once:

"Oh, it's—someone I've quarrelled with, that's all. He—you see, he wanted me to do something that I didn't want to and so we sort-of quarrelled. That was three months ago (gosh, it seems like three years). He did say I was to ring him up if I changed my mind, but I haven't, of course."

"Why 'of course'?" Louise lit a cigarette and held out the case to Pauline, but she shook her head.

"Oh—well—I just can't. But I'm so—so *horribly* miserable"—
she gave a quivering sigh—"I feel as if I can't stand it much longer
and I'm sure he's miserable too. I saw him this morning and he
looked so fed up."

Louise nodded.

"And there's—there's another thing. I suppose it's silly of
me but I'm terrified he'll do something frightful. Something—
well, he might kill himself, Louise! He said so!"

There, it was out. And she looked longingly, fearfully, at
Louise, hoping to see her laugh and hear a comforting "Don't be
so crazy, Pauline!" But Louise slowly turned her head sideways
so that the brassy light from the west illuminated one dark cheek,
and did not reply.

"It's awfully silly of me, I know," almost whispered Pauline at
last.

Louise turned to her again.

"It's not silly at all," she said, and Pauline felt a pang of dread,
"I was just remembering . . . when I was about your age someone,
a boy down in New Orleans, wanted me to do something that
I wouldn't do. Not because I had any notions about it being
wrong, I never was that way, but because I liked to tease, the way
girls do."

Pauline was staring at her.

"I teased once too often," said Louise, getting up and going
over to the window and touching the petals of a cyclamen plant,
"he said he'd shoot himself, and he did."

There was a long silence.

"So I don't think you're silly at all," said Louise, returning to
her chair and sitting down again. "I think you're quite right to be
worried. But I think you're a silly girl to say 'no', and mean, too.
After all, honey, we're here for such a short time. Why not be
happy? I'd call him up, really I would, and say 'you win'!"

"Oh, I can't!"

"Why not? You don't want to be the sort of girl that holds a
man off until she's got him safely tied up with a wedding ring,
do you?"

Louise's voice was still gentle and yet there was warmth in it:
the impersonal warmth of the soul or body hunter, eager to con-
vince and convert.

Pauline did not answer, but her silence was now caused by
embarrassment. It was plain that Louise thought someone
wanted her to live in sin, and it would be an anti-climax, to say the
least of it, to confess that he only wanted her to go to a nudist
camp with him.

9*

"Ungenerosity's the meanest thing——" Louise ended softly, looking at her with slightly glistening eyes.

"I'm not ungenerous!" Pauline answered, her temper beginning to rise, "and as a matter of fact he hasn't actually—well, asked me to live with him. It's just that he wanted me to go to a nudist camp with him."

"Well, why not?" cried Louise, her pretty voice going up like the cry of a dove. "All the more reason to call him up and say 'you win', if that's all he wants. Honestly, you Englishwomen get me down. You're so horrified if a man asks you for what's natural and right——"

"Well, I don't think it is natural and right, I think it's funny," said Pauline, dejectedly, her flash of temper over, "I should feel such a fool. Besides, I——"

She paused, frowning at the floor. The story of the young man of New Orleans was beginning to reinforce the dread in her own mind, and in spite of her confidential mood she could not quite bring herself to tell Louise that she was *frightened* to do what Brian wanted; frightened of herself and her own feelings, and of him. Her experience was limited, and she had never been the type of girl who says confidently "I can take care of myself."

"What's funny about it? I think it's very serious. He's miserable, and you're miserable, just because you won't be kind to him."

"How about him being kind to me?"

"Ah, honey, if you'd once let him see you like that he *would* be kind to you! He'd ask you for the rest quick enough, I'm sure."

"Do you mean—ask me to marry him?"

Louise shook her head.

"Maybe. But why are you so crazy on getting married?"

"I'm not crazy, but I'd certainly—well, I suppose everybody wants to get married. I'm no keener on it than anyone else," proudly, "but when I think about—about later on, I always sort of imagine myself married. And I don't see——"

"A girl can have a lot of fun if she doesn't get married," said Louise, smiling. "Marriage isn't all jam, you know."

"Marriage is dearest lovers and having children!" suddenly said Pauline, the words seeming to rise suddenly from the deepest longings, the desires she hardly knew were there, half-awake in her heart; and then to her shame the contrast between her brave, warm words and the cold facts overwhelmed her, and she began to cry.

"Don't cry, honey," said Louise, but lazily and not very sympathetically, watching her.

"Frightfully sorry," said Pauline after a minute or two, blowing her nose. "It's the weather or something."

"You English never tell the truth about anything that matters. You put everything down to your precious weather."

"So what? We manage." Pauline took out her flapjack and did her nose. The desire to confide in somebody had gone completely, as it has a way of doing after we have indulged it, and she was regretting that she had given way to it, for she was worse off than before. Her pain had been exposed to uncomprehending eyes, she had been reproved and blamed, and left with a story, a legend, so tragic that she dreaded lest it should at last persuade her to give in to Brian.

"Well, thanks awfully for letting me get it off my chest," she said, looking for the first time since her outburst at the charming dark face bent over the purple flowers. She meant to be kind, she thought desolately. "I'm sorry to have been such a bore."

"Oh don't be crazy, Pauline! How *could* I have been bored? I was very interested. That's you English all over again, always pretending. I don't know—you never seem to get close to things, somehow." (She was following Pauline down the conservatory towards the dining-room door.) "It's all—like people playing a game."

"Cricket," murmured Pauline, a little maliciously, taking comfort (as many wounded English have done before her) in the bewildered comments of a foreigner upon the Island Race. Suddenly there floated through her mind as though a voice had said the words:

This precious jewel, set in the silver sea

and for an instant she had an extraordinary picture of a green, flowery, smoky, lazy shield tilted in the midst of slowly running pewter waves. Then it had gone again. But, though she did not know why, she felt comforted.

"It's the way you've been brought up," Louise was saying. "You won't *give* until you've *got*. No wonder your boy's miserable."

And I'm dancing the Lambeth Walk, I suppose, thought Pauline.

"You won't take my advice, I know, but if I were you I'd do what he wants. It would be the best thing for you. Help you to grow up and get rid of your—inhibitions, don't they call them?"

"Probably. Well, thanks awfully, again. I must be getting along."

"Won't you stay to tea? Mr. Early'll be in any minute now."

"I don't think I will, thanks, Mother expects me back. Give my love to Ted, will you?"

"I will. Good-bye."

"Good-bye."

She went through the hall, now illuminated by rays of fierce sunlight that made the turbans and sashes in the old prints sparkle magnificently, and out through the tangled front garden where spiky crimson and purple dahlias were blowing about. The cold seemed to have abated and although the wind still blew roughly the heavens were all broken up into clearest blue reaches and golden white clouds.

The next person, she thought, the very next person who tells me I'm inhibited, I'm going to *hit*.

But all the time, deep below the surface of her thoughts, the words tolled: *I teased once too often. He said he'd shoot himself, and he did.*

CHAPTER XXXII

A S she opened the front door of "Dorna" she was met by the urgent sound of the telephone bell, ringing and ringing through the silent house, and hurried to answer it.

"Hullo?"

"Oh! Oh, hullo? Is that you, Pauline dear? This is me, Vera Pask. Mrs. Pask. Can you hear me?"

"Yes, perfectly, Mrs. Pask. How nice of you to ring up. How are you?"

"Oh, I'm very well, I always feel well in this wonderful stormy weather. Pauline, dear, this is very short notice and I don't expect for a moment you will be able to come and I'm afraid Jean wouldn't like it at all if she knew, but as a matter of fact she's gone to London for the day to see her father and I was wondering—it's such a wonderful evening! Do you think we could go for a walk?"

Pauline laughed. "In all this wind? You'd be blown away!"

"Oh no, dear, I'm very wiry, you know, and I could always hold on to your arm. I used to hold on to Lionel's, my dear husband's, you know, when we went for our walks together. I thought we might take the bus out to the First Tower, to Happy

Sands, I mean, and walk along the shore. But I expect you're engaged, are you not?"

"No, I'm completely at a loose end, as a matter of fact."

"Oh, that's splendid! Then do you think we could go, dear? I should enjoy it so much, I haven't had a good walk for—it must be years. How soon could you meet me?"

"In twenty minutes?" Pauline's tone was indulgent and amused, as if she were talking to a child. "Shall I come and fetch you from your house?"

"Well, dear, I think we'd better meet at the bus stop, it will save time. These lovely clouds may go at any minute and the wind may drop and I *do* so long to be out in it!"

"All right." Pauline was laughing. "I'll meet you at the bus stop in twenty minutes."

"I'll be there, dear. It *is* kind of you, Pauline, I do appreciate it so much."

"Not a bit. It'll be fun. Good-bye."

"Good-bye, dear."

Pauline hung up the receiver and went upstairs to put on the pair of old brogues she kept for walks along the sands, relieved to be going out into violent weather with someone she would have to take care of, so that she would have no opportunity to think about the young man of New Orleans.

Exactly twenty minutes later she was approaching the bus stop opposite the Hotel Bristol. It was so late in the year that there were scarcely any visitors in the town, and as the inhabitants were too familiar with East Coast winds to desire to walk about in them, the roads near the sea were deserted.

Whooo! rushed the wind at her, coming in from the magnificent grey and green sea. Everything was moving. The hedges of witch's hair streamed in the gale, the waves rushed towards the shore with their white crests foaming over, above them hurried the grey and gold clouds pierced with stormlight from the now hidden, now suddenly glorious, sun. A dead leaf blew stingingly against her face and clung there for a second before the wind snatched it away. She could hardly get her breath, and as she waved to Mrs. Pask, whom she could now see sheltering in the bus-stop, she began to wonder whether her old friend would be able to keep her feet, much less march gaily along the sands.

But there was not time to hesitate. A bus was approaching and Mrs. Pask was frantically signalling. Pauline ran across and was just in time to help the conductor hoist Mrs. Pask's small person on to it.

They turned to each other with smiles of excitement and triumph as the bus started.

"There!" said Mrs. Pask. "Wasn't that fortunate! There wouldn't have been another for half an hour."

Pauline agreed, and they chatted cheerfully while the bus covered the few miles between Seagate and Happy Sands.

A record number of gadgets had Gone Wrong in the Pask home that day. After lying awake as old people often do from the early hours until the arrival of tea at a quarter to eight, Mrs. Pask had been greeted by Ellen with the news that the refrigerator had ceased to freeze. At breakfast Miss Gaye had announced a strike on the part of the electric iron, and during the morning the infection spread to the Hoover. By tea-time, the electric toaster was useless, although this last rebel later thought better of it and was working again by the time Mrs. Pask set out to meet Pauline.

"Good heavens," said Pauline at the end of this saga. "All at once."

"Yes, wasn't it strange. They often do go wrong, of course, but I never remember them all going together like that. Jean said it might be an omen."

"How cheerful. What of?"

"Something unpleasant, I'm afraid. But she didn't say. Oh, here we are! Just *look* at the waves!"

The last rays of stormy sunlight had retreated behind the clouds and only a copperish glow lingered in the west, colouring the waves that were rushing in and bursting with a wonderful effect of unleashed passion and triumph along the beaches of Happy Sands. The fragile little houses that had been built for pleasure and painted pale blue or yellow to look pretty under a summer sky now seemed livid and desolate. Newspaper was blowing about and the stunted plants in the sandy gardens made tiny hissings as the wind poured through them. Most of the houses were shut up and deserted, but in one or two of them where people lived all the year round lights were already shining. Save for these, there was loneliness and the stormy sea as far as the eye could reach; far, far along the coast, where the mists of evening were beginning to descend, the curving line of foam could be seen, glimmering and moving. It was just four o'clock.

"I say!" said Pauline, as they stood with the rough wind snatching at their clothes and breathed the cold smell of the sea, while the bus with its disapproving conductor turned round and made for Seagate again, "this is a bit rough, isn't it. Are you sure it won't be too much for you?"

Mrs. Pask, who was already on her way to the sands, pretended not to hear. She was so tired of people asking her if things mightn't be too much for her. Dear Pauline meant it kindly, but *really* she was old enough to know what she could and could not stand.

As she did not answer, Pauline concluded that she had not heard, and thought no more about it. She was enjoying the angry sea and the wind blowing in spray from the great waves; it was impossible to brood or feel sad in the midst of so much fighting movement, and unhappiness became a small and unreal thing.

Mrs. Pask had gone right down to the sea's edge and was standing there with her back to Pauline, gazing out across the seething white crests as if she had forgotten her.

Dear old squoo, she is loving it, thought Pauline, and went down the stone slope towards her.

The cold sand crunched under her feet. No one had walked here for days, and there was a wonderful border of shells and sea-weed spread out beyond the rage of the waves; mussels embedded like the dark backs of miniature sea monsters, mussels sunk in the sand with water trembling as the wind smote it along their blue pearly cups; tassels of clear red seaweed, ribbons of dark weed and fringes of glistening green; the moss of the sea that rises and falls on the rocks with the washing of the tides. There were pink crab-shells and crab-legs worn white and transparent; pieces of bleached grey wood that had been in the sea for so long that they were halfway through their long journey towards a complete differentness, and it was impossible to imagine that they had ever waved with green leaves on them in a forest and felt the sap rising in the spring. There were long moony white shells, always broken, and strips of sodden cardboard and old black boots and plimsolls, already acquiring poetry (as any ordinary object does as soon as it is broken and useless and nature gets to work on it with water or grass or mere air). Sponge-like growths, pale cream in colour, blew along among the ruffled pools and once she saw a big rusty starfish. And there were the commoners of the sea; the millions of grey and brown and white stones, the grinders and beaters and rollers that help the sea in its unending work of changing everything that it takes. "Sea-change" is one of the most astonishing phrases ever given to mankind, in which poetry *fully* expresses an immemorial natural fact.

Pauline came up to Mrs. Pask and stood beside her.

"Enjoying yourself?"

Mrs. Pask turned quickly, smiling and nodding.

"Isn't it glorious! I'm so glad we came." They began to walk on. "I was just remembering that poem dear Lionel was so fond of. He always used to quote it about our walks along the shore together:

"It was many and many a year ago
In a kingdom by the sea
A maiden lived whom you may know
By the name of Annabel Lee——"

She turned away and gazed out to sea for a moment.

"I always used to think that part about 'the demons down under the sea' was so frightening," she said dreamily. "One always thinks of demons in a hot burning place, of course, it's so queer to think of them in a wet cold one."

"Don't think of them at all!" said Pauline with one of her healthy laughs and ignoring the faint thrill that as usual went down her spine at the sound of poetry.

"Oh, I don't mind thinking about them, dear. I like it. Lionel and I often used to read poetry aloud to each other in the evenings."

Pair of old pets, thought Pauline.

They walked on. The wind tore at their hair and scarves and took their breath, and the sand wearied their feet while the ceaseless hissing of the waves assaulted their ears; and the thunder of the whole ocean, the colossal mass of water agitated by the autumnal gale, made a commotion that was no less exhausting because it was familiar to these two, who had both been born within a mile of it. From very far away, the deep undertone to the hissing and foaming seemed to come. *The demons down under the sea.* But New Orleans was a dreamy place, half asleep above a warm, sleeping ocean. . . .

"Had enough?" Pauline suddenly turned to her companion. In the midst of her own painful thoughts she had been increasingly aware that Mrs. Pask was walking slower and slower; and even as she spoke Mrs. Pask falteringly put out her hand as if to lay it upon her arm. "It really is a bit much, isn't it?" The hand was immediately withdrawn and Mrs. Pask quickened her pace.

"Oh no—I'm enjoying it immensely, aren't you?"

"Rather!" almost shouted Pauline. A tremendous gust of wind hit them, and Mrs. Pask gave a cry as her hat, wrenched from her head, sailed out to sea. A monstrous wave leapt on to it and they saw it rolling over and over among the foam wreaths, a dark object with a gleam of mauve, for a moment before it passed under the wave and was lost to sight. From that moment the twilight seemed to descend; Pauline suddenly found that she had to peer to see her companion's face, about which the grey hair was now streaming.

"Oh dear, oh dear!" Mrs. Pask was saying as she tried to smooth it down. "What an adventure!"

"I'm so sorry—was it a pet of yours?" and they went slowly on for another minute or two without speaking.

Mrs. Pask shook her head.

The wind was increasing in power and coldness and Pauline, forced to move at her companion's slow pace, was beginning to feel chilled, while the thought of hot tea and a fire suddenly became very attractive. She was on the point of turning to say firmly that they really must go back now, when Mrs. Pask stood still, and put out her hand.

Pauline took it instantly with a feeling of deep dismay, and as she did so the first drops of rain dashed coldly against her lips.

"I'm so sorry—it's a bad pain—I'm afraid I can't—just for a minute——"

"Of course. It's all right. Just lean on me and don't worry." Pauline put her arm about the little figure, and the loosened grey hair blew disagreeably across her young face. The rain was increasing and darkness was coming down rapidly as the clouds grew thicker.

Mrs. Pask clung more and more tightly to her arm and suddenly gave a little moan.

"Oh dear! Oh dear! Such a dreadful pain—there! There it is again! In my heart——"

She swayed forward and fell limply across the arm that supported her.

The sudden weight took Pauline by surprise and she nearly let her fall on to the damp sand. She was really frightened now; her heart was beating hard and her confusion was increased because she could not put up a hand to wipe her eyes clear from the streaming raindrops; but she supported Mrs. Pask as best she could and tried to remember all she knew about first aid while she stared about her for help.

Not a soul was in sight. Before them stretched the angry sea, now veiled in a rainy mist out of which the waves rushed forward with an extraordinary and terrifying appearance of coming from the lowering sky itself, and behind lay the deserted pleasure village with its pallid houses glimmering in the twilight.

But to her great relief she suddenly realized that they were standing almost opposite the turning leading to the bungalow where Wally Wade lived with his sister. The house could be seen from the shore, and even while she looked eagerly towards it she saw a light appear in one of the windows.

She hesitated for a moment, undecided whether to leave Mrs. Pask on the shore while she ran to the bungalow for help or to try and carry her, but a sudden increase in the rain made up her mind for her, and she awkwardly bundled Mrs. Pask up and began the staggering walk up the beach towards the house.

Mrs. Pask was a small old lady, but she was a dead weight, and the rain was pouring down on her and rapidly soaking her thick clothes and adding to their weight. Once she nearly slipped from Pauline's grasp, and the distance between the sea and the bungalow, and the time it was taking to plod over the sodden sand, both seemed very long.

She felt sure that Mrs. Pask was dead. She had not felt such a lumpish weight, with just that frightening limpness, since the morning years ago when she had lifted a poor old dog, Jumps's predecessor, from his basket at the end of his last illness.

And it all seemed so unreal! At one moment they had been chatting about poetry and admiring the waves, and the next she was staggering in the twilight across endless sands with the rain streaming down on a dead woman in her aching arms.

The steps leading up to the bungalow were slippery with rain, and she stumbled as she reached the top one and again nearly dropped Mrs. Pask. She tried to support her with one hand and ring the bell with the other but the burden began to slide to the ground, and when she endeavoured to support her by raising one knee she nearly overbalanced herself. So she put her gently down on the doormat, and after one distressed look at her livid face, rang a long peal on the bell.

She was in the middle of the second peal, wondering in an agony of apprehension and impatience what on earth they could all be *doing* in there, when the door opened rather quickly and there stood a man, a stranger to her, looking indignant.

"All right, all right, I'm coming!" he said sharply. "There's no need to deafen anybody."

"Oh please—is Wally there, or Estelle? This is Mr. Wade's house, isn't it? I'm a friend of theirs, Pauline Williams—look—it's the old lady—we were out for a walk and she fainted—and I'm afraid——"

He glanced down and for the first time saw Mrs. Pask, who was almost invisible in a deepening gloom that was not lessened by any light from the hall. Alarm and astonishment came into his face.

"Good heavens—here—we must get her into the house—sorry, I didn't see—Estelle!" he shouted over his shoulder, half-turning towards the hall across which Pauline could see firelight flickering. "Here's a friend of yours—someone's fainted—an old lady. Come out a minute, will you, dear? Here——" and he stooped and began to work his hands awkwardly under Mrs. Pask's body; "give me a hand, will you?"

Pauline took her feet and together they lifted her and carried her into the hall. Pauline glanced up as the man kicked the front door shut and saw the cripple girl's sturdy figure outlined against the door of the firelit room. The next instant the hall was full of light and Estelle exclaimed:

"Pauline! What on earth—who's that? Whatever's the matter? Here, Jack, bring her into the drawing-room, I'll put the light on——" and she moved back into the room with her awkward rocking step.

Jack Caldicott lowered Mrs. Pask on to the sofa and put a cushion under her head, and Pauline slowly stood upright, and rubbed the rain out of her eyes and sighed deeply.

Estelle looked at her curiously with a not completely friendly expression. She was dressed in one of her favourite bright woollen frocks, a jade green one with dressy kiltings on the skirt and sleeves, and looked slightly flushed, and ruffled about the hair.

"Whatever's the matter?" she asked again. "Who is it, poor old thing? What on earth were you——?"

"Mrs. Pask. She's a friend of mine. Hadn't we better get a doctor?" said Pauline rather distractedly, blowing her nose. "I'm afraid she's—I'm afraid she may be dead."

"Oh no, she's not dead," said Jack Caldicott decidedly. "Poor old thing. Lives at 'Avonlea' in the High Street, doesn't she? Nice bit of property though the neighbourhood is going down. We'd better get a doctor. Who's the nearest? Oh damn, we haven't got one. They all say there aren't enough of us here in the winter. Who's her own doctor, do you know?"

"Doctor Eames."

"I'll try for him at once. I suppose you don't know his number?" (Pauline shook her head.) "Oh, well, he'll be in the book."

He went out into the hall and snatched up the telephone directory.

Both girls glanced at the unconscious woman. Her face was bluish and she had begun to breathe heavily As they watched, a jabbering sound came out between her lips and died away into a bubbling sigh.

"Can't we *do* anything?" said Pauline distractedly, bending over her.

Estelle shook her head.

"Better not. You might make her worse."

"Hullo? Is that Dr. Eames's house? Is he there? Can I speak to him? At once. It's very urgent. A matter of life and death."

There was a pause.

"Sit down, won't you, Pauline." Estelle seated herself in a

chair by the fire and arranged the folkweave cushion at her back.
"We can't do anything till the doctor comes."

Pauline took the chair opposite and leant forward, gazing
troubledly into the dancing fire.

Estelle took up some knitting.

"What on earth were you doing out here on such an awful afternoon?" she began. Her bangles jingled and slid over her wrists
as she worked.

"She wanted to go for a walk. She was—she is, I mean—she's
crazy about the sea in rough weather, and she rang me up this
afternoon and asked me if I'd go with her."

"*You* must have been crazy to let her do such a thing," said
Estelle bluntly. "You must have known she isn't strong."

"She seemed perfectly all right this afternoon!" said Pauline,
roused to a little indignation. "And the weather wasn't all that
bad, either. It seemed to get worse so suddenly. The whole thing
happened so suddenly! I can't get over it."

"Well, I think it was a mad thing to do," said Estelle firmly.
For a moment she knitted in silence, while Pauline stared into the
fire with a disagreeable feeling of guilt added to her anxiety and
grief. But she was also annoyed with Estelle, sitting there so trim
and comfortable with her kiltings and her bangles and giving
judgment in her rather sharp voice. She never did like me, she
thought, but I've only just realized it. I wish Wally had been here.

"Oh, will you?" Jack's voice, relieved and grateful, sounded
from the hall. "Thank you very much. Yes. That would be best.
We have got a car but the ambulance would be much more comfortable. We'll expect you in about twenty minutes, then, Doctor.
The house is quite easy to find, it's on the corner, the third turning
past the Express Dairy. It's called 'Daree.' Thank you very
much. Good-bye."

He came back into the room.

"That's all right. He'll be here in twenty minutes and he's
'phoning for an ambulance in case she can be moved."

"In *case* she can be moved!" Estelle glanced up quickly, and
stopped knitting. "You don't mean to say he thinks she *won't*
be able to be moved—that she'll have to stay here?"

"Now, now, dear, I didn't say anything of the sort. All I said
was—all *he* said was—that he can't tell us anything until he's seen
her. If he thought it wasn't likely she could be moved he'd hardly
be phoning for an ambulance, would he?"

"Well, I hope to goodness she won't have to stay here," muttered Estelle, resuming her knitting. "I don't know how I should
manage, I'm sure—with my wedding coming on and everything."

There was a fainter murmur about "a beastly nuisance" before complete silence fell.

Pauline, with crimson cheeks, stared into the fire. She was longing to get up and march out of the house, but felt that this would only complete her humiliation. She was responsible for all the trouble, or so they seemed to think (for the man's manner was far from cordial), whatever her feelings were, and she must see it through to the end.

"Oh—I must apologize—I never introduced you two," said Estelle presently, with a little laugh but not looking up from her knitting. "This is my fiancé, Pauline, Mr. Caldicott. Jack, this is Pauline Williams, an old friend of Wally's."

"Pleased to meet you, Miss Williams. I'm only sorry it couldn't have been under happier circumstances. Poor old lady—— glancing at the figure on the sofa—"whatever possessed her to come out in such awful weather?"

Estelle said nothing. The diamond in her engagement ring flashed as she lifted her work up to the light.

"She phoned me and asked me to go with her," said Pauline sulkily, at last. "She was crazy about the sea in rough weather and——"

"But surely you tried to persuade her not to? It's mad—an old lady like that—not very strong—anyone could have seen——"

"She seemed perfectly all right this afternoon," repeated Pauline, with a growing despairing feeling that these sentences were going to be her signature tune for some time to come.

Estelle put her knitting away in a bag with a crinolined lady appliquéd on it and glanced at the mantelpiece.

"Five o'clock. It's a bit late for tea but I suppose we may as well have some. I'll go and get it."

But at that moment the front door bell rang, and a few seconds later Jack Caldicott brought in Doctor Eames.

He was a quiet, stout man of sixty, with grey hair and a greyish face and a guarded look in his eyes. He greeted Pauline with surprise and pleasure; he had brought her into the world, and watched her grow up, but if he ever made a comparison between her girlhood and another girlhood that he had also watched from infancy, it was in his secret heart and was only rarely expressed in a deep sigh.

While he was taking off his coat and washing his hands in a basin brought by Jack, Pauline told him what had happened. He made no comment, much to her relief, and at once set about his examination.

The girls went into the kitchen while this was going on, and

Jack waited in the hall with the front door open to guide the ambulance.

"Is that your ring, Estelle? Isn't it a beauty! May I see?" said Pauline, feeling a slight relaxation in the atmosphere as they moved about the spotless and glittering kitchen, and anxious, in spite of her annoyance, to take advantage of it. Open disapproval from anyone was a new experience for her, and she was not liking it at all.

Estelle held out a carefully tended red hand.

"I don't like to take it off," she said proudly. "It *is* rather nice, isn't it?"

"It's beautiful," said Pauline. But it was the things represented by the flashing watery drop that gave it charm for her. She looked at it respectfully. Try as she might not to have the feeling—how she wished that she had a ring too!

"Jack says nothing but the best's good enough for me," said Estelle, arranging triangular cups of shaded pink and green on a tray covered with an embroidered white cloth. "This cost forty pounds."

"*Gosh*, Estelle!"

"It's worth seventy but he knows a man in the diamond business who got it for him for forty."

"It's marvellous. I love just one enormous diamond like that, it looks so *good*."

"Oh, so do I. Nothing common about it. Will you put the biscuits on that plate with the roses, and then I think we're ready."

The tea preparations and the little gossip had occupied Pauline for a quarter of an hour and driven her anxiety and remorse to the back of her mind, but as she carried the tray across the hall to the dining-room all her forebodings returned.

Doctor Eames was standing by the fire, slowly arranging his shirtcuffs. He glanced up as the girls entered.

"It is a stroke complicated by heart trouble," he said. "At least, that's the simplest way I can explain it to you. She can be moved, and she must be, to-night. The ambulance should be here any moment now, and Mr. Caldicott is telephoning her home."

Estelle had seated herself at a little table in front of the teacups and now looked up at him.

"Tea, Doctor?"

He shook his head. "No, thank you. I have had tea. But I expect Pauline is ready for some, aren't you, my dear?"

She nodded. For the moment she could not speak.

Estelle handed her a full cup and an elaborate sugar biscuit on a rose-wreathed plate.

"Doctor Eames——" Pauline managed to say, as she took them—"(thank you, Estelle) is she—I know doctors don't usually like telling people—but—is she *seriously* ill?"

He hesitated; then answered quietly:

"Very seriously ill," and no more was said until Jack came in from the hall announcing that the ambulance had come.

Pauline could do nothing but drink her tea and nibble the sugar off the biscuit while two uniformed men were carrying Mrs. Pask (but it did not seem like Mrs. Pask any more) out of the warm and brightly lit house into the stormy darkness. The raving of the sea could be heard coming out of it, and showers of glittering raindrops whirled across the beam of light from the hall door and vanished into the blackness beyond.

But when the men had stepped outside with their burden and were going carefully down the steps, Pauline stood up.

"Oh, Doctor Eames, can't I go with her? Sit beside her in the ambulance, I mean? If she recovered consciousness she might be frightened, and if I was there with her it wouldn't be quite so bad, perhaps."

He shook his head.

"She won't recover consciousness yet, if she does at all. I'll try to drive you home after I've settled her in. He glanced round the room. "Her hat? Mrs. Pask's hat? Where is it?"

"It blew off," said Pauline, bewilderedly, suddenly remembering what seemed to have happened in another life, "into the sea. That was really the start of everything. She kept on trying to smooth her hair down——"

"And lifting her arms up and down and struggling all the time against the wind and putting a strain on her heart—— "He shook his head. "What were you about, letting her go out in such weather? You're not usually thoughtless. You must have known she wasn't strong. But never mind now. Come along home, you must be tired out. Good night, Miss—Wade, isn't it? Good night," with a nod to Jack. "Come along, Pauline."

Jack accompanied him to the door, and Pauline lingered a moment.

"Good night, Estelle. I say, I'm most awfully sorry to have given you such a lot of trouble."

"Oh, that's all right, Pauline. We shouldn't have been human, should we, if we hadn't taken the poor old thing in. I'm sure I hope she'll recover but I doubt it. I'm afraid her number's up. But don't you worry. We've all got to go some time, and she's had her life; it's not anybody's fault—really. Good night."

"Good night. Give my love to Wally."

"I'll tell him all about it. Good night."

Pauline went slowly down the steps into the darkness. Cold raindrops mingled with spray blew into her face, bringing the smell of the sea, and in the dimness she could just discern pale shapes that were the toy houses built for summer, and beyond them a line of white crazily dashing and writhing.

She climbed slowly into the car beside Doctor Eames.

"Wouldn't you rather sit at the back? It's much more comfortable," he said as he backed the car down the road.

She shook her head.

"Please let me sit with you."

"Of course, my dear. We'll be at Avonlea in a few minutes and then, if you'll wait, I can drive you home, I expect."

He meant to be kind, but he made no attempt to cheer her by saying that Mrs. Pask had a chance of recovery, or that she had not been to blame for taking her for the disastrous walk.

They were nearly home, driving in silence beside the ambulance along the deserted sea front, when she remembered the young man in New Orleans.

CHAPTER XXXIII

PAULINE was surprised when she did get home to find that it was only half past six. The darkness of the winter evening and the experiences of the last three hours had made her feel that the time must be much later.

Her mother and Marjorie were sitting gossiping by the drawing-room fire and glanced up when she came in with no more than ordinary interest; but the sight of her shocked and exhausted face made them both exclaim; and as she sat down wearily by the fire Marjorie hurried to get the sherry and poured her out half a tumbler.

She sipped it while she repeated for the third time the story that she was already sick of telling. At the end of it her mother asked her why she had been so silly as to take an old lady, who was not very strong, out in such wild weather, and expressed the hope that Mrs. Pask would leave her something if she passed over: but all Marjorie said was: "What a sweat for you."

Her sister glanced at her gratefully. Really, there were times and situations when no company was bearable but that of one's contemporaries. Even Estelle thought it was a damned nuisance, underneath all that stuff about being so shocked, thought Pauline, finishing her sherry. Of course I'm most awfully sorry and I hope the poor old pet doesn't die, but honestly, it *is* a damned nuisance. Only somebody else young could see how utterly unnecessary and maddening it all is. And how many more times am I to be asked what she was doing out in such bad weather? The next time someone asks me I shall scream.

But she felt too depressed to scream at Miss Gaye when the latter telephoned a little later. Her usually acid voice was very subdued, and this frightened Pauline more than ever.

Mrs. Pask was much worse.

"I thought it best to tell you," said Miss Gaye.

"Oh . . . thanks . . . I'm most awfully sorry, Miss Gaye."

"What I cannot understand, Miss Williams—what none of us can understand—Doctor Eames says so too—is how you came to be out in such dreadful weather when you *know* that poor Vera has a weak heart and had been told to avoid all exertion."

"She did ask me to go, Miss Gaye. I thought——"

"So odd. So very peculiar and strange. Out in all that rain. I simply cannot."

"It wasn't raining when we started. It was rather rough but it was a gorgeous afternoon, really. She—she was quite enjoying it, really."

There was a pause, in which it was certain that Miss Gaye was compressing her lips and raising her eyebrows and shaking her head. Then she said:

"Well, she has been getting steadily worse ever since Doctor Eames brought her home just after six o'clock. I myself have not been home very long. What a home-coming for me! Poor Ellen is very much upset, too, and Jack. Poor old doggie——" her voice changed as she spoke to the Airedale, who was evidently standing near the telephone, "he loves his missus, don't you, boy? And poor Gladys, too! Gladys and Ellen have been with us for fourteen years. If only you had only been a little less thoughtless, Miss Williams. That keeps going round and round in my head, try as I may. *Surely*, as I said to Doctor Eames, you must have *known* poor Vera's heart was weak?"

Pauline was so angry that for a moment she actually could not speak. She began once more to feel as if she were in a nightmare, forced to listen to person after person accusing her and unable to say a word in her own defence.

"I'm most *awfully* sorry," she said at last, trying to keep the anger out of her voice and let only unhappiness and anxiety come through. "I—I simply can't tell you how sorry I am, Miss Gaye. It all happened so suddenly. One minute we were walking along quite happily and the next—it all happened so suddenly—you see——"

Her voice died miserably away.

There was a pause. Coming through the silence at the other end of the line Pauline suddenly heard a faint sound, secretive and wretched. Miss Gaye was crying.

"Well—good night. If there is any more news I will telephone you again," snuffled Miss Gaye at last.

"Good night, Miss Gaye, and—and thanks awfully. My mother asked me to tell you"—in response to a muffled call from the drawing-room—"how very sorry she is—and my sister too—and we do hope, all of us, I mean—you'll have better news soon."

"Oh, I do hope so, too, but I'm afraid . . . good night."

Pauline hung up the receiver, and as she did so Marjorie came out into the hall.

"You come along to the Fisherman's Rest with me and have a drink, my girl," she ordered quickly, in a low tone. "I'm meeting a crowd there—oh, come on! It's just what you need. You'll go nuts if you sit here all evening waiting for the bad news to break."

"Gosh, I'd love to—but suppose she rings up and finds me out?"

"Let her. The thing's done now."

The sherry had gone to Pauline's head, because she was both upset and hungry. Her only longing was to get out of the house and forget about Mrs. Pask, and she did not pause to think what she was doing or take any notice of her mother's warning remark as she put on her hat—"Pauli, you aren't going out again, are you? Suppose Miss Gaye rings up—it will look so bad if you're out, dear"—but followed Marjorie quickly out of the house and slammed the door.

The Fisherman's Rest was a modest pub in a back street near the theatre, which the repertory company had adopted. It was about eighty years old, with small dark rooms and bulging yellow plaster walls, and had no attractions for such sophisticates as there were in Seagate. But upstairs there was a long narrow room overlooking the street where an excellent supper, of cold ham and salad in the summer and roast beef with apple tart in the winter, was served to such commercials or stray motorists as might wander in and discover that it was to be had. Of course the Fisherman's Rest never advertised it; why should they want people to come in, eating their food and making extra work and keeping the girls on their feet all hours?

Here, at the long table covered with a thin but ample white tablecloth and adorned by a complicated cruet with accommodation for at least four sorts of vinegar, Pauline had supper and a lot to drink with Marjorie, who had her usual egg, and Marjorie's friends. The tired lively faces of the girls were friendly under their turbans and she took a huge fancy to Lenham Browne, who flirted with her and tried to make her tight. I do like stage people, she thought, looking round muzzily at their faces. They give you such a lovely feeling that you can sit here and laugh and make silly jokes for ever and there's no need to get up and go on with the next boring job. It's like having supper at the Rich House. Of course—I was forgetting Mr. Early had been an actor.

"Where's Ted?" she asked dreamily.

"The great man won't be back from town until to-morrow," said Lenham Browne, filling her glass again.

"I'm always trying to loathe Ted and can't," said one of the girls.

"He's really a grand person, you know, but has he got a lot to learn!"

"He's ham," pronounced Lenham Browne.

"*Ted* is?"

"Lenny *dear*!"

"But ham acting is coming back again so he'll be all right," went on the actor. "If he'd come to the front ten years ago he wouldn't have had such a chance of success. The public wouldn't have been ready for him."

"I should have said Ted would always have been good. He just can act," said somebody.

"So can lots of us but we haven't got what he has," muttered Marjorie.

"Especially if there's going to be a war. That throw-away-your-lines stuff will go right out."

"In the last one they wanted the lightest stuff they could get."

"Light, Sylvia, but not sophisticated. There's a big difference."

"*Need* you babble about the bloody war, darling? Every time I see a tank on the movies little Joanie nearly fwows up."

"Sorry."

"It's getting late."

"Darling Marjie. Such a little worker."

"She's quite right," said Lenham Browne, standing up. "Let's have the bad news, will you, dear," to the waitress.

Pauline walked to the theatre arm in arm with him. "I've fallen heavily for your sister, Marjie darling," he announced as they said good-bye at the stage door. "It's a case, isn't it, Pauli?"

She nodded, laughing up at him, and he took her face gently in his hands and kissed her on the mouth.

"There."

"Thank you," she said demurely.

"Come in and sit in the dressing-room, I get off at the end of the second act and you can't go home now, you're tight," said Marjorie, leading her sister down the odorous corridors.

Pauline giggled happily. She was not thinking, but was interestedly observing her sensations. Her legs felt as if they ended at the knees and were moving through deep cotton-wool. and every time she shut her eyes everything went swinging round in one long delicious swoop.

"I do think it's heaven being tight," she said earnestly, stumbling into an old arm-chair.

Marjorie, sitting at the mirror and preparing her face for paint, gave one of her ironical and affectionate looks.

"Honestly, Pauli, you're just so sweet . . ." she murmured.

The tightness lasted satisfactorily until Marjorie was ready, at about half past nine, to go. There were even traces of it left after the walk home through the cold air cleared by the afternoon's rain.

When they got into the quiet dimly-lit house and Marjorie was shutting the front door, their mother came out into the hall with a grave face.

"Pauli, Miss Gaye telephoned," she said, and then she nodded. "Yes. Poor old thing. She's gone. About two hours ago."

Pauline pulled off her hat and her eyes filled with tears.

"Beastly," she muttered.

"Miss Gaye asked to speak to you. I had to say you were so upset you'd gone to bed. But I don't really think she believed me. I wish you hadn't gone out like that, dear. It looked so heartless."

"Well, it wasn't," said Marjorie coolly, arranging her hair in front of the hall mirror. "What one can never get old people to see is that we go out and get tight because we do mind things, not because we don't."

"Well, that may be so, Marjorie." Mrs. Williams did not like the reference to old people. "All I can say is that it looked very rude and heartless."

"So what?" murmured Marjorie, going into the drawing-room and picking up the evening paper. "Is Connie in? I'd adore some coffee."

Pauline lingered unhappily in the hall.

"Mother, do you think I'd better phone Miss Gaye?"

"I shouldn't now, dear. It would look so peculiar after I'd said you'd gone to bed."

"Mums, do I get my coffee?"

"Really, Marjorie, you are tiresome. Connie has cleared everything up for the night now and she's listening-in. Besides, we're short of milk."

God, thought Marjorie, scanning the paper with grave eyes and a smooth forehead, how much longer have I got to live at home? When I've got a place of my own I'll have mussels in Dutch sauce at three in the morning if I feel like it."

"I suppose I'd better go to bed," said Pauline.

"I should, dear. You must be worn out."

"Is the water hot? I'd adore a bath."

"Not very, I expect. Connie let the fire down; I told her no one would be wanting one this evening."

"Doesn't matter." Pauline went drearily up the stairs to bed.

During her miserable affair with Brian she had become used to secret unhappiness and anger, but it was a quite new sensation to set out for the bank dreading what people might say to her. No one said anything about Mrs. Pask, although she thought that the manager looked at her curiously once as he went into his office. Eric was more silent than he used to be, but then he had become more silent lately. The hollows in his cheeks were filling out and his eyes looked cheerful and he went about with lists which he pulled out of his pockets and earnestly studied. Pauline, reading over his shoulder, saw: "See about Gas. Fire-irons. See about Hooks. ? Green Carpet. Cornfield or Cypresses? Ask M." He was in the thick of it.

She was feeling calmer at the end of the day, and had made up her mind to go round to "Avonlea" that evening and leave a note saying how very sorry she was that her old friend had gone and how deeply she regretted having taken her on the walk.

She was indeed very sorry. Walking home through the bitter wind (for the first savage cold of the East Coast winter had seized the town) she remembered how kind Mrs. Pask had been to her; how glad to see her; what delicious lunches she had taken pleasure in giving her, and how interested the old lady had always been in all her doings. Just as if she'd been an unusually nice grandmother, thought Pauline.

She remembered Mrs. Pask's innocent and friendly pleasure in the affairs of the town; she had never made spiteful or envious or disapproving remarks. It was almost like being with somebody young, really, thought Pauline, walking quickly home in a charming Esquimau hood of brown fur, her latest treasure, tied with ribbons under her chin. Well, not quite, perhaps (hastily withdrawing this overwhelming tribute) because she did make you feel you wanted to shriek and kick stones to let off steam after you'd been with her. But she was far and away the nicest old lady I've ever known and I shall miss her very much. I do hope she's with Dear Lionel. Sweet, that was. And we never found out who sent those letters! But she'd almost stopped worrying about them; I made her.

She turned into her own road, giving one glance towards the sea hidden in the black winter night. The waves were making a far-off hissing and rustling, very remote and cold: it was impossible to believe that the thing making that sad far away sound had ever been bathed in and sailed upon by human beings.

For a moment Pauline thought of death. But it was useless; the fur was warm against her cold yet glowing face and she walked full into the icy wind without shrinking because of her lively blood. I don't believe I'll ever die, she thought suddenly and did a little skip for joy of the cold weather and her fur hood.

Poor old darling, she had her walk by the sea, anyway, and I'm glad I gave it her even if it did kill her, she thought, opening the gate of "Dorna." It was what she wanted, and she was enjoying it almost up to the end. And the last thing she must have known was the feeling of my arm round her. She must have been glad I was taking care of her, poor old squoo.

No matter what people say, I'm *glad* I gave her that last walk.

But a few minutes later, when she was reading the letter she found waiting for her, this calmer mood completely disappeared.

DEAR MISS WILLIAMS,

I feel that I must do my duty to poor Vera, *unpleasant though it may be*, and tell you how very strongly I and others feel about the way you have behaved. It was bad enough to take her for a walk in *such dreadful weather* when you must have known that she had a weak heart and was told by Doctor Eames to avoid *the slightest exertion*. That was bad enough. But to go out as you did last night and to *such a place in such company* when you knew that she was dying, and I might telephone at any minute to let you know all was over is far worse. She might have asked for you. How should I have felt if I had had to tell her: she cannot come—*she is at a public house*. Doctor Eames is much shocked and upset also and cannot think what your mother is

about to let you, *but perhaps she did not know*. I tell you this
for your own good. The funeral is to be to-morrow at St. Anne's
at half past twelve, *if you care to follow.*
            Yours sincerely,
                        JEAN C. F. GAYE.

Pauline put the letter down with an angry little laugh.
" 'She cannot come—she is at a public house!' " she mocked.
But a blush came up into her cheeks.
"What is that, dear?" Mrs. Williams looked up from her book.
"Aren't you frozen? Come to the fire." Her tone was affection-
ate, for once. Instinct made her feel closer to her daughter now
that Pauline was being disapproved of by outsiders: such criticism
was an indirect attack on Pauline's mother.
Pauline handed her the letter.
"Well, dear, I did tell you not to go, didn't I?" she said, with
control but pressing her lips together, when she had read it. "I
told you at the time how peculiar it looked."
"I know you did, Mother."
"All the same, she had no right to send a letter to you like
that!" burst out Mrs. Williams, crumpling it and flinging it into
the fire. "Interfering old maid! Of course it's all dreadfully sad
and I'm very sorry, but there's no point in saying anything about
it now—the thing's done. Did you do anything about flowers,
dear?"
"I wonder how on earth she knew I went to the Fisherman's
Rest?" muttered Pauline. "(No, I'm afraid I didn't, I was in such
a state. I'll phone now, it's not too late.) Someone must have
seen me. Ellen, perhaps."
"Order a wreath, dear, with a card from all of us. White
chrysanths would be nice, those big spiky ones."
"You and Marjie send those, I want to send something special."
Pauline hurried out to the telephone, adding: "About how much
do you want to give?" Her mother's habits made the question
necessary although she disliked asking it.
"Oh, about ten-and-six. It isn't as if Marjie and I knew her,
but it looks better to send something. Are you going to the
funeral?"
"I suppose so. I don't want to. I hate——"
Her voice died away as she searched for the florist's number.
I hope to heaven there won't be crowds of people there all
staring at me as if I'd murdered her, she thought, as she undressed
that night. She sighed. The events of the last two days had driven
the thought of Brian to the back of her mind; but now, at the end

of an unpleasant day, his sad handsome face returned and haunted her, without hope of happiness.

I feel as if I'd got a cold coming, too, she thought. Oh dear, I do begin to feel old.

In the night a freezing east wind sprang up and raced over the land. At dawn the sky was grey, with strips of cloud like darker grey wool scattered across it. The pavements looked yellow and the sea was a dark and treacherous green. The branches of the trees seemed made of iron. It was going to be a day without mercy.

"*God!*" said Pauline, as she came out of the house and the wind hit her. At once her nose and eyes began to stream, and the wind, thin and piercing rather than savage, passed straight through her thick clothes on to her flesh and chilled it to the bone.

On her way to the bank she called at the florists and gave them two pounds with the order to make up a round wreath of dark red roses and carnations with violets. The woman looked at her curiously when she heard where the flowers were to go: Pauline's cold made her look as if she had been crying heavily.

She gazed drearily round the shop, at the beautiful faces of the flowers lifted quietly up in the warmed air. Small crimson tulips were here already, and curled blue hyacinths and the fairy mimosa.

Suddenly she said:

"I've changed my mind. I'll have all mimosa. Just the same plain round wreath."

"Mimosa, madam? Just as you wish, of course. It won't last any time, you know."

"I'll have it, please."

"Very good, madam."

She walked out of the shop suddenly feeling bitter with all the world. Everyone was so damned mean. No one ever had a gorgeous riot of reds and blues and riding and laughing and mimosa. Don't forget to turn the oven out. How much will it cost? Mind you shut the door after you. Don't make yourself cheap. It won't last any time, you know.

Hell! What does it matter how long it lasts so long as it's beautiful while it does?

There was more trouble when she got to the bank. The manager was irritated because she had left it until the day of the funeral to ask for leave of absence, and got his own back at her, although he gave the desired permission, by remarking that he had "heard all about" Mrs. Pask's death, at the same time giving her a pompously disapproving look. When she was halfway across the room, however, he repented (for she still looked as if she had been crying) and said that she could have the rest of the day off as well.

"Thank you, Mr. Green," she muttered.

"What's all this I hear about your being arrested for murdering an old lady?" enquired Eric cheerfully, and was surprised and a little hurt when she snapped at him. Happiness was making him less morbidly sensitive than he used to be to other people's moods; a delicate yet solid happiness that increased every day, every hour. The coral reef of misery was crumbling rapidly. A tender and peaceful delight unlike any other feeling he had ever known was now his daily state of mind. And he knew that Mavis felt it too. She was less shy, she laughed more often. He could not know, of course, that "Mr. Somers" and "Eric" were now nearly one. But Mavis knew. And such happiness was opening before her, splendid yet completely real like an unclouded sunrise in summer, that she often shut her eyes while choosing a bath-mat or a tea-towel and said a prayer of thanksgiving. *Dear God, thank you ever so for letting me be so happy*, prayed Mavis in the Hardware Department of Brown's The Household Word; and then hurried off to lunch with Reenie, who naturally took the greatest interest in all the arrangements for the wedding, and the new flat facing the sea on North Parade (although she continued privately to think the bridegroom A Bit Washy).

At half past eleven Pauline packed up her things and hurried away. The wind was colder than ever and everyone looked wretched. Curdled white crests, frothy and evil, were now spreading along the tops of the dark waves that appeared to move disconnectedly up and down with no motion of approach to the shore. St. Anne's looked sombre and dreary against the lowering sky, and as she walked along with her head down against the unbearable wind something colder than rain struck her cheek. She glanced downwards and saw fine crystals clinging to her coat: snow.

Heaven! was her first thought; which proved that, although she might say she felt old, she was in fact young.

She had not allowed enough time to get to the church, and the first half of the service was over when she arrived, breathless and half-running.

She crossed the churchyard between the gravestones now covered with a thin dusting of fine snow and made her way towards a little group of people standing under umbrellas, near an open grave by two large ancient yews. There was Miss Gaye with her arm through that of a cross-looking old gentleman, and Ellen with two others who must be the cook and the housemaid, and a pale

10

elderly woman in an unbecoming hat and brown fur coat with a seat to it, and one or two more.

Everyone looked up as Pauline approached, and stared; then the three servants deliberately turned their heads away. Miss Gaye bowed without smiling and made a nervous movement of the hand that was not clutching the old gentleman; he raised his hat and frowned. The pale elderly woman stared angrily.

Pauline had never felt so miserable and uncomfortable in her life. She retreated to the shade of the nearest yew and stood there, a figure plainly in disgrace, while the small coffin on the shoulders of the bearers was slowly lowered into the ground. She could see upon it her mother's wreath of white chrysanthemums, and her own large circle of mimosa. But now it was an ugly thing, all its plumy delicacy withered away by the fierce cold.

It looks frightful, she thought, appalled. They'll think I got it cheap or something. Her card—"With love and deepest sympathy and sorrow from Pauline"—had been blotted in the haste and distress in which she had written it, and looked untidy and too large, and it seemed to her that everyone was staring at it with disapproval.

The service continued. The wind blew more fiercely and the snow whirled across the gravestones. The three servants stared at Pauline the whole time with the same serious, sad, stupid look on their faces; Ellen was remembering that bottle Pauline had smuggled out the day she came to tea; that bottle from nowhere; and thinking that it All Went To Show.

I'm sure *she* doesn't blame me, anyway, thought Pauline, watching the coffin; and then the Vicar's quiet voice asked of the grave the two superbly triumphant questions.

But it seemed to her suddenly that just by being there, unmistakable in depth and shape and purpose, the grave answered *Here*; and she was overcome by such misery that it was all she could do not to turn around and run out of the churchyard.

The old faces with their angry look, the biting wind and the snow so thin that it did not seem like the snow she had loved from childhood, the sight of the little coffin with kind harmless Mrs. Pask in it, killed by thoughtlessness—all these suddenly struck upon her spirit with almost unbearable force, and without thinking she drove her trembling fists into her pockets to help her to stand her ground.

There's disrespect for you. Not my idea of a young lady at all, thought Ellen, looking severely at the sturdy figure among the shades of the yew branches with her brown, troubled young face in the Esquimau hood. Going into publics with men, too. Poor madam, it was a bad day for her when she first took up with her.

Everything's so freezing cold and mean and beastly, thought Pauline. I wish I had something warm and beautiful to comfort me: a huge bunch of wallflowers or a horse's nose to stroke or someone to love with all my heart who'd love me too.

Louise said the English weren't generous and never got close to things somehow, and she's quite right.

Why can't the old fools *see* how sorry I am?

I can't say more than I have. I'm absolutely no good at showing my feelings anyway.

Perhaps if I'd shown Brian I was really crazy about him and gone with him to his old nudist place everything would have been all right by now.

Perhaps I've been wrong all along?

It was over. They were turning away from the grave and picking their elderly way carefully between the stones and over the dry snow. Not one of them took the slightest notice of Pauline except the Vicar, who remembered her because he had confirmed her (although he had not seen her more than two or three times since that occasion five years ago): he now gave her a little smile.

She made a sort of grimace in return, and hurried away.

CHAPTER XXXIV

AFTER hesitating miserably outside the church for a moment or two in the tearing wind, while all the old people carefully packed themselves into several cars, she decided to have lunch at the Fan, and walked away quickly in that direction.

The place was emptier than usual, for of course all visitors had left the town, and there would be no more until Christmas, and the weather was so disagreeable that no one was out shopping to-day or treating themselves to lunch before the pictures. She ordered her pet liver and bacon and was not too wretched to relish it.

But she was very wretched: more wretched, it seemed to her, than she had ever been in all her life; and the fact that she had a holiday for the rest of to-day and need not keep an eye on the time while she lunched did not cheer her at all. Everything was strange

to-day; the early and unexpected snow, the sinister colour of the
sea, the knowledge that many of the people in this little town
where she had been born must be talking about her over their
lunch with disapproval and morbid interest, as they did about
Madeleine Eames; and strangest of all was the conclusion she had
just quietly arrived at a little while ago; that she had been wrong
about Brian.

It was so queer to sit in the Fan and eat apricots and cream and
think: What an ass I've been. All this misery for all these months
and none of it necessary. I could just have phoned him, as Louise
said, and said "You win," and everything would have been all
right weeks ago.

I feel absolutely different about it now. All those old beasts
disapproving of me. . . . And the poor old thing dying. Suppose
I were to die suddenly without having made it up with him?

Everything's cold and beastly and mean.

I've simply *got* to have something warm and beautiful. Generous, like Louise said.

I've given in.

"You win," I'll say.

After lunch I'll go round to the Bristol and see him. That'll
be better than phoning.

Heaven, to see him again.

Slowly she began to feel happier.

She leaned back in her chair and stared out in silence at the sea,
now ice-grey, and the grey sky whence the snowflakes, darker
against its clouds, were spinning down. The cream-coloured
houses along the sea-front looked startlingly pale in the dreary
afternoon light. Snow lay along their roofs and ledges.

She lingered until two o'clock, smoking and dreaming. It was
so simple to give in. Why on earth didn't I do it before, she wondered, over and over again. I must have been crazy.

At last she got up slowly, still in a dream, paid the bill,
and went out. Snow was falling thickly now, more like the
"white birds," the "Mother Goose's feathers" of fairy tale. The
hedges of witch's hair were beginning to nod under the weight
of it.

She walked sedately towards the Hotel Bristol with her heart
full of love and peace. It did not occur to her that Brian might be
out or might be unkind to her. Her longing had run ahead of her
body, and built up a glowing picture, and towards this warm and
beautiful and desired vision she was steadily moving. The unhappiness of months, ending in the tragedy and shame of the past
few days, had thrown her into a waking trance. Love and beauty

and the music of the gipsy orchestra were in command now, not
the will-power of sensible Pauline Williams.

She went up the hotel steps. On either side of her the fig-vine
was in its brown winter sleep and the little tables were stacked
up. She pushed open the swing doors and went through into the
hall.

No one was on the reception desk. A dull little fire burned at
one end of the hall and by it an old waiter was studying a newspaper, turning it about and shaking it in a searching way as if for
some reason he was discontented with it, and muttering to himself
as he did so.

He looked up and saw such a pretty young woman smiling at
him, in one of them fancy fur hoods with a lot of that red stuff
they put on their mouths nowadays.

"Is Mr. Kingsley in?" she asked.

Dunfee hesitated. He knew who she was, of course. Had he
not seen her sitting with young Smartyface on the veranda, summer before last, and riding horseback on the beach lars' summer?
Miss Williams. Nice young lady, his great-niece Connie said, if
she did get a bit la-di-da sometimes.

He stared at her, and she stared peacefully back at him. Her
brown eyes were bright and yet sleepy, like the eyes of a child who
has been allowed to stay up late for a treat.

Too good for 'im, brast 'im, thought Dunfee.

And suddenly, as he stared at her, an idea hit him; an idea so
clever yet so simple that his heart began to beat fast and sweat
broke out over his old skin.

"Mr. Kingsley, miss?" he enquired in a voice slightly hoarse
with excitement, straightening his thin trembling shoulders in their
carefully cleaned jacket and beginning to fold up his *Daily Mirror*
and put it away in his pocket. "Yes, he's in. Will you come this
way, please, miss."

And Pauline followed him as he set off in a hasty shuffle up the
stairs that led to the second floor.

She was not wondering why he had not conducted her to
Brian's little office. All her thought was moving forward, ahead
of her body, towards the moment when she should see Brian and
say to him: "You win." Even when Dunfee paused at a closed
white door at the end of the corridor, and noiselessly opened it,
muttering: "Mr. Kingsley. There you are, miss," without turning
his head towards her as he spoke, she did not think his sly and
excited manner peculiar. She answered "Thank you" with a
radiant absent smile that he did not see because he was shuffling
away down the corridor as fast as he could shuffle, and pushed

open the door and went forward into the warm and beautiful and desired vision, into the room.

But Brian was not there. The room was one of the handsomest in the hotel; a lofty square chamber with two french windows opening upon a balcony facing the sea and curtained with white net and thick green velvet below an ornate pelmet. There was no carpet on the floor and the narrow boards were so brilliantly waxed that they reflected the furniture, of which there was not much; a narrow severe bed like those seen in hospitals, a patent folding table with copies of *The Yachtsman* upon it, an open shelf filled with books and on the walls some large faded photographs of sailing ships, a seascape or two and some old prints of naval battles. The room smelt of the wax polish and that sweet tobacco —shag—of which she had sometimes caught a whiff when a workman passed her in the street. It was an odd room, un-ordinary; and she felt this at once in spite of her disappointment and surprise.

A deep voice said:

"Hullo! You've come to the wrong place, haven't you?" and she turned quickly, startled, as a wheeled chair moved forward from *behind* her, where its occupant had been helping himself to a book from another shelf.

Mr. Kingsley had a disagreeable smile on his square yellowish face, that must years ago have been as sunburnt and handsome as Brian's; it was still so like Brian's that the sight of it gave her an indescribable emotion. The smile was mocking and appraising, and his gaze lingered upon her ankles.

"Oh—I'm so sorry," she stammered, putting out her hand towards the door. "The waiter must have thought I meant——"

"That's all right." He moved the chair suddenly forward, passing behind her, and shut the door. "I'm glad to see you. I don't often get pretty girls up here." His smile grew wider, showing false teeth. "I haven't had a visitor like you since your sister was up here back in the spring. She's a pretty girl too. Not so healthy looking as you are, though. You're the one that plays all the games, aren't you?"

While he was talking he was rapidly manœuvring the chair across the room and into a position near the window that was obviously the one he usually occupied, and she was watching him. She was embarrassed by his manner and yet sorry for him and also dismayed at the old waiter's mistake, for Brian had always made it plain that he did not want her to meet his father, and if he came up and found her here he would be annoyed. The mood of dreamy surrender in which she had entered the room had gone completely.

"Sit down, sit down, can't you," he went on. "I suppose you want to see Brian?"

"Yes, I did, really. I just looked in for a minute as I've got the day off from business."

Her manners had now come to her aid and she was speaking without nervousness or haste. But her wish to get away from him grew stronger every minute. This room, with its close peculiar smell and look of being dominated by one idea—a passion for the sea that its occupant could never indulge—oppressed her; and her mingled dislike and pity for the invalid increased.

"Been to the old lady's funeral, have you?" he went on. "There's been a lot of talk about that business. People are making some very nasty remarks about you, and I think you ought to know it. Oh, I hear most things, although I do sit up here all day like a stuffed image." He held out a cigarette case. "Have one?"

She shook her head. "No, thank you."

"I usually smoke a pipe but I keep these things in case I feel like a change. God knows any kind of a change is a godsend, up here. Yes," taking out a little black pipe and beginning to pack it, "they're saying you're getting something under the will. Is that so?" giving her a sharp look.

"I really don't know, Mr. Kingsley. I shouldn't think the will has been read yet," she answered, putting her hand on the door and looking at him steadily. She was beginning to get angry.

"All right, you needn't fire up—though I must say you look very charming when you do; I like to see a pretty girl in a temper." (So does Brian! He *is* like him, she thought.) "Do you know what else people are saying?"

"I don't care what they're saying."

"Very silly of you, then. They're saying you knew you were due for something handsome under the will, so you took the old girl for a walk in a thunderstorm just to hurry things up a bit."

From rage and dismay she was silent, staring at him.

"Nasty minds people have got, haven't they?" he went on, lighting the little black pipe. "But that's what the world's like, and when you're my age you'll know what devils men and women are."

He leant back, puffing, and staring at her through the smoke.

"I must go," she said coldly. "Good-bye."

"Oh, don't go yet, Brian'll be here any minute, he usually looks in to see me about this time every afternoon. You aren't angry with me, are you?"

She was silent. She could think of nothing save that he was Brian's father and a cripple, and therefore she did not want to be rude or hurt him. But how horrible he was! like an old, embittered Brian.

"Come on, sit down and make yourself comfy. Don't take any notice of me, I'm a lonely devil and not used to talking to charming girls. Now that I've seen you I'm damned sure it isn't true, anyway. You aren't the type. Now if it was your sister! She's a clever, cold little devil! I can imagine her doing anything for money or to get on on the stage. Oh do for god's sake sit down! You fidget me, standing there."

She sat down reluctantly on a chair by the door. If Brian isn't here in five minutes I'll go, she thought.

Mr. Kingsley was sitting with his back to the windows past which the snow was now thickly whirling, and his face and body were against the light so that he sat in shadow; sinister shadow, it seemed to her, for although his legs were covered by a light rug and he was leaning back in a way that emphasized his crippledness, there was no weakness or gentleness about him.

"You're in love with Brian, of course," he went on, and her heart leapt at the words and she looked away from him, longing to get up and go but not quite daring to. "(My god, what a waste of a lovely thing like you!) Because he's no damned good, you know. Not a pretty thing for a man to say about his own son, is it? But it happens to be true. Has he ever asked you to marry him?" he demanded.

She shook her head and then tried to say something, but he hurried on:

"I thought not. Too fond of his own comfort. All the same, he *is* going to be married, and soon. Ah! that's a surprise, isn't it?"

"It isn't true!"

"Oh yes, it is! And do you know who he's going to marry?"

"It isn't true!"

"Eve Cunningham. That's the lucky woman. Suit each other down to the ground, won't they? For my part I'm damned glad. She'll take him away from this place and I can run it as I please again."

Suddenly the door opened quickly and in came Brian.

"Pauli——" he began agitatedly, holding out his hand to her.

"He says you're going to marry Mrs. Cunningham," she interrupted him loudly, going up and putting both hands on his arm and looking up into his pale angry face. "It isn't true, is it?"

"Of course it's true," he answered at once, but going even whiter and looking down at her with miserable eyes. "You've made such an utter damned fool of yourself over this Pask affair

that I got fed up and asked Eve last night. I've—I've been meaning to for some time, and then you didn't seem to——"

She took her hands away from his arm and quickly, like a child,
put them behind her back as if to stop herself from touching him.

"You wouldn't do what I wanted you to," he ended.

"I came to tell you that I would. 'You win,' I was going to say."

"It's too late now, anyway. You should have come before."

Pauline nodded, still staring at him.

Mr. Kingsley sat quiet, looking from one young face to the
other.

"You've been such a *fool*," Brian said, following her as she
walked slowly to the door. "Everybody's talking about you. It
got me down. On the top of everything else——"

She nodded again. She was standing with her back to him and
feeling for the door-handle.

"You know I always did hate a girl to be conspicuous, Pauli.
I'm—I'm sorry. Oh, my dear," he said, under his breath, turning
his head away from the watching figure by the window, "you've
been such a fool! You could have had me so easily!"

"I don't want you," she said, and found the handle of the door
and opened it and went out of the room, shutting the door after
her.

The snow was falling thickly. The streets were deserted and
the pavements covered. Large fluffy flakes clung to her coat
as she walked steadily on, with her hands in her pockets, towards
the Rich House.

The wind was so cold, and the streets and the distant grey sea
so desolate, and she was dreadfully miserable; and in the Rich
House there would be a big fire and all the lights shining cheerfully out into the winter gloom, there would be Louise's pink and
purple flowers in the warm greenhouse, and Mr. Early dreaming
over the cakes and cream of a luxurious tea; and Ted.

At the Rich House there would be something beautiful and
warm and comforting, just as there had always been ever since
she was a little girl.

She walked quickly on. The iron gates with the pattern of
leaves and grapes came in sight, their crevices now filled with
crystal snow. The leafless elms above them were heaped with
snow and the carriage way where she had seen Ted playing with
the luminous cricket ball a year ago was covered with dimpled
whiteness. She pushed open the gates and walked in and came
round the shrubs and saw the great lawn, a wonderful sweep of
snow, with fantastic bushes nodding in the midst of it. And there

was the house, a castle of purple brick against the grey sky, with every turret and ledge outlined in fairy white.

She went up the wide steps with tears running down her face. The door was shut against the cold and the string with which it was usually pulled open had slipped inside. So she rang the old-fashioned bell and waited, searching in her handbag for her handkerchief. Silence; the sea was silent and the winter wind; the only sound was the tiny crisping fall of fresh snowflakes upon the snowy ground.

Suddenly the door opened and Ted's voice, tender and alarmed, exclaimed:

"Why, what's the matter, my darling Nut Brown Maid?"

CHAPTER XXXV

SHE felt his arm go round her, and heard the door shut, and then she was led across the dark hall to where a splendid fire was now dying down, and by its red glow he made her sit on an old sofa that was drawn up to the warmth. Still keeping an arm tightly round her shoulders, he sat down beside her and began to pull at the broad ribbons fastening her fur hood. The gesture was so clumsy and loving that she cried harder than ever, and at last he stopped trying to untie the ribbons and pulled her head down on to his shoulder, where it rested more comfortably than it had rested anywhere in her life before, and let her cry while he silently held a handkerchief to her face. Once or twice she felt a kind of spasm convulse him, and on the third occasion she lifted her head and said hoarsely:

"You aren't crying too, are you?"

"No. Feeling sick," he answered in a weaker voice than usual.

"Oh, Ted darling! I am so sorry—and I come and roar all over you. I am a beast."

"It's all right, my sweetheart." (She heard what they were calling each other, but the whole occasion was so dreamlike, the dark hall, the glare from the motionless fire, a sort of distant roar of voices and what sounded like music coming from upstairs, and her own swollen nose and aching head—that she could not take it in properly.) "It's my own fault. We had lunch to celebrate my getting the Gielgud job. Heaven!—lobster à la americaine and champagne and potato salad and turkish coffee and ice pudding—and it's given me a bilious attack, that's all."

"Poor darling," she said dreamily, and suddenly soft firm lips were pressed upon her own, and with an exquisite flowing of comfort back into her heart she returned his kiss.

"Have you actually *been* sick?"

"Oh yes, but only the first time. I'm always sick twice, you know."

"I know." (And indeed she did, having heard about, and not infrequently been a witness of, his bilious attacks ever since he was four years old.) "Wouldn't you like to lie down? I'll make room." She did so, and he leant back with his head on the cushions while she reclined beside him, the broad old sofa comfortably supporting them both.

"Whatever's that noise upstairs?" she asked presently.

"Grandfather throwing a party."

"Good heavens."

"I know." He put his hand out and gently turned her face towards him and kissed her again. Absolute heaven, kissing Ted, she thought dreamily.

"Darling Nut Brown Maid, I do love you so."

"Oh Ted, so do I you! And I love it when you call me Nut Brown Maid."

" '*Shall never be said the Nut Brown Maid was to her love unkind.*' I found that in a poem one day when I was very miserable and it made me think of you. How long do you suppose we've felt like this? (Oh god, I'm sick again.)"

"(Just lie still, darling.) Oh, ages. I can't think properly. I seem to have loved you ever since I can remember, only sort of underneath, without knowing it."

"Me too. I'm so exquisitely happy if only I didn't feel so ghastly."

"What on earth does your grandfather want to give a party for *now*?"

"To celebrate my getting the Gielgud job."

"I *am* so glad."

"I know. Isn't it heaven. He's got the house full of incredibly ancient old troupers—Myra and Beamish Vaughan and Clarice Thoroughgood and Arthur Keate and thousands more. Every now and then one of them comes doddering downstairs and smites me feebly between the shoulder blades to congratulate me. I did try to go to bed once, but in vain, in vain."

He sat up suddenly.

"I say, I'm terribly sorry but I must go and be sick again."

He rushed off into the dimness, calling over his shoulder: "It's the second time, you know. I'll be better after this," and disappeared.

While he was gone Pauline lay back on the sofa and stared into the fire, not thinking about anything, only filled with happiness and peace and waiting for him to come back.

Suddenly a figure loomed up out of the dusk and bent over the sofa, and a cracked but rich female voice exclaimed: "Ah, asleep, poor boy. Worn out with excitement. All temperament, just as I used to be at his age. Well, sleep on, dear lad, and dream your dreams. I won't disturb you." Here she patted Pauline on the shoulder. "He'll never be good looking as poor Archie was. Now where are those stairs . . . ?" and the figure, which appeared so far as Pauline could make out to be extremely fat, and streaming with scarves and beads and shawls, slowly receded into the twilight again.

"That's better," said Ted, coming back in a few minutes and sitting down beside her. He took her hand and kissed it.

"Somebody came and patted me, thinking I was you," said Pauline.

"They're all as blind as bats and stone deaf. None of them are dumb, however, and Grandfather's adoring it. Dear sweetheart, when will you marry me?" and he suddenly but gently put his head on her breast.

"Oh——" she said, and then was silent, overcome. "Oh Ted, whenever you like," she went on after a moment. "Do you know what I'm afraid of—I know it's silly but I can't help it, I'm so choked up with feelings and I've simply got to tell you them all——"

"I'll never get tired of listening, so tell away."

"Oh Ted, I do love you!"

"Oh dearest, so do I!"

"It's almost too much."

"Never. I can take it, don't you fear. Now tell me what you're afraid of."

"Well, only that if I get to love you so much and show you I do you might stop loving me."

"Listen, Pauline." He sat up and spoke earnestly. "However much you love me I shall only love you more and more. I know that. I feel that in my heart, right down where I feel about acting. I can't say I won't ever look at another woman, because I have a roving eye, like Grandfather, you know, but I can and do promise you from my deepest heart that you'll always come first. Always, for ever and ever, till death us do part."

They exchanged a long kiss.

"After—all," he said unsteadily as they drew apart, "there was my father, you know."

"What about him?"

"Well, Grandfather always says he was 'a poor thing, a poor thing,' but he did make my mother perfectly happy for the short time they were married, and when she died he died too, of a broken heart. I may be like Grandfather in acting and my father in loving. I hope I shall. Acting and you are all I want."

"You are all I want. Oh Ted, it's so lovely to be allowed to *say* it!"

Thicker and faster fell the snow. By the time the shops put up their lights, hardly anyone was about, and the sea was strangely hushed, breaking in long smooth waves on the untrodden sands covered with snow. Towards tea-time there was a considerable flurry at the front door of Railway Cottage due to the sudden and unexpected arrival of Uncle Herbert. With his Things. Come to stay just for a day or two until he went into the Houses at Nunby. Yes, it was all fixed up. Mr. Brian had come down into the kitchen in ever such a rage.

"Comes right up to me where I was sitting finishing up me coffee," narrated Dunfee to a breathless audience over the tea and shrimps. "Dunfee! he says. Yes, Mr. Brian—quite calm, I was. Dickson tells me you showed a young lady up to Mr. Kingsley's room. (Dickson's the pageboy; regular brat he is too. Must a' been hidin' somewhere an' seen us.) I never stands up. I just looks at him, quiet like. Yes, Mr. Brian, I says. (All Them Others was listening.) Oh, he was in a taking! Never see anything like it. How dare you! he says. You fool. (Standing over me with his fists clenched. Threatenin' me, see.) You knew perfectly well it was me she wanted to see. What have you got to say for yourself? Nothing, I says. Nothing, eh? he says. All right, then. Very good. You're fired. Go on, get your things and clear out. You won't get your wages nor no testimonial from me, he says, marchin' to the door. Beg parding, I says, Mr. Brian, Mr. Kingsley pays me my wages, not you, and seeing I've been here forty years he'll give me a testimonial if I want it. He never says another word. Just marches out. Oh, there hadn't half been a flare up, I'll lay."

"Fancy, Uncle. You always said you'd have to do something horrible to get yourself sacked, didn't you?" said Connie.

"Yes. I was just about desperate and that's straight. I saw meself *dyin'* over them veranda teas one summer and bein' *buried* there, in that bit o' garden under young Smartyface's window."

"Why was he so wild?" enquired the slow voice of Connie's father from his place beside the hob.

"Afraid the Master 'ud show him up, I reckon. Tell her all his goin's-on. Oh, he's no use, young Smartyface isn't. No respec', no natural feelin's. Why, you'd hardly believe how he was carryin' on to Miss Williams's sister, the actress one, larst January it was, one evenin'. Him and her was havin' dinner in the little dinin'-room and I was waiting. Telling her his poor mother wasn't right in the head, of all things. Kind of hintin' about it. All lies. She was no more wrong in the head than I am. Delicate, yes, and always the worryin' sort. And enough to make 'er, poor lady, with the Master bein' crippled and young Smartyface like he was. But mad! Never heard such wicked nonsense in all my life."

He felt in his pocket and produced a greasy little black notecase and held it up, while they all watched. Slowly he drew out, amid an excited chorus, a clean five-pound note.

"See that? The Master give me that. Forty years of faithful service. *And* a letter to the Nunby Awards Committee. I took that along to them afore I come here. And it's all fixed up. I move in on Saturday. Nice little room. Read the *Daily Mirror* every mornin' all the way through. Bit o' garden and grow lettuces. Nunby! That's the ticket."

And, surrounded by cheerful and relieved faces (for there had been at first some natural apprehension least he had come to spend the rest of his declining years at Railway Cottage), Dunfee took the first bite at a huge shrimp sandwich, prepared for him by a dutiful great-great-nephew while he talked.

Presently the slow voice of Mr. Letter observed:

"Five pound. Don't seem much for forty years work. Sixpence a year, I make it."

But Dunfee pretended not to hear, nor did the faintest rustle in the old pocket-book betray the presence of three more five-pound notes.

At four o'clock, just as the dusk was beginning, the snow ceased to fall. A faint brightness from the hidden sun crept into the air, followed by a wonderful clearness, in which every burdened tree and buried road and lawn seemed twice as white and gleaming. Mr. Early, standing at the window in the drawing-room that gave a view of the distant sea, announced that he would take his usual walk.

"Archie, darling! Is that wise?" asked Myra, putting an arm in a grubby lace sleeve through his. Her head was covered with tight little red curls; under the other arm she held the wheezing Vinny. The wireless was playing airs from "Carmen" and one of the ancient actresses who had also been a singer was chanting in a cracked voice while the others stood round her applauding and waving their glasses.

"If you were not so charming you would sometimes be a little tiresome," absently returned Mr. Early, patting her veined hand. Louise came up at that moment with his coat with the astrakhan collar and a cap of the same fur, high and picturesque, with ear lappets.

"It's so cold to-day," she explained, "here's your fur one."

"Going out, Archie?"

"Dear fellow, in this weather?"

"Isn't he naughty!"

Mr. Early, arrayed in the cap and coat and looking exceedingly impressive and handsome, brushed off his friends like so many fruit flies and having recommended them to the fire, the sandwiches and the tray of drinks, went out of the room and down the stairs.

He passed through the hall without glancing towards the sofa by the fire, and out through the front door, shutting it after him.

Once outside in the silent afternoon air among the snow-laden trees, he breathed loudly through his nose and began to march along with his head well up, surveying the scene and not taking in a single detail of it. Down the drive he went and out of the gates, swinging a malacca walking stick and relishing the marvellously pure air.

He was even happier than usual to-day, because Edward had secured an excellent part in this new play, and because Edward had found his work, and had The Spark, and would carry on the acting tradition in the Early family. And while he had been standing at the drawing-room window waiting for the snow to stop and never once doubting that it would because he. Archibald Early, desired to go out, he had seen the charming little Pauline coming up the drive, evidently in some distress. Even now, Mr. Early was sure, Edward and she were comforting one another in the proper and natural manner. That was why he had been careful not to glance towards the sofa.

O spirit of love! how quick and fresh art thou, muttered Mr. Early, striding along with the malacca stick swinging, and went all through Duke Orsino's opening speech in his head. *And my desires, like fell and cruel hounds, E'er since pursue me*, he went on presently as he approached the pillar box which marked the lim

of his daily promenade. No, no, he thought, shaking his head.
A deplorable state of affairs. I have never experienced that, and
neither will Edward, I am certain. I am not of the stuff of which
victims are made and neither is he. Besides, nothing must be
permitted to interfere with our work. I shall advise the young
people to marry soon. An early marriage, contracted when the
senses are fresh and the heart is innocent, provides an admirable
safeguard against Entanglements. And should Entanglements
come later, mused Mr. Early, walking towards the post-box, they
can be more readily and pleasantly managed if the affections are
already firmly rooted in the joys and sorrows of married life.

Lights were shining in the houses near the pillar box, for it was
tea-time. The box stood on the edge of a part that was not yet
built on; the last mark of civilization before the rough fields
that ended in a low cliff above the sea. It had recently been
painted, but this afternoon its brilliant scarlet was dimmed against
the dazzling snow. Red pillar box, white fields, grey sky, dark
grey sea and the golden lights of tea-time. Mr. Early strode on.

A figure was slowly approaching the box, dressed all in black,
with a letter in its gloved hand. Cautiously, as if she were nervous
of slipping on the already lightly frozen pavement, the woman
drew near to the box. Just as she came up to it, Mr. Early reached
it from the other side, and saw the pale blue envelope she carried
and the round childish writing on it. She had given one quick
incurious glance at him, her hand was outstretched to put the
letter into the box, when out came a large authoritative paw in a
fur glove and snatched it from her.

"Here!" she squeaked with a look of terror, starting back.
"What are you up to? Give that to me!"

Mr. Early, towering over her, pulled off his gloves and dropped
them in the snow, gave her one short stare of stern distaste, and
began to open the letter.

Time was never very real to him. He knew of course that the
season now was winter, but last summer was as real, and still as
present to him, as were this grey sea and snow, because he lived
in his own timeless world. The last occasion on which he had seen
a letter exactly like this one had been in the summer garden when
Pauline had asked his advice about the anonymous letter written to
Mrs. Pask; and he had immediately assumed this to be another
of the same sort. And—the millionth chance coming off—it was.

He read it through and gave a contemptuous exclamation, then
crumpled it and handed it back to her.

"How dare you!" she said, trying to face him with a hard stare.
"Opening people's letters. I'll report you to the police."

He clasped his hands upon the head of his stick and leant forward a little, looking down at her. After a second or two she could look at him no longer, and her eyes fell.

"You must once have been an unusually pretty woman," began Mr. Early calmly. "You are still not without attractions. You must know, therefore, what pretty women are put into the world for—to give delight, to fill the dreariness of everyday life with warmth and colour. But *this*," shaking the crumpled letter, which she had not taken, "this is the action of a plain woman who has neither known nor given delight. How can you, a pretty woman, have done such a thing?"

She stared at him, then bewilderedly shook her head. The anger and hardness had gone out of her face and only suspicion was left.

"It was an unnatural act," pronounced Mr. Early, "come now, wasn't it?"

"It was because of my business," she said, as if against her will. "Some of my clients took their custom away and I got wild. There wasn't any harm in it. It was only a bit of fun."

"You alarmed and distressed a number of harmless ladies."

"More fools them, then. Can't take a joke. Going to London for their corsets and bras. That's my business, see, making corsets and——"

She stopped, for he was holding up a protesting hand.

"I do not wish to hear. These things are mysteries, and I prefer them to remain so."

"Sorry," she muttered.

"I believe that you are. I can see that you still possess delicacy of feeling—and warmth, too, I am sure, yes, and remorse for what you have done."

"I don't know about that," she muttered, staring up at him. Barmy, she thought, but could not help being awed by his height and ancient beauty and manner. She had never in her life encountered such an impressive combination. And he had said that she must have been unusually pretty! More than I am now, she thought. Let him try having four kids and two misses and see if he'll be pretty.

"I s'pose you'll tell the police," she said sullenly.

"I am sure that it will not be necessary. Now that it has been pointed out to you that what you have done is not in keeping with your appearance, I know that you will write no more of these letters."

It was not even a question. He spoke as if the matter were at an end.

"I used to get a lot of fun out of it, though." she said, as if to herself, and staring down at the snow.

"We must ignore such satisfactions. They make our faces ugly."

Mrs. Voles shook her head as if she gave it up, and suddenly shivered. The brightness had gone out of the sky and it was rapidly becoming dark.

"I suggest that you go home," said Mr. Early, drawing himself up in readiness to walk on. "Where are my gloves? Ah—thank you—oh, do not trouble, I beg of you——" She was dusting the snow off them against her skirt. "Thank you."

And as he took them from her, he lifted her hand and kissed it.

"Good day to you," he said, smiling at her, already miles away, and set off on his walk home.

Barmy, decided Mrs. Voles, also walking home and wondering who on earth he was. Then she suddenly recollected the stories of the famous old actor who lived in a big house up this end of the town and decided it must be he. Buttering me up like that! Still, I was lucky, really. Might have turned out far worse. How on earth did he *know*? Got the shock of my life. Must have seen one of my letters in someone's house and guessed. Pretty smart, at his age.

Kissing my hand! No one 'ud believe it.

All the same, he's about right. I shan't do any more. That little softie getting married and the other old fool passing out, that only leaves Mrs. S. She and that little fool might get together and tell the police. I used to get a good laugh over that little fool's face sometimes. Stuck-up prig.

Still I'd better lay off it now.

It was a good idea while it lasted, though. Putting the wind up them by buttering them up instead of writing the usual poison-pen stuff. Quite original, really.

And Mrs. Voles went on, arranging in her mind to destroy the pale blue notepaper and envelopes and special pen and ink she used (which she kept hidden in the Outside W.), to-morrow morning after Reenie had gone to work.

She happened just then to be passing Beard's, and suddenly she went in and bought a jar of anti-wrinkle cream.

There was a faintly disagreeable thought at the back of Mr. Early's mind as he marched dreamily home, and at last it emerged into his consciousness as the recollection of a greasy black kid glove against his lips. But his thoughts immediately retreated from the memory and began to wander among other memories; of the same kind, but how different! He remembered little hands gloved in white kid and smelling of violets, a smooth brown hand where rubies flashed, a soft hand put suddenly, lovingly, across his mouth to silence passionate words.

He sighed and smiled and went in through the gates of the Rich House.

Reenie at work in her little den coated with fish scales in Cousins's shop, fat and pale, her energies unused and the influence of her mother strong upon her, was one person; and Reenie after two years as a mother's help in New Zealand, sunburnt and friendly and happy, was quite another; and no one but her mother was surprised when she married a prosperous sheep farmer and proceeded to have eight children. ("Disgustin'," said Mrs. Voles as Reenie and the years and the children rolled on.) Spring after spring, back to Lavender Road came snapshots of Reenie and the kids; she smiling in the midst of them and they in all stages of toddling and darting and hopping, all about her.

In the background there sometimes appeared her husband (invariably referred to by Mrs. Voles as "that poor feller") looking patient and humorous, two useful qualities in a man who lives with an energetic woman and eight children.

Mavis also received these snapshots, enclosed in affectionate letters, and studied them with wonder and respect; for she herself found it took most of her time to keep little Pamela and little Brenda as they should be kept. What it must be with eight! And all those sheep, too. But of course, New Zealand was a bigger place than Seagate and there would be more room for them to run about: that would make a difference.

After Eric and Mavis had enjoyed two idyllic years in the elegant flat on the sea-front with its pale blue walls and modernist windows, they had had to give it up. Little Pamela was delicate and cried a good deal and their neighbours complained. So the young Somers took a small house out on the way to Happy Sands and here little Brenda was born.

It was wonderfully healthy and open out there, of course, only rather lonely in the winter and a long way from the nice shops in Seagate; and the garden wasn't very nice; not so bad as those horrid sand gardens out in the bungalow town, of course, but not really a proper garden like Grannie and Grandpa had in Station Avenue. Still, the house was ever so pretty and easy to run and there were a lot of advantages, really.

It will be gathered that Eric was up to his neck in it.

So he was, but happier than he had ever been in the romantic years of his prolonged adolescence. He made such efforts to retain intellectual interests in his life, in spite of the longer journey to and from the bank and the fact that he was almost always tired, that some of the refreshing magic of poetry and music actually did sift into the pleasant ordinary life at "Glendene" (domestic life is consciously exciting and beautiful only to poets and saints; see Thornton Wilder's *Our Town* for confirmation) and his daughters grew up with good tunes in their heads (Grandpa helped with those) and tags of Rupert Brooke and de la Mare on their tongues.

The Rupert Brooke bits came from Mummy. When she worked in the library Mummy was ever so fond of his poems and used to read them in the evening in that little blue room the two children loved to hear about. To Pamela it was as entrancing as a palace in a fairy story, and she never tired of being told about the blue cups and saucers and the rug with the roses on and the unkind men who came and took it all away from poor Mummy because she had no pennies.

To Mavis also, relating these events while she made a pudding or ran up a little frock on the machine, her story was as satisfying (and as faraway) as a fairy tale.

She and Eric loved each other tenderly and were as nearly completely happy as two people can be in this world; and should any orchidaceous person doubt that complete happiness can exist on a small income in a small house with two growing children, we can only reply that this (from a large body of evidence) appears to be how God intended the greater part of the human race to live; throwing in, as sweeteners, the sense of His Presence and the beauty of art. So, conforming to The Pattern, the Somers were happy.

It cannot be denied that the sex of Brenda and Pamela was a disappointment to their grandfather, who had looked forward to bringing up little grandsons as sturdy atheists; but Brenda was almost as satisfactory as a boy; for she had a lively, enquiring and sceptical mind. Her company and conversation was a continual interest and pleasure to him. He had begun to give her simple music lessons and every Sunday morning, in fine weather or bad, the two went a walk along the sands together. Brenda's most frequent demand was "Temme about it," and Mr. Somers never fobbed off her questions or teased her about them but conscientiously tried to answer them all in a way that she could understand. Mavis sometimes feared that her father-in-law would one day return from a Sunday morning walk carrying his younger granddaughter in a state of high brain-fever, but Brenda seemed to take no harm from their discussions.

The high-spot of her relationship with her grandfather occurred when she was four and he seventy-five years old.

He had been eagerly awaiting the moment when she should ask

who made the world, her parents having refrained from touching upon the question in front of her until her own curiosity should have been awakened. How Mr. Somers hoped that *he* would be the person she would ask! How thoroughly and carefully he would instil Materialism into that virgin and infant mind! What an opportunity, which the less intellectually active Pamela had never presented, of gaining a soul for Atheism!

The moment came. Grandfather and granddaughter were proceeding, she hopping and he pacing, along the sands on a magnificent morning in early summer, when, apparently moved by the size and splendour of the scene all about her, and yet at the same time so absorbed by the shell-hunt upon which she was engaged that she could not give her full attention to the question, Brenda asked casually as she hopped over a pool:

"Grandpa, who made everything?"

Now, now was the moment. Mr. Somers looked down at the top of her fair head, opened his mouth, drew a deep breath, and prepared to instil materialism.

Seconds passed. Brenda, unused to silence following her questions, looked up from her shell-hunt and shook the hair back from her face, put her legs apart, gazed at her grandfather, and repeated:

"Who made everything?"

Mr. Somers looked down into her eyes, wonderfully clear in her little sunburnt face. And it was no use. He could not do it. To that question, on such a morning, from such a questioner, there was only one possible answer, and at last he gave it.

"God."

"Temme about it."

And Mr. Somers tried.

An even more satisfying experience befell Mrs. Williams, who became three or four different grandmothers. The children of Pauline (born into a world of luxurious houses, swimming pools, long train and car journeys, sudden delightful holidays with Mummy and Daddy and equally sudden and sad partings from them when Daddy had to go to Australia or Brazil to act and took Mummy with him) were completely different from the one pale and precious little son born to Lenham Browne and Marjorie, (after the adamant cow had at last seen the light and divorced him and Marjorie had faced and conquered a strong fancy for Ted).

Pauline's four were lively, precocious and cheerful, and flatteringly fond of "pretty Granny"; they all inherited love of bodily beauty from their mother and their paternal great-grandfather;

and Mrs. Williams found admirers, more affectionate and satisfying than any since her husband died, in her three grandsons and
her granddaughter.

But the deepest love her shallow nature had ever known was
given to Marjorie's delicate Hugh; while her daughter and son-in-
law were on tour, Hugh stayed with her at Seagate, enjoying the
sands and benefiting from the pure keen air while his grandmother spoilt him and basked in his love and admiration.

Mrs. Williams's life, indeed, was fuller and more satisfying in
its last twenty years than it had ever been in her first fifty; a state
of affairs that few people are lucky enough to experience and that
she hardly deserved. And it was not without gaiety, for a back-
wash from the supper parties, camellias, lovely clothes, first nights,
famous dramatists and all the rush and glitter of the life of an
actor of genius overflowed into Seagate and coloured her life
there, to the immense and satisfying interest and envy of all her
cronies.

Another person who enjoyed the last ten years of his life more
than he had enjoyed the first seventy was Dunfee; in his little
room, among his few treasures, in the almshouses built by a
benevolent nobleman in 1743 at Nunby. The lettuce-growing, the
rabbit-keeping, the leisured perusal of the *Daily Mirror*, were all
achieved and relished. Of course, there was always the business
of that Dratted Uniform; why they wanted a man to wear a hat
like an organ-grinder's monkey and a sort of an overall-thing,
passed anyone's knowledge. But as the wearing of these garments
was not compulsory but was left to the grateful instincts of the
almshouse men and women, they all derived a stimulus for their
declining years by getting out of wearing them whenever they
could and rejoicing together (Dunfee not the least) when they
succeeded in doing so.

The poetry and passion hidden in Pauline's nature opened fully
in the exquisite happiness of her marriage; but to the end of her
days she had a secret conviction that she did not get enough
exercise and fresh air.

They were going slowly up the staircase in the Rich House
towards the statue of Mercury glimmering in the dusk, and their
arms were about one another.

"I never asked you what you were crying about."

"Yes, you did, only I forgot to answer. I'd forgotten I had
been crying, as a matter of fact."

"What was it, love? The Melancholy Double-Crossing W.,
I'll be bound."

"Oh yes—him, and everybody being so horrible to me about poor Mrs. Pask. Did you hear about it?"

"Louise told me. I was coming over to see you this afternoon only I came over all queer."

"Ted?"

"What, angel?"

"You don't mind, do you?"

"What about? Of course not."

"Well, poor old thing, it *was* my fault, in a way."

"Now look here, Pauli. Who suggested going for that walk? She did. And I'm sure she was enjoying it, before she was taken ill?"

"Oh yes! I know she was."

"Well then, comfort yourself with that. Just before she died you gave her something that made her happy. That's all that matters."

"Don't you mind *at all* what people say?"

"Why should I?" he returned absently, with exactly his grand-father's royally dreamy manner.

"Nor about Brian either?"

"Not now." He clasped her waist tighter. "I did mind a little bit before, but I was always quite sure you'd see how cruel and tedious he was in the end, and so you have."

"*Gosh*, I have!" she said feelingly.

"Let's go into the little room with the books for a moment. We can see the sea from there and I adore it against the snow."

It was almost dark. Still entwined, they felt their way across the little room to the window, and stood there, looking out.

There lay the sea, a dark grey line beyond the black trees and the glimmering lawn. Suddenly Ted opened the window, and across the evening air came the sound of the waves, regular and soft, strangely hushed in the silence brought to the coast by the snow. The Northstone Light was flashing.

"Heaven," he whispered. "Smell it."

She too leant forward, feeling the firmness of his young waist under her arm, and gazed out at the twilight.

Suddenly the room behind them was filled with light. They both turned, and saw Mr. Early standing at the door, smiling at them, blinking slowly in the brilliance.

"Hullo, Grandfather."

"Edward, my dear boy. How are you now?"

"Perfectly restored, thank you." He kept his arm about Pauline's waist as he spoke.

"You have had exactly the medicine I should have prescribed," said Mr. Early, and came forward and kissed Pauline's hand. He kept it in his for a moment, while he looked down affectionately into her happy face.

"Do you feel equal, Edward and you, my dear, to coming in, and meeting our friends?"

"Oh yes. Don't we, Pauli? No doubt there will be a hailstorm of nods and becks and wreathed smiles, but we can take it."

They went towards the door. Ted's long fingers were now linked in hers.

"Did you have a good walk?" he asked hastily, seeing his grandparent drawing himself up with the obvious intention of asking a most important question and suddenly wishing to postpone the moment.

Mr. Early paused, and appeared to think.

"Yes," he said at last. "At least, I imagine so. I seem to have a recollection of some disagreeable incident occurring, but as I cannot recall what it was it cannot be of any consequence." He went on majestically: "Are you and Pauline betrothed, Edward?"

"Yes," said Ted at once, turning to smile at her. But she had gone off into a dream. O beautiful word! And through the sea dusk came the music of the gipsy orchestra.

In the snowy gardens, among the black and motionless elms, the Rich House, following Mr. Early's fancy, stood with all its lights shining. Now the night had almost come, and the sea was concealed under a blue snow mist, but its voice sounded clearly. From turrets and pointed windows shone the lights, glittering towards the hidden waves and making gold upon the snow.

"I shall announce it to all our old friends," proclaimed Mr. Early. "They must share my delight and yours."

And he flung open the door and in a voice of music began to make a speech.

THE END

VINTAGE CLASSICS

Vintage launched in the United Kingdom in 1990, and was originally the paperback home for the Random House Group's literary authors. Now, Vintage is comprised of some of London's oldest and most prestigious literary houses, including Chatto & Windus (1855), Hogarth (1917), Jonathan Cape (1921) and Secker & Warburg (1935), alongside the newer or relaunched hardback and paperback imprints: The Bodley Head, Harvill Secker, Yellow Jersey, Square Peg, Vintage Paperbacks and Vintage Classics.

From Angela Carter, Graham Greene and Aldous Huxley to Toni Morrison, Haruki Murakami and Virginia Woolf, Vintage Classics is renowned for publishing some of the greatest writers and thinkers from around the world and across the ages – all complemented by our beautiful, stylish approach to design. Vintage Classics' authors have won many of the world's most revered literary prizes, including the Nobel, the Man Booker, the Prix Goncourt and the Pulitzer, and through their writing they continue to capture imaginations, inspire new perspectives and incite curiosity.

In 2007 Vintage Classics introduced its distinctive red spine design, and in 2012 Vintage Children's Classics was launched to include the much-loved authors of our childhood. Random House joined forces with Penguin Group in 2013 to become Penguin Random House, making it the largest trade publisher in the United Kingdom.

@vintagebooks

penguin.co.uk/vintage